HOPE ISLAND

ALSO BY TIM MAJOR AND AVAILABLE FROM TITAN BOOKS

Snakeskins

HOPE ISLAND

TIM MAJOR

TITAN BOOKS

Hope Island
Print edition ISBN: 9781789092080
E-book edition ISBN: 9781789092097

Published by Titan Books
A division of Titan Publishing Group Ltd.
144 Southwark Street, London SE1 0UP
www.titanbooks.com

First Titan edition May 2020
10 9 8 7 6 5 4 3 2 1

A CIP catalogue record for this title is available from the British Library.

Printed and bound by CPI Group (UK) Ltd, Croydon CR0 4YY.

Rose, this one's for you.

CHAPTER ONE

All chatter ceased the moment Nina slammed her heel onto the brake, yanked the wheel to the left and then, as she remembered which side of the road she ought to be driving on, hard to the right. The unfamiliar Chrysler saloon groaned and shuddered but barely slowed. Its front wheels struck the dark grass bank, throwing Nina forwards. The car hissed in complaint, bumping to a lopsided stop.

Nina worked her jaw. The silence was like deafness.

'Everyone okay?' she said. She twisted to look into the back seat, wincing at the spike of pain in her neck.

'Shit, Mum,' her daughter Laurie said, her eyes shining.

Nina's de facto mother-in-law, Tammy, was sitting in the back seat beside Laurie. 'Lauren Fisher! We don't appreciate that kind of language, do you understand?' She glared at Nina, who understood the subtext: scolding Laurie ought to be Nina's job. 'What in heaven's name are you doing to my car?'

Nina had swerved because there was a child on the road.

Through the grimy windscreen she could see the girl

still standing in the centre of the track, illuminated by the car headlights. She stared at the car with no suggestion of alarm. She looked to be around ten years old, certainly younger than Laurie, and wore a cardigan, long socks and a pleated skirt. What was she doing out at this hour?

None of the passengers in the car had noticed the girl.

'I think your brakes need seeing to,' Nina said. 'Is there a garage on the island?'

'My Bobby never has any problem when he visits,' Tammy replied in her loud, flat drawl. 'He drives it like a dream.'

Nina's knuckles whitened.

'But Bobby – I mean Rob – isn't here, is he?' she said as coolly as she could manage.

Tammy removed her fur hat and placed it in her lap like a cat, then smoothed her hair which had remained unmussed despite the lurching of the car. It was held fast with lacquer, the smell of which mingled with her perfume to make the air in the car heavy and sweet. The Fishers' scent was probably ingrained into every atom of this old heap. Tammy fussed with her handbag, tutting as she rifled through it, as if the sudden stop might have somehow robbed her as well as startled her.

Nina turned to Tammy's husband sitting in the front passenger seat. His head was bowed as though in prayer. 'Abram? You okay there?'

Abram raised his head, blinking in surprise. A red horizontal smudge gave him a third eyebrow in the centre of his forehead. Now the blood began to seep down at both ends of the wound.

'Oh hell,' Nina said. 'Here. Let me help.' She pulled a tissue from the inside pocket of her jacket, spilling crumpled tickets and English coins as she did so. Abram smiled as she dabbed at his forehead. The injury wasn't as bad as it looked, only a nick from bumping against the dashboard. Abram's old skin looked thin as paper; it wouldn't have taken much to puncture it.

Nina sensed movement at the edge of her vision. The girl on the road. Her small body slackening, her knees buckling. The car hadn't even come close to hitting her, but the shock of a near-miss must have terrified her. She fell to the ground; her limbs, her torso, then her head disappeared as she slipped into the gloom beyond the headlight beams.

Tammy and Laurie made protestations as Nina pushed open the door and stumbled onto the grass bank. The car pinged its soft alarm as a complaint at the door being left open.

Nina edged around the bonnet, shielding her eyes from the headlights. The world beyond the yellow light was a black ocean.

She squinted into the dark, where the girl had fallen.

'Hello?' she said quietly. 'Are you there?'

She knelt to put a hand on the ground where the girl had been, then felt a fool. What was she hoping to find? A trace of heat?

'I just want to check that you're all right,' she said, unsure where to direct her voice. Her words were swallowed by the darkness as soon as they left her mouth.

The wind rolling up from the harbour was as regular as breathing.

Another sound overlapped it. More breathing.

Nina turned to her left and was relieved to see that the girl was on her feet again. Only her silhouette was visible, blacker than the darkness behind her.

'You shouldn't have been on the road,' Nina said. 'Were you hurt when you fell?'

More breathing.

The girl replied, 'I'm okay.'

Nina exhaled. 'Do you live very near here?' Then she remembered where she was; the island was tiny. 'Of course you do. Would you like me to drive you home?'

She took a single step forwards. Immediately, the girl retreated a step, stumbling on the gravel.

Nina held up her hands.

'You don't need to be afraid,' she said. 'I just want to know you're safe.'

'Keep away,' the girl said. 'Leave me alone.'

Nina didn't move. She felt desperately tired after her long journey and her many attempts to summon enthusiasm from a recalcitrant Laurie.

'Do you want me to scream?' the girl said, without inflection.

The breeze from the ocean snuck around Nina's neck, making her shudder.

'What?' she said. 'Why would you scream?'

'I said keep away.'

At first, Nina's only clue that the girl was backing away was the sound of her feet, but then she recognised that the black shape was diminishing. The girl was moving downhill, towards the harbourside. Surely there were no homes down there.

'Look, this is silly,' Nina said. She couldn't let the girl continue wandering in the opposite direction to her home. 'Won't you tell me your name, at least?'

The girl moved faster. It was hard to be certain, but it seemed that she was still facing Nina, that she was walking backwards down the hill, though the idea seemed absurd. Nina followed, matching her uneven pace. In this stop-start manner they approached a plain building, an ugly concrete structure directly at the foot of the steep hill that hung behind the harbour.

The girl came to a halt at the corner of the concrete building. A slice of moonlight fell upon her pale face. The skin below her eyes appeared cracked and raw. She craned her neck to look past Nina. Nina turned and was shocked to realise that the car wasn't far away – they had barely walked any distance. Inside the vehicle, Tammy and Laurie were deep in conversation. In the front passenger seat, Abram was staring at the wad of tissue in his hands.

Nina turned back to the girl, annoyance flaring within her. At precisely the same moment as Nina began to stride towards her, the girl stepped backwards again, disappearing into the narrow gap between the rear of the concrete building and the rock face at the foot of the hillside.

Nina swore softly.

'Please come out,' she said.

Then, 'You've told me that you're okay. So you can head on home.'

As she closed the distance to the building, she heard scuffling sounds from the narrow gap.

She stretched both arms before her, like a sleepwalker.

More scuffling. The lightest of sounds, barely anything, but becoming more frantic with each passing second.

'It's all right,' Nina said, more to herself than to the girl.

She turned her head, listening for the girl's breathing, but she heard only that same skittering sound.

She placed her right hand on the rock face, her left on the rough wall of the building. Reluctantly, she dipped her head into the gap.

The scuffling sound was amplified within the narrow passage.

Nina took a breath and eased herself fully into the gap.

But as the sound grew, so did a strong sense of the wrongness of all of this.

That sound.

It was too light, too flimsy.

The thought of pushing further into the gap was suddenly unimaginable.

'Please,' she said, but got no further, because the skittering sound grew louder and wilder. Something brushed against her stomach, tugging at the fabric of her T-shirt.

The need to retreat became overwhelming. She toppled backwards awkwardly, not trapped within the narrow gap but unable to turn. The loose rocks beneath her feet prevented her from launching herself away effectively, so that when some tiny, frenzied thing emerged from the depths of the darkness, batting against her forearms as she struggled to protect herself, she could do nothing other than continue to fall backwards.

Then she was on the ground, her already aching neck now singing with pain. She held her arms crossed before her face as something small and unpredictable flashed down. It nipped at her forearms then snuck past them to fling itself at her face. She gasped but didn't cry out as some hard, sharp part of it dragged across her throat, a clean vector on her skin that she visualised as a line of bright light rather than an injury. The creature's crackling flurry was as loud and calamitous as a cresting tidal wave.

It flittered upwards, puncturing the strip of moonlight – a panicked, skittering thing. A bird.

✳

Tammy and Abram's house – that is to say, Rob's childhood home – was not as Nina had expected. She had seen photos over the years and had dismissed the white porch and its white trellis as outdated Americana, envisaging Tammy and Abram sitting before their vast homestead, glaring at their neighbours. But Cat's Ear Cottage really was a cottage, reminiscent of the small homes on the Scottish islands Nina had visited, albeit with red cladding as opposed to slate or stone. The view from the porch was not of a neighbourhood but the endless Gulf of Maine dotted with tiny hillocks of islands nearer to the mainland. The moonlight skidded on the surface of the water, delineating the stark horizon and making Nina's breath catch at its geometric beauty.

She dallied on the porch after the others had entered the house, scanning along the rough dirt track, wondering about the girl on the harbour road. After her absurd encounter with the bird, Nina had forced herself to return to the gap between the building and the hillside, but it had been empty – the girl must have wriggled around two walls to evade her. She was probably at home now, sniggering about having fooled some clueless Brit.

When Nina had returned to the car it was clear that not only had her passengers failed to see the girl when she had been on the road, they hadn't seen or heard anything that had happened afterwards, either.

Laurie emerged from the cottage and tugged her arm, pulling her indoors. 'Come inside, Mum. It's cold out here.'

If the exterior of the house had surprised Nina with its simplicity, the interior had the opposite effect. Behind the low, brown leather furniture the walls of the wood-panelled sitting room were crammed with framed photos of Tammy and Abram on their travels. They stood before geysers and campervans and restaurants; they wore sunglasses, garish floral patterns, hats with slogans. The images were selfies from a time before selfies, reliant upon Tammy asking passers-by to operate her camera. Nina tracked the images from right to left, travelling backwards in time. Tammy's outfits became progressively less enveloping, her skin less pale. Her hair its usual dyed caramel, then dazzling white, then merely peppered with bright flecks, then her original dark blond. Abram grew in stature, his back straightening and his creases flattening, until he stood a head taller than his wife and his eyes became Rob's eyes, shining and laughing.

The papery Abram of today emerged from the dining room and gazed up at the photos with polite interest.

8

'You're sure you're not hurt too badly?' Nina said. Now the wound on his forehead looked more like a bindi or a dab of paint.

Abram turned both of his palms upwards and frowned at them. 'Never better. It's wonderful that you can be here, Emma.'

They had known each other for almost fifteen years.

'Actually, that isn't—'

Laurie yanked at her elbow again. 'Hey, Mum. You should see your room.'

Nina frowned at Abram but then allowed herself to be led back into the hallway. She turned towards the staircase.

Laurie shook her head. 'No, you're downstairs. Gran calls it the den. You'll laugh when you see it.' She pushed open a door.

Nina didn't laugh.

This room, too, was wood-panelled and had its walls filled with photos. But these photos were all of Rob. Here was Rob as an infant in pictures arranged alongside the den's built-in cupboard with its slatted double doors; Rob as a child aging incrementally along a wall otherwise interrupted only by a flat-screen TV and a dartboard; Rob as a lumbering teen; and then recognisably *her* Rob, his laughter lines already established as his likenesses edged closer and closer to the doorway in which Nina stood. She missed him suddenly. She had an urge to slip her arms around the waist of any of the men in these pictures. Surely she had a claim over some of them? She searched for a picture of herself but found none. Judging from this display, Rob's life had ended around the time that he and Nina had first met. Perhaps they ought to have got married, if only so that the wedding might have warranted a single framed photo somewhere in Tammy and Abram's house.

Laurie skipped to the centre of the room, to the foot of the futon that took up most of it. She had become herself again: a fourteen-year-old as opposed to the surly late-teen she had playacted on the journey.

'Hi Dad,' she said as she whirled around, looking up at the photos.

'I can't sleep in here,' Nina said without thinking.

Laurie stopped spinning. She tilted her head. 'No? All right. I will, then. You can sleep up in the box room between Gran and Grumps.'

Nina shivered. It was difficult to decide which was the less appealing repercussion of switching rooms: the idea of trying to sleep surrounded by Tammy and Abram in their respective bedrooms, or the thought of Laurie sleeping down here, watched over by Rob.

'No,' she said hurriedly. 'I'll be fine down here. It's cosy.'

'You're the boss.'

Nina watched her daughter carefully. That was what Reeta and Laine and the rest of her newsroom team said when they disagreed with her instructions: *You're the boss*. She had told herself that with Laurie she could shed her authoritarian stance. Being on Hope Island was supposed to be an escape from all that. A new start.

It was important that Laurie felt friendly towards her, before Nina broke the news.

She flinched as something bumped against her arm.

Tammy held a tray of cookies. She peered into the den.

'Bobby *said* he was coming. Not that I'm complaining, of course. It's always a blessing having Laurie stay with us. No matter the circumstances.'

Nina took a breath before beginning her rehearsed excuse. 'I'm sorry it's come as a surprise. Rob had already booked the plane tickets to come here, and it would have been a waste not to use them.'

In her too-loud voice, Tammy said, 'We'd been looking forward to seeing Bobby for forever. I still don't understand why he isn't here.'

'Dad's away,' Laurie said. 'He's been away yonks.'

'What's a *yonk*?'

Laurie giggled. 'Ages. Weeks.'

'He hasn't been away weeks,' Nina corrected her daughter. 'A week. And a bit. He sends his apologies, Tammy.'

Tammy smiled. 'One of these days Laurie will be able to make the hop on her own, I suppose.'

'But not yet,' Nina said. 'I hope you don't mind me being here, Tammy?'

'Why should I? Goodness me.' She paused. 'You're one of the family.'

Nina noted the pause. She was certain that Tammy had almost said '*practically* one of the family'. Despite Nina's long relationship with Rob, despite her having brought Laurie into the world, her status was still up for debate.

'And I can't remember if you told me – Bobby is…'

'In the Czech Republic. Somewhere near Prague.' It was the same lie Nina had used when Laurie had asked the question more than a week ago. She had no idea why she had answered 'the Czech Republic' in the first place; she had never been there. Strange how the mind worked sometimes. 'A holiday, sort of. He's with friends.'

'Well, I should hope he would be,' Tammy said with a gruesome smile. 'What's a holiday with people who *aren't* your friends?'

Nina pressed her lips together, uncertain how much to read into the question.

She realised Laurie was watching her carefully. The image of the girl on the harbour road flashed into Nina's mind, the face superimposed onto her daughter's, yellow-white as though still lit by car headlights. That same baleful expression.

'Well. Cookies are in the other room for those that can risk indulging,' Tammy said brightly. 'Your suitcases are still in the car. Can you manage, Nina?'

She escorted Laurie across the hallway before Nina could answer.

CHAPTER TWO

Nina slept in and jet lag turned everything inside out. She blinked sleep out of her eyes to see a hundred Robs smiling down at her. She groaned and rolled onto her face. The slats of the futon pushed through the thin mattress and dug into her chin.

Her phone gave the time as 10.30 a.m., but blearily she remembered that it would have set itself to local time automatically, and that UK time was five hours ahead. She hadn't slept this long for a decade or more. Not that she felt any benefit. Last night, after making her excuses and turning in 'early', she had stared at a patch on the ceiling, trying to ignore the Robs, listening to the enthusiastic rise and fall of Laurie's voice, the strident tone of Tammy's, the infrequent bass rumble of Abram's as they exchanged anecdotes in the sitting room.

Nina had an irrational sense that Laurie was being stolen away from her by Tammy and Abram, by Hope Island itself. She reminded herself that yesterday's journey had been fraught from the off. Their booked taxi hadn't arrived, the replacement had rolled up to their house late, the man behind the American Airlines counter had disputed the dimensions of Nina's suitcase, and another man operating the full body scanner had detained Nina almost long enough for them to miss their flight due to a cheese knife that somehow had remained in her jacket pocket after a friend had returned it following a dinner party. The flights were long, uneventful slogs enlivened only by pilot episodes of TV shows she would never watch again and her abortive attempts to make headway with *The Sound and the Fury*. The stops, at Philadelphia International and then Washington Ronald Reagan, had been fluorescent-lit and bland. When they had arrived at Portland, Maine, it had taken three circuits of the conveyor belt to determine that Nina's luggage was missing – though Laurie's had appeared almost immediately – and then four members of staff to ponder and finally alert them to an alternative conveyor belt where, inexplicably, her suitcase had chugged around and around in a slow, solo waltz.

All of this might have been bearable. Nina had hoped that the journey would feel part of the trip, that she and Laurie would bond over the daftness of the obstacles put in their way. The whole point of Nina visiting Hope Island for the first time, after all these years of refusing invitations, was to put her daughter at ease. But Laurie had jammed in her earphones early on and had slept – or pretended to sleep – on each flight. At one point, Laurie's phone had slipped off the armrest and into Nina's lap; when returning it Nina had flicked on the lock screen, only to discover that no music was playing.

It was only when they boarded the ferry at Boothbay Harbor that Laurie began to come alive. On the choppy twelve-mile crossing they had gripped the white barrier side by side and Laurie had used it as a makeshift ballet barre, performing swift pliés and speaking with growing enthusiasm. She gabbled about this same journey in the past – seemingly made wonderful because of the presence of Rob in place of Nina – while Hope Island grew from a smudge on the horizon to a wide crescent, its harbour nestled at the centre and Tammy and Abram waiting at the tip of its jetty.

As soon as they were given the signal to disembark Laurie raced to her grandparents, leaving Nina to struggle with both suitcases. The roar of the ferry's engine combined with Tammy's accent, made even less intelligible due to her foghorn shout, meant that their hellos were a pantomime of confusion. So much for the promised peace and quiet of Hope Island. So much for the welcome embrace of what remained of Nina's family.

Nina pulled on yesterday's clothes and lumbered out of the den. The air reeked of bacon. She followed the smell to the dining room. Her family were sitting at the table, one on each side.

'Moments too late!' Tammy chirruped, still in the process of forking the last thin rasher of bacon onto her plate. She wiped the serving tray clean with a piece of kitchen roll. 'There's melon still left over – no, look, it's past its best – or at least there's oatmeal.'

'Oatmeal would be lovely,' Nina said, but Tammy only glanced at the kitchen without rising.

In the kitchen, Nina found a crumpled packet of oatmeal in a cupboard. When she shook it, it rattled hollowly. She sighed and tossed the packet in the bin below the sink.

When she rose, movement outside the window caught her eye. She thought of the bird that had attacked her and she reached up to touch the graze that ran across her throat. It didn't hurt, and when she had checked in the mirror last night she had struggled to make out the line.

She pressed her hands on the cold sink and leant over it, peering through the grimy glass.

At first she saw nothing amongst the dense bushes beyond the scrubby cottage lawn. It was only when the figure shifted its position again that she identified its contours, its bare arms, its eyes peeping through the leaves.

It was a child. Could it be the same girl?

Before Nina could make out any further details, the figure retreated. The window was single-glazed, thin enough for her to hear a high-pitched laugh from outside.

Back in the dining room, she slumped into a chair and helped herself to coffee from the pot. Abram attempted to pour her cream from the jug. He frowned as she put her hand over the top of her cup, then instead poured it into his own empty cup and sipped it.

'The children seem to roam quite freely here,' Nina said, not quite managing an offhand tone.

Laurie raised an eyebrow as she munched a slice of toast.

'You should have left your preconceptions back in the UK,' Tammy replied. 'Kids here are wholesome. They enjoy simple pleasures.'

'The girl yesterday that I told you about. She was out very late. And she acted kind of strangely.'

'You said she gave you a shock?' Tammy said, though without any suggestion of sympathy.

'Well, not exactly. I tried to check on her, but a bird surprised me. I feel silly about looking so rattled by something so tiny. It must have been nesting behind one of the buildings at the harbour, I guess.'

Abram came to life. 'What did it look like?'

Nina blinked. 'I don't know. Small. Mottled wings, as if they were dusty. Black patch on the top of its head.'

He nodded enthusiastically. 'Blackpoll warbler. Should be nesting up in the woodland, never on the coast. It has this lovely song.' He raised his chin, then released a series of high-pitched *tsi* sounds.

Without understanding why, Nina shivered. But she would have preferred the bird making its call rather than that panicked rush of tiny beating wings. The sound echoed at the back of her mind even now.

'How are you feeling, Mum?' Laurie said.

Nina felt a pang of shame at her daughter's almost maternal concern. 'Bit fuzzy. You don't have any jet lag?'

Laurie shrugged. 'I never have. Dad doesn't either. He says it's made up, like homeopathy.'

Rob never seemed to fall ill or experience ailments of any sort. By willpower alone he staved off jet lag, colds and hangovers.

'Ever since I was a kid, I'd always get ill on the first day of holidays,' Nina said. 'Your grandparents – your *other* grandparents, the ones you never met – were teachers. I think it's genetic.'

She wished her own parents were still alive, to provide Laurie with an alternative template for adulthood. They had been good people, but frail. They hadn't even stuck around to see Laurie born.

Laurie smiled. 'You realise that's the first time you've said that word? Holiday, I mean.'

'That's ridiculous.'

'It isn't. You've been calling it a sabbatical.'

Nina felt acutely aware of Tammy watching their exchange. 'Well, it is. A month off work is a big thing, you know.'

'It is for you.'

Nina's executive producer hadn't so much as raised an eyebrow when she had requested the time off. 'About time,' he had said with a grin. A month off would hardly make a dent in the holiday entitlement she had accrued over the last five years.

Tammy raised her eyebrows. 'A month? My word.' She raised her voice to speak to her husband. 'Do you hear that, Abram? We'll have Laurie with us for a whole month. We can celebrate Easter together at the Sanctuary, how wonderful. That'll show narrow-minded folks what's what.'

This was exactly the sort of discussion Nina had hoped to avoid. She had successfully avoided the subject of religion during their previous encounters, and had instructed Rob to remain vague if Tammy ever enquired. Confessing to atheism might drive a permanent wedge between her and

Tammy. Despite everything, she would prefer to have her on her side. It would help in the long run.

'No,' she said forcefully.

Tammy's eyebrows lifted higher still. 'No?'

'We'll be staying for no more than a week.' Long enough to drop the bombshell and then escape.

Laurie threw down her slice of toast. 'Mum, but you said—'

'I said we'd still be coming to Hope Island, and here we are. But I had the idea that we'll travel around a bit, see more of Maine and maybe other states too.'

Tammy sat up straighter in her chair. 'Hope Island is America at its finest, I guarantee you that. The grand, great outdoors, honest people, real food, none of your McDonald's and In-N-Outs. You'll find nothing in New England to rival one of Si Michaud's lobsters.'

'I'm sure you're right,' Nina said, 'but I want Laurie to see more of the world.'

When Nina had discovered the flight booking printout in the cabinet on Rob's side of the bed, her plan had seemed so clear. She wasn't coping, and this opportunity ticked every box. She could escape from the bustle of work and the city, reconnect with the real world, come to terms with everything that had happened recently, spend enough time with Laurie to soften the blow when she delivered the news. Hope Island was important to Laurie, a safe space. Being here would lessen the impact. As a bonus, there was always the chance of Nina establishing some kind of a relationship with Tammy and Abram before giving them the lowdown on what a shit their son really was.

However, in the days leading up to their departure from Salford, the instinct to evacuate Hope Island at the first opportunity had become stronger.

'I'm right as rain here on the island,' Laurie said.

Right as rain. Since when did a fourteen-year-old use a phrase like that?

'I do like an In-N-Out burger,' Abram said thoughtfully. His upper lip still bore a stripe of cream. 'If anyone's going.'

Tammy rolled her eyes. She reached across the table and grasped Nina's hands. In a tone more like an announcement than conversation, she said, 'So it's settled then. You'll stay with us until Eastertime. Exciting!'

Nina withdrew her hands and sipped her cold coffee. She nodded noncommittally. When she finally mustered the courage to tell Tammy that her perfect son Bobby had abandoned his partner and his firstborn child, Tammy would be stunned, weakened, and more than happy for Nina to get out of her sight.

But things had to be in the right order. Laurie must be told first. She had to hear the truth from her own mother.

'It's Sunday, isn't it?' Nina said, genuinely uncertain. 'Tammy, will you be busy attending a service this morning?'

Tammy's forehead became a collection of tight wrinkles. Distantly, she said, 'Bobby could have been a choirboy if he'd wanted. The most beautiful voice, as a child.'

Abram began humming a hymn that Nina couldn't place. It grew louder and louder as Abram fidgeted with something below the table.

Nina clung to her line of reasoning. 'So, Laurie and I will head off after breakfast, just the two of us.'

Tammy began clearing away the dishes. 'No. I mean, there aren't any Sunday services on the island.'

'Oh.' Nina looked to her daughter, trying to appeal to her silently. 'Still, I'd enjoy it if you'd give me the tour of the island, Laurie. It's my first time here and I know it's meant a lot to you over the years. I'd love to see the place through your eyes.'

Laurie shrugged. Good enough.

'Don't mind us,' Tammy said. 'Feel free to use the cottage as a base camp. You'll show up when you get hungry.'

Nina would have to learn the cues that signalled Tammy's true emotions – she had no idea whether her tone indicated nonchalance, offence having been taken, or a vindictive streak. How many times had she met Tammy and Abram in the past? Four, five? But all the meetings had been brief and scrupulously polite, and all had been in England during European tours that culminated in visiting Rob. Nina had only met them once since Laurie had been born; she had been away during Tammy and Abram's final jaunts. Then, following Laurie's sixth birthday, Rob had begun carting her all the way over to Maine each year and Nina had always managed to make her excuses.

Abram leant over to his granddaughter. 'Hey, watch this,' he said. He wafted the napkin from his lap to cover an empty eggcup on the table before him. When he pulled it away again, an egg had appeared. Laurie grinned, then frowned in concentration as Abram held up a hand. With the restraint of an orchestra conductor, he tapped at the tip of the egg with a butter knife. Then he prised away its uppermost part and daintily retrieved a plastic dinosaur from it.

'Grumps, that's brilliant!' Laurie lifted and peered at the egg, which seemed to Nina to be otherwise normal and untampered-with. She paraded the plastic dinosaur around the table, roaring.

Rob had always done magic tricks like that for Laurie too – he must have learnt them from Abram. Until now Nina had never thought to wonder how much preparation went into these sorts of illusions.

*

Hope Island was only two miles across at its widest point, but the woodland along its central spine made the journey from west to east coast slower than Nina expected. The breeze made the air colder; she chided herself for wearing a skirt. Laurie strode ahead, clad sensibly in denim, swiping at red spruce with a stick and knocking cones to the forest floor.

'We're nearly there,' Laurie called over her shoulder.

Nina jogged to catch up. When she returned to Salford she would reactivate her lapsed gym membership. Too much standing around at work, then consecutive Netflix addictions in the few waking hours at home. Rob had always been careful not to flaunt his healthy social life – his evenings out at the snooker club or the pub – and had always understood about Nina being so tired after work.

'Nearly where?' she said.

Her question became redundant as they pushed through a final boundary of foliage and suddenly the world fell away before them.

Beyond the cliff, the Atlantic was a vast, uninterrupted plane and the sky its mirror. Nina remembered something she had once been told about ancient civilisations having no word for the colour blue, instead using terms like 'wine-looking' or 'shield-like'. At this moment neither the ocean nor the sky appeared blue, even though objectively she perceived that they were dazzlingly so. Instead, they were twin voids.

She was struck by the thought that this trip might really be a positive turning point. The water sighed and the wind caught at her jacket, and she imagined her problems as dandelion seeds on the cusp of being blown away. The outside world was larger than it appeared on the monitors of her TV newsroom. There was beauty in it.

Without turning from the ocean, Laurie snaked her right arm around Nina's waist, drawing the two of them gently together. They were almost the same height. Nina wished that Laurie had inherited her dark hair, or that she herself could be granted the same tightly curled blond hair as her daughter. She wished that they were more identifiably family.

There was no sense in waiting. This was the ideal moment. The revelation about Laurie's father abandoning her would be put into perspective, measured against the scale of the ocean.

'Did you know there are three Hope Islands?' Laurie said, interrupting her thoughts.

'What?'

'Dad says there are millions of islands off the coast of Maine. And three of them are called Hope Island. Isn't that funny?'

It didn't seem at all funny to Nina. A strange idea occurred to her: that each of the alternative Hope Islands might be dedicated to only one of the wonky trinity comprised of her, Rob and Laurie. Clearly, this Hope Island belonged to either Rob or Laurie. It wouldn't be kind to her.

She tried to shake off the feeling. 'Laurie. I'm happy that we have some time together.'

Laurie squeezed her tighter. 'Yep. Come on. You wanted me to show you around.' She shrugged herself free and darted towards the cliff edge.

'No!' Nina yelled.

Laurie spun around at the precipice. 'Don't be silly. It's nowhere near as steep as it looks.'

Nina followed and sure enough, the ground sloped away shallowly to the bare rock. What she had assumed was a cliff was actually a pile of huge boulders that appeared frozen in the act of tumbling down to the water's edge.

Laurie had already begun to make her way down, sliding gracefully on her bottom to land lightly at the next level of boulders.

'And your father lets you do this?' Nina called out.

'He never said either way. Isn't that an American thing? Don't ask, don't tell?'

Nina shuffled to the edge of the first boulder and slid down, copying her daughter's route precisely. Her bare thighs rubbed painfully against the pitted stone.

'Where are you taking me?' She pointed down to the waves hurling themselves at the sea-level boulders. Each one connected with a slap. 'We're not going all the way down there.'

'No, we aren't.'

Instead of clambering any further down, Laurie hugged a boulder to her left and then edged sideways along a flat, narrow outcrop. Below it the piles of rocks were less staggered, producing a sheer drop. Soon she was out of sight.

'Laurie?' Nina whispered.

'Still here,' Laurie replied, her voice made small by the rock barrier.

A few moments passed before Laurie screamed.

Nina lost her footing immediately. She grabbed at the rock behind her but couldn't find any purchase. She yelped as her flimsy sandal caught in a fissure.

'Laurie!' she shouted. 'Laurie!'

Her daughter's scream became something deeper, something thick and drawn up from deep within her body. Nina fumbled her way along the same slim outcrop, her belly pressed against the stone, not looking down.

Laurie's shouting continued uninterrupted. Dimly, Nina noted that it still came from the same location; Laurie hadn't fallen any further down.

The outcrop narrowed to a point. Now Nina realised that there was no longer anything pressing against her stomach. She bent awkwardly to examine the rock she had sidestepped around to discover a cave-like depression and, within it, her daughter. Laurie peered up at her impishly. She stopped screaming.

'What the actual fuck was that about?' Nina snapped.

'Sorry. It's just what I do.'

'Is it? Screaming like a lunatic is what you do?'

Laurie fluttered a hand to wave Nina away. 'There isn't room in here for two. Go back around and I'll follow you. Then you can have a go.'

Lacking any other option, Nina obeyed. Within seconds Laurie reappeared, navigating the outcrop with ease.

'Go ahead, Mum.'

'I'm not doing that. And what *were* you doing, anyway?'

'Primal screaming. It's ace. I used to call this place the Crow's Nest, because I liked pretending to be on lookout, but these days I like it for the... what's the word? Not echo, exactly. *Acoustics*. Try it?'

The rising inflection was meaningful: a request more than an invitation. This was a personal thing. Perhaps it was the way to earn Laurie's confidence.

Nina made a show of huffiness. 'If you absolutely insist.'

Once again, Nina worked her way around the outcrop, then rotated her body carefully and eased herself backwards into the depression Laurie had vacated. The outcrop path disappeared from view. All that she could see was sea and sky.

Vertigo was something she had heard about but had never experienced. Now it was as if she slumped forwards on an axis without having moved, and suddenly the hidey-hole became a vertical tunnel, and she was hurtling towards the flat solid slab of the ocean, and in her panic she wondered whether she would crack through its surface and plunge into its depths, or whether she would skim like a flat pebble far away and out of sight. She braced herself against the uneven walls of the cave, pushing and pushing to prevent herself from being sucked into the vortex.

She pushed and shook and cowered in silence and then heard Laurie's faraway voice say, 'Now scream.'

Her daughter's voice reoriented her. The ocean plate swung to become horizontal. Her stomach lagged behind, coffee swilling in its emptiness.

Now scream.

Nina opened her mouth, wondering if she would do it. The air was thick with salt and the wind spiked directly into her throat and her lungs.

The ocean sighed its disappointment.

'I don't want to scream,' she said.

'Everybody needs to let rip sometimes. You're on your own now.'

Nina hesitated. 'What did you say?'

'Pretend I'm not here. It's only you and the big wide sea. Scream and let it all out, Mum.'

Nina opened her mouth wide again, but then gagged. Abruptly, hot tears stung her eyes. She stared out at the void and thought of the note from Rob she had discovered on the kitchen table upon returning from work: *I'm sorry, but I've gone for good.* She thought of her frantic looting of the house while Laurie was staying at a friend's house overnight: Rob's passport gone, and maybe a few items of clothing and a couple of books, but pretty much everything else left behind. Her careful repositioning of every disturbed item the next morning in preparation for Laurie's return.

Her glassy denials to her daughter, and at work, and to her friends, that anything was wrong.

If she could only channel it all. A single scream. It would solve nothing, but it might establish an outlet. A statement of intent that she was ready to start afresh.

No sound came from her mouth. She grabbed her knees and rocked, bumping her shoulders on the hard cave walls.

Minutes passed without any sound other than the waves, a hum made somehow threatening in its journey into the cubbyhole, a roar in all but volume. She rubbed her forearm across her face, more and more rapidly as if she might prevent the tears with heat.

She struggled forwards and made a crouched one-hundred-and-eighty-degree turn in the opening of the little cave. After she had made her way along the outcrop and onto the relative safety of the boulder platform, she found that she couldn't meet her daughter's eye.

CHAPTER THREE

Nina frowned when she saw the boy. He stood at the crest of the hill as they trudged along the worn track at the cliff edge. With the sun behind him he looked like a Giacometti statue, the light turning his limbs into barely-there spindles.

He was watching them, like the girl on the road last night. Nina felt a surge of coldness and glanced instinctively at the sea to her left and far below, as if the water level might suddenly have risen and begun to creep along her skin from the feet up.

She shielded her eyes and looked again at the crest of the hill, but the boy was already gone.

Laurie hadn't noticed, staring at her feet as she walked ahead of Nina. Her fluid movements as she navigated the rocks and clumps of grass revealed her nascent maturity. The malleable, formative years of Laurie's childhood were over. Somehow Nina had missed them.

She forced herself to look at her surroundings instead.

Hope Island was beautiful. No aspect of the environment

was motionless; even the cliffside rocks were alive with shifting shadows. Herring gulls wheeled in the sky, graceful stringless kites whipping in the irregular gusts. The wind from inland pointed the meadow grass towards the water, green waves hurrying to meet blue. The ocean embraced the island, insulating it from the real, hostile world.

This was a place in which she, too, ought to feel safe. It would allow her to reach out to her daughter in a manner made impossible by their respective lives at home.

She took a deep breath and relished the clear, cold air in her lungs.

There was no sense in waiting.

'There's something I need to talk to you about,' she called out.

Laurie stopped and turned. Her eyes shone glassily. People had always commented that they were Rob's eyes, not Nina's.

Once again, Laurie interrupted her. 'What's your problem with Gran?'

Nina blinked. 'What? I don't—'

'She's only trying to make you feel welcome.'

Nina shook her head, in order to clear it rather than as a refutation. 'I don't have any problem with Tammy. And Abram's a sweetheart.'

'You don't even want to be here.'

They stopped walking. Nina reached for Laurie's hands, but they slipped away.

'I'm sorry,' she said. 'I know I've been on edge. I'll calm down. It's work.'

30

'It's always work, Mum. What's the point of a holiday – I mean *sabbatical* – if you're still at work, really, in your head?'

Nina had no idea how to demonstrate her innocence. In truth, work had only been on her mind in fits and starts. Tammy and Abram's house had no Wi-Fi; she had spied a desktop computer on the upstairs landing, but stifled the impulse to ask to use it. Before they had entered the woodland, she had finally found a patch of 3G reception, but after a couple of forced refreshes her inbox had insisted that it had *Updated just now*, with not even a spam email to show for it. Anyway, she had left minutely detailed instructions about ongoing projects and everyday routines for her team and Hannah, the acting producer, at the *North West Tonight* studio. They'd be fine without her.

'It takes a lot out of me, that's all,' Nina said. 'Don't be cross about it.'

'I'm not cross.'

'No. Okay.'

This must be about the primal scream. Nina had been given a chance to participate in Laurie's private ceremony, and had turned her down.

'Today is today,' Nina said. 'I'm grateful to be here with you. And I know it's strange that I've never visited Hope Island before, and that I really don't know your grandparents all that well. I know it's weird and I suppose I don't really have any good answer for why. But I'm here now, and I'm happy about it.' She smiled to prove it.

'You're lying,' Laurie said.

Nina shivered even though the breeze had died down. 'What do you mean?'

Laurie watched her, breathing deeply. Her concentration and intensity were unlike a child's. 'I can't be doing with lies, Mum.'

This was the time for the truth.

But suddenly Laurie was shouting at her. 'You're *not* happy to be here! I don't understand what you're *doing* here!' All her earlier poise had disappeared and her eyes glittered silver. 'You want to ditch me and go travelling – well, fine, do that, then. It would be better if you didn't pretend. You're just bringing everyone down, don't you see that?'

Laurie's face tilted up towards the sky and its skidding clouds. Nina wondered whether she might scream again. But then Laurie scraped her blond hair behind her ears and gazed at Nina. That round, open face. Nina experienced twin impulses, both equally alien and wrong: firstly, to embrace Laurie and prevent anybody else from influencing her; secondly, to shove her and watch her plummet into the ocean.

Nina wondered what Laurie's equivalent impulses might be.

Even though Nina hadn't moved an inch, Laurie whispered, 'Don't come near me.'

Nina held up both hands in surrender.

'I need to talk to you about your dad,' she said slowly.

Laurie frowned, then reached up to rub tears from her eyes.

Nina realised that her daughter was no longer looking directly at her. Her attention was directed over Nina's shoulder.

With a heavy-bellied certainty that Rob was standing behind her, Nina turned.

She gasped and recoiled. Pain shot through her stiff neck.

The boy – that same boy from the hillside – was standing directly behind her, far too close. His arms were loose at his sides, but his proximity had connotations of an attack.

'What the hell?' Nina snapped. 'Why would you sneak up on someone like that?'

The boy stared up at her, one eyebrow raised. He didn't speak. He looked to be a similar age to Laurie. His limbs emerged from his baggy T-shirt like sticks from a bundle.

He must have been walking fast to have made it all the way around the inland hillock in such a short time, to approach them along the cliff path from behind.

'Thomas!' Laurie called out. Gently, she pushed Nina aside.

The boy gazed at Laurie impassively.

'Thomas? It's Laurie. Remember me?'

Thomas's eyes narrowed.

'We're not from the island,' Laurie said. 'Well, obviously. I mean, there's hardly anyone living here so it'd be weird if you'd only bumped into us now.'

'What are you doing here?' Thomas asked in a neutral tone.

'Visiting Gran and Grumps.' Laurie's face flushed. She *liked* this boy. 'My grandparents. They live here. You must remember me. I was here only the Christmas before last.'

Thomas's eyes darted to Nina again.

Laurie waved a hand dismissively. 'Mum's never been to Hope Island before. My dad was born here. Rob Fisher.'

Thomas nodded slowly.

They stood in an awkward triangle. All of Laurie's rage appeared to have evaporated, but Nina felt no relief at all.

Thomas seemed immune to any sense of having interrupted them. There would be no opportunity to speak to Laurie about her father now.

'Shall we keep walking?' Nina suggested. She took a few strides along the cliff path, then turned. Behind her, the two children still appeared to be sizing each other up. Laurie shrugged and set off. After a moment Thomas caught up and kept pace alongside her. Nina continued and decided that she ought not to look back at them again. She heard Laurie's light laugh. It sounded forced.

The woodland ended abruptly and now Nina could see all the way to the southern tip of the island. There, the land fragmented into enormous, slick rocks dipping into the water; the fractal image deceived the eye so that the precise coastline was impossible to identify. Nina saw a series of small bays with stony beaches and occasional small shacks. Nearer to where she stood, a dozen houses built on the slope were raised at their front ends to keep them horizontal. They were mostly identical weathered wooden buildings, nothing fancy, but it occurred to Nina that the views of the gulf from each of their porches must all be equally impressive and that they had been positioned carefully for precisely that reason, like cinema seats. For a brief moment, Nina fancied that the buildings were snapshots of a single house scudding down the hillside.

She listened for Laurie's and Thomas's footsteps, but heard nothing.

Turning, she found that the children were no longer visible, hidden by the outcrop of trees. She waited for more than a minute before retracing her steps.

She froze, just as the two children were frozen in a peculiar tableau.

Fifty metres away, Laurie was perched on the very edge of the cliff top, looking at the ocean below, the tips of her shoes protruding over the edge. Thomas was standing directly behind her, just as when he had appeared behind Nina on the path. His arms were outstretched so that his palms pressed against Laurie's shoulder blades.

'Laurie!' Nina cried out, bursting into a sprint.

Laurie shook her head, but whether it was in response to Nina's call was impossible to tell. The wind picked up, pushing against Nina as she ran, diminishing her cry.

'Get away from her!' Nina shouted. Drawing closer, she could see the taut tendons in Thomas's scrawny arms. He was strong enough to push Laurie over the cliff edge, if he wanted to. Why didn't Laurie turn around?

When Nina reached Thomas, she gripped his right shoulder and spun him away from her daughter. He recovered quickly, but his expression remained sullen and unashamed.

Laurie still didn't turn to face her.

Nina reached up to put her hands on her daughter's shoulders, but the action was too like the boy's. She clasped her hands together instead.

Finally, Laurie turned. There were no tears in her eyes but her cheeks were pink. Her eyes raised to look at Thomas, then dropped to the ground.

'Get a grip, Mum,' she said quietly.

Laurie set off towards the houses on the slope. Thomas followed and Nina brought up the rear, taking gulps of air and watching the boy for any sudden movements.

They came parallel to the edge of the woodland. One building at the top of the slope, hidden until now, was different to the others. Its horizontal pure-white slats reminded Nina of the Baptist churches she had seen alongside highways on the journey from the airport.

A woman hopped from its porch and headed directly towards Nina. She was carrying something in the crook of her arm. A baby. Now Nina could hear its wailing. The woman wore a pale, floral skirt that floated away from her and her long hair became a horizontal streak, making her appear lopsided as she navigated the grassy slope.

'Thomas!' she called out. Of course. The boy's mother. 'Come on in now. You haven't eaten a thing all day.'

Thomas trudged sullenly towards the house without saying goodbye to Laurie.

The woman grimaced as the baby in her arms shrieked and pulled at her hair. She turned her attention to Nina and Laurie. 'Lord! Laurie Fisher, is that you? Aren't you a beanpole now! I'd give you a bear hug, but His Highness here wouldn't allow it.' To Nina, she said, 'He's been grizzling all week. I'd say it was teeth but a three-month-old with teeth? Doesn't bear thinking about, does it?'

Nina tried to shake off her earlier shock and offered a smile. She could barely remember Laurie's first six months. Her brain had blanked it all out. When she had abandoned breastfeeding within the first week, Rob had been perfectly understanding about it; in fact, he had been pleased that bottle-feeding would allow him to be more hands-on, sooner than many of the other dads. The idea of something with teeth near her nipples was gruesome, but only slightly more so than the idea of breastfeeding at all.

'I'm Laurie's mum,' she said, holding out her hand. 'Nina.'

'Marie Maddox.' She laughed at the awkwardness of using her left hand to shake Nina's right. Her wide face was freckled and the gap between her front teeth made her goofily likeable. 'This little beast is Niall, and I guess you've already met Thomas. I love your accent. British, but not high-and-mighty, you know? So, you're with Rob?'

'He isn't here, I'm afraid.'

'Mine neither. Fallon works on the mainland, in haulage. It sucks, right?'

Nina paused. 'Yep.'

Marie gestured at Thomas, who had almost reached the white house. 'Fallon being away so much of the time is getting him down this year. Look at the slump in those shoulders. He's been like that since the end of the semester. Still. You here for long?'

Laurie spoke before Nina could answer. 'A whole month. Mum's taken a sabbatical from work.'

'Attagirl!' Marie said.

'She's a high-up producer on a news show,' Laurie said. Nina wanted to hug her, though her suddenly positive attitude was puzzling. 'She works really hard.'

Marie beamed. 'You deserve a break then. So, what are your plans?'

Nina spread her arms wide: no plans.

'Hey,' Marie said, now speaking to Laurie. 'I know this is your vacation and all, and you're too old for our little school—'

Nina peered again at the building. It wasn't a church; it was a schoolhouse.

'—but if you'd like to join in,' Marie continued, 'the island kids have set up a little weekday club to occupy themselves. You'd be very welcome.'

Laurie looked doubtful.

Marie chuckled. 'It isn't only the young ones. Thomas joins in each day too. His school's on the mainland, of course. He comes home each day full of wild stories about the 'real world', as if Hope Island isn't part of it. But he was as keen as anyone to set up this little club, seeing as he's stuck here for the vacation. I guess you'd say he's the ringleader.'

'Thank you. I'd love to,' Laurie said, before Nina could interject. Laurie stood on her tiptoes to watch Thomas as he climbed onto the porch of the schoolhouse and disappeared inside.

'There you go then. Tomorrow at ten or thereabouts.' She patted Nina on the arm. 'It'll give you more time for R and R. Let's do coffee.'

She flinched as the baby shot out a tiny hand, scraping his nail all the way from her neck to her breast, leaving a thin track. His scream scrambled Nina's thoughts.

'Christ, that one hurt,' Marie muttered. 'He'll be a bruiser like his dad.'

Laurie bent to the baby. 'Hello, little Niall. Nice to meet you.' She enclosed his tiny fist in hers. The baby's yelling stopped abruptly.

Laurie looked up at Marie quizzically and then, to Nina's surprise and odd revulsion, she threw her arms around Marie on her free side. Marie reciprocated one-handed. Her grin directed at Nina contained no hint of gloating.

'We'd best be moving on,' Nina said.

Marie peeled Laurie away from her gently. The baby resumed his crying.

'Come now,' she whispered to him. 'You'll get what you want, once we're back inside.' She rolled her eyes at Nina. 'Give my love to Tammy and dear old Abe, will you?'

'You know them?' Nina's face flushed. 'Of course you do. What's the total population of Hope Island?'

'Seventy-eight.' Marie looked down at the child in her arms. 'Seventy-nine. But sure, I know the Fishers well. Had plenty of my meals in their little kitchen when I was a kid.'

Nina's cheeks became hot. Perhaps Rob and Marie had been childhood sweethearts.

'They're having a tough time of it,' Marie continued. 'Well, Tammy is, anyways. You'd never know it, but there's a whole lot of tension on this little island. A whole lot of politics.'

'Is it anything to do with the Sanctuary? I got the impression that Tammy has a bee in her bonnet about it.'

Marie smiled. 'You're a quick study. You should be a journalist.'

'Actually, I am.' She frowned, testing the label against her current role at Salford MediaCity. 'Or at least I was.'

'There you go then. Sure, it's about the Sanctuary. Down at the harbour they're plotting counter-insurgency. You been over to the Sanctuary yet? Met the Siblings? They're good folk, all told.'

Nina shook her head. 'We really should be getting back to Tammy and Abram. It was lovely meeting you.'

'Likewise, Nina Fisher. See you tomorrow.'

'Scaife. Nina Scaife.'

'Oh, sure. Scaife.'

Nina ushered Laurie down the hillside.

*

The sounds of the harbour grew in volume as they approached. Nina had always liked seaside holidays as a child, though her experiences were of the garish promenades of Bournemouth and Brighton, the amusements and ice-cream kiosks. It occurred to her how much of a landlubber she was: even though she had lived in Manchester for almost six years, the only time she'd been to any of the Lancashire coastal towns was a single trip to Blackpool, and that had been only for the illuminations. They had set off late because something had cropped up at work, and Laurie had slept in the car the whole time, missing everything.

In fact, she wasn't sure she'd ever visited a working coastal village. Perhaps the constant shouting between the men hopping from boat to boat, the fishermen dragging plastic crates filled with ice and red limbs, the woman standing with arms folded outside the tiny grocery store and the locals criss-crossing the cobbles between the shops and a hotel were normal and necessary to the smooth running of life on the island.

As they passed the concrete building where the girl had disappeared last night, Nina glanced into the gap between it and the rocks. She saw pebbles and crisp packets. There was nothing unnerving about the space.

She forced a bright tone into her voice. 'How about I treat you to something?'

Laurie hadn't spoken during their struggle down the hillside from the schoolhouse. The misunderstanding about Thomas's intentions made Nina reluctant to push her luck by trying to start a conversation. Silence was better than being shouted at again.

Laurie smoothed down the collar of her denim jacket which she had pulled up against the wind. 'Like what?'

Nina tried to judge a correct answer. Not comics, not beer. 'A bar of chocolate?'

'Have you tasted American chocolate?'

'Something else then. Sweets. I mean candy.'

'Yeah. Okay.'

The woman outside the grocery store ignored them as they approached. Instead, she continued bellowing, '— and my sister doesn't even *have* a cat, so there's no telling where it came from. All I know is that she's pissed, and she's going to set traps, you can bet your life on that!' Nina turned to follow the woman's gaze, but her shouts appeared to be directed towards nobody in particular, as if she were conversing with the harbour front itself, a hundred metres away.

As Nina and Laurie entered the tiny shop, the woman clomped in behind them.

The shop was small, but the junk overflowing from its floor-to-ceiling shelves and pinned to the walls made it even more claustrophobic. It felt to Nina like a cave with its walls covered with sharp barnacles. Everyday provisions seemed to comprise only about half the stock. Most of the items in the doorway and leading up to a counter littered with paperwork and stacks of boxes were tourist tat and toys: water pistols, fridge magnets, pink sombreros, police officer dress-up sets.

'Saw you arrive yesterday!' the woman shouted, her voice even more blaring in the confined space. 'You're not little Laurie Fisher no more. Getting to be quite the young lady, aren't you? Bet the boys are all crowded round you these days.'

Laurie actually blushed. 'It's nice to see you again, Mrs Rasmussen.'

'You know, if I'd had her looks when I was young, I'd have *used* them,' Mrs Rasmussen said, winking at Nina. 'You her mom?'

Nina nodded. As the shopkeeper busied herself by ineffectually reordering the mess on the counter, Nina glanced at each of the woman's ears in turn, looking for any sign of a hearing aid. Nobody had any reason to shout like that in normal conversation. 'We're here for a bit of a break.'

Mrs Rasmussen raised her head. She squinted at Nina. 'What's that? You English are so shy and retiring. Don't know why. You don't look a bit like Laurie. You sure you're not stealing her away? You're not some kind of a nut?' She cackled, a sound so sharp and loud that Nina actually covered her ears.

Nina's heart leapt when Laurie rolled her eyes, a response clearly at the expense of the shopkeeper. Nina couldn't remember the last time she had shared a private joke with her daughter.

'So, hey, Laurie,' she said. 'Want to pick some candy? Anything you like.'

'Anything?'

'Sure.'

As Laurie moved up and down an aisle crammed with confectionery, Nina made a show of looking around, mainly to avoid eye contact with the shopkeeper, who continued muttering to herself about her sister's rodent problem and her assumptions about predators luring children with candy. She clicked on a portable radio balanced precariously on top of the till, then cranked it to maximum volume. The words that came from it were barely discernible in a sea of static, pops and something like whale calls.

Nina had to raise her voice to be heard. 'Do you have today's newspapers?'

'No.'

'A recent one, then?'

Mrs Rasmussen only shrugged. She bent to put her ear closer to the radio speaker.

'I could tune that in a bit better if you want,' Nina said, miming turning the frequency dial.

'You some kind of an expert?'

'Sort of. I mean, you don't need to be an expert to—'

'I like it like this.'

Laurie returned with her crooked arm laden with colourfully wrapped sweets. 'I couldn't decide.'

'That's fine,' Nina said. Then, to Mrs Rasmussen, 'That's all, thanks.'

The shopkeeper took an age to note down the prices of all the sweets, returning to the confectionery aisle twice to consult handwritten signs, and then in the end Nina had to calculate the total for her. By the time they exited the shop Nina's head was ringing from static and anxiety. Laurie had already unwrapped and begun munching a wilting, yellow-and-pink-striped stick.

Nina pointed along the uphill track. 'Perhaps we should head on back—'

She stopped as she spotted a figure silhouetted on the hillside overlooking the harbour, her face obscured by her hair whipping in the breeze. She couldn't tell if it was the same girl from last night.

'Laurie, do you know—'

But when she looked back, the girl was gone.

CHAPTER FOUR

'Keep following this road,' Tammy said in her flat, loud voice. She was gripping the handle of the car door with both hands in what Nina assumed was an implied criticism of her ability to control the Chrysler.

Nina obeyed. In the central rear-view mirror she saw Laurie pop in her earphones, humming as she watched the view out of the window. Abram had stayed at home, and with the entirety of the rear of the car at her disposal Laurie had somehow found a way of sitting sideways, her legs sprawled across the back seat, whilst keeping her seat belt on.

'Where are we going?' Nina asked.

'You looked a little lost when you showed up at the house this morning,' Tammy replied.

'No, only thoughtful.' It took Nina a few moments to decipher the implications. There were numerous possible reasons for Tammy bearing a grudge against her, but Rob shacking up with an atheist presumably rankled – surely there was no mistaking Nina as anything other than a godless liberal? And of course, she and Rob had never married, though he had offered twice.

'Listen, Tammy,' Nina said, 'I'm as interested as anyone in traditions and all that. But if you're taking us to your church then I really—'

'Watch out,' Tammy said. 'The road dips away sharply.'

Within seconds, the combination of the steep incline and the still-unfamiliar stick shift (hadn't all American cars become automatics long ago?) meant that Nina had to focus all her attention on wrestling with the heavy car.

'Follow the bends.'

Nina grimaced. What else could she possibly do? Eventually she got the measure of the sweeping curves of the road, and she allowed the car to coast around each bend. The road was wide enough that the bulky bonnet of the car, as it swung around, wouldn't impede oncoming traffic – not that there was any traffic anyway.

As the road straightened, she allowed her gaze to rise from the asphalt.

They were fast approaching the northern tip of the crescent-shaped island. The land ahead tapered away almost to nothing, but then became a lumpy mass. It looked as if the island was a claw, tapping at the outcrop upon which stood a thin white lighthouse. Even from this distance Nina could see that it was in bad shape. Stains marked its walls and paint had flaked away to produce grey staircase-like patterns. A glinting, ragged outline on the curved window of the lantern room suggested the glass was smashed.

'The Sanctuary,' Tammy said loudly, startling Nina.

Nina frowned. 'That lighthouse?'

'This whole place.' Tammy drew a shape in the air.

Nina swung the car around another bend, then leant forwards to see what Tammy indicated. The entire northern coast of the island was enclosed within a tall wooden fence, the type one might normally expect to see on a construction site. Most of the land within the enclosure was meadow, with the odd large rock poking up from the green expanse. A collection of buildings stood in the centre of the enclosure, far away from the lighthouse. By far the largest and grandest of these buildings was a blunt-faced mansion with a dozen or more windows and, in the middle of its wide roof, a snub tower that appeared rather like a dovecote. It looked like it might once have been a fancy hotel, though it was now decidedly unkempt; long grass reached halfway up the windows of its ground floor. Dotted around in the shadow of the mansion were a church with a thin spire and a handful of oblong cabins positioned at odd angles, as though they had been tossed carelessly from above.

'Technically, it's only the mansion that's named the Sanctuary. And it's prettier from the other side,' Tammy almost yelled over the struggling engine. 'It's all about the sea view.'

'I think I know what this is,' Nina said slowly. 'Rob mentioned it once, and I looked it up online. Wasn't there some sort of artists' colony on the island?'

'There sure was. It's been through a few proprietors since then. Seen better days.'

'So what is it now?'

'The Sanctuary. And don't we all need sanctuary sometimes.' It wasn't a question.

Nina decided to hold her tongue. It wasn't hard to see what might have drawn artists to stay here in the nineteenth and early twentieth century, back when being an artist was a legitimate occupation, at least among the privileged classes. From the upper windows the view over the ocean must be incredible. Nina caught glimpses of a lawn stretching from the far side of the building, where she imagined painters working at their easels. She thought of Laurie's cubbyhole, the Crow's Nest: her daughter's own method of blocking out the world and focusing only on the unending water. She shivered and shut off the car's fans.

The latticed-wire gate in the tall fence was propped open, so Nina trundled the car directly into the compound. They passed a man in a white wide-brimmed hat and then a young couple wearing baggy trousers and loose shirts.

'Over there,' Tammy said, pointing.

Nina parked up alongside three vehicles in the shadow of the main building. Two were battered four-wheel drives, the other a filthy flatbed truck. Nina stepped out of the car and gazed up at the main building. Now she saw that it was in a far more dilapidated state than she had realised. All of its windows were dark and several of the shutters hung loose. The horizontal grey boards of its walls – a visual continuation of the grey tiles above, as if the roof were gradually enveloping the entire structure – were warped and untidily overlapping. Through the upper windows Nina could see glimpses of the sky.

From somewhere, she heard the sounds of construction. A screech of metal against metal.

'Wrong way,' Tammy barked behind her.

Nina turned to look at the small church. Structurally, it was in as poor condition as the mansion, but its white paint must have been applied recently. Even where the struts bent away from the front porch, no longer supporting its roof, thick paint covered the snapped ends. The sight made Nina unaccountably nauseous.

Laurie exited the car and grinned as Tammy gently plucked the earphones from her ears. Tammy then put one of the buds to her own right ear, her nose wrinkling at the music. She shook her head and handed it back.

To Nina, Laurie said, 'Dad says this place will be nice when it's finished.'

'We'll have none of your cheek,' Tammy said, prodding her in the ribs.

'You've been here before?' Nina asked. 'You've been to the church?'

Laurie stared at her blankly.

Tammy gripped Nina's shoulders firmly and spun her around. The three long, low prefabricated buildings formed a rough semicircle, a visual echo of the crescent-moon shape of Hope Island itself. The construction sounds seemed to be coming from the open double doors of the middle cabin. Like the periphery fence, the prefabs would have looked more at home on a construction site. Correspondingly, the man who emerged wore a lime green high-visibility jacket and goggles that covered most of his face. He pushed the goggles up to become tangled in his blond, chin-length hair.

'Tammy!' he yelled. 'It is around time!'

He was younger than Nina, though the crow's feet at the corners of his eyes suggested worldly experience or, at the very least, dedication to some outdoor occupation. His nose must have once been broken and then set oddly. Far from making him appear threatening, Nina thought the lack of symmetry made him unconventionally handsome.

'And who have you brought here for us?' he said with a grin. His teeth were bad. It occurred to Nina that everybody she had encountered in Maine so far had perfect smiles.

She held out a hand, determined not to let Tammy relegate her to a passive role. 'I'm Nina Scaife. Me and my daughter are staying with Tammy for a while. We're visiting, over from the UK.'

'I am Clay,' he replied, taking her hand in a dry grip without shaking it. 'Your voice is good. Strong.'

For the first time, Nina detected his accent. 'You're not American?'

'Finnish. I am born in a town named Uusikaupunki, which is funny for you to say. It is a small town, but not as small as Hope Island, and it is on the coast, but a coast not so beautiful as Hope Island.'

Nina recalled Laurie's fact about there being three Hope Islands in the Gulf of Maine. Were the other two as picturesque, or as large? Might there be a Sanctuary on each of them, and a Clay, and now a Nina?

'And what brought you here?' she said.

Clay looked around, taking in the church, the mansion, the ocean. 'All of this. But this same question to you. What brings you to here?'

'Like I said—'

'*Here here.*' He jabbed a finger downwards. 'The Sanctuary.'

Nina looked at Tammy.

'I was determined to show Nina the old place,' Tammy said. 'It's important. To me.'

Clay beamed, his skin crinkling concertina-like at the corners of his eyes. 'That is good enough for me too. Come, we have coffee all ready for the cups.'

The interior of the prefab smelled like burning. Nina winced as the shriek of an angle-grinder grew to an unbearable volume. It took her eyes a moment to adjust to the dimness, during which time she was aware only of a suggestion of clutter and the flash of sparks at the far end of the cabin. Clay moved to a bench upon which stood a kettle and a collection of mugs. The room was filled with timber beams and metal struts, piled up or leaning against the metal walls.

The angle-grinder powered down. Now Nina realised that another sound had mingled with it to produce the cacophony she had heard from outside. Chaotic guitar music and a vocal delivery that was more a bellow than a melody came from some unseen stereo. Nina had always assumed it was a cliché that everybody in Finland listened to death metal.

Something moved in the gloom. From behind a workbench appeared an enormous man several decades older than Clay. He wore a grimy white vest, and beneath the wiry white hair of his upper arms was an array of tattoo smudges. In his right hand he held a long steel bracket.

Tammy greeted him with a hug.

Clay handed Nina a mug. When Tammy extracted herself from the newcomer, he said, 'My pleasure is to introduce to you Mikhail Zieliński.'

Nina nodded at Mikhail, who only blinked at her over Tammy's shoulder.

'He is Polish,' Clay said. 'But he does not speak.'

Nina waited for somebody else to say something. The death metal continued blaring from somewhere in the darkness. She looked at Laurie, who appeared unflustered.

'Is it a vow of silence?' Nina said finally.

Clay laughed. 'Is it hell. Mikhail used to speak plenty. He got sick of his own voice, am I right, Mikhail?'

Mikhail smiled. He patted Tammy's arm, then lifted the metal bracket to examine it. He blew on the angled joint, which turned from silver to crimson momentarily. Behind him on the workbench, Nina noticed a blowtorch propped up. That explained the smell.

'I'm sorry,' Nina said. 'I'm not sure I quite understand the setup here.'

Clay tipped backwards and, as if by sheer luck, landed in a low armchair. He pointed at other chairs positioned in a ring near to the kitchen area. Tammy and Laurie took seats, but Mikhail held up the metal bracket and then slunk to the other end of the cabin. Nina perched on a stool, sipping her coffee. It tasted of washing-up liquid.

'No setup,' Clay said. 'The Siblings are the Siblings. Family.'

'A brotherhood?'

'Women can be Siblings also.'

'What denomination are you?' When Clay only looked puzzled, she added, 'What do you practise?'

Clay gestured towards Mikhail, who had bent to examine the bracket on the workbench. The roar of the blowtorch merged with the screams of the singer. Nina was impressed Tammy was remaining calm despite the racket. If anything, Tammy seemed more content in the cabin than she had been outside. Her mouth hung slightly open and her head nodded in time with the throbs of distorted guitar.

'We practise this,' Clay said.

Laurie shouted over the din, 'He means his art.'

Nina frowned. 'The Sanctuary isn't a religious group? A commune?'

'Commune, yes,' Clay said. 'But religious, no. Not in the way you mean.'

'But you're artists? That's what brought you together?'

Clay pointed again. 'Mikhail and Elliot, who did the purchasing of this place, they brought us together. But your answer is yes. We create. We make art. The Sanctuary has a history that is long. You have heard of the Pennsylvania Academy of the Fine Arts? The New York School of Art?'

Nina shrugged agreement, struggling to hear him against the background noise.

'They all came here, once upon a time.' He counted on his fingers. 'Edward Hopper, Harriet Beecher Stowe, Thomas Cole...'

'Rockwell Kent,' Tammy added.

Behind them, a screech signalled that Mikhail had resumed working with the blowtorch.

'There were artists' colonies on other islands in the gulf too,' Tammy shouted. 'The outer islands.'

Clay nodded. 'Many transformed? No, converted – into military forts. A sad thing. Guns instead of paint, you know? But Hope Island resisted and kept its art and artists. In Uusikaupunki we had a history of great art. Robert Wilhelm Ekman was born there! But nothing like Hope Island. Less artists now than before, but still very great.'

'And you, Clay,' Nina said. 'What do you do?'

'Most days, I do building. Mikhail and me, we are fixing up the old house. It will take no more than one more year, maybe two. We are working hard and one day it will be a colony all over again. Like bees working together, yes? But that is not your answer. I work hard with art too. I am lucky that Mikhail likes working on metal, so he is helping me with my installation.' He pronounced the four syllables of the final word carefully and deliberately. 'And I think we are ready to add to it now. If you would like to see?'

Without waiting for an answer, he leapt to his feet. 'Mikhail? Is it done?'

Mikhail reappeared, brandishing the metal bracket. Now it had another strut fixed onto it to make a rough tripod. Clay received it, daintily holding the part that had been recently welded.

'Come,' he said. 'To the church.'

*

Clay put his weight against the door of the church to heave it open. Light spilled from an oblong hole in the angled roof. Dust motes were sent whirling by the inrush of air.

The church must have fallen into disuse long ago. Only the four rearmost pews remained. The space before them was empty of furniture and the floor was covered in a thick layer of sawdust tracked with footprints. There was no altar. The wall at the far end of the room was filled from floor to ceiling with a stack of black boxes.

Something moved to Nina's left. From the darkness emerged a man and a woman. They were young, perhaps in their early twenties. The man's black skin and shaven head contrasted with the woman's pale complexion and her dirty-blond dreadlocks. As she passed into the light Nina saw that the woman's pupils were dilated, and she fiddled with her belt around a sack-like dress as she scurried towards the door, giggling. The man slung a threadbare blanket over his shoulder and shot Clay a grin as he departed.

'They are Zain and Mischa,' Clay said, gesturing at the door. 'Do not mind about them. They will fuck just about anywhere.'

Nina glanced sideways at Tammy, who appeared nonchalant. Perhaps she hadn't heard what Clay said.

'They're members of the commune?'

Clay shrugged. 'We have no membership, no ID papers. They came here and they are welcome. Maybe they will find art in them, who knows. Come this way.'

As they passed the pews Nina had to squint against the light. The stack of black boxes at the far end of the room was actually an untidy pile of speakers, their black grilles rimmed with dust. There must have been at least forty. The largest looked like guitar amplifiers; the smallest were portable radios. The speakers at the foot of the pile had been arranged neatly, but those at the upper reaches had tipped precariously. The topmost ones were restrained with striped, elasticated cables more commonly used to fix items to the roofs of cars.

'Please, sit,' Clay said.

He gripped Nina's bare shoulders and guided her to sit on the frontmost pew. Flustered, Nina smiled up at him, admiring his dark eyes, the gleam of his sunburned skin. Tammy and Laurie sat too, Laurie positioning herself on the other side of her grandmother. Nina noticed her daughter staring wide-eyed at her, then glancing up at Clay, and she felt a rush of shame at ogling him. As far as Laurie was concerned, Rob was still very much part of Nina's life.

'Mikhail?' Clay called. The two of them moved to the left side of the room, where another speaker, larger than the others, stood. Clay placed the metal bracket on top of it, then they both bent to shuffle the speaker across the floorboards, which groaned under the weight. Clay indicated its destination with a nod and a grunt, and they were both breathing heavily by the time they set it down. Mikhail tipped the speaker backwards a little and Clay inserted the tripod bracket beneath its front, angling it by fifteen or twenty degrees.

He stood. A little breathlessly, he said, 'This speaker is from public address system for Hope Island summer fair. I fixed it but I borrowed it for a while too, a fair deal.' He wiped his forehead. 'I wanted to put it up high, but Mikhail made a good point. Angle does the same job better.'

'What's it all for?' Nina asked.

'You would like a demonstration?'

'Okay. Sure.'

Mikhail was bending over something on the floor beside the foot of the tower. Nina heard a loud click. Pinpoints of red light appeared across the array of speakers, indicating that they were all now receiving power. Then Mikhail returned to Clay, carrying a small device in his cupped hands. A thin black wire trailed behind him. Nina found herself fascinated by the whole setup, whatever it was. All this technology reminded her of her own safe place, the production gallery in her Salford newsroom.

'Thank you very much, Mikhail,' Clay said with a bow. He held up the device: a MiniDisc player, very like one Nina had owned at the start of the century. 'Tammy, you will do us the honours.'

Tammy gave a girlish giggle as she pressed a button on the device, then rejoined Nina and Laurie on the pew and gazed up at the speakers.

Nina heard nothing. Or close to nothing. A low hiss, perhaps, along with something less like sound and more like a change in the atmosphere, as if the air had become charged. Or it might only have been a physical rumble, a vibration travelling from the speakers, through the floorboards, and up through her feet and into her body.

Tammy appeared rapt. Her eyelids fluttered closed. Clay and Mikhail each had their arms folded, looking at the speaker stack with the formal, critical manner of engineers.

To Nina's relief, Laurie appeared nonplussed. When she noticed Nina watching her, she made a face.

'I don't hear anything,' Nina whispered.

Tammy's eyes opened. Were there tears forming in her eyes?

For a moment Clay's mouth twitched in an expression of annoyance, but then he gave a wan smile. 'It is not as wonderful as once it seemed. Tammy?'

Tammy wiped her eyes and shook her head, though whether it was sadness or something else was impossible to tell.

'But this is only the first part of my project,' Clay continued. 'I add to my collection.'

'Your collection of speakers?' Nina said.

'No, no. Not the speakers. The sound.'

'But there *is* no sound.'

Laurie stood up, glaring at Clay before addressing Tammy. 'I'll see you guys outside, okay? It's stuffy in here.'

Nina waited until Laurie had left. 'I'm not trying to be obtuse. Nothing happened.'

'But it was a recording, nonetheless,' Tammy replied.

'Of what exactly?'

'Silence. No, don't laugh. Clay has been all over the island, collecting recordings.'

'Of... silence?'

'Exactly right. And that recording, Clay...?'

Clay double-checked the readout on the MiniDisc player. 'Yes. This is your house, Cat's Ear Cottage. Empty. Even I was outside of it, starting this recording with remote control.'

Tammy nodded. Her breath caught sharply. 'Thank you.'

To Nina, she said in a loud voice as if to somebody with impaired hearing, 'Each silence has its own quality, you see. I think it's a wonderful project. But I have to say, hearing *that* silence is kind of eerie. Like it's my life, but without me or Abram in it.'

Nina had no idea how to respond. The concept was compelling enough in theory, but in practice it seemed nonsense.

Clay clapped his hands, startling Nina. 'A little bit of fun. Part two is more interaction.' From the side of the church he produced a tall metal stand and another trailing wire. He hooked up a microphone and placed it onto the stand. 'I thought to myself, what could I do with this big amount of speakers? I have become interested in feedback. Feedback... how should I say?'

'Loops,' Tammy said loudly. 'Feedback loops, they're called.'

'Quite right. Nina, would you please?'

Clay tapped the grille of the microphone, producing a sharp thud from the speaker stack that made Nina wince. Moments later, the thud repeated, less harsh this time. It repeated again and again at intervals, becoming diffuse with the slight latency between the speakers in the stack.

'The sound plays and then it is heard – I should say picked up – by the microphone once again,' he said. 'And on and on and on and so on.'

Tammy was looking at Nina expectantly.

Nina rose from the pew, though she didn't really want to. This felt like a test.

'What do I need to do?' she said.

'Come here to the microphone. Speak into it a single word.' Clay held up a hand. 'But not any word. Speak a word that you would like to understand. A word and my installation will reveal the…' he paused to consider, '…essence.'

Nina felt their gazes upon her. She trod slowly to the microphone. It was hard to shake the feeling that this was some sort of a trick. She reached up and cupped the microphone in both hands, producing a sharp *pip* that reverberated around the room, echoing and then deteriorating into fuzz.

To Nina's surprise, she realised that she didn't want to disappoint Tammy.

Clay was watching her carefully, his expression as serious as a surgeon examining a patient.

What was the answer? A word she would like to understand. Possibilities occurred to her. *Loss. Anger. Purpose.*

She raised her face to the microphone, which Clay had placed a fraction too high. She wet her lips.

She said, 'Laurie.'

The speaker stack spoke the name back to her. She had always hated hearing recordings of her voice, but this was different. She blinked rapidly, experiencing the sound as a gust, her own breath amplified and heated.

Laurie.

It was loud without being loud. She could have believed the speakers weren't turned on, that the voice was inside her.

And then, after a second or two:

Laurie.

This time the name was rounded at its front, the attack on the 'L' softer.

Laurie.

Laurie. The repetition came around faster, or perhaps it was only that the previous utterance lingered.

Laurie.

The name became part of the air within the church, became the air itself.

Nina wanted to move away but she remained standing there, no longer holding the microphone, her hands lowered but still cupped around the ghost of its shape.

Laurie.

It was barely distinguishable now. The 'L' had become a breath that began and ended the name, the only rise in pitch the 'au' sound which now was only a soft moan.

It repeated. It kept repeating.

It no longer repeated but only continued, a drone with only the slightest inflection acting as a hillock within the waveform.

Now it was only a hum, flattened and reverberating so that every few moments Nina found herself unable to hear anything at all, experiencing the sound as something very distant but also very close, physical against her skin, moist and cloying. She spasmed and fought the urge to rub at her bare arms. Nausea rose up, flooding her throat with sweetness.

'I—' she blurted out.

This new sharp sound punctured the drone, then it did so again and again, and each time she felt it sting like a blade piercing her belly.

She turned and fled.

CHAPTER FIVE

'Laurie.'

'Like a truck?' Nina replied. 'Lorry?'

'Lorraine. Laurie. Like Hugh Laurie.'

Nina snorted. 'That's hardly better. I like Hugh Laurie as much as the next person, but that's no basis for naming our child.'

Her eyes moved from Rob's face to the baby in his arms. He had a natural way of crooking his left arm to support the head, even though he had never really held an infant before, as far as she was aware. A muslin cloth was draped over his shoulder, as they had been shown at the antenatal classes, and his posture in the low bedside armchair appeared totally comfortable. Only the top of the baby's head and one rounded cheek were visible to Nina from her position propped up on the bed. The soft fuzz of the baby's sparse hair mingled with the thick, fair hair on Rob's forearm.

'You look good,' she said. 'You're a natural.'

'You too,' Rob said, but it might easily have been a kneejerk response. She wasn't the one holding the child, after all. All she had done was push it out of her.

She wet her lips. 'I'm really tired. That's pretty much all I am right now. I'm not a person, I'm a tired.'

'I know, love. I don't understand how you had the energy.'

'I did eat three Yorkies.'

He grinned. 'Want another?' He reached into the holdall positioned at his feet. He had been prepared for weeks, had packed the bag himself, following online guides and NCT photocopies scrupulously, then adding flourishes of his own. He knew Nina inside out. Her nose wrinkled at the unsavoury thought. Rob took her expression to be a refusal and withdrew his hand from the bag to resume stroking their child's back.

It took Nina a few moments to register that she was crying. She sniffed and rubbed at her nose with the back of a shaking hand.

Rob looked up. 'Hey. Hey, what's up?'

Nina shook her head. She waved a hand to mean: all this.

Rob started to rise from the chair.

'Don't,' Nina said. 'She's sleeping.'

Rob settled again but now he was watching Nina carefully. She had been watched – by Rob, by a succession of midwives, then by a male doctor with a perfunctory manner and an eye on the clock – constantly since she and Rob had arrived at Saint Mary's. That had been before six in the morning, yesterday.

'So,' Rob said softly. 'Talk to me.'

Nina stared at the ceiling. The aircon dried her tears faster than was natural, making the skin of her cheeks taut. 'It all happened very fast.'

Rob chuckled. 'You would have liked a few more hours of labour?' He wilted under her glare. 'Sorry. Misjudged that one.'

'You don't feel it? All this, so soon?' She pointed at the sleeping baby. 'She's our responsibility, us together. How long have we even known each other? A year? We don't even have a joint bank account, Rob.'

'One year and one month,' Rob replied. Wincing with caution, he raised the child to allow him to shuffle the heavy chair closer to the bed. 'Who cares about numbers? We know each other, Nina. We know what we want. We know where we're going.'

A sob swelled up within Nina's throat. She pushed it back down, then nodded without conviction. 'But we didn't want this, did we? Not actively, I mean. It wasn't the plan.'

'Fuck the plan,' Rob said cheerfully. 'My plan is to be with you. To take the journey, with you. And now we are three.' Carefully, he twisted to show the baby to her. 'Look at her. She's on our team.'

Nina stared at the scrunched-up face, the screwed-shut eyes. Nina hadn't had a chance to see what they looked like open, but weren't all babies' eyes blue in colour at first, like Rob's? What evidence could she rely upon to determine whether the child looked anything like her?

'I know this means we're bound together now,' Rob said. 'More than a shared bank account. More than a mortgage or a marriage.' His eyes flicked up, then down again to the baby. 'And I like it. I like the idea of being bound to you.'

Nina opened her mouth to reply. A midwife entered, knocking on the glass panel as she pushed the door open.

Her uniform was blindingly white under the fluorescent strip light: she must have only recently started her shift. Her name tag read *Magda*.

'Okay, Mum,' Magda said. 'It's about time we had a go at a feed. All right with Dad hanging around?'

Nina looked at Rob, who gave an *it's up to you* shrug. She nodded.

'You're right-handed?' Magda said. 'Then let's start with the left boob. I'll help support her to begin with, then you can take over.'

Rob rose and offered the baby to Nina, but Nina made a show of fumbling with the tie of her gown. Magda received the child effortlessly, holding her against her body with one arm as if she were a rugby ball or a draped towel. Her breast now freed, Nina pushed back against the pillows to straighten herself, though she wondered whether it appeared like an attempt at a retreat. Magda lowered the child onto Nina's lap. The baby's eyes remained closed even as she raised her face towards Nina's breast.

'There she goes,' Magda whispered. 'She knows what to do.'

Nina only wished that she did too. She had paid diligent attention at the NCT classes, but from this angle the process was alien. She waited, frozen, for the baby to find her nipple. Magda put her hand on her bosom, pushing it towards the encroaching lips.

Nina looked up at Rob. He was hovering between the chair and the bedside, trying not to look more interested than was appropriate.

'Isn't Laurie your mum's middle name?' Nina said.

He shook his head. 'No. Louanne.'

The lips grazed Nina's nipple. She didn't look. If she kept pressed against the pillow, Magda's hand blocked any clear view of what was happening. She had a flash of certainty: *This isn't going to work.*

'Whatever name we pick for her,' she said, 'should be meaningful.'

Rob's face crumpled. He eased himself to his knees on the floor, elbows upon the bed, the same pose in which he had been fixed during her final hour of labour. 'You're not listening. Don't you see? *Any* name will have meaning, once it's attached to our daughter.'

CHAPTER SIX

Nina made a circuit of the ground floor of the house, looking for alternative distractions before she poked her head into the tiny kitchen.

'Can I help?' she said.

Tammy turned from the open freezer. Loudly, she said, 'You're the guest, dear.'

'Please don't think of me like that. If Laurie and I are going to stay for a while—' she winced at her accidental emphasis on 'if', '—then you need to let us make ourselves useful.'

'All right then.' Tammy straightened and smoothed down her apron. 'How does it all work at home with you and Bobby?'

'I'm sorry, how do you mean?'

'He was always a good little chef. Did he give it all up when he found a woman?'

'No. Quite the opposite, in fact. He's very much the boss in the kitchen. Always searching through celebrity cookbooks for new ideas, always picking up tips from the other mums.'

'And you?'

'Don't get me wrong, I can cook. I just don't have the time.'

Tammy nodded slowly. With distaste, she said, 'You're a modern woman.'

Tammy shivered, then glanced down and laughed. She closed the freezer door, then crossed to the small kitchen table with its thick laminate cover, swivelled one of its two chairs and sat down heavily. She rubbed at her calves.

'The only thing that surprised me,' she said, '– at the church, I'm talking about – is that your word was 'Laurie'. If you were going to pick a name, I'd have expected you to say 'Bobby', or I guess 'Rob'. Absence makes the heart grow fonder, after all.'

There was nothing overt in her expression to suggest animosity or that her observation was a test. It was impossible to know whether she had any inkling about what Rob had done to Nina.

'Clay told me I should say a word to learn its essence,' Nina said slowly. 'Rob and I have been together for fifteen years. I know his essence.'

Tammy smiled. 'But your own child will always remain a mystery.'

Nina refused to reply. Perhaps there would be a thrill, after all, in seeing Tammy's dawning response about what kind of child she herself had raised.

'You're a modern woman,' Tammy said again. 'I never did understand what it is you do.'

Nina's lips tightened. 'I'm a producer for *BBC North West Tonight*. It's a TV news programme.'

'When I was a girl, produce was what farmers sold in the marketplace.'

'It's hard to explain. Basically, everything that appears on the TV screen is there because I decided it would be.'

Tammy's laugh was light and tinkling, and fake. 'Goodness. You make it sound as though you make the news. As if you hide the cats up trees, loot the stores, murder the call girls.'

'You're teasing me. It's difficult to explain. Do you want me to try to?'

Tammy sighed. 'I guess we ought to be thinking about dinner.'

Nina bowed her head. 'Quite. What was it you had in mind? Or I could rustle something up, maybe.'

She watched on as Tammy struggled to her feet again, crossed to the freezer, then bent down slowly. After almost a minute of rummaging, blowing on her thin fingers, then more rummaging, she produced a thin box. 'Pie,' she said simply, and flashed a smile that, for the first time, seemed perfectly genuine.

She pressed it into Nina's hands, patted her shoulder, then plodded out of the kitchen and into the sitting room. Nina listened as Tammy spoke to Abram, who had been dozing when Nina had passed through the room earlier. Abram must have severe hearing problems: he and his wife both tended to shout when they were addressing one another.

After several minutes fiddling with the controls of the tiny oven, Nina registered that Tammy had fallen silent, whereas Abram was still speaking. From the little she knew about his character, it was rare for him to hold forth at length. She placed the pie, on its baking tray, into the oven and closed the door gently.

'—all a matter of timing,' Abram said in the adjoining room. 'Yes. That's it.' A pause. 'I wouldn't have believed it either. Do you think— No.' Then again, louder, 'No.'

Soundlessly, Nina crept to the doorway and pressed herself against the wall.

She jumped as Abram spoke again, loud enough that he might be standing directly on the other side of the thin partition.

'I said fuckin' no,' he said vehemently.

Her eyes darted. If he walked into the room now, she would appear entirely unoccupied.

She exhaled as she heard footsteps padding away on the threadbare carpet.

It was ridiculous, hiding like this. She adopted a neutral expression and stepped out of the kitchen. Abram was alone in the sitting room, as she had suspected. Oddly, he was already facing her: he must have walked backwards. They stood in silence. Then Abram raised both his hands and rubbed the skin below his ears, working his jaw from side to side, as Nina had done during each of her flights yesterday to restore her hearing. The old man yawned and loped out of the room and into the hallway. His clumping up the stairs took more than a minute.

*

Nina swore softly as she carried the two plates into the dining room. She had over-warmed the plates, and the oven glove had a hole in it, resulting in her palm being scalded. Each slice of pie had sunk at its vertex to become almost liquid, and if she hadn't seen the packet she would have been hard pressed to determine that the grey lumps were chicken. She had scoured the kitchen for anything resembling fresh food, and had added tinned sweetcorn and frozen peas, plus a jaundiced squash she had discovered in a cupboard and which she had somehow turned into a thick puree.

Both the dining room and the sitting room were empty.

'Laurie?' she called.

A pack of playing cards was spread face-up on the dining room table. Abram might have been practising another magic trick, or perhaps it was a game of patience. She deposited the plates, fetched the other two, then swept the cards into a pile.

She could hear voices upstairs.

'Dinner's ready,' she called as she made her way up the steep staircase.

The muttering continued.

'What's the matter?' she heard Tammy say. 'I thought youngsters were supposed to be whizzes at this sort of thing.'

'It's slow, that's all,' Laurie replied. 'Old and slow and tired.'

'If that's a dig at your grandparents, young lady...' But Tammy's tone was light.

Nina reached the landing to see Tammy and Laurie huddled before the desktop computer positioned beside the laundry bin. Abram stood behind them, an index finger scratching away within his right ear.

'Dinner's ready,' Nina said again, quieter this time.

Laurie's eyes flicked in Nina's direction, but she didn't acknowledge her.

'Nearly there,' she said to Tammy.

With a sinking feeling in her stomach, Nina recognised onscreen the blue window of a Skype call.

'There,' Laurie said.

The small speakers emitted a tinny ringing sound. Tammy leant forwards and cranked up the volume, then nodded along with each insistent, crackling trill.

'Why isn't he answering?' she asked.

'I sent him a text to tell him we'd call,' Laurie replied. She maximised the window. 'Here we go.'

The screen fizzed with colour. Nina gripped the banister and descended a step to ensure she was out of the field of vision of the bulbous webcam mounted on the monitor.

There he was.

'Bobby!' Tammy squealed. 'We can see you!' She bent close to the screen, so that Nina had to duck, too, to examine the image.

The connection was awful, the digital artefacts coalescing into recognisable shapes only every few seconds. Rob was wearing aviator sunglasses. The bright light that illuminated one side of his face suggested he was outside, having taken the call on his iPhone.

'—um! Laur—' The audio stuttered constantly, making sharp burps and flattened drones.

Rob appeared unaware that his words were inaudible. His mouth moved in fits and starts, the artefacting freezing it into different open positions.

'You sound like a robot!' Tammy shouted. 'Speak slowly!'

'It needs a kick!' Abram yelled.

Laurie opened another window and clicked various settings. 'I don't think there's anything I can do. Your connection can't cope, Gran.'

Tammy stared at her, uncomprehending. She pointed at the screen. 'It's not me, it's him. He's gone funny.'

Addressing her father, Laurie pointed at her ears. 'We can't hear you, Dad. How are you doing?'

Abruptly, Rob disappeared out of shot. Nina squinted, trying to make out the details. A lawn. The corner of a building – was that a bike leaning up against the wall?

'Where is he?' Tammy demanded. Behind her, Abram tilted his head to the right, as though he expected Rob to emerge from one side of the monitor.

Rob reappeared in a flash, a magic trick worthy of his dad. He was holding a small piece of lined notepaper, held sideways. On it he had scrawled a crude smiley face. One eye was a U-shape, a wink.

Laurie gave a thumbs-up sign in response. 'Where are you, Dad?'

Nina descended another step. Maybe they hadn't even noticed her arrival. She could go to the dining room and wait for them. It would give her a chance to prepare an excuse for her lie about the Prague holiday.

But the image of Rob was now completely inert.

Laurie clicked on more settings. None of the buttons responded. 'It's frozen. Dead.'

Tammy put her hands to her mouth, aghast.

Abram shrugged and walked away.

Laurie grinned. 'It's all right, Gran. Happens all the time. We'll get you set up on FaceTime or something. Do you have a phone?'

Tammy wrinkled her nose and pointed at the cordless house phone charging on its base beside the computer.

'Dinner's ready,' Nina said from the staircase.

Tammy and Laurie turned. After a moment, Laurie offered a smile. Nina knew the expression well, from subjects in TV interviews. It was a smile using only the muscles around the mouth rather than the eyes.

'You go down,' Nina said. 'I'll shut the computer off.'

After they had left, and before she started the shutdown, Nina peered at the frozen, pixelated image of Rob. Frustrating though it was not to be able to see his expression fully, the sunglasses were inadvertently helpful: he really did look as though he might be on holiday. He looked healthy and happy, but then he always did.

The backdrop was harder to make out now that Rob and his smiley face took up most of the frame. But on the bright green lawn Nina saw the long shadow of somebody standing just out of shot.

CHAPTER SEVEN

It was impossible to find any trace of threat or malice in the push of the wind, the circling birds, the boots tramping on dry, packed earth. But Nina's long shadow unnerved her. Its arrowhead tip protruded over the cliff edge.

'Are you happy here?' she said.

Laurie shrugged, making her rucksack jostle. Nina hadn't known whether to pack a lunch for her. The bag contained only a packet of crisps, a bottle of water and one of Rob's old baseball caps.

'How about your Gran and Grumps?'

'They wouldn't live here if they didn't like it,' Laurie said sharply.

'That's not what I meant. Does everything seem okay with them?'

Laurie shot her a sideways look. 'What do you mean?'

Perhaps attempting to describe Tammy's passive aggression would be too complex. 'People get old, that's all.'

'They talk loud now.'

Nina nodded. 'They're probably both a little hard of

hearing. Or even if only one of them is, they'll have got into the habit of loud conversations. It'd be weird for one person to shout and the other not to.'

As if to illustrate the point, Laurie's 'Yes' was barely audible, mingling with the wind that rolled up the hillside.

'And you shouldn't be alarmed if Abram seems a bit mixed up every so often.'

Another glare. 'He seems all right to me.'

'Yeah.' Nina concentrated on her feet for a while. 'Last night I heard him talking to himself.'

'You do that too.'

'Only on purpose. When I'm trying to work something out.'

'Maybe Grumps is working something out.'

Nina saw that her daughter was searching for a way to end the discussion. 'That's a fair point. All right then.'

Laurie had been quiet at dinner yesterday. She hadn't so much as prodded at her pie, though that was reasonable enough considering the state of it. Abram, in fact, had been restored to something close to normality. While his interjections were often non sequiturs, his warmth shone through his muddle. Nina tried to imagine Rob at that age, at the family dinner table, then pushed the thought away.

It was obvious that Tammy had been rattled by the inability to speak to Rob via the computer. She had slipped away from the table; when she returned, she complained that she had tried to call Rob's mobile phone but she had been put through to 'some woman'. Nina's throat constricted until it became clear that Tammy was referring to a pre-recorded answerphone message.

Nina had resolved that she must speak to Laurie as soon as possible. And yet here was an ideal private moment – again – and here she was watching the window of opportunity close.

'You know I love you very much, don't you?' she said.

'Mum.'

'I'm just saying. I think you're all kinds of wonderful.'

'You *have* to think that.'

'I don't.' She stopped on the rough track. 'I really don't, Laurie. I know you and I—'

Laurie kept walking. 'What?'

'Well. I know I haven't been as present in your life as I should have been. I know your dad has done all the heavy lifting so far.'

Now Laurie stopped too. Her hair hid her face, but Nina saw her shoulders slump.

'Heavy lifting?' she said slowly.

Shit.

'It's a turn of phrase.'

When Laurie spun around Nina expected her eyes to be red, or teary, but she appeared totally in control. She would be a confident young woman soon enough.

'First off,' Laurie said, 'you're lucky I don't have any hang-ups about how I look. I know a bunch of people who'd freak out at being called "heavy".'

'I'm sorry.'

'I told you I don't have a problem with it. But you make me sound like something that just needs carting from place to place.'

'That's not how I feel. I swear.'

'No. But you count yourself lucky that someone else is good at heavy lifting.'

Nina's mouth opened but no words emerged. What was the appropriate response?

Laurie turned and resumed her climb. Nina followed on leaden legs.

Within a few minutes the schoolhouse rose into view behind the hillock. As they approached it, Laurie turned. 'Mum, listen to me.'

Nina listened.

But Laurie didn't speak. They stared at each other.

Laurie scratched her forehead and winced, an absurdly adult combination. Then she said, 'Look, you're trying your best. That's good enough. Okay?'

'Yes. Okay.'

'Do you want to come inside with me for a minute?'

Unable to disguise her gratefulness, Nina replied, 'Of course.'

The door was ajar. Laurie pushed it open and stepped inside. Beyond the hessian-carpeted hallway with its narrow staircase, Nina saw light spill from a large room. She followed her daughter inside.

The schoolroom was larger and friendlier than she had expected. Its dimensions and the blue expanse visible through the ceiling skylight reminded her of the church at the Sanctuary. The sun's rays seemed more dazzling than they had been outside, reflected off the pale varnished floorboards. The open-plan spaciousness made the room appear far less old-fashioned than the exterior of the building, and this sense of modernity was emphasised by a large interactive whiteboard that took up half of the back wall, a laptop computer on the desk beside it and a desktop PC on a bench before one of the windows. On the other walls were neat displays with encouraging slogans, photocopies of scientific diagrams and pinned examples of children's writing and drawing.

Marie appeared from a side door. 'Laurie! I'm so glad you came.' She grinned at Nina. 'She'll be taken good care of, don't you worry.'

Nina offered as warm a smile as she could manage. 'When are the other children due to arrive?'

'Oh, they're already here. In the canteen.'

She kicked backwards to open the door. To Nina's surprise, it led directly into a kitchen full of the bric-a-brac of a family home.

'You live here in the schoolhouse?'

Marie beamed, showing the gap in her teeth. 'I never did like a long commute.'

It was only as Nina entered the kitchen that she saw it was occupied. Seven children of different ages sat around a large, square pine table. Before each of them was a plate with a thick slice of bread, and beside each plate a tall glass of milk. Nina scanned their faces, trying to determine which of the girls was the one she had encountered on the harbour road. The tallest of them, perhaps? She couldn't be sure. None of the children said a word, but they swivelled in their chairs to regard Nina. Their expressions were blank.

Then, almost in unison, they all smiled.

Out of the corner of her eye, Nina registered that Laurie had followed her in.

Marie bent to a Moses basket in the corner of the room. The baby lay within it, his eyes open and watching the other children. When Marie tried to lift him, he squealed and his hand punched upwards. She straightened again, leaving him be.

'Kids?' she said. 'This is Laurie Fisher and her mom. Laurie would like to join in with the vacation fun, if that's all right with you guys.'

None of the children spoke, but they were still smiling. Nina recognised Thomas, who was a head taller than any of the others. Both of his hands were laid flat on the surface of the table.

Laurie raised a hand. 'Hi. I remember some of you.'

Marie waited a moment before adding, 'That's good. Thomas, I know you know Laurie pretty well already, so I'm counting on you to make her feel welcome. Understand?'

Almost imperceptibly, Thomas nodded.

'Okay,' Marie continued, unruffled by the muted response. 'Clockwise from the top. There's Thomas, of course. Then Ali, then Eugenie – I should say Genie, as she likes to be known these days – then Sally and Landon – they're brother and sister – then Chase, then David. Thomas is the oldest – no kidding, right? He's a regular Stretch Armstrong. He's fifteen. And Landon's the youngest at seven, but he's no pushover. Actually, we'd normally have one even younger. Noah Hutchinson's only six. He and his sister, May, have been absent for a few days. Some sort of bug.'

Laurie said, 'Hi.'

'So, are you guys going to welcome Laurie?' Marie said.

Nina flinched at the abrupt scraping of chairs being pushed back. The children rose and padded over to stand before Laurie. Their motions appeared more dutiful than enthusiastic, with no particular curiosity. They were all still smiling, though, which was something. They rearranged themselves to make a tight circle around their new playmate.

Nina marvelled at Laurie's composure under such scrutiny. When Nina had been at school, being watched like that would have turned her into a shy, stuttering fool. Laurie had Rob's confidence.

But then Laurie glanced at her, and Nina saw uncertainty in her expression. Nina gave a smile of sympathy. Laurie's expression hardened but as she turned back to the children her body language changed, her limbs looser, her smile broader.

'Did I see a Nintendo out there?' Laurie said, addressing Thomas. 'And a dance mat?'

'Yes,' Thomas replied dully. Maybe that was it, Nina thought: videogames had made him unresponsive.

'Fancy a tournament? I'm no good past intermediate level, but it's always a good laugh.'

The other children looked at Thomas.

Something happened to Thomas's smile. Its tight formality melted so that it became wide and genuine. 'Later, maybe,' he said. He reached out and clapped a hand onto Laurie's shoulder. Nina shuddered, remembering the momentary illusion of him on the verge of pushing Laurie from the cliff. In a far more animated tone, he said, 'We like playing outside. We have this game where we gather sticks and then patrol the island. It's fun.'

Sally, who looked the next oldest after Thomas, reached out to take Laurie's hand. 'You're tall so you'll be good as a lookout.'

Laurie's eyes flicked to Nina. Now Nina felt certain this display of confidence was for her benefit.

'Sure.'

Within moments the group bustled into the main schoolroom, shuffling about as they pulled on their shoes. They didn't speak.

Nina felt off-balance with Laurie no longer at her side. 'It all sounds a touch military,' she said to Marie.

'Are you going to lecture me about American kids being all guns and fighting? That British children are innocent as lambs?'

It had crossed Nina's mind – the first part, at least. 'Not at all.'

'Don't worry. It's all really sweet. It's more Davy Crockett than all that.'

'You mean they hunt? And wasn't he a soldier?'

'All right. Not Davy Crockett, then. How about Robin Hood and his Merry Men, to go with an English theme.' She eased herself into a chair and glanced at the baby, who was beginning to grumble restlessly.

Through the doorway Nina saw that the children were ready to leave.

'Thomas?' Marie called out.

Her son sloped back into the kitchen.

'If you're back by midday I'll have a spread all laid out.'

Thomas nodded stiffly.

A sharper sound came from the Moses basket, the beginnings of outrage. Marie dived to it, scooping up the baby. As she did, she said, 'Thomas, be a love and fetch a mug for Nina, would you? And bring the coffee pot?'

'You don't need to,' Nina began, but Thomas had already clomped to a cupboard and retrieved a red mug, then crossed to the stove. The coffee pot was angled with its handle to the wall. Nina winced as the boy curled his hand around the steel pot rather than using the handle, but was relieved to see that as he carried it to the table his expression was neutral: it mustn't have been hot.

'Thank you,' she said as he placed the items on the table. She reached out to the pot, then withdrew her hand quickly, staring at her scalded fingertips.

Thomas looked at his left hand, too. The heat of the steel pot had left red streaks on his palm.

'Shit. Sorry for swearing. Are you okay?' Nina said. She glanced at Marie, who was busy soothing the baby.

Thomas blinked rapidly, still gazing at his hand. He held it before him at arm's length, watching it as if it were untrustworthy, then walked out of the kitchen slowly, his face a blank mask.

Nina watched him from behind as he approached the group of children, all ready to leave. Silently, he ushered them towards the front of the building.

Laurie was in the middle of the pack. She didn't look towards the kitchen as she left.

Nina heard the click of the door closing, then the whoops of the children and Laurie's unmistakable and genuine laughter.

Nina pressed two fingers to the coffee pot, but after a few seconds it became too uncomfortable to continue. She blew on her fingertips.

Marie had returned her youngest child to his basket. Now she was watching Nina.

'You're very alike,' she said. 'You and your daughter.'

The thought of broaching the subject of what she had witnessed made Nina feel a fool. Thomas had been fine. She must have missed him changing his grip on the pot.

She tugged at her hair and grimaced. 'Nobody says that.'

'I don't mean your appearance. She's Rob Fisher through and through.' She laughed. 'I'm sorry. I don't know you and I barely know Laurie. I can't possibly know what you're both like. So. You're a TV producer? That's awesome. Is it awesome?'

'I like it. It's very hands on. And frantic and stressful – all the preparation feels worth nothing once you're in the midst of a live broadcast – but to be honest I like that too. Spinning plates. The adrenalin rush you get from the chance that everything might fall apart at any moment. And I guess I get off on being in charge.'

'I hear a "but".'

Nina's eyes flicked up to the ceiling. 'I suppose.'

'You must be very busy.'

'Yeah. Of course.' She exhaled loudly. 'To be honest, it's pretty weird, not being there. Not being in control of my newsroom. I know I need a break, but…' Without thinking about it, she had drawn her phone from her pocket, unlocked it, opened the email app. 'Still no reception.'

'The main mast down at the harbour copes all right with calls from landlines and, most of the time, mobile signals – if the weather's fairly clear, that is, but then of course there's a radio line in the fire department for emergencies. Hope Island's never played ball with the internet. There's a hardwired connection on the classroom computer, if you need to get hooked up right now?'

Nina smiled gratefully, looked at the door, but then shook her head. 'Cheers. To be honest, the guys at work seem to be getting on fine. I just have to suck it up, this dictatorial streak of mine.'

'Well, any time. So it's been getting in the way, this being so busy?'

'Rob always made clear that he understood.' It wasn't quite an answer to Marie's question, but Nina sensed that the question wasn't literal anyway.

'Is he still in computers?'

'Databases. Barely. He takes on the odd project from old contacts. I think it's hard for him to get back into the game after taking so much time out.'

Marie nodded vaguely. 'Was it an active decision, you being the breadwinner?'

'It isn't like that. Rob's work is always lucrative when it comes in – he seems to attract money without effort. It's only bad luck, I suppose, that my job requires me to be somewhere else physically, and work unsociable hours.'

Marie tutted at her mug, rose and refilled it from the pot. The baby wailed at Marie as she passed. She sat down again. A muscle under her right eye twitched several times in succession.

'You must be pretty lonely,' she said, staring at her coffee.

Nina frowned. She had conducted enough face-to-face interviews in the past to know when someone was on edge.

'I get by,' she replied softly. 'I've always been a loner. You seem more the gregarious type, am I right?'

When she looked up, Marie's eyes were glistening. 'Don't get me wrong. I've got a heap of fun-loving kids around most of the time. It's not that I lack company.'

'Yeah. Still, how many young parents are there on the island?'

'A handful.'

'But living on an island is a bit like living with family, I suppose. You don't get a free choice of who you end up hanging around with.'

Marie sighed. 'You nailed it. I was quite the socialite, back in my college days. Now I feel old before my time. Maybe I should ask the kids if I can join in their fun, building dens up in the forest. Recapture my youth.'

Niall coughed in his Moses basket. Marie heaved herself from her chair and bent low to the basket. She jerked backwards as the baby flung up his hand.

'Shit. I'm sorry,' she said when Niall had quietened again. 'Offloading on you. I'm so starved of company. I'd have confided in you even if you were some serial killer, I reckon.'

She downed her coffee then fell silent, rolling the empty mug between her hands.

Nina would go crazy, too, living on an isolated island. At least Rob had never asked that of her. Even if that were the only thing to make their relationship work, it wouldn't have been worth it.

Partly to break the silence, she said, 'It's been tough on Laurie, the way I've arranged my life.'

Marie only raised an eyebrow.

'Actually, that's not right,' Nina said, turning the concept over in her mind. 'Laurie's never complained. Maybe it's been tough on me. I've watched her grow up, but as if it's been through a window, you know what I mean?'

Marie sipped her drink.

'Getting the producer gig was supposed to be a compromise. Before then, I worked abroad for a while.'

'When Laurie was young.'

Nina examined her face but saw no hint of censure. 'Yes. That's when the opportunity came up. Did Rob ever tell you how we met?'

A shake of the head. Nina felt gratified that Marie and Rob weren't close enough for her to know his entire history.

'I was a runner on a morning TV show. *Rise and Shine.* I'd only been doing it for a few months, and it sucked. Rob was a guest – this was after the point when he went public as a whistle-blower. He worked for Quinch, the soft drinks company?'

Marie shrugged. Her eyes flicked to Niall, whose grizzling had become louder.

'They're bust now,' Nina continued. 'Partly because of the fallout from Rob's revelations. All that tax dodging and data-skimming. Anyway, I was told to look after him when he was off camera, and we hit it off. If you watch the interview back, there's this bit where he's explaining to Pat, the host, how he managed to gather so much information without being discovered. "I'm pretty good at keeping secrets," he says, and then he does this wink. That was directed at me, standing to one side of the camera.'

'He always made a good first impression.'

Nina's lips tightened.

'Rob and I never had a thing together when we were younger,' Marie said, 'if that's what you're wondering.'

'No. Okay. Sorry. Anyway, we hung out, which was great, but all the time the Quinch story was building and building. And Rob had more, far more, than he revealed in the *Rise and Shine* piece. And he knew that I wanted into *proper* journalism. So, he gave me the story.'

'So then you were, what, a newshound?'

'It was what I wanted. Pretty soon afterwards, I was offered a position at Al Jazeera, in their London bureau. But then we found out I was pregnant.'

'So you never got to do it?'

'No, I did it all right. They kept the position open for me. But I could see it was shaky – the chance could easily slip away. I guess that was partly why...'

After a few seconds of silence, Marie said, 'Laurie?'

'Yeah.'

More silence.

Carefully, Marie said, 'Not all women take to motherhood right away.'

Nina's eyes flicked up.

'Sorry,' Marie said. 'Sorry, I shouldn't have said that. It's nothing to do with me.'

The kitchen seemed smaller. Nina could stand and leave. There would be no repercussions.

But instead she said, hoarsely, 'There were probably a ton of reasons. But the itch I couldn't scratch was this career being taken away before it had begun.'

'You chose the career.'

Nina examined Marie's expression. There was nothing in it that suggested censure.

'Objectively, I know I did nothing wrong. Men go back to work. Women too, especially here in the States, right? With your non-existent maternity leave? But yeah. I took the job partly to escape. And then I compounded it with an *actual* escape.'

'You ran away?'

'Of course not. But Al Jazeera offered me a post in Qatar. It was a big deal. Rob was fine about it. He was basically unemployable anyway, having been branded a snitch after the whole whistle-blowing incident. And he was deeply in love with the idea of fatherhood. He was everything to Laurie, even as a baby. Whenever he left the room, she'd be inconsolable.'

On cue, Niall emitted a wail. Marie bent to lift him out of the basket. His eyes opened wide and his little mouth contorted in an expression that in an older child one would describe as fury. He screamed.

'Hungry, huh?' Marie said.

Nina pulled out her phone as Marie slipped her shirt off one shoulder and put the child to her breast. No signal. Niall snuffled unhappily as he fed.

'Go on,' Marie said. 'It's interesting.'

'I want to hear more about you.'

Marie waved at the kitchen. 'This is me. Those kids out there are me. Fallon works away for most of the week, but we're all good.' There was no sign of her previous vulnerability.

Marie winced and lifted Niall, peering into his face. Without warning, he thrust out a tiny hand and his nail caught on her cheek, drawing a speck of blood. He shouted. Nina imagined she could see Marie's hair blown by the force of the yell. Marie pulled her shirt back in place, rose and danced around the kitchen, holding him close but angled so that his blows didn't connect.

'When he gets like this he won't let up for a while,' Marie said.

'I'll let myself out,' Nina said. 'I know where I'm going. Thanks for the coffee. And, you know. You're a good listener.'

Niall's screams grew in volume as she collected her jacket and bag. When she closed the outer door of the schoolhouse after her, the roar of the wind seemed a whisper in comparison.

CHAPTER EIGHT

It was true, Nina thought as she trudged northwards along the cliff path. Marie was a very good listener. It was a real skill. The trick of getting a story was to allow the subject to talk, only ever pitching in to keep things on track. Not like in a TV newsroom. Nowadays her job was all *telling*; her responsibility was to broadcast, not only in terms of what appeared onscreen but also in terms of issuing commands to her studio crew. She had a vision of the required output in her head, and her colleagues were her tools. She often wished she had more hands. Relying upon a team felt like a necessity, a weakness.

She was rarely required to listen, these days.

Had she listened to Rob over the years? Certainly not recently – the fact that his departure had come as such a surprise was evidence of that. But what about in the early years of their relationship, or the early months, before Laurie arrived?

She laughed bitterly. She could see his face clearly in her mind's eye, but she could barely summon the sound of his voice. No, she was not a good listener.

Fifteen years ago, alongside the antenatal classes, Rob had signed them both up for a one-off mindfulness session. He'd been worried about Nina's inability to switch off. They had sat with three other couples in a small treatment room in a clinic in Kennington with their eyes shut while a well-meaning therapist encouraged them to concentrate on each part of their bodies in turn, loosening each tight joint. Then the therapist had turned off the stereo playing godawful muzak and asked them to listen, to *really* listen, and to name each sound they heard, however insignificant. Nina had done as she was told: she heard and named the creak of the plastic chair, the scrape of her jeans against its hard surface, the tap of the zip on Rob's fleece jacket against his belt buckle, the rustle of the breeze from the open window pushing against the mobile of Perspex geometric shapes that hung from the ceiling in the corner of the room, the slam of a car door outside on Opal Street and the less distinct hum of traffic from the main road beyond, all punctuated by the heavier rumble of lorries, raised voices not quite arguing but perhaps negotiating a delivery to one of the local shops, the drawn-from-the-belly barking of a dog. And then she tried to shift her focus from these external sounds to those within herself. The air through her nostrils, sounding more ragged with each passing second. The sickening thud of her throat constricting as she swallowed. The pulsing of her blood experienced not as a sound, quite, but as a series of momentary deafnesses, like the blindness of blinking which, when noticed, becomes maddening. And then she turned her attention lower, trying to perceive something –

anything – that might prove to her that the thing in her womb that made her so uncomfortable, both physically and mentally, was something real and capable of making sounds and therefore, perhaps, one day would be capable of speaking to her and explaining itself. But she heard nothing from it. Her belly was a stretched-tight, full, silent void.

Now, on Hope Island, she closed her eyes and forced herself to listen to the birdsong and the wind. They were good, clear sounds, the soundtrack of a world that was alive and alert.

She may have lost Rob already. Retaining Laurie was a matter of communication, of listening.

But falling from the cliff wouldn't be a good start.

She opened her eyes.

Without realising it, she had walked far enough north that the lighthouse outpost of the Sanctuary was now visible. She looked at her watch: half past ten. But time meant nothing on Hope Island. She shielded her eyes to gaze down at the bright white church in the shadow of the Sanctuary mansion. A couple of figures moved to and fro in the area between it and the prefab buildings. She thought of Zain and Mischa, their obvious physical bond that suggested other intimacies, and she thought of Clay, his confidence, his health, his stack of speakers.

She began to make her way down the slope.

*

Clay waited for her in the centre of the gravelled area, his arms open wide, almost Christ-like with his straggly hair and beard.

'I am glad you have returned,' he shouted.

But she hadn't returned so much as ended up here. Wasn't that right?

'I worried about you some,' Clay said.

'Why?'

He gestured with a thumb at the church.

'Sorry about that,' Nina replied, her cheeks flushing. She added a lie: 'I had a headache, that's all.'

'It is something, huh? It is good that my installation made such a response from you. That is what it is for.'

Nina offered a weak smile. 'It's wonderful, it really is. I've never known anything like it. The first part, especially.'

A raised eyebrow. 'Why so? I feel not so sure about the project of silence recordings. Too quiet is what it is. A place like Hope Island has enough quiet. It is our job to add noise.'

'No.' Her cheeks became hotter still. 'Sorry. I don't mean to be so vehement. I don't think I *got* it, at first, your reasons for recording an empty house. It's all about listening. Listening is the way to connect yourself to the world. Otherwise everybody's broadcasting endlessly, and everything else is just background noise.'

Clay gave no response to indicate whether he agreed.

'You're doing it right now,' Nina said. 'You're listening, and I'm talking. I think I'm tired of talking.'

He was watching her closely. Nina wondered whether his body was as lean as his face, under all that loose clothing.

She shouldn't be thinking like this. She couldn't remember the last time she had felt any particular sexual urge for anyone other than Rob, and he was barely out of the door. Then again, she struggled to recall the last time she had felt that way about

Rob, either. She felt a sudden certainty that it wasn't due to their becoming parents, or seeing each other less often.

Clay wet his lips and nodded. 'And you want to listen?'

'I'm trying to remember how. I used to be good at it – professionally, at least. And then I stopped.'

Clay nodded. 'Please wait here, Nina.'

He darted away, leaping up the couple of steps to the prefab workshop. Within moments, he had returned. He was holding a pair of headphones.

She shook her head. 'You don't understand. Sorry, something must have got lost in translation. I meant that I want to listen to *real* things. Not music, not recordings.'

Clay smiled and offered the headphones to her. At the end of the trailing cable was the same MiniDisc player he had used inside the church.

Nina took the headphones and turned them in her hands. They were the bulky, old-fashioned type with a thick band connecting two cushioned cups that would entirely cover the ears. There was something unusual about them, though. On the outside of each headphone cup was a thick, furry pad. They looked as much like peculiar earmuffs as headphones.

It took a few moments to work it out. 'They're microphones?'

Clay beamed. Carefully, he enunciated, 'Binaural microphones. You try them.'

She slipped them over her ears. The silence was alarming. Sounds that she hadn't realised she had been hearing suddenly ceased. She tried to recall what the background noise had contained. The sounds of construction work from the mansion? She was only guessing.

Clay was still holding the MiniDisc player. He gave a thumbs up then tapped a red button labelled *Rec*.

The external sounds returned, louder. There were no sharp noises from the building after all. Instead, Nina was aware of the hum in the air, fluctuating with the wind that she now realised was catching at her shirt in time with the swell of the sound. The calls of gulls punctuated the hum, the distance softening their squawks into something pleasant, like the murmur of children playing. Beyond, or perhaps behind or underneath, she perceived something regular which she imagined as a smooth sinusoidal waveform. The waves on the sea rising and falling, rising and falling.

She closed her eyes and turned her head from side to side. The sounds shifted in their hierarchy of volume as well as their locations. She could hear Clay's feet shuffling on the gravel and she could hear the creasing of her own jacket. A strange effect of the microphones was that while external sounds were amplified, she heard nothing that she could attribute to her own body: no breathing, no creak or click of limbs. She turned again and – with a laugh that she heard as something other than herself, far away and dislocated from the usual hum within her chest that ordinarily accompanied her voice – she realised that she had wound herself tightly within the cable.

She opened her eyes to see Clay offering her the MiniDisc player. She took it and tucked it into her jeans pocket. She pulled the headphones back and down to make a bulky necklace.

'They're wonderful,' she said.

'They're yours,' Clay replied. 'Until you leave. Record sounds, listen to sounds. It is good for you.'

'You don't need them?'

'They are good at teaching you to listen. I have learned. I do not need them now.'

Nina exhaled. She wanted to hug him, but as much as anything the thought of the amplified sounds of their impact put her off. 'Thank you, Clay. I think I'm going to enjoy using them.'

Clay seemed to be appraising her. There was a possibility he might construe their conversation, the very fact of her being here, as a come-on. And there was a possibility that she was pleased about it.

'There is something else I would like you to see,' he said. 'Or I should say hear.'

'Another art project?'

'No. Not *my* project, at the least. You will find it interesting. You have good shoes. It is a walk.'

✳

They tramped for more than ten minutes in silence, heading towards the northern tip of the island. The lighthouse grew in size on the horizon. Every so often, Nina slipped the binaural microphones onto her ears, the MiniDisc player still recording, and she relished the amplification of the sounds of the island. Removing them resulted in deafness until the same noises slowly seeped in again, muted but intact. Clay swung a thick walking stick, only setting it to the earth every few paces. Wearing the headphones and watching him ahead of her, Nina noted that the sound of the impact of the stick and his footsteps lagged behind the reality by a fraction of a second.

'All is beautiful here,' Clay shouted over his shoulder. 'More inspiration than you can shake a stick.' Accordingly, he waved his walking stick in the air.

Nina looked beyond the land's end to the grey sea. More impressive than the view was the sound of the waves breaking against rocks out of sight, amplified by the headphones. Clay's voice sounded booming and godlike through the earpieces.

'It really is,' she said. Her voice sounded grand and outside of herself too, dislocated from the environment like the voice of a documentary narrator.

Clay turned. 'For me it is the sound. For others it is the vision. The painters, like Edward Hopper. Like Tammy Fisher.'

Nina yanked the headphones down. 'Hold on. What did you say? Tammy's a painter?'

'Of course. A very fine painter of…' he paused, '…sea-sky-scapes, perhaps.'

'She never mentioned it.'

'She is a shy painter. I tell her, you bring them to the Sanctuary, we will display them for certain. She says, "And get them all covered in brick dust? No way, no way."'

Clay set off again and as Nina followed she stared out at the sea, unable to fully process the idea of Tammy having any kind of artistic ability. Of all the surprises Tammy might have thrown at her, this seemed among the most unlikely.

'Here we are,' Clay announced suddenly, startling her. He hopped onto a wide, disc-shaped boulder, the only large protuberance in an otherwise barren landscape.

'I assumed we were heading to the lighthouse.'

'Lighthouse is disabled. This is where I headed to.'

The clumsy statement struck Nina as strangely profound. *This is where I headed to.* A statement that was always true, in a way, but coming from Clay it seemed an expression of deliberate intent. If she applied the same logic to herself, it would come out slightly altered and more passive: *This is where I am now.*

'What is it you wanted to show me?' Nina said.

Clay didn't answer. Instead, he tapped the boulder with his stick. Then he rose, turned, and pushed the stick beneath one edge of the boulder.

'Takes some push,' he grunted. He worked the stick further into the crevice between the rock and the dry, packed soil. Then he took a breath and pressed downwards.

The boulder lifted a fraction. Clay renewed his grip and then heaved. The rock moved. In a single, fluid motion, Clay released the stick and then in a flash his hands were beneath the boulder, his fingers scrabbling for purchase as he eased it aside. Soon he was able to use the weight of the rock to assist him. The boulder flipped over and landed with a thud that Nina felt in her knees.

Clay wiped his forehead. 'I wasn't one hundred per cent I can do it. Mikhail helped me before, always.'

'I could have helped, if you'd told me what you were doing.'

He shrugged. For a moment Nina considered accusing him of sexism, but her curiosity won out. Where the boulder had been was a hole, roughly the dimensions of a coffin. The rock had been a lid.

Clay pulled a battered smartphone from his pocket. Its screen was a lattice of cracks. 'You have phone too?'

'Yes. I haven't been able to get any reception.'

Clay prodded at the screen with his index finger. Nina blinked as a bright pinprick of light shone from its back.

'It is dark down there,' Clay said.

With that, he walked confidently into the hole.

The sight made her laugh out loud in her confusion. Standing to one side, at first she didn't register that Clay was actually descending – instead, she thought of an illusion that Rob used to perform for the delighted young Laurie. He would stride behind the sofa, bending with each step, pretending to go down non-existent stairs. Laurie would clap and call him back and there he would be, rising out of the floor.

But Clay really was going into the earth. Soon he had disappeared entirely.

Nina squinted up at the sun, then looked at the hole. She could see the first step – dark, packed soil – but nothing more.

She flicked on her phone torch. She took a step into the dark.

The passage was narrow, with no more than a few centimetres of space either side of her shoulders. The tail of her jacket scraped lightly against the packed earth as she descended. She aimed the torch downwards. Clay was nowhere to be seen.

'Is not far.' His voice echoed oddly, reverberating more than seemed right. She heard a strange crunching sound too.

Nina plodded on, taking care to find her footing on each rough step. The bulk of the headphones around her neck made a brace that prevented her from looking directly down.

The torchlight seemed to dim. She flipped her phone around and then squeaked at the intensely bright light shining in her eyes. She blinked to dispel the green ghosts on her retinas. When she shone the torch ahead again, she realised that it had seemed dimmer because it was no longer picking out the shapes of steps, or the narrow passage. She had reached the bottom, and the light now dispersed into a wide cavern.

It was about ten metres in diameter, roughly circular, perhaps two metres in height. Clay stood in its centre, the top of his head only a hair's breadth from the roof. For a moment Nina forgot about the journey from the gravel circle within the Sanctuary buildings to here, and imagined one above the other, as if they had descended directly to this underworld equivalent.

'It is impressive,' Clay said, purely a statement of fact.

Nina shone the torch around. Thin roots protruded from the black, low ceiling. The walls shone with lichen: pale, sickly greenish-white, the colour of cabbage white butterflies.

'Up is okay,' Clay said, 'but down is better.'

Nina pointed the torch down to see that Clay was standing on a thin board placed upon the surface of the cavern. But it was what lay either side of the board that commanded Nina's attention. At first, she thought that they were ceramic pots, broken like landfill. Then she took them to be something softer, like plate fungus. She bent down to examine those nearest to her. The larger objects were smooth, white stones, cousins of the disc-shaped boulder that had formed the trapdoor to the cavern. The smaller items were shells. Some were intact, but most were smashed, their sharp edges rising like tiny stalagmites. There must have been hundreds of them. Thousands. Some she recognised as mollusc shells, others oysters. With a lurch in her stomach, Nina registered other pointed shapes rising from the chaos. Thin bones. The cavern was a pit of white knives.

Nina heard the whooshing of blood pumping in her ears.

'It is nothing you should be afraid,' Clay said loudly. Nina winced at the volume of his voice and its peculiar soft echo, as if he were shouting in a cathedral. 'Is called a shell midden. Is not so unusual in these islands.'

'How old is it?'

'Depends. Top layer is maybe one thousand years. Lower is older. Many thousands of years. Many.'

'So it was, what, some kind of processing site for food? Is that it?'

Clay shrugged. 'So people say.'

'I've heard of shell middens. I think I saw a documentary once. But I don't understand. I thought they were normally found at ground level, beside rivers or on the coast.'

Another shrug. 'Hope Island is coast all around.'

'But we're up on the cliff, not at sea level. So the oyster shells and all the rest—' she peered again at the animal bones, '—would have had to be brought up here. And then down these steps into a cave? I don't get it.'

'Nina Scaife. Perhaps you look too much. You look and don't listen.'

That shut her up.

Clay continued, 'Wind has died down out there. We will wait. Then you will hear what made me fall in love at Hope Island, what made me listen to the world. Come to me.'

Nina made her way along the wooden board to join him. She grimaced at the sound of cracking beneath the wood as she put her weight upon it. The Siblings had laid the plank directly on top of the shells. The artefacts.

Clay lowered himself to sit cross-legged upon the board. Nina copied him.

They faced one another and waited. Nina glanced over her shoulder at the passageway that led up to the surface, the only way out.

'Now,' Clay announced. 'Listen.'

She watched his face, his closed eyes. She pulled her headphones over her ears and checked that the MiniDisc player was still recording.

At first, she thought the sound was coming from Clay: the 'Om' of a Buddhist or a yoga enthusiast. She turned and the movement of her head helped her locate the source of the groan. It was coming from the passageway. Her eyes widened. Had somebody followed them?

But there were no footsteps.

It was only the wind.

She turned from side to side, tracking the sound. It seemed to travel around the wall of the cavern. She remembered a water slide Laurie and Rob had once insisted that she try, which had deposited her into a disc-shaped enclosure, in total darkness, and she had been flung around and around like a coin in a dish, gaining speed until she had fallen shouting from a hole in its middle. She looked down, now, to reassure herself that there was no hole in the floor of the cavern.

The groaning air swung around her. She could distinguish the original sound from the additional gusts that hurried heaving into the cave, merging and amplifying the song. And it was a song. A long, sustained single tone like the tuning-up of an orchestra, with all of the subtle variations and individual cadences that suggested. It grew louder and louder, more and more beautiful.

It really was—

Nina realised that she was weeping.

She pulled down the headphones. Clay was watching her, but his interest wasn't voyeuristic, only indicating his happiness and confidence that they were experiencing something in precisely the same manner.

The reverberating hum transcended language. Nina struggled to determine her response to it. It was as if it was replacing the air with something fluid. And this fluid *something* connected the pair of them, she and Clay, and also tethered them to the rock, the lichen, the packed soil, the roots, the gleaming white shards.

Nina raised her hands and the song tingled on her fingertips.

It really was—

And then it began to abate. The orchestra had readied itself, but the symphony failed to come. Each individual player dropped away.

When the final steady drone lessened and then ceased, Nina was aghast at her sense of emptiness.

CHAPTER NINE

The sense of weightlessness and disorientation continued long after Nina had made her excuses and left. She stumbled through the Sanctuary gates and up the slope, soon abandoning the road to trudge wearily through the long grass.

What she had experienced in the shell midden had been a celestial song. Rationally, that thought made no sense to her, but instinctively she knew that it was true. It was no wonder that Clay had found it so inspirational. On their return journey to the Sanctuary he had watched her closely, smiling all the while. Back when he had first experienced the sound, his response had been to dedicate himself to Hope Island. Nina wondered what hers would be.

At the very least, the experience reinforced her resolve to listen. She detected traces of the song in the ambient sounds around her. The whispery chuckle of the blown grass. The wind catching in the trees on the hilltop, billowing with tiny booming noises like puffs of breath into paper bags. The cumulus clouds scudding overhead.

But all of these things were too quiet. The thought appalled Nina. The beauty of the song in the cavern diminished everything else in comparison.

The headphones were still around her neck. Perhaps they were the antidote to this sense of loss. She pulled the cups over her ears and clicked *Rec*.

There they all were. All those sounds, amplified and clarified. She stopped and turned on the spot. Her eyes closed and she spread her arms wide to invite the sounds in.

Yes.

Yes, she could hear it all. She was small and the world was vast and cared nothing for her. It was good to not be at the centre of things.

She resumed her climb, smiling at the introduction of new sounds, cocking her head to pay each new one attention, giggling. A gull cawed overhead: she saw its beak widen half a second before she heard its call. That was the only drawback to the binaural microphones, that slight lag. She couldn't quite trust what she saw. Or, at least, the visual couldn't quite be reconciled with the aural. But the sound was a better reflection of the truth.

As she reached the crest of the hill, she realised that her route had taken her far from the road which wound east around the woodland. Of course, the island was small, and either way around the trees would take her to Cat's Ear Cottage or the harbour. She wet her lips, tasting the salt air, and imagined the delicious array of sounds to be heard at the harbourside.

She frowned as she registered something new, insistent and regular, rising and falling as the wind pushed it her way.

It was music.

She spun to locate it. West. There were no forested areas in this direction. The ground undulated in gentle valleys and hillocks.

She set off, her head bobbing to pinpoint the sound. A sustained note, a voice, and something underpinning it, a clang that became more defined as she moved closer.

At the top of each new hill she expected to find it. She kept searching. The music grew louder. It was nothing like the song of the cavern. The voice was impure, the pitch high and wavering. The clang was a messy chord, repeating each second with careless variations. The air fizzed with dissonance.

Nina yanked the headphones down, sucking in air to calm herself. She pressed herself into the grass and crawled over what she knew must be the final hillock.

Two people danced in the pit of the tiny valley. A man and a woman. Both of the woman's arms were raised above her head and she pirouetted and whooped. Every few steps she returned to a wooden crate and slapped her palms upon it, producing twin thuds. The man's back was to Nina. His arm windmilled as he brought his hand down to crash upon an acoustic guitar, letting the chord ring out and echo around the clearing.

She recognised them. Zain and Mischa, the young couple who were staying at the Sanctuary.

The thought of alerting them to her presence filled Nina with revulsion. She watched their cantering about, Zain's stamping feet. She listened to their awful song.

The pair grew louder and louder. Zain attacked the guitar with a fist, Mischa pummelled on the box and screeched. Zain shouted, too, their voices merging into a discordant scream.

Nina put her hands over her ears.

Then she took her hands away. The mixture of sounds was shrill and strange, but there was joy in it too.

She surprised herself by laughing.

She shook her head to clear it, eyes darting between the man and woman in the valley. They hadn't heard her.

At the crescendo of their performance Mischa leapt back from the box, her arms spread. Her shirt was torn, perhaps having snagged on a splinter. Zain struck the guitar a final time, then raised the instrument above his head.

And then he brought it down.

The guitar hit the wooden crate with a crack of thunder that thrilled Nina. Instantly, both the instrument and the box exploded into shards that knifed outwards in a perfect radius. Involuntarily, Nina ducked down even though she was far out of reach. Neither Zain nor Mischa flinched. Nina couldn't tell whether either had been injured. For a second, they stared at the debris in the centre of the valley.

And then they ran at each other, trampling over the splinters. Zain lifted Mischa off her feet and whirled her around in an embrace. She pressed herself tightly to him, her hand clawing at the back of his head to push his lips to hers.

Then they were tearing at each other's clothes, and then their upper halves were bare. Nina realised she was still watching, and she felt ashamed.

In comparison to their music, their lovemaking was almost silent. But there was another rhythmic sound, and it wasn't being made by the lovers. Regular and sharp. A clapping of hands.

Wincing with concentration, she shuffled forwards a little further to see directly down the near side of the valley.

A man lay sprawled comfortably on the slope, one leg bent and his head raised by the incline.

It was Mikhail, the silent leader of the Siblings.

He was watching Zain and Mischa intently and he was applauding loudly and slowly.

*

Almost an hour later, Nina stumbled down the track to the harbour.

She needed a drink.

The only building that halfway resembled a pub was the hotel with a swinging sign that announced it as the Open Arms. Passing from the bright light outside to the dark interior reminded her uncomfortably of the entrance to the shell midden. However, in every other respect the two locations were entirely dissimilar. Wall-mounted TVs with their contrast turned up high blared chat shows and sports commentary. There were a dozen or so customers in the wide room, some on the black leather sofas, others standing at the bar or propped up on tall stools.

They were all shouting. Their words might have been in any language: Nina could only hear a cacophony. She waited uneasily on the entrance mat, squinting into the depths of the barroom, an alien observer. Her eyes adjusted. The barman and a few of the customers were looking at her, though their conversations continued uninterrupted. If you could call them conversations. None of them appeared to be listening to what any of the others were saying.

You're a trained journalist, she told herself. Walking into unfamiliar situations is what you do.

But really, she just needed a drink.

The barman was prodding his finger to make a point – something about a disappointing politician – but the woman he was addressing didn't seem to be paying attention: she was watching the baseball game showing on an overhead screen, and she was talking over him.

Nina waved to catch the barman's eye. When he slid along the counter the woman kept muttering to herself.

'What are you having?' the barman bellowed over the din. The capillaries in his cheeks and nose had burst, which at first glance made him appear sunburned or ashamed.

'Pint,' Nina said. She couldn't hear her own voice. 'What would you recommend?'

The barman pointed at his ear and shook his head.

'Pint of beer!' she yelled.

The barman pointed at the Coke dispenser.

'Beer!' she shouted again, exaggerating the shape of the word and breaking it into two distinct syllables.

He swung around, opened a fridge door, and when he had completed his revolution he was holding a bottle of Budweiser.

'Do you have anything on tap?'

The barman stared at her.

She nodded and held out a note. 'I'll take that.'

By the time he had returned with her change he was already absorbed in an argument with another patron. Further along the bar, two men were bellowing at each other even though their body language appeared friendly and they were sitting so close that their heads were almost touching.

Nina sipped her drink and surveyed the room, attempting to triangulate the TV screens, though she found she couldn't decide whether she preferred an area where their blaring wouldn't infiltrate, or whether they were a comfort. She slumped into a corner seat, her posture immediately undone as she slid down the slick faux leather.

She had visited the States a few times before. Never with work, as the Middle East had been her specialism, but in her late teens she had taken a lengthy Green Tortoise 'adventure bus' tour from California to the east coast, and then she had returned in adulthood for short city breaks in New York and Chicago. She had always felt that, despite the cultural differences, people were people. But sitting here on this shiny couch, swamped in noise and aghast at the hotel patrons who seemed more brash and belligerently American than any caricature, she had never felt more alien.

She wished she had a book to make herself appear occupied. She pulled out her phone and frowned at its lack of reception. She fiddled with the controls of the MiniDisc player Clay had given her and pulled the headphones over her ears, but the cushions barely blocked out the noise within the room and she could hear nothing of her recording of the Hope Island soundscape. The thought of replaying the ethereal song from within the shell midden in this context made her nauseous. She tapped the *Rec* button and the LCD level markers became tall, solid blocks representing an input of pure noise with barely any variation. Despondently, she cast the headphones onto the black marble-effect table.

A man sat at the table to her left. His facial features were smooth and rather androgynous; though he was almost entirely bald, he couldn't have been older than forty-five. Unlike the other customers, he was silent. His eyes were closed. He, too, was listening to earphones, the type that came bundled with iPhones. As if aware that he was being watched, his eyes flicked open. His gaze moved from Nina's face to the binaural microphones on the table. He smiled and raised his bottle of lager, then downed the little that remained. Beside it on the black tabletop was another, full, bottle.

He shuffled sideways on the padded bench, drawing nearer. He plucked out his earphones. Even against the backdrop of loud TV broadcasts, Nina could hear the music coming from them: a pounding, insistent beat.

He gestured at the binaural microphones. 'What are you into?' His voice was nasal and wavering, though it was as loud as any of the other customers in the bar, as if he couldn't modulate his volume. Perhaps his hearing was bad.

Nina shook her head. 'I don't listen to music much these days.'

The truth and sadness of this struck her suddenly. She tried to summon a tune in her head, but all she could muster was the opening sting of her programme, *North West Tonight*, less a song than a factory whistle indicating that work was about to begin.

'I used to,' she added hopelessly.

'Like what?'

'Britpop, I guess, back in the day. Indie.'

'The Rolling Stones?'

She scowled. 'How old do you think I am?'

The man flushed and retreated visibly, a shy tortoise. He picked up his earphones and made to put them back in.

Nina held out a hand. With a broad smile of relief, the man passed her one of the earphones. She held it a few inches from her right ear: the music was too loud to bring it any closer. Her mum would have said it was all thumps and clicks. It was fucking terrible, that's what it was. Rave, or happy hardcore. An unlikely choice for a conventional-looking, middle-aged guy, and loud enough to damage his ears. That explained the weird pitch of his voice.

'What is it?' she asked.

'I've no idea!' he yelled. His earphone was jammed right in. 'But it rules!'

He must have registered her disbelief. He pulled out the earphone again and reached into a pocket. The thudding stopped.

He held out a hand, this time empty. Nina shook it.

'Nina Scaife,' she said.

'Gavin Frears. Glad to meet you, Nina.'

While the TVs continued to push out noise, Nina realised that the nearby customers at the bar, two red-faced men, had fallen silent and were watching them. Abruptly, the men guffawed. One of them snorted beer from his nostrils.

'Don't let him tell those lies,' the other man, whose checked shirt was the same shade of crimson as his face, bellowed at Nina. 'Only his mom calls him Gavin.'

Beer-snorter elbowed him in the ribs. 'She don't, Jeb. His mom's fucking dead.'

Now they were both laughing.

'So then nobody in the world calls him Gavin,' checked-shirt announced. 'His name's Egg. On account of his fucking head.'

'Which looks like an egg,' his friend added.

This information delivered, they appeared satisfied that the conversation had ended. Still chuckling, they turned to face one another, resuming their loud discussion about some superhero film.

'Morons,' Nina muttered.

If her companion heard her, he didn't show it. 'They're right. My name's Egg. Always has been.'

'I can call you Gavin.'

He sighed. 'No. Call me Egg.'

'All right. But keep me updated. I'm perfectly flexible, if you decide to change it.'

Egg gulped from his bottle. 'There was a time when my name was respected round here. Not *my* name. My family name, Frears. My great- or maybe great-great-grandfather was a big deal. Built this harbour, for one thing. Frears have always been important on Hope Island.' The implication was clear: *until now.*

Nina grinned. 'Names shouldn't matter, but I know exactly where you're coming from.'

'Scaife's a good strong name.'

'No. It sounds like a knife going in. Not like Fisher. What could be more wholesome, especially on an island with an economy dependent on lobsters and shellfish?'

Egg stiffened. 'Fisher?'

'Abram and Tammy, up on the hill. They're sort of my in-laws.'

'You're married to Rob Fisher?'

'That's my point. We never did.'

Egg nodded vaguely. 'Saw Rob in passing when he was last over here. He's looking good. We're the same age, if you can believe it.'

So he was thirty-eight rather than forty-five. It *was* pretty hard to believe.

'You hung out when you were kids, I suppose?' she said. 'You were at school together? What was he like back then?'

'We were up at the schoolhouse together, sure.' He left her other questions unanswered. 'Funny thing. It was Rob who gave me my nickname. Must've been only five or six. Rob had a way about him, could make an idea stick.'

Nina's stomach lurched. She could picture it clearly. Charismatic young Rob – he must always have been that way – working the crowd in the schoolhouse. Given that there was only a single class, he and Egg would have been the youngest, and yet Rob had insinuated the nickname so that all ages had taken it up. He could have caused real damage if he'd turned to the dark side in adulthood and worked in politics or advertising.

'I'm sorry,' she said. She wasn't certain if she meant it as condolence or an expression of her own confused guilt.

Then she added, 'Rob isn't here. Just me and our daughter, Laurie. I've never been to Hope Island before. I'm looking forward to exploring.'

Egg brightened a little. 'There isn't a whole lot here.'

'Sure there is. It's beautiful, for a start.'

Egg nodded without conviction.

'And there's always stuff going on, even in a small community.'

'There really isn't.'

'What about the situation up at the Sanctuary?'

'Situation?'

'The shell midden.' She watched his face carefully, wondering if the phrase would mean anything to him.

Egg's forehead creased. 'It's only a hole in the ground.'

'It's more than a hole.'

'Suppose so.' Then, with an abrupt grin, and pointing at his earphones lying limp on the table, 'It's better than this racket, that cave song.'

Nina was surprised by her sudden wave of annoyance. Clay's manner had suggested that he was showing her something special: a scoop.

'You've been inside too? So why have the Siblings put up that huge fence around their property? I assumed it was to stop people going in there.'

'The Siblings do their own thing. There's not a whole lot of crossover with the islanders. They're up there and we're down here. But yeah, they let us in, always with a couple of them around as chaperones.'

'Surely it's private property.'

'It's their land, from the busted-up lighthouse to the

old mansion. That's all above board. And they're not out looking for a fight. They understand we're all curious.'

Nina took a gulp of beer but watched Egg over the top of the bottle, noting his adjustment of his sitting position, his shiftiness. There was something stirring within her, a voice she hadn't heard in a while. A compulsion to uncover the truth.

'I get the sense that a divide has opened up,' she said.

Egg glanced around before replying. 'You know what you said before, about Hope Island relying on lobsters and shellfish? That's not enough these days. Lobsters and shellfish don't make the kind of money this place needs. And even if the Sanctuary does end up an arty commune like it once was – which is the Siblings' masterplan, I guess – that wouldn't solve it. Artists don't spend. They sit on their asses all day, painting or, I don't know, making their own soup instead of buying shit from stores.'

'And Hope Island needs tourists. Tourists who are prepared to spend.'

'You got it.'

'And you think the discovery of the shell midden might attract that sort of person.'

'Not me specifically. Pretty much everyone. Like Kelly Brady over there.' He pointed.

'The barman?'

'Owner.'

Despite the fact that he was in the act of handing change to another customer, Kelly Brady had noticed Egg gesturing at him. He plodded away from the bar and stood before their tables, his meaty arms folded over his chest. Burst capillaries made crimson river deltas on both of his cheeks.

Egg wilted. 'I was just telling Nina here about your campaign.'

Kelly turned to Nina. 'You from the press, kid?'

'Sort of. I work for the BBC.'

Kelly's expression was somewhere between disdain and approval. 'That shell midden? It's a *major* archaeological site for certain. Teams ought to be in there, digging away with those tiny trowels. And then there ought to be a museum, a cafe, a store packed with fucking sweatshirts and pencil cases. Might be on Sanctuary land, but that place was part of Hope Island long before it was snatched by those communist fucking fairies. It belongs to *America*.'

Nina knew his type. To people like him, *America* was always synonymous with *white America* or, better still, *white third-generation-or-greater America*. She was tempted to point out that the layers of shells and bones predated European colonists by many centuries, having been dumped there by Native Americans and, long before that, by prehistoric tribes with skin colour that would presumably make Kelly furious.

'And these tourists would stay here at the Open Arms?' she asked innocently.

'Benefits us all. Got to have footfall, got to bring in the money.'

She thought of the dilapidated mansion that Clay and Mikhail were slowly renovating. 'At least the Siblings aren't building a hotel.'

Kelly's face reddened. 'That's beside the point.'

Nina wondered if he'd have liked to have bought the old place himself.

'So it was Kelly here who started the campaign,' Egg said. 'To petition the Siblings to open up the land, make it accessible to all.'

'But they aren't playing ball,' Nina said.

He shook his head. 'But that's not to say that they're obstructive. Any of the islanders can rock up to the gates and ask to visit the shell midden, and pretty much everyone has done at some point. It's only that the Siblings refuse to let tourists in. Which is their right, I guess.'

Kelly swung a hand down at Egg, who flinched and then gasped in relief when Kelly only grabbed the empty bottle. As the landlord turned away he yelled over his shoulder, 'Spread the word, BBC. Tell everyone there's *injustice* right here on Hope Island, okay?'

When Kelly's attention returned to his other customers, Nina puffed out her cheeks. Egg rolled his eyes in response. He was about to speak when a sharp sound from the barroom entrance made him and everybody else turn.

In the doorway, one hand pressed against the glass door which rattled against a chair, was a thin man in his fifties. His face was a concertina of vertical lines, within which his mouth and eyes seemed interruptions of a neat pattern. His fleece jacket and his wide, floppy hat were stained with white patches.

He said something that Nina couldn't hear. Evidently, neither could anybody else. None of the customers reacted but only continued to gawp at the newcomer.

'Where's Egg?' the man croaked finally.

Nina watched as Egg rose slowly from his seat.

'Right here,' he said loudly.

As the man stumbled over to their corner of the barroom, Egg said to Nina, 'I'm head of the fire department, you see. Told you that Frears held positions of importance.'

Nina made an impressed face. It was for real.

'*Volunteer* fire department, I should say,' Egg added. 'But same difference. It's all there is in the way of emergency services on the island. There used to be a coastguard stationed at the lighthouse, but the base has been disused for a decade or more.'

To Nina, the idea of an island without a coastguard seemed an invitation for trouble.

When he joined them, the newcomer only stared at the seat Egg was gesturing at. He looked at Nina doubtfully. Egg nodded and he toppled into the seat.

'Nina Scaife,' Egg said, 'this is Si Michaud. Works on the south coast. He catches lobsters and shellfish.' He gave her a look to emphasise the significance. 'What's the problem today, Si?'

Si stared hungrily at Egg's drink, then grabbed it and downed it in one. He wiped his mouth and stared at Egg. 'You got to come with me and see.'

'See what? You having trouble with any of the other catchers?'

Si swallowed noisily. 'It's not me having the trouble. You got to come.'

'First tell me what it's all about.' Nina had the impression that Egg was playing a part for her benefit, this pillar-of-the-community role.

Si's head dropped. He grunted, perhaps gathering himself. But when he raised his head again his eyes were still wild.

'I heard a shout,' he said hoarsely. 'A scream, I guess you'd call it.'

Egg looked at Nina, then back again at Si. 'Who screamed?'

'I followed the sound,' Si said. 'Had to scramble down from the bluff.'

He lapsed into silence, his eyes darting.

Nina leant forwards over the table. Her heart rate had sped up. Her pounding journalist's heart. 'What did you find?'

'Wasn't nothing to do with me, you got to believe me,' Si said, still addressing Egg.

'What happened?'

Si stood and pushed his seat back noisily. 'You got to come. Right now.'

Egg's eyes flicked to Nina. He leapt up too. His upper body wavered as though it were too heavy for his legs.

'Is it far?' Nina asked. Then, cautiously, 'Can I come with you?'

'I got the car out front,' Si said glumly. 'Nearly crashed it coming here.' He held up his hands. They were shaking terribly.

'I'll drive,' Egg said. He stifled a belch.

'How many beers have you had?' Nina asked sternly.

Now Egg held up his hand, too, as if inviting her to count the fingers.

'Then you're just as much of a liability. I'll drive. No arguments.'

She passed them and strode towards the exit. Out of the corner of her eye she saw both men follow her meekly.

CHAPTER TEN

Nina brought the four-wheel drive to a stop where the coastal track ended at a rough turning circle. A teetering pile of lobster pots made a wall, as though to defend the southern tip of the island from anything emerging from the ocean beyond.

Si stumbled out of the back seat. He pointed to a worn trail that led down the hill through a tall corridor of marram grass. He hadn't spoken a word during the ten-minute journey. He stared at the grass passageway, puffed out his cheeks, and then entered.

Nina allowed Egg to follow the fisherman, and brought up the rear. Both men had already disappeared into the grass, but she heard the sounds of their stumbling and the scuff of the marram against their clothes. Even though the ground was uneven, she felt in control of her footing. She realised that she was exhilarated by this development.

The ground fell away gradually. When she emerged from the corridor, she found the two men staring out across a small inlet with steep grassy slopes on three sides. The rocky beach was littered with abandoned lobster pots, their ropes frayed and fluttering. The bay permitted a view of a narrow vertical slice of the Atlantic; Nina thought of the Crow's Nest and its similarly limited outlook. The ocean roar made her wish she hadn't left the binaural microphones on the driver's seat of Si's car.

Si pointed again, out to sea. No, not quite that far, but further out along the beach.

Egg shielded his eyes. Nina did too.

There was something there, beyond the lobster pots, where the seawater lapped at scattered rocks.

'What is it?' Nina asked.

'I was up there,' Si replied distantly. He gestured over his shoulder with a thumb, without turning. His voice shook. 'Couldn't see a damn thing. I heard the shout.'

Nina looked at Egg squinting into the light.

'Shall we?' she said.

Egg blinked. He nodded.

As they drew closer Nina didn't take her eyes off the black shape at the water's edge. At first, she thought it was a seal – they must have those around here? But it was big, and the part that rose from the ground was rounded, not tapered like a snout.

Then she saw the neatly bent legs beneath the raised part. What she had taken to be slick animal hide was actually man-made material, shining wet.

'Who is that?' Egg said.

It was an adult. Knees bent, feet splayed. Buttocks raised in the air, a seesaw consequence of the head being so low to the ground. The body pointed away from the approaching trio. It looked for all the world as though the person were praying to the ocean. Shivers rippled up and down the body.

Si stopped several feet short of the figure. Nina and Egg exchanged glances.

'Hello?' Nina called out. There was no answer. Behind her, she heard Si's shuddering inhalation.

She led them the rest of the way.

The short hair suggested that it was a man. His head was tucked within a circle made by his arms. He faced directly downwards, his nose and chin resting on the rocks.

'Are you okay?' Nina said. But she knew that he wasn't.

She watched the tide push in. The man's shivers were synchronous with the movement. They were produced by the water.

Nina and Egg bent beside the man. Nina reached out but then waited, giving Egg a chance to take over. He said and did nothing, so she took the bent man by the shoulder and gently pulled.

He rolled towards them with a series of wet slaps, his legs and arms unfolding and splaying to flop into the rockpools. His trousers and jacket were black waterproof fabric. Rivulets of water trickled from them, tiny waterfalls on a dark mountainside.

His scruffy beard glittered with moisture. His mouth was open and his lips were white and torn, the lower one bitten through.

Nina felt a strange empty feeling in her stomach; she wondered if her lack of breakfast would be a blessing or a curse.

Above the mouth was a smashed nose, and above that only a hint of eyes. His forehead had caved in. Shards of skull protruded from the messy, dark hole. Nina stared into it, strangely fascinated and unblinking despite the tears welling in her eyes. She saw no hint of colour in the hole, but neither was it blackness.

Slowly at first, but then in a flood, blood poured from the void. It mixed with the sea water and made its way along the man's pale neck to be lost in the black folds of his clothing.

Nina felt Egg clutch at her. She rubbed away her tears and dragged him away from the body before he puked.

*

'I haven't seen him since yesterday morning,' Si said haltingly. 'He does his own thing. Did.'

Egg rose from his position leaning on a stack of lobster pots. He had run here to retch behind them but Nina didn't think he had puked again. 'His name is Lukas Weber, right?'

'Just because he was staying in my barn, doesn't mean I know anything about him.'

Nina frowned. 'He isn't an islander?'

It was Egg who answered. 'An itinerant worker. We usually get a few each summer. Not as many in winter and early spring. He'd been here since New Year. Is that the case, Si?'

Si jerked his shoulders; it might have been a shrug.

Once again, Nina felt a compulsion to investigate, a voice within herself, urging her on. If it was a distraction from her own life that she craved, this situation more than fit the bill.

'Tell us again what you saw,' she said quietly.

Si shook his head. 'Nothing. I told you that. I was at my workshop, then I heard the shout and came running.'

'And then?'

Si raised a shaky arm to point at Lukas's body. It was bobbing a little more now – the tide must be coming in. They would have to move the body soon if they didn't want it to float away. It would mean tampering with the crime scene. Nina noted how easily the phrase 'crime scene' came to mind, and how she savoured its taste.

'You saw nothing else?' she asked. 'You didn't see anybody?'

Si stared at the body, blinking fast. He shook his head vigorously.

'You're sure?'

Another shake.

Si raised both his hands to his face, rubbing his eyes hard. It was wrong to make assumptions about people – she had learnt that from years of interviews. But what seemed strange was that he had been unable to tell them what he'd witnessed, when he burst into the Open Arms. If there was a thread to tug, that was it. But that would have to come later.

Nina made her way over to the body. This time, she made an effort not to be drawn in to looking at Lukas's mangled face. She cast around for any sign of a scuffle. All of the rocks beyond the body were slick now. Any traces that might have been left had been erased. She turned, shielding her eyes to survey the steep hillsides on both sides and the slope at the rear of the bay. Even the track that she and Si and Egg had taken was invisible. There would have been an infinite number of ways for somebody to make their way up onto the headland from here.

CHAPTER ELEVEN

Nina transferred the carrier bag to her left hand to knock on the door of the schoolhouse. Her fingers were shaking, though perhaps that was only due to the handle of the bag nipping at her skin. She checked her watch: it was just before three. She heard a scuffling sound from inside the building, then Niall's wailing. Poor Marie.

Egg had been in a state after she had driven him back to the harbour. Nina had been momentarily unnerved to discover that the headquarters of the volunteer fire department was the breeze-block office behind which the girl had disappeared and the bird had emerged on her first evening on the island. Egg had sat at his desk and had barely been able to hold the phone receiver as he called the Maine Marine Patrol. After he had managed to pass on the information about Lukas in stop-start, stuttering fashion, his eyes had glazed over as he listened to the voice at the other end of the line. Then Nina had made him coffee in an attempt to sober him up before the helicopter arrived. It seemed to work: half an hour later Egg declared himself back to normal. He insisted that Nina leave him to work, that this was official business and no concern for civilians, and that he was relying on her discretion until a formal statement could be released. He had escorted her out of the building.

Nina had felt self-conscious at her lightheadedness as she had left the fire department. Not shock, but exhilaration. In her energised state the thought of returning to Tammy and Abram's house and slotting into their dreary routine was the true horror. She had stopped at the fishmongers, bought two huge lobsters and a bagful of Atlantic surf clams and several oysters on the recommendation of the short, strident man behind the counter. Nina had swung the bag back and forth, humming loudly as she climbed the hill to the schoolhouse.

The door opened. Marie's face was pale, and she was holding Niall at a distance from her body. His tiny hands were claws and he shrieked and shrieked.

Even so, Marie looked Nina up and down, frowning first at the headphones around her neck and then at the expression on her face, and said, 'You look tired.'

'Oh. I feel fine.' But the lightheadedness had become a giddiness, perhaps exacerbated by the steep climb and by the flashes of memory of the hole in Lukas's head. She nodded at the baby. 'He's still playing up?'

'I want to say it's only a phase. But second time around that kind of talk gets to sound hollow.'

'Thomas was a difficult baby?'

Marie grimaced and turned Niall's body to prevent him from nipping the skin of her arm. 'Yeah. Maybe not like this. But he was a shouter all right.'

'It's hard to imagine. He might be the quietest kid I've ever met.'

'That's only recently. Christ, puberty's going to be a whole new world. First this introversion. Then eventually he'll be jacking off all over the house. No sock will be safe.' She laughed, though the sound was overwhelmed by Niall's loud complaints. 'A teen and a newborn on my plate all at once. Talk about timing, huh?'

Abruptly, Nina's right leg buckled. She flung up her right hand, swinging the carrier bag as she supported herself on the door frame.

Marie's concerned face hung above her. 'You'd better come in.'

Nina stumbled into the schoolroom. She had been aiming for the kitchen but it seemed safer to stop sooner; with every step, her legs felt less capable of supporting her. She slumped into a hard plastic chair at a melamine table. The chair was small, designed for a child, which completed the effect of the wrongness of her body. She overflowed the chair, and it forced her to sit with her knees drawn up tight. The posture reminded her of Lukas.

Marie hovered beside her, shushing the baby. She worked a dummy into his mouth, which partially muffled his shouts.

'Sorry,' Nina said. 'It's been a funny day since I last saw you.'

'Take your time. Breathe.'

Nina looked around. 'Where are the children?'

'Still out and about. You can stay and wait, or I'll send Laurie safely your way if not.'

Nina nodded, a long, slow bobbing of the head. She gripped the seat of the chair and arched her back, gulping air. Her ears were ringing a little, like they had on the aeroplane. She held her nose and forced a breath in an attempt to pop her ears. It didn't help.

Marie disappeared. When she returned, Niall was gone and in his place she carried a small, half-filled glass. Nina took it gratefully and drank even as Marie said, 'Hold on,' and then Nina spluttered.

'Sorry,' Marie said, taking the glass and placing it on the table. 'Vodka. Thought it might help.'

Nina wiped her mouth and grinned stupidly. 'Cheers.' She took a smaller sip and relished the burn on her lips.

Marie perched on a seat opposite and they sat in silence, facing one another. Nina's gaze travelled upwards to the skylight, but its brightness threatened to turn the ringing in her ears into a full-blown migraine. She focused instead on the displays on the walls of the room. Above Marie's head was a mind map comprised of cloud-shaped paper cut-outs on a mint-green background. In the central cloud were the neatly handwritten words, *When I put the shell to my ear, I hear...* and connected to this with strands of red string were statements in children's handwriting: *the sea; the wind; my dad's snoring; planet earth spinning round.* Alongside this was an array of pictures, multiple photocopies of a single line drawing from a textbook. They appeared to have been coloured by young children, the crayon marks bleeding over the lines. Neanderthal men and women bent to the task of prising open shells with sharp, flat stones. And beneath that were a series of decorated shells, oysters and clams, stuck onto the green paper background.

'You've been teaching about the shell midden?' Nina said weakly. She tried to summon a little of the calm she had felt when she had heard the song in the cave. Her hands only shook more.

Marie smiled. 'As a teacher you learn to grab every learning opportunity gratefully. And the kids demanded it anyway. They were thrilled after their visit.'

'They went inside?'

'Sure. The Siblings offered. Most of the parents came along too.'

Nina imagined the group of schoolchildren tramping around upon the fragile shells and bones in the cavern. She shuddered.

Marie anticipated her train of thought. 'It's not as though the Siblings are too precious about the place. Which I know is probably sacrilege, and plenty of folks here are horrified, but I guess not really for scientific reasons so much as financial. But like I say, you take learning opportunities when they're there. And if the Siblings tell us to go ahead and take a few shells to display in the schoolhouse, who am I to say no?'

Carefully, she plucked a clamshell from the wall: it had only been Blu-Tacked on. One of the children had glued green glitter into the valleys between the ridges of the shell, and stuck plastic jewels onto the raised parts.

Nina took the shell. Slowly, she raised it to her ear.

She closed her eyes and heard the sea.

CHAPTER TWELVE

Before Nina entered Cat's Ear Cottage, she cupped her hand around her mouth to smell her breath, like a teenager afraid of punishment. The vodka and her dizziness had made the journey faster rather than more awkward. It was as if she'd floated above the hillocks and tracks.

Tammy was waiting for her: she must have heard Nina's footsteps on the porch. Her arms were folded tight across her aproned chest.

Nina's forced smile became a silly grin. *Now I'm for it*, she thought. *Mum looks mad.*

She held up the carrier bag. 'I brought us all some dinner.'

'What's in there?'

Nina held it open and raised it to Tammy's face as if it were a nosebag. Tammy's nose wrinkled and she backed away.

'But you said there was nothing to rival Si Michaud's lobsters,' Nina said with undisguised petulance. 'Aren't these Si's? There are clams in there too, and oysters.'

'I was going to make ham and eggs.'

'We could have both?'

'You do as you like, Nina. But Abram likes ham and eggs.'

'And he doesn't like lobsters or shellfish?'

'They're a bit too much fuss, aren't they?'

'I thought that was part of the appeal of living on Hope Island. I thought that everyone here loved seafood.'

Tammy shrugged, wiped her hands on her apron, and padded away. Nina followed and found her on one of the sitting-room sofas, crossword puzzle book in hand, her tongue protruding from her mouth in concentration.

'Mind if I go ahead and get started?' Nina said, swinging the bag in the direction of the kitchen.

'Sure. The ham's in the freezer so it'll need thawing first.'

Nina rolled her eyes and sloped into the kitchen. One by one, she removed the items from the carrier bag and placed them on the small plastic-covered table. The carapaces of the lobsters were almost black, their claws pendulous and knife-like at the tips. They looked more like cockroaches than anything edible. Nina bent before the freezer, retrieved a vacuum-sealed packet of individual gammon steaks, then jammed both lobsters in, tail-first. She wrestled with their thick claws for a minute or more before she managed to shove the drawer closed.

She turned her attention to the clams and oysters. She'd eaten them many times before – she had never liked the sensation of oysters going down but understood that it was a pleasure that had to be learnt – but had never cooked them. There were no bookshelves in the kitchen, and she hadn't noticed any recipe books elsewhere in the house. Judging from Tammy and Abram's diet, they had no need of recipes. Nina pulled out her phone and thumbed to the internet browser. No reception.

The kitchen window gave a partial view over the lane that curled around the house. As Nina cleaned the shellfish at the sink, she watched as a gaggle of children made their way up the hill. Laurie and Thomas were at the centre of the group, tall and silent, their faces shining in the golden light of dusk. The other children were satellites orbiting these twin suns. As they drew closer to Cat's Ear Cottage, Nina saw that the younger children were all gazing up at Thomas, the whites of their eyes gleaming, and Laurie shot glances at him too. Thomas only looked ahead. His fixed facial expression was peculiar: he appeared mature and resolute and – though Nina couldn't pin down quite what made the word come to mind – *ravenous*.

✳

'I've already eaten,' Laurie said without inflection as Nina handed her a plate.

Tammy and Abram had already begun tucking into their ham and eggs. Abram's head was bent to the task, whereas Tammy's back was pressed into her chair, her arms outstretched to cut her gammon into strips, as though the food had a distasteful odour.

'What did you have?' Nina asked.

Laurie made a stop-asking-me-stupid-questions face. 'Camping food.'

'At the schoolhouse?'

'Why would I eat camping food at the school?'

Uncertain how to respond, Nina returned to the kitchen to collect the steaming bowl of shellfish. Tammy only glared at her plate but raised a hand to waft at the steam.

'This is all fresh,' Nina said. 'It's good stuff. You should try it.'

'Thanks,' Laurie replied, but didn't move.

Nina sighed and leant across the table to ladle shells onto the stiff spaghetti on her plate. She sat gratefully: her dizziness had barely abated since she had returned to the house. She rooted around for a clamshell that was already open, then plucked out the soft interior with her fork.

'It's really good,' she said, chewing slowly to savour the taste. 'Better than in restaurants, even.'

Laurie gave a tight-lipped smile.

'So,' Tammy said to Laurie, 'tell us about your day.'

Laurie brightened. 'It was fun! They're all so *nice*.'

'And is Thomas still your favourite?'

Laurie's cheeks reddened. 'Gran!' She lengthened the vowel into two parts, a teenager's complaint.

'He always was a sweetheart, huh?'

Nina chewed on another clam thoughtfully. Perhaps Thomas really was pleasant and fun, when he was away from adults. It was hard to imagine, though. Perhaps Laurie had entered a new phase: the surlier and less communicative the boy, the more appealing he became in her eyes. Or perhaps her opinion was informed by their previous encounters, her memories of having once been happy.

In an attempt to insert herself into the conversation, she said, 'What kinds of things did you get up to? When you were out exploring?'

Laurie's shoulders stiffened. 'We were mucking around, Mum.' Then, more freely, 'They've set up a kind of den in the woods. It's pretty cool, actually. There's a hammock and some tarpaulins strung up so you can huddle underneath. And they've been stockpiling supplies.'

'Like what?'

'Tins, packets of stuff. It's not stealing, it all came from their own houses.'

'I wasn't going to suggest it was stealing.'

Laurie's eyes met Nina's for a moment. 'Thomas reckons we could all last out for weeks if we needed to. But he'd ration the tinned stuff and then we'd hunt too, to make it all last longer. There are rabbits up there, tons of them.'

Nina prodded at one of the oysters on her plate. Its gnarled, layered surface looked a thousand years old. She put a butter knife to its sealed lips and tried an investigatory wiggle.

'Why would you need to "last out"?' she said.

Laurie's only response was a twist of her hands upon the table so that they lay palms upward. It could have meant anything.

Tammy squeezed Laurie's arm. To Nina, she said in her flat, loud drone, 'It's a game, dear. It's what children do. You should know that.'

You should know that.

Perhaps there was a safer topic of conversation. In a tone as close as possible to what she imagined a dutiful daughter-in-law should sound like, Nina said, 'Tammy, Clay told me about your paintings – he said they were wonderful. I'd love to see some of your artwork some time, if you'd show me. I had no idea. I think it's terrific.'

A sequence of emotions flashed across Tammy's face. First pride, then self-consciousness, then something a little like shame. Her eyes flicked to Abram as she replied loudly and clearly, as if speaking to a child, 'Yes, dear. Maybe later on. I don't know when we'll find the time.'

Nina gave them all a chance to substitute their own topic of conversation for her failed attempt. Nobody spoke. With a sigh she turned her attention to her plate. She forced the knife a little further into the sliver of a gap in the oyster shell, grimaced and then pressed harder, pushing at the rounded end of the knife handle. The blade skidded on the rough surface and jabbed into the webbed tissue between the thumb and forefinger of her left hand. Though the knife wasn't particularly sharp, the wound produced a line of blood immediately. Its sting matched the hiss in her ears as though they were one and the same. She hissed, 'Fuck,' as she sucked on the flesh.

Tammy and Laurie were staring at her scornfully. Abram's lack of reaction was even more offensive: he continued scooping forkfuls of wet egg and pushing them messily into his mouth.

'I don't think it *wants* you to open it,' Laurie said. Her tone wasn't harsh. Perhaps Nina was misreading her daughter's expression. 'Are you okay?'

'Fine,' Nina mumbled, her hand still pressed to her mouth.

She wasn't going to let it beat her. She attacked the oyster again, this time bridging her hand over the shell, pressing it firmly to the plate, then carefully working the knife within its jaws. It yawned open with a creak.

She stared into the darkness within the shell. She thought of Lukas, his open head, the wetness within.

She didn't want the oyster, but before she could consider what she was doing she raised it to her lips and tipped. The soft flesh slid into her mouth and slipped straight down her throat, leaving behind a pool of brine.

Her eyes watered. She swallowed, then gulped from her glass of water.

'So good,' she managed to say.

'You don't have to have any more,' Laurie said softly.

'I *like* them.' Nina took another gulp, then dabbed at her mouth with a paper napkin. 'I think I'll have another.'

'Bobby always loved seafood,' Tammy almost shouted. 'He'd be able to show you how to go about it.'

Abram finished shovelling egg, then tossed his knife and fork onto his plate with a clatter. In a voice as loud as his wife's, he said, 'Where is Rob anyhow?'

Tammy didn't answer. She looked at Nina.

'He couldn't be here, Abram,' Nina said. 'We've been through this.'

Now she was grateful for the amount of work involved in opening the oyster. All eyes were upon her but at least she wasn't being asked questions. There was a knack to fitting the blade between the lips. Keep pressure on at all times, find the weak spot, always push.

'He's good at fishing, too,' Tammy said.

'Dad's good at everything,' Laurie added, laughing. 'This one time he had to help me get my stuff together for a school fashion show, and he kept saying, "This is one for your mum really," but then he got totally into it and he ended up doing more work than me. Sewed bits of three different dresses together and it was *awesome*. And then I got the biggest applause of the whole night.'

Nina grunted at the oyster. When it opened it leaked something black.

They were watching her again. She raised the oyster to her mouth.

'Tell me again, when does Bobby's vacation finish?' Tammy said in a wheedling tone.

Nina tipped her head back. She blinked to dispel the speckles on her retina that made constellations on the beige ceiling.

The oyster skidded into her mouth and instantly she wanted rid of it. It tasted sourer than brine, a sickly, dark flavour that surged up immediately; she imagined it staining the inside of her cheeks black, her gums too. She panicked, ballooning her cheeks and clamping her throat tight in an attempt to trap it. But it no longer seemed a solid thing. Her eyes widened as it teased its way in, trickling into her body.

She shook her head again and again, as if she could command it not to do what it was doing. Along with the nausea was the hissing sound in her head that rose correspondingly in volume.

She lurched to her feet, inhaling noisily through her nostrils.

This wasn't how it was supposed to be. At that moment, she hated everybody in the room and everybody outside of it. Look at what they were doing to her.

'Mum?' Laurie said, somewhere far away.

Nina opened her eyes that she hadn't even realised were closed. She had become too tall, or everyone else too short. She gripped Abram's shoulder for support, and he smiled up at her.

Drunkenly, Nina realised what she was about to do.

This was it. The dropping of the bomb.

'Rob isn't on holiday,' she said between gasps for breath. Then, faster, 'And he's a fucking bastard.'

Instantly, Laurie rose too. She dropped her unused napkin onto her empty plate.

All of Nina's hate evaporated in an instant. 'I'm sorry.' Another wave of nausea shuddered its way upwards from her stomach. 'This isn't how I wanted you to find out about it.'

Laurie's expression was more pity than anger. Nina rubbed at her eyes to clear the tears.

Then, slowly, Laurie shook her head. 'Mum. I'm not a moron. I know. I found out back when I wondered where the hell Dad had got to, and I sent him a text message, and he told me. I know he's left you.'

'Us,' Nina said involuntarily. She couldn't bear to look at her daughter, so she addressed Tammy instead. 'He's left us.'

Tammy took Abram's hand – he seemed not to be following the conversation and was still looking up at Nina with only mild concern – and took a deep breath. 'I guess I figured as much.'

'Seriously?' Nina's cheeks puffed as the sour taste bloomed in her mouth again.

'It was obvious, dear.'

Nina bowed her head. Calculations about risk had become impossible. 'Then you should know something else, both of you. It's worse than that.' She took a gulp from her glass, but the water tasted fetid. 'Rob didn't just walk out on us. Me. He left to be with another woman.'

They were still looking up at her. Evidently, everything she had said was still obvious. It wasn't fair. It wasn't fair for her to be put through all of this and then be made to feel that she was being needy.

'You want more?' she said. 'Then how about this – he left to be with another woman and her two kids. *Their* two kids.'

The two children were formless in Nina's mind. She didn't even know how old they were, or their genders. They were black silhouettes standing beside an equally obscure woman and beside Rob, who no longer belonged to Nina but to *her*.

The room was spinning now. She was still gripping Abram's shoulder, but it wasn't a secure enough anchor point. Nina leant heavily on the table, her palms skidding with sweat upon the cloth.

'It turns out that Rob started another family, years ago,' she managed to say. 'And now he's chosen them over us.'

That image of Rob on the Skype call. The sunglasses, the lawn, the bike – a child's? – the long shadow of his preferred spouse.

One purge followed another. Nina felt a glimmer of relief amid her horror as the swill in her belly rose up and forced its way, burning, into her mouth and then finally *out* in a dark, spattering arc.

CHAPTER THIRTEEN

Nina gazed up at the sky unblinking. Beneath her bare body the waves undulated, making her spine stretch pleasingly as she bobbed on the surface of the water humming around her, the breaking of waves punctuation to a crowd in cheerful conversation. Her arms had been at her sides: now she spread them wide, splaying her fingertips so that each grazed the surface of the water without puncturing it. She imagined a meniscus layer stretching all the way from the Maine coast to Britain, subtly concave and cupping her.

Clouds appeared at the periphery of her vision. She smiled. She would make them into shapes. The clouds brushed past one another, growing greyer and more numerous. There were no shapes, only uniform coverage that erased the blue sky.

She could no longer feel the water beneath her fingertips. She turned her head from side to side awkwardly – her neck was stiff as though something solid was wrapped around it. She gasped at the realisation that her body was no longer resting on the water. With sharp movements she tried to bend her arms back, as if there might be something there to grasp. The motion only propelled her upwards. She struggled, unable to determine how far above the waves she now lay. The murmur of the ocean sounded mocking from this distance.

The dark cloud cover had become solid, its lumpen shapes more rock than gas.

The wind threw her hair over her eyes. She clawed at the wet clumps, trying to pull them aside, but could only clear her vision for seconds at a time.

It was intolerable, lying prone like this. With a rising sense of panic and of being trapped, she wrenched her body left; the sudden motion made her retch. She tried again. This time she managed to turn a little, rocking sideways as if supported by something, though beneath her was nothing but rushing air. The wind roared its disapproval and renewed its efforts to blind her with her own hair. She glimpsed streaked water below. She was moving above it, fast. The thought occurred to her that if she succeeded in flipping herself she would be staring down at the ocean as she flew. Nausea blossomed in her stomach.

No, she must put herself upright.

She fought against the screaming gale, writhing and clutching at nothing. Her mouth was open, but she made no sound. The black clouds – which appeared sharper now, with jagged points – descended slowly so that she hurtled within a narrow vertical space between the water and this stalactite-riddled roof.

She gasped with relief as she pulled herself upright. The contents of her stomach swilled and settled. But she was still travelling, faster than ever. The wind shrieked at her back. Now it felt not as though it were blowing at her, but as if she was falling into it, horizontally above the ocean. It made her hair a dark tunnel before her. She tried to yank it away, but she had lost all sense of proprioception – her hands were impossible to locate – and she couldn't tell whether her body was still beneath the tunnel of hair or whether it, too, was missing. Beyond the corridor of hair, her only view was of two horizontal, mirrored surfaces, both equally black, with blinding white between. She could no longer blink. She thought she saw something in the centre of the blackness, but her vision was littered with retina floaters.

She gained in speed. The wind shouted and became her own shout.

CHAPTER FOURTEEN

Nina's hands became claws, bracing against the door frame to prevent her from toppling into the sitting room.

Tammy looked up from her puzzle book. 'Lord. You look like death.'

Nina squeezed her eyes shut. When she opened them, Tammy and the sitting-room sofa had stopped rocking from side to side. 'I'm fine now. Where's Laurie?'

'Sit down, won't you?' Tammy said. 'But maybe not on the good couch.'

Involuntarily, Nina glanced into the adjoining dining room. There was no sign of the mess she'd made, but the tablecloth was missing. She eased herself onto the sagging cushions of Abram's chair and regretted it. She was so low to the ground that she might never be able to rise from it. Her stomach groaned and she forced a bitter taste back down her throat.

'I'm sorry for yesterday,' Nina said. Then, noticing the bright sunlight at the window, 'It was yesterday, wasn't it?'

'Sure. And now it's lunchtime. You'd be better off eating plain food.'

'I slept that long?' Her first thought was of Egg and the mystery surrounding Lukas Weber's death. The Marine Patrol would have arrived yesterday evening. By now the police would likely be involved and a formal investigation initiated. After having found herself in the thick of the situation the day before, being absent now felt like a demotion, only made worse by Tammy's and Laurie's reactions to her other 'scoop'.

Weakly, she said, 'Where's Laurie?'

'Young Thomas Maddox called for her this morning. Smart young thing. Polite.'

'So she'll be back in a few hours? I need to talk to her.'

Tammy shook her head. 'Marie called on the telephone. The children are all having dinner together. Some kind of bonfire setup, I guess. S'mores and candy don't do any harm once in a while.'

Nina ignored this assault on her maternal instincts. She was no longer certain she had any.

She sucked in a lungful of air. 'Tammy, you and I should speak about last night.'

'It was the oysters.'

'Yes. No. That's not what I mean. We should speak about Rob.'

Tammy frowned at her puzzle book.

'It's all true,' Nina continued. 'He walked out and didn't explain why. I had to figure it out myself. I hacked into his email account and saw the messages going way back.'

'Isn't that sort of thing illegal?' But Tammy's tone was light, offhand. She was searching for diversions.

'Her name is Kaytee,' Nina said. She wondered if crying would help, either in terms of her own state of mind or to elicit sympathy from Tammy. Sourness rose up into her mouth again. It tasted like rust. 'K-A-Y-T-E-E.' Her head dropped. 'Fucking hell, I hate the way she spells it. It tells me everything I need to know about her.'

'This is my house. We don't swear in this house.'

Tears pricked at Nina's eyes. 'Seriously? That's your response to all this? *That's* your response to the news that your son abandoned his long-time partner – no matter what you might think of me, that's what I am – and his eldest child?'

Tammy tapped at her book with the tip of her pencil.

Nina cupped her hands over her mouth, breathing into the enclosed space to stop herself from hyperventilating. The house was heated far too high. Her head was on fire and whatever was still in her belly was clawing at the walls for escape.

Tammy scratched a few letters into her crossword.

Suddenly Nina understood. This reaction wasn't only calmness, it was complacency. It was anticipation.

'You're fixated on the children,' she said hoarsely. 'You like the idea of more grandkids.'

Tammy's eyes snapped upwards. 'Those children are Bobby's responsibility, as much as Laurie is.'

'But *I'm* not his responsibility? He doesn't owe *me*?'

'That's different.'

'Because we never married, is that it? Because we were never really together, in your eyes?'

'I don't appreciate having words put in my mouth, dear.'

In a flash, Nina saw how this was going to pan out. The next time Laurie came to Hope Island, it would be with Rob, not her. And they would bring his two other children along, and Rob's lover too. A big, new family for the grandparents to gush over. There could be no room for Nina in that scenario.

'I'm going to be sick,' she muttered. But she didn't move. If she really was going to be sick, she wouldn't stop herself from doing it right here in the sitting room.

'It's playing Russian roulette, eating oysters,' Tammy said pleasantly. 'All sorts of ways they can upset you. I figure yours was a bad one – some bacteria, maybe the norovirus, that's the one they're always talking about these days, isn't it? But who knows? I had an old maiden aunt once got a tapeworm or some such from shellfish. The sickness, my Lord! I heard she had diarrhoea and cramping for *days*. Really not pretty. But she lived past ninety, so go figure.'

'Thanks, Tammy,' Nina said. She heaved herself onto her feet and staggered towards the kitchen. 'You're a big help.'

✳

When she came downstairs after a shower in the mint-green bathroom – an act which required adopting an uncomfortable crouching position in the bathtub, made worse by the churning within her stomach and the wrangling with the too-short, limescaled pipe of the showerhead tap attachment – Abram had been substituted for Tammy. Almost literally, in fact: he sat not in his usual low chair, but on the same sofa cushion where Tammy had been sitting, and her puzzle book was on his lap, though it was unopened.

'Morning, Abram.'

Abram twisted to look at the window.

'Afternoon,' Nina corrected herself. 'Now I'm the one getting confused.' She winced. 'Sorry. I didn't mean to suggest anything.'

Abram's placid smile was wide enough to force his eyes up at the corners. The expression was so like Rob's, the same warmth, but with any sense of meaningful content stripped away. He could have been smiling at anything.

'I get confused too,' he said in his foghorn voice. There was no trace of sorrow.

Nina's grandmother had suffered from Alzheimer's. It had been awful to watch her deterioration, so much so that as a teenager Nina had found as many excuses as possible to avoid visiting the care home. It hadn't been the forgetting of specific details so much as the vacant way that her grandmother had watched Nina when she entered the room. The suspicion that she regarded Nina in precisely the same way as she regarded any of the staff, or the actors on TV, or even the furniture. When Nina's own parents had died before Laurie was born, it had been difficult to shake a sense of gratitude that they wouldn't have to face that vacant fate. These days, whenever Nina considered the concept of old age, her first reaction was always a twinge of guilt at her absence back then.

'Have you seen anybody about it?' she asked quietly.

The smile faltered. 'I didn't catch that.'

'I asked if you'd been to the doctor.'

'I'm perfectly well.'

'But you get confused.'

A nod. 'I do get confused, yes.'

Nina sat on the opposite seat. She ran her hands through her wet hair. Her stomach felt far less awful than it had that morning. The dizziness persisted as a faint hiss, a product of the mind like the tinnitus she had once suffered after a three-day stint at a music festival in Camber Sands. But she could handle it.

She thought of Lukas Weber, with no accompanying revulsion. Perhaps this was a good opportunity for some background research.

'You must know everyone on Hope Island pretty well,' she said.

Abram's smile returned to full power. 'Oh, yes. Good people here.'

'Do you know Si Michaud? The fisherman?'

'Oh, sure. We go way back.'

'You're friends?'

Abram made a croaking noise that might have been a laugh. 'Used to fight tooth and nail! Always after the same girl.'

'You mean Tammy?'

She was surprised at the vehemence of his refusal. 'Not on your life. Tammy grew up in Durham, South Carolina. I met her at a kind of Bible camp.'

He pointed up at a collection of framed photos beside the window. Nina could see none that showed him and Tammy as a young couple. Either he was mistaken, or they had revisited the site of their first meeting later in life.

'Not that I was religious, you understand,' Abram continued. Nina reminded herself that it wasn't unusual for distant memories to remain perfectly accessible to people suffering from dementia. 'I was only passing through. And those places are full to the rafters with young women. Tammy was fifteen. I was, what, twenty?' Another barking laugh.

Nina frowned. 'It's hard to imagine Tammy as anything other than strong-willed, even back then. I bet she didn't let you take advantage of her.'

Abram shrugged. 'Not that year. We didn't hook up right away, although I wasn't such a sap to go away empty-handed. Next time around was another story. Let me tell you, her girlfriends told tall tales about me. Guess I was the big challenge.'

It was difficult to imagine this tall, lean gentleman as anything other than a one-woman man. Funny how far people could subvert your expectations.

'Does Tammy hate me?' Nina said, then blanched; she hadn't meant to ask that question.

Abram shrugged. 'She's her own woman. There're big thoughts going on in that head.'

'She's an artist, I suppose. At least, so I'm told. She doesn't seem to want to let me see her paintings.'

Abram nodded thoughtfully. 'You don't want to see them. And she doesn't need to see them either.'

'Why do you say that?'

'Some things are best left alone. Tammy doesn't paint no more, and that's for the best. Didn't make her happy. Didn't make me happy. But now we're happy.'

But he didn't look it. Dimples stippled his chin and his lips spasmed, clamped tight.

'Anyway,' Nina said after a pause. 'We were talking about Si. You said you didn't fight with him about Tammy.'

Abram sucked in a breath and nodded gratefully. 'I was handy back then. Never a fighter as such, but a few drinks and I'd step up.'

'And Si?'

'Likewise. Thing is, he never grew out of it. One time I had to step in and cart him away when he broke old Matt's jaw. Spent a night in the lockroom in the fire department, shouting up a storm, kicking down the doors. He was starting brawls aged fifty, same as when we were back on the island in our twenties, in the downtime from being on the road.'

'You both drove trucks on the mainland?' Rob had often spoken about his father's work, how it had taken him away from Hope Island for days at a time, often returning only at the weekends and then too exhausted to do much of anything. She had taken it as read that Rob's hands-on attitude to Laurie's upbringing was a correction to his own childhood treatment, consciously or unconsciously.

Abram shook his head and stared at the photos on the wall. In a quieter voice than his usual tone, he said, 'She wouldn't.'

'Who wouldn't?'

'She wouldn't,' he said again, glaring intently upwards.

Was he talking to Tammy, in the photos? Nina leant forward. 'Abram? Are you okay?'

He shook his head again.

'Can I get anything for you?'

The shaking of his head continued, faster and faster. The puzzle book fell to the carpet as Abram reached up with both hands. He pressed his index fingers to the skin behind his ears, rubbing them in circles, hard.

'Is your hearing causing you trouble?'

She put her hand on his arm. He flinched and turned to face her. She withdrew at the sight of his contorted features. It wasn't an expression of pain, quite. The twisting and rolling of his open mouth was like somebody clearing blocked ears.

'Fucking noise!' Abram yelled, with such rage that Nina pulled her hand away and leapt to her feet.

She watched as Abram continued to rub at his jaw, then pressed both hands over his ears like headphones. 'Don't you fucking *start*,' he said in a loud, flat tone.

Then he stood. He already had his shoes on. As he strode to the front door Nina rummaged for her shoes, which had been pushed to the back of the rack, and pulled them on.

The chill of the air outside was glorious compared to the stifling atmosphere of the house. Despite the circumstances, Nina was suddenly conscious of her wellness, and she felt a rush of confidence that she might, after all, be able to head down to the harbour, meet with Egg, find out the situation with Lukas's death.

But she couldn't abandon Abram. He had already left the main track and was scrambling unsteadily up the hillside, yanking clods of grass in his attempts to haul himself up the roadside bank. She would have to escort him back to safety before she could consider herself a free agent.

She jogged to catch up with him. He had surmounted the bank and was heading directly up the slope; he was far faster on his feet than she would have expected.

'Where are you going?'

'Clear the mind,' he said loudly, as though he were shouting through a storm. Then, barely quieter, 'I like to hear the sea.'

He had found a worn path that led directly to the crest of the hill, though whether it was by familiarity, chance or instinct, Nina couldn't tell. It crossed her mind that perhaps the track had been created solely by Abram. His route took them around the small patch of woodland rather than through it as Laurie's had done. Before long they passed the trees and the ocean once more came into view, looking like a mossy blue carpet, as if one's toes and heels might sink into it but nothing more. The sound of the merged wind and waves was majestic – in it, Nina could hear distinct, clear tones, all in harmony. She wished that she had brought Clay's headphones. She wished all the sounds were louder.

Abram stopped and Nina slowed her pace to approach him cautiously. His hands were on his ears again, then rubbed at his jaw. She realised that he was making a sound, too. An open-mouthed 'ah', long and low. It continued even as she drew up to stand beside him.

She didn't want to interrupt him. She pulled her phone from her pocket to check the time: just after two. She swiped to unlock the phone. Still no reception. It had been more than a day since she had refreshed her inbox. Were they all still coping back at the TV studio?

Abram's moan petered out. In his flat, loud voice he said, 'Only fucking thing that shuts them up.'

She turned. The old man looked almost content.

'Shuts who up, Abram?'

His hands were still pressed beneath his ears. He pulled his hands apart, then pointed at his jawline. 'Chatter. All the time with the chatter.'

His eyes were wet with tears now, though Nina realised that the chill wind was producing them in her eyes too.

'I'm sorry,' she said. 'I didn't know.'

But he grinned. 'Maybe they hate it out here, maybe they love it. Either way, they quieten down some.' He took his hands away from his head, brushed down his clothes. 'Gotta keep walking. Change it up.'

To their right was the point where Laurie had descended to the Crow's Nest, and far beyond that the schoolhouse. Neither destination felt at all desirable. Nina pointed left, where the hillside rose sharply, its front cleaved away to reveal bone-white cliffs facing the sea. There might even be phone reception at that altitude. 'There'll be more wind and better views up there,' she said.

Abram took her arm as they ascended the steep slope. His grip was strong, but his pace was slowing. He must get tired easily, and perhaps he had already used up his reserves of energy walking this far.

At the crest of the cliff Nina's stomach flipped. The wind yanked her hair and billowed her T-shirt, pulling first in one direction and then the opposite. She planted her feet firmly and turned to help Abram up.

The grass bank was narrow, and though one could simply bear left along the headland and descend the sine-curve hillock to reach the same level from which they had started, here the cliff felt as thin and precarious as a diving board.

Beyond the strip of grass, the ocean was a blue whirling pit. To her surprise, she saw a land mass not far away.

'Which island is that?' she said, pointing.

Abram bent to place his hands on his knees. Breathlessly, he replied, 'Monhegan.'

'Is it nice?'

'It's exactly the same as here.'

Thoughts of the other two Hope Islands in the gulf flashed through Nina's mind. She shuddered. Then, partly as a distraction, she surreptitiously checked her phone. No messages, but nine new emails. Six were irrelevant circulars, one a reminder to book an appointment with her dentist. The most recent two were from Laine at the studio. She prodded at the first eagerly. *Hey Nina, hope all's well. Sorry to bother you but any idea where the OB tripod ended up after we used it last?* But then she scrolled down to read the follow-up: *Ignore that – Yvonne found it – have a fab hol. L.*

'They don't need me,' she muttered.

To her surprise, Abram put his arm around her waist. She flinched at his papery skin against her arm, but then leaned in to him.

'You'd be surprised,' Abram said. 'Everybody needs somebody.'

'Are you referring to Rob?'

Abram didn't answer.

They stood like that for several minutes, before Abram eased her away. Nina watched him sidelong as he raised both his arms. He clamped his palms onto his temples, pulling his head back until he faced directly upwards.

She flinched as he began to shout.

At first there were no words, only a howl. His body shook with its force. Nina gripped his shoulders but he shrugged her away with surprising delicacy.

'Get fucked!' Abram roared, not to Nina but to the sky and the sea.

Then he reverted to his wordless howl. His fingers were pressed hard against the skin below his drooping earlobes, rubbing in tight circles.

Nina's horror ebbed away, replaced by exhilaration. Abram's cry became one with the tumult of the ocean, the buffeting of the wind against the cliffs, the whip of the long grass that scattered the plateau.

Abram reached for her left hand and raised it up, as somebody might raise the arm of a triumphant but punch-drunk boxer. Unbidden, her right arm lifted too.

Abram turned his head. He shouted, 'Now you!' and Nina felt his breath push against her skin.

She blinked at him. He gestured, with a sideways nod, at the ocean.

She turned to face the roiling water.

She opened her mouth but nothing came forth.

Why did everybody keep telling her to shout?

And why were they all so frustratingly good at it?

She said, 'Why is everybody shouting?'

Abram's dry hand squeezed hers. *Again.*

Louder than before, she repeated, 'Why is everybody shouting?'

The sea and wind laughed at her voice.

Nina drew all of the air – *all* of it – into her lungs. With exaggerated, slow enunciation, she called out, 'Why is everybody shouting?' and let the final 'ing' lengthen and become louder and louder.

Her shout was nothing so impressive as Abram's – or even the bellowing customers of the Open Arms, come to that – but it felt real and good.

But when Abram lowered her hand and then turned to her again, his expression was one of pity.

'Keep working at it,' he said in his usual voice, which nevertheless seemed louder than Nina's attempt at a roar.

The sense of having failed once again to find her voice was devastating.

Several seconds passed and the relative quiet was almost unbearable.

'Rob might need somebody,' she said haltingly, 'but I'm pretty sure it's not me. It's Kaytee and whatever the hell their two kids are called. I don't even know what gender the brats are, or how old.'

It was hard to determine whether more information would make the situation easier to digest, or harder. When had Rob first met Kaytee, and in what circumstances? How long had they been seeing one another, in the evenings when Rob claimed he was out with his snooker pals or in the pub?

Abram nodded. It struck Nina as remarkable how calmly he was taking the news about his son. She had assumed that he hadn't even registered what was happening.

'There's little Laurie,' he said.

'Abram. She isn't little, that's the point. Did you see how she looked at me yesterday? Soon she'll be old enough to make her own decisions about who she spends her time with. And it won't be me.'

Abram prodded a finger into his right ear. He leant forwards to look over the edge of the cliff.

'Folks are selfish,' he yelled.

Nina put her hand over his, which was still holding her waist. 'Including you?'

He turned. The wind billowed his cheeks, like a squeezed empty envelope. 'For sure!' He looked almost proud. 'We're not so different, me and Robert. A whole lot going on under the surface, like that big old ocean. Currents that could snap your legs. People like us, we're not to be trusted all the way, you understand?'

'But you wouldn't have done what he did. Would you?'

His smile broadened. 'Not for want of trying.'

'You'd have cheated on Tammy?'

'I would, and I did. Time and again. I'd say it was another era, but that's horseshit. I got away with it is all. No other kids to show for any of it, least none I ever knew of. So Tammy could deny it happened.'

Nina had no idea how to respond.

Abram peered out again over the edge. A swell, a roar, rose from the ocean and the wind flattened the creases on his cheeks. 'I learned one thing. Kids don't need to get muddled in all that. That was my mistake. Tammy claimed Rob for herself and I let her. Collateral damage, you could call it. I should've hung on. Can't remember the last time he and I talked – I mean really *talked*. It's the saddest thing.'

CHAPTER FIFTEEN

When Tammy entered the house, Nina helped her remove her coat; in her hurry to shed it the old woman's arms had become tangled in the sleeves.

'I've heard the most awful story!' Tammy squealed, her delight evident. 'Down at the store they're all talking about it.'

Nina made a noncommittal noise.

'Abe?' Tammy craned her neck to see into the sitting room. 'Abram? Some young farm worker, down at the south bay. Dead!'

Abram looked up from his low seat. His eyes had glazed over. He had been silent, exhausted, since he and Nina had returned from their walk several hours ago, and hadn't responded to her offers to fetch him anything. At one point, Nina had walked to and fro before him, to check that his eyes followed her. He kept rubbing his jaw. Despite her desire to head to the harbour, Nina had felt unable to leave him alone.

Tammy turned back to Nina, sizing her up as if to determine whether she was a worthy recipient of the news. Then, 'His head got smashed in, right there on the beach!'

Nina nodded. She had always been bad at playacting innocence, had never been a good liar. 'I heard about it, yesterday.'

Tammy's face darkened. 'Where's Laurie?'

'You said she was having dinner at the schoolhouse.'

'But how's she getting home? Not on her own, with all these goings-on.'

The blood drained from Nina's face. There it was: an encapsulation of her maternal failings. Her response to Lukas's death had been purely one of morbid curiosity. Whether it was an accident or something more rotten, her interest was factual, investigatory. Being holed up in the house had been a frustration, but only because she craved news about the police enquiries. She hadn't considered Laurie's safety for a moment.

'I'll take the car,' she said, suddenly breathless. 'I'll go and get her.'

Her fingers fumbled to retrieve the keys from a bowl full of glass pebbles on the sideboard. Tammy watched with arms folded as Nina flung open the door.

Laurie was standing on the porch. Beside her was Thomas Maddox. His eyes were as vividly blue as the ocean and endlessly deep. It occurred to Nina to wonder whether she had ever seen him blink. On an impulse, she burst forwards and took her daughter's hand, yanking her over the threshold and into a clumsy kneeling embrace. Nina pressed her daughter's head against her chest.

'Thank you for bringing Laurie home,' she mumbled.

Her eyes flicked up. Thomas was watching the pair of them huddled on the mat. His expression gave no suggestion of emotion. A cold shudder ran through Nina's body from the toes upward, as if she had stepped in icy water. She rubbed at Laurie's back as if her daughter were the one who was cold and to disguise her own shivering.

To her horror, Thomas started shuddering, too. His feet remained planted on the doormat, but tremors shook his body. He blinked again and again but didn't look away from Nina.

'You'd best head back to your mum?' Nina said hurriedly. She hated that it sounded like a plea.

When Thomas still didn't leave, she reached up and pulled sharply at the door handle. The door swung shut and the latch clicked. Through the mottled glass in the upper part of the door she could still see Thomas's silhouette. It remained for several seconds before it slid away.

It was only now that Nina realised how stiff Laurie's body was against her. Nina pushed her away but remained on her haunches.

'Can we talk, love?'

'We don't need to.' Laurie wasn't anywhere near as emotionless as Thomas, but she was calm.

'But all that news, yesterday.'

'I told you—'

'I know. Sorry. You already knew about your dad. But even so, you must be reeling.'

Laurie gazed at her. More pity. Nina wanted to curl up into a ball, right there on the rug in the hallway. Out of the corner of her eye she saw Tammy edge into the sitting room. Nina felt a surge of gratefulness towards the old woman.

'I wanted to talk about it sooner, just me and you,' she said. 'It was… hard. But I want you to know that that isn't why I'm here. I want to spend time with you, Laurie. I really do. All this other stuff between me and your dad, we'll figure it out. Somehow. But you and I are family and I will always love you.'

Laurie wrapped her thin arms around herself. She nodded. 'Thank you for telling the truth.'

This role reversal was unbearable. And Laurie had known the truth anyway, so all that Nina had achieved by blurting out her confession was to redeem herself fractionally in her daughter's eyes. Up to that point, her silence had been a black mark against her character.

But now the truth was out. She may have lost Rob, but her relationship with Laurie could be salvaged.

Nina couldn't prevent herself from gabbling. 'And I'm so enthusiastic about having some adventures of our own! That trip around Maine? Let's do it, hey? Me and you on a road trip, like Thelma and Louise.' She hoped her daughter had never watched the film.

Laurie shrugged. 'I like it here, Mum.'

'Of course. And that's fine. We can have adventures anywhere, can't we? And it's wonderful that you feel so welcome here.' Nina glanced at the bright glass of the front door.

Now Laurie smiled. 'They're so *funny*, Mum. They make me laugh.'

'Those kids? Really?'

'Hey. Don't be down on them. They're my friends.'

Nina's eyes stung. When she rose from her crouched position, hypertension made her ears sing. 'I can't imagine any of them telling a joke, that's all. Thomas most of all. There's a phrase Americans might use about people like him: *Looks like he's got a stick up his ass.*'

Laurie stared at her in disbelief. Her arms were folded tight over her chest, an echo of her grandmother.

'You know what, Mum?' she said in a small, calm voice. 'Fuck you.'

And then she turned and walked in measured steps to the sitting room. Through the ringing in her ears Nina heard her greet her grandparents brightly.

She shook her head. She rubbed at her jawbone.

There was no way she could face anyone right now. She slunk into the den, eyes down to avoid seeing the Robs. She scrabbled on the bedside table for the binaural microphones, prodded at buttons on the MiniDisc player, set one of her recordings running.

The snarls of the wind and ocean swirled around her. Her eyes fluttered shut. She turned up the volume.

After a minute she flicked through the tracks to locate her recording of the interior of the shell midden. She visualised Clay sitting before her, a single fixed point in the midst of the whirling song that had made her so off-balance and giddily joyful. She pulled the duvet over her head to create a fabric cavern, turned the volume higher, imagined Clay now beside her, and placed her hand between her legs.

CHAPTER SIXTEEN

This time she spun constantly, and the water was far below her. If she had a body, she would undoubtedly be sick. The waves hurtled from all directions, spewing salt water at her, even this high up. Each droplet stung like a needle.

Something shrill punctured the bass rumble.

Her eyes opened. The sea was beige, not blue, and as she oriented herself she found that it was hanging above her. Then with a snap she was in the den. Light penetrating the gaps in the wooden slats made slashes across the photos of Rob.

That sound.

She bent at the waist to sit up, then gasped as something clung at her neck. Her hands went up to the bulky headphones. She pulled them down and disentangled herself from the cord.

But the shrill sound continued. A shout, nearby. Within moments it became ragged and fell away.

She stumbled to the door and opened it.

There in the hallway she saw a family. For a moment, in her confused state, she imagined that she might be part of it. Wasn't that her, kneeling on the rug, embracing her daughter, watched on by Tammy? She could still feel Laurie in her arms. She could still sense the presence of Thomas Maddox at the door.

But then the crouching figure turned. It was Egg. He blinked at Nina uncertainly. Laurie clutched at his shoulder and neck. Her blond hair had fallen over her eyes, but Nina could see her wide-open mouth, now soundless.

'What's going on?' Nina managed to say.

She looked to Tammy. The old woman's posture was strange, too. She gripped the coat rack as though it were a staff. Her knees were bent, her body slack.

'Egg?' Nina said. 'Talk to me.'

Laurie didn't allow him to rise, so he simply gazed up at her as she approached. 'I'm so sorry,' he said. 'We found him this morning.'

Nina squeezed her eyes shut. Even without her recordings she could hear the wind as if it were within the house. 'Who? Rob?'

Egg frowned at her confusion. 'No. Your father-in-law.'

The term threw her. She raised both hands in a show of dismay. She didn't have a—

'Abram?'

Now Tammy and Laurie were watching her too. Three accusing stares.

The imagined sea took her legs from under her. She felt nauseous at the sense of bobbing, of being adrift.

'What happened?'

'It might have been an accident,' Egg said slowly. 'He might have been out for a walk. Though it seems that all this happened late last night, so it would have been dark. One of the catchers was coming around the north-east coast by boat when he saw the body – sorry Laurie, sorry Tammy, that's an inappropriate word to use – saw Abram lying there.'

Nina bunched her hands into fists. She wanted to hit Egg in the face to stop him telling her awful things. She wondered why she couldn't speak, suddenly, and felt as ashamed as when she hadn't been able to scream in the Crow's Nest.

'He was right there at the foot of the east cliff,' Egg said.

That was the cliff that Nina had led Abram to, yesterday. She had shown him the way up there and she had checked her phone as he stared down into the abyss.

Tammy released her grip on the coat rack that had been supporting her, and stumbled to her granddaughter. Still on her knees, Laurie nestled her face against Tammy's stomach. She didn't let go of Egg, who was drawn into this new, three-way embrace.

Nina stood to one side, only watching.

CHAPTER SEVENTEEN

Against a wall of the Open Arms somebody had propped an enormous portrait of Abram comprised of twenty letter-paper printouts pasted onto a board backing. It looked like an old passport photo. Its faded scratchiness and Abram's baleful stare reminded Nina of a 'Wanted' poster in some old Western.

She glanced around. Nobody else seemed to be fixated on the picture. Perhaps this was what funerals were like here: everything bigger than it needed to be.

Of course, this wasn't even a real funeral. Egg had beat around the bush the day he had delivered the news about Abram's death, but had finally, reluctantly, told Tammy that a formal funeral would be delayed due to the need for an autopsy on the mainland. Tammy had only groaned at the prospect of her husband's body being carted away on the next ferry. Nina had wished that she could go with him.

The last two days had been almost unbearable. Tammy had refused to speak about Abram's accident. She had collected flowers from the front garden – milkweed, harebell and boneset – and had draped them messily over the back of Abram's sagging chair in the sitting room. Then she had deposited herself onto the sofa, turned on the TV, and had barely moved from that position from morning until night. While her daytime soap operas and quiz shows blared at incredible volume Tammy had become almost mute, ignoring Nina's offers of help. Nina had suffered from constant headaches; no part of Cat's Ear Cottage was spared the TV's bellowing.

Laurie's reaction had been entirely different. Beneath her stiff civility Nina detected simmering rage, along with grief. Laurie made her polite excuses and left the house, dismissing Nina's faint objections. She had spent the last two days with her new family, the children at the schoolhouse.

Nina had found herself at the fire department twice, but each time Egg had brushed away her questions about Lukas Weber, perhaps due to a sense of impropriety given Abram's death. It was clear that he had no information to impart anyway, other than that he had been told to wait to hear from the mainland authorities once they had assessed the evidence.

She had distracted herself with chores, and when the obvious ones had run out, she scrubbed the front and rear doorsteps of the cottage, trimmed the hedge and washed the curtains, though she left Abram's room untouched. She recognised that her activities were a penance. It boiled down to this: if she hadn't led Abram to those towering cliffs on their walk, surely he wouldn't have thought to go there in the night-time, in the midst of whatever delusion he was experiencing? Neither Tammy nor Laurie knew of this, but their attitudes seemed accusatory all the same. Nina's presence had been the only new factor in Abram's day-to-day life. He might have been fine if she hadn't shown up.

It seemed that the entire population of the island had squeezed into the barroom. Nina turned in her seat to scan the crowd of faces: Egg, Marie, Si Michaud, Clay, Mikhail and other scruffy-looking men who must have been members of the Siblings, along with people she had encountered in the Open Arms as well as fishermen from the harbour. At the rear of the room, behind the rows of folding chairs, the island children stood in a silent huddle. Thomas stood slightly away from the others, staring straight ahead and blinking rapidly as if stifling tears. Nina was grateful that Laurie hadn't joined the other children and had instead taken her seat between Nina and Tammy.

Laurie took Nina's hand – and Tammy's too, at the same time – and squeezed it. For a moment Nina imagined that things might be different after the wake, but then reminded herself that the situation with Rob and Kaytee and his two alien new children would remain the same. If anything, Rob might have even more claim over Laurie, now that he represented a last link to beloved Abram. Nina felt ashamed at her relief that he wasn't there. She had phoned, emailed and sent text messages about the urgent need for them to speak, but Rob hadn't replied. It would only be matter of time before he showed up, and that might be the end of everything. Nina squeezed her daughter's hand in return and didn't let go.

Kelly Brady lumbered onto the makeshift platform before the enormous portrait. His checked shirt was open at the collar, his limp grey hair slicked to one side, and he held a beer glass in his left hand. When he grabbed the microphone stand for support, he looked for all the world like the worst kind of stand-up comedian.

'Folks!' he bellowed. Nina winced as the speakers at the back of the room squealed with feedback. Kelly's booming voice required no amplification.

'This is a shitty day,' Kelly continued. He suppressed a belch, then swung his beer to indicate the Wanted poster. 'We're here to mourn Abram Fisher in the only way we're allowed to.'

Nina followed the direction of his glare to see Egg's cheeks turn pale. He must have been taking a lot of flak, as the island representative of the mainland authorities. Nobody would have been happy for Abram's body to be taken away.

'But it's not for me to speak about Abram,' Kelly said. 'For a start, he wasn't a customer, the old bastard. But we all do our bit for the community, so I'm only too happy to host this whole jamboree. Anyhow. Without further ado, I present to you Abram's granddaughter, Laurie, over from Britain, or England, or whatever they call it now. Up you come, darling.'

Nina's eyes widened as Laurie extricated her hand from her grasp and stepped up to the platform. Kelly Brady sloped towards the bar.

Laurie looked tiny standing on the wide stage. She looked out at the crowd, then up at the microphone on its stand. For a few moments she fumbled to bring it down to her level.

'Hi,' she said. Her quiet voice, amplified to an absurd degree by the speakers, reminded Nina of the sound installation in the Sanctuary church. Soft but loud. Laurie cleared her throat and said again, 'Hi. My name is Laurie and Abram is my Grumps. That's what I called him. But he wasn't grumpy, or mean, or anything like that. He was sort of beautiful.'

Nina heard shuffling sounds from behind her. She turned to see a number of people in the audience fidgeting in their seats.

'I wanted to tell you what he was like, to me,' Laurie continued in a higher pitch. 'There was this time. Maybe two summers ago? And I was upset. It doesn't matter about what.' Her eyes raised briefly, perhaps looking at Thomas at the back of the room. 'And Grumps always had this way of doing the right thing to snap me out of it. He showed me how to bundle together everything I was angry about, and then deal with it.'

Nina felt a chill in her toes and against the skin of her ankles. The door of the hotel had blown open, though nobody had entered. Other members of the audience coughed and muttered.

Laurie's voice was becoming quieter. 'He did this trick. A magic trick, I suppose, but the magic was only part of it. He told me to go up to the woods and collect one twig for each thing that was making me angry or worried. I came back with maybe six.' She scanned the crowd, not settling on anybody in particular. 'Grumps gave me a shoebox and I put them inside. He chucked in a few bits of string too.'

In the row behind Nina, a husband and wife were muttering to one another. She glared at them. Other people were squinting up at Laurie. Their mouths hung slackly open and their heads tilted in an attempt to concentrate. Thomas was standing alone at the rear of the room, his hands gripping the seat backs, a stricken expression on his face.

'Speak into the microphone!' somebody called out.

Laurie's cheeks reddened. She stood on tiptoes and pressed her lips against the microphone grille, producing wet popping sounds from the speakers. Her voice became distorted and alien. 'And then he opened the lid. And it was amazing. All those twigs, that string, had got bundled up together, like magic. It made a little person, a stick doll.' She stretched her finger and thumb a few inches apart.

More shuffling from the audience, more restlessness. What was wrong with them? Nina could hear her daughter just fine.

'And Grumps told me that all my worries and fears, everything, were bundled up in that doll made of sticks. He asked me what I wanted to do with it.'

She stared at the ceiling above the congregation as more and more members of the crowd made noises of impatience. Nina glanced at Tammy, who seemed on the verge of nodding off. The lack of respect was appalling.

'I—' Laurie began. She cleared her throat. 'I told him I'd deal with it. And he was happy that I took him seriously, I think. He gave me the biggest hug. And then later that day I went to this place I like, this little hole in the rocks on the east coast...'

As Laurie's eyes fixed on hers, Nina felt the shame of letting her down at the Crow's Nest all over again. She ought to have screamed.

Laurie said, 'And I threw that little doll off the cliff and it hit the rocks and then went into the water. And I was so happy. And now I can't think of anything else, whenever I think of Grumps. Because he was…' Her voice faltered and tailed off. The murmurs in the audience had grown louder. Out of the corner of her eye Nina saw one or two people rising to their feet. Laurie stared at them, blinking rapidly.

Just as Nina was about to turn and confront the crowd, Kelly Brady marched up onto the platform.

'Can't blame the girl for being a bit shy,' he bellowed. 'Show her some appreciation, would you?'

The audience began to applaud, first sporadically but then growing louder and louder. Tammy only stared ahead without seeming to register what was happening. Nina stared at the congregation, some of whom had begun to stamp their feet. What were they all thinking? This was no way to behave at a wake.

Kelly watched as Laurie made her way down from the platform and back to her seat, then turned his attention to the crowd, drinking in the applause.

'You were wonderful,' Nina whispered to Laurie. 'I know that was really hard for you. And I could hear every word. Ignore those idiots.'

Laurie responded with a tight-lipped smile, then nestled into position leaning against Tammy's shoulder. She pulled her phone from her pocket and thumbed at the screen, which was angled away from Nina. Nina faced the front so that her daughter couldn't see her twitching lips.

Kelly consulted a scrap of paper. 'Christ. Looks like we have more live wires up next. As you're all aware, there's no love lost between me and the Siblings, but this joint is called the Open Arms for a reason. So join me in welcoming to the stage… Elliot Vance and Mikhail Zieliński.' He enunciated each syllable of Mikhail's surname carefully, highlighting its alienness: *zye-lin-ski*.

The pair had to make their way around the edge of the seating, stepping over bags and coats piled on the floor, and members of the audience frowned at them as they passed. Elliot was stouter than Mikhail, with receding hair and a waistline that required him to lead with his belly. His suit was too small around the shoulders, and Mikhail's grey linen jacket was hopelessly creased. They couldn't have much call for formal wear up at the Sanctuary. Mikhail had scraped his usually curly hair into a dark skullcap.

Mikhail stood to one side of the stage as Elliot ambled to the centre. Mikhail appeared not to know what to do with his hands: first he crossed his arms, then thrust his hands into his trouser pockets, then pulled them out to hang stiffly at his sides.

Elliot seemed far more at ease. He took the microphone from its stand and held it loosely. Perhaps he had once worked onstage, before joining the Siblings.

'You may wonder what we might have to say about Abram Fisher,' he began. He laughed and gestured at Mikhail. 'Or what *I* might say, anyhow. Mikhail here doesn't talk a whole lot.'

Nobody in the crowd seemed to appreciate the joke.

Undeterred, Elliot continued, 'See, we're newcomers here, in the grand scheme of things. We all met Abram only, what, three years ago? Mikhail had big plans for renovating the big house. You've all seen the state it's in, and it was worse before. Abram might have come across as pretty mild, I guess. But put him in front of a problem that needed solving and you'd see all those skills get to work. All those years in construction and haulage on the mainland, he picked up a few logistics tricks. Without him we'd have floundered from the start. If the Sanctuary ever had an architect, it was Abram Fisher. It wasn't only us that benefitted from his wisdom, either. He was a mentor to countless people. I think I'm right in saying that he helped out young Fallon Maddox in his career – weren't you something of a tearaway before then, Fallon?' Elliot shielded his eyes to look out across the sea of faces. He frowned. Nina turned and saw Marie, a pinched look on her face. The baby's hand was clawing at her neck. To either side of her sat other women. Fallon must still be on the mainland.

Elliot shrugged. 'And it was sad to see Abram in decline, let me tell you. Those stories he'd tell about his trucker days—' He scanned the front row of the crowd, then coughed. '— are best saved for another time.'

The crowd were becoming restless again. Nina's attention shifted to Mikhail, who had shuffled even further to one side, out of the glare of the lights. His eyes were wet with tears and his body trembled.

'He was a terrific guy,' Elliot continued. 'And not only smart on the job. He was as much an artist as his dear Tammy, and an entertainer too. Those magic tricks he'd do, they're a testament to a creative mind. And of course, his treasured collection of vinyl—'

'Music!' somebody in the audience bellowed.

The interruption released others from the shackles of decorum. Nina heard hisses of, 'Get those hippies off of there,' and, 'Aren't we done with *talking*?'

Elliot looked stricken for a moment, then grinned. In a louder voice than before he said, 'As it happens, we thought it might be appropriate to play one of Abram's favourite tracks. If now's the time?' He looked sideways to Kelly standing in the shadows. 'Okay then. Clay, would you cue it up please.'

Nina saw Clay at the side of the room, bending before a hi-fi unit. He gave a quick thumbs up.

Suddenly the sound of a distorted guitar blared from the speakers, a woozy wavering note produced by a guitar string bent too far. Beneath it was a splash of reverberating snare drums and a bassline that, over-amplified through the poor-quality speakers, sounded like nothing so much as a series of farts. It was only when the vocals began that Nina recognised the song as 'Everybody Knows This is Nowhere'.

Somebody whooped. Several people rose from their seats immediately. Heads nodded. Nobody complained that the music was too loud or that it was inappropriate at what was surely supposed to be a sombre event.

It was clear that the service was now considered over. Nina took Laurie's hand, though Laurie still held onto

Tammy so that they all crossed to the edge of the room in an awkward conga line. They stood behind the speaker where the raw guitar line could only be heard rather than sawing into Nina's brain. She watched in horror as the congregation abandoned the seating area, shoving one another to get free, and gathered in the open space behind the folding chairs. Then most of them began to dance, or at least bob their heads like teens in a moshpit. The floorboards bounced with their lumbering motion and the thudding from the speakers.

Laurie worked her hand free of Nina's before she guided Tammy to the back of the room. Tammy's body seemed to slump further with every step. Laurie gently deposited her onto a bench, then joined the other children in their huddle. None of them acknowledged the loud music or showed the least interest in dancing.

Like Nina, many of the adults who weren't part of the dancing throng were watching the children. Couples who might have been parents of some of the kids hugged one another and frowned at the little group. To Nina's consternation, she noticed Si Michaud standing close to the doorway of the barroom. He was muttering to a short man that Nina had never seen before. Both of their gazes were fixed on the group of children.

If anything, the huddle was growing tighter. Laurie was at its periphery at first, but then the younger children stepped aside to allow her entry. Nina was reminded of animations she had seen of white blood cells surrounding and digesting bacteria.

If only the music would stop. It was scrambling her thoughts.

Though perhaps that was preferable to dwelling on the possibility of having influenced Abram's death. A voice within her told her that the islanders were right, losing themselves to noise as a means of cutting themselves off from the real world, just for a short time. Perhaps she, too, would dance.

'You are okay?' a voice said. It was Clay. He had pulled his blond hair up into a high ponytail, revealing more of the crinkled skin around his eyes. His was a kind face.

Nina gulped, pushed away her strange impulse to lose herself in the music, and smiled. 'As much as I can be. Bit of a weird time, I'll be honest.'

'Your daughter is a wonder. She is much like you.'

Nina glanced at Laurie at the same moment her daughter looked her way. Laurie's eyes flicked from Nina to Clay.

Nina's cheeks flushed immediately. Clay was younger than she was, and very attractive. She didn't want Laurie coming to the wrong conclusion. She turned and, without speaking to Clay again, took a few paces and leant against a rail to watch the children.

Thomas was still standing apart from the group. His face was utterly white.

Neil Young's voice dropped out of the track, replaced with the falsetto voices of the backing singers.

Thomas lunged forward, away from the other children. At first Nina thought he was going to dance, then that he might be making his way over to her, but after a couple of faltering steps it was clear that he was falling. Adults stepped aside as he crumpled to the floor in a dead faint. One of his arms was splayed out and the other was draped behind his neck. It seemed an almost impossible pose, as if he were a wooden puppet with cut strings rather than anything made of flesh.

Nina darted forward, almost colliding with Marie who also dashed to his aid. Thomas stirred immediately, flopping onto his side and looking up at them groggily. Marie's baby shrieked in her arms, his voice rising to a crescendo as the backing singers began to fade out.

'I'm okay,' Thomas said weakly. 'Help me up, Mom?'

But the baby renewed his attack on Marie, so it was Nina who eased Thomas up into a sitting position, then slowly back onto his feet. The song had ended, and she was aware that everybody was watching her. Why didn't they help?

Thomas regarded her with glassy eyes. 'Thank you,' he said in a formal tone.

Then, absently, he rubbed at one of his ears, turned, and walked to the group of children. They appeared wary of Thomas at first, but then their expressions cleared. The white blood cells parted and then absorbed him.

Nina didn't know whether to be relieved or enraged when another track began playing over the speakers. It was even louder than the last song; some modern rock band that surely couldn't have been in Abram's record collection. The adults on the dance floor bobbed their heads with their mouths hanging slackly open; a couple of people yelled something wordless. They all grunted with exertion and bent to their spasmodic dancing.

*

Nina found Marie standing outside the porch of the Open Arms, struggling to clamp Niall's two hands in one of hers. She shivered and light rain speckled her bare shoulders.

'Need any help?' Nina said. She held out her hands.

Marie passed the baby to her immediately. Nina stiffened, but she forced herself to cradle the child rather than hold him like something diseased. To her surprise, Niall's claws retracted, his arms fell, his eyelids closed. He nestled against her breast, nuzzling until his nose was squashed flat.

'Jesus,' Marie said. 'You're good.'

Nina stared down at the boy. 'I swear that's never happened before. I mean, even with Laurie.'

'Late bloomer?'

Nina shrugged, but carefully. She had no desire to disturb the kid so soon after this triumph.

Marie's hands shook as she rummaged in the small bag slung around one shoulder. She retrieved a pack of cigarettes and a lighter, then waved them at Nina, who shook her head.

Marie took three attempts to get her cigarette lit. 'Haven't smoked for maybe twenty years,' she said. 'I didn't even like it as a teenager.'

'So,' Nina said after allowing Marie a few puffs in silence, 'what the hell's going on in there?'

Marie glanced at the hotel door. Through the glass the jerking figures on the dance floor were visible against an orange glow. Out here, only a bass rumble was audible, a smacking sound that bore no relation to music. It might as well have been the sound of roadworks.

'People cope in different ways,' Marie said distantly.

'I don't think Abram would have enjoyed this.'

'No. Or the fact that Rob's not here.'

Nina stiffened. 'I've tried to contact him – we all have – but he's not answering, and he never was one for checking his emails. As far as I can tell, he doesn't even know about what happened to Abram yet. I think maybe he started to feel hounded, even from across the Atlantic.'

When Rob did learn about his father's death, Kaytee would comfort him. Then he would rush to Hope Island to be comforted by his daughter and his mother. The idea of watching on from the sidelines was unthinkable. Nina had to escape before then.

She considered explaining the situation to Marie. She was a decent sort; she might be able to advise or at least comfort her.

But Marie didn't even appear to be paying attention. She held the cigarette to her lips, inhaling again and again, smoke billowing from her nostrils. Her eyes watered. Nina realised that it wasn't from the smoke: tears began to streak her cheeks.

'Hey,' Nina said softly. 'Talk to me?'

Marie squeezed her eyes tight. Her voice rose in volume as she said, 'I don't think I can live with him any more!' She threw the cigarette down and ground it under her heel.

Nina was more alarmed by the force of this action than Marie's outburst. She looked down at the sleeping baby in her arms – his presence was so comforting, so *right*, that she had almost forgotten he was there.

No. Marie wasn't talking about Niall. Perhaps there was some issue with her husband – she had talked so little about him – something that Nina in her ignorance had failed to spot. It would be consistent with her inability to notice anything amiss in her own relationship. She had always told people that she and Rob were solid.

'Fallon?' she said.

Marie glared at her. 'What? No, of course not. Fallon's fine.'

'Oh.' Then, 'Shit. Sorry. Thomas. That was pretty fucking weird, in there. Has he done that before?'

'Only once, yesterday. One more episode and I guess I'll take him to the doctor next time we're on the mainland.'

'Okay. But it's not that you're worried about.'

'Laurie's a teenager. You must have to deal with odd behaviour. Right?'

'Of course.' No such thing occurred to Nina at this moment, though. 'What are we talking about, exactly?'

Marie pulled out another cigarette but didn't light it. She pointed with it towards the door. 'I guess you'd call it a morbid attitude. But more like a lack of empathy. Compassion.' She exhaled, as though she really were breathing out smoke. 'So this is it: when I told him the awful news about Lukas Weber? Nothing. No reaction.'

'Kids that age… there's no telling what a normal reaction might be.' It was the sort of thing Nina imagined another mother saying.

'Yeah. But that was the start. Or maybe this whole summer

has been the start – his silences, his total focus on being nowhere the hell near me and spending all his time away with his friends. Anyhow, it was the night after Lukas's death. I was awake most of the night, like always these days.' She gestured at the sleeping Niall, then rolled her eyes at his angelic appearance. 'Christ, Nina, I'm *tired*.'

'I can help you. I'll, I don't know, babysit. Get you some rest.'

Marie's posture crumbled in her gratefulness. 'Thanks. Maybe it'll come to that, but even if not, it's good to know someone's got my back.'

'Please. Go on?'

'Sure. I was awake, so I heard Thomas moving around. And then I saw him leave the house.'

'This was late?'

'One, two in the morning. Yeah.'

'Where did he go?'

'You don't think I wanted to know? I was crazy with worry. I bundled Niall up – we have one of those crappy slings, but they're a bitch to get on and I was tying myself up in knots, so I left the house holding the kid in my arms, like you're doing now. And I looked all around, of course. There was only a half moon but enough to see by. But I didn't know where to start. Thomas was nowhere nearby. I figured maybe he was up at the den they've been building, up in the forest. But there's barely anything to it. I found their tarpaulins soon enough, some boxes of Cheerios, all that.'

'But no sign of Thomas.'

Marie shuddered. 'I must have been out for more than an hour. It was *cold*. But then I headed on back. And what do you know? Thomas was right there in his bed. I actually shook him, to make sure I wasn't seeing what I wanted to see. Fast asleep, or at least the best impression of it I've ever known.'

'But you're certain—'

'I won't deny I'm strung out, Nina. There's not much let-up, the way Niall's been scratching and shouting at me. It's not like first time around. But no. I was certain. And I had proof, of a sort. Once I'd got the baby down finally, I didn't go straight to bed. I couldn't help myself – my mind was on fire. I sneaked back into Thomas's room, checked the pockets of his jeans, flipped off the blankets to see that he was wearing the same T-shirt as when he went to bed. But then as I was about to give up, I saw it.'

Niall squirmed in Nina's arms. She rocked him gently. 'What did you see?'

'The floor. The floorboards outside Thomas's bedroom and leading all the way to the stairs and the back door, the door we use instead of tramping through the schoolroom. There were streaks on them, where there hadn't been before. The whole corridor had been mopped clean.'

CHAPTER EIGHTEEN

Nina tried to tune out the blare of the TV in the sitting room. It was impossible. She found herself absorbed in the quiz show, a *Deal Or No Deal* far glitzier and brasher than the version she had seen once or twice at home. She stood in the centre of the room, still clutching the bathroom bin which she was intending to take to the kitchen to clean inside and out. She stared at the rows of identical hairsprayed women in identical red dresses, all holding numbered signs, and she let the wave of the audience's applause wash over her. It sounded so much like the sea that her imagination played tricks on her: she pictured herself submerged in that water, that sound. It was beautiful and at the same time overwhelming and obscene.

She gasped, fighting for breath. Then she lurched to the coffee table, grabbed the remote control, and turned down the volume.

'You'll damage your ears,' she said to Tammy.

She was startled by Tammy's open mouth, her vacant stare. It took several seconds for the older woman to register that Nina had spoken.

Tammy peered up at her. 'It hurts my head,' she said in a flat, loud tone.

'Me too. Maybe we could turn it off for a bit? Go for a—' She stopped herself before she said 'walk'. She still hadn't determined whether Tammy blamed her at all for Abram's death. Perhaps she didn't even know that Nina and Abram had been to the cliff on the day of his death. She didn't want to find out. 'We could see what Laurie's up to.'

Tammy's face screwed up in an expression of revolt. 'That's not what I meant. It hurts my head *now*. Would you turn the volume up again?'

Nina obeyed without comment. Tammy lapsed into something like contentment, her jaw hanging open again as the TV presenter bellowed at her. Nina forced herself not to pay any attention. She hurried out to the kitchen and set to her cleaning task furiously.

When she returned Tammy had slumped to one side. She was awake and yet she hadn't even put out a hand to right herself, though her back was as stiff as if she were sitting primly at a table. It was as if the room had changed its orientation rather than her.

Tammy stared through Nina when she blocked the view of the TV. Then she barked, 'I'm very tired.'

'I'll help you up to your room,' Nina said. She reached for the remote, then thought better of it.

Tammy waved her away. 'I want Bobby to help me.'

'I'm sorry, Tammy. He's not here.'

'He should be here.'

'I'm doing my best. I can't reach him.' A strange idea

occurred to Nina – that Hope Island was floating further away from the mainland, further away from the world she knew. Rob *should* be here, and she should not. It was all a terrible mistake.

Tammy's head swayed as Nina raised her awkwardly from the sofa. As they staggered to the doorway, Tammy's head turned from side to side continually. Her mouth was still hanging open. Now it appeared like concentration, like a jazz musician absorbing the sound of the other players in a band, determining when would be the perfect moment to join in.

The stairs were only just wide enough for them to climb side by side. If Tammy had had any meat to her body, it would have been impossible. She hadn't seemed so thin when Nina had arrived on Hope Island. It must have been an illusion caused by her flapping long skirts and her bulky cardigans.

Finally, Nina elbowed open the door to Tammy's room and heaved her into a sitting position on the single bed. The decor was immaculate, all pastel shades. On a pine chest of drawers beside a full-length mirror was a smaller drawer unit for jewellery. Upon it lay a brush that appeared pristine and unused. The only sign of real human occupation was a pile of books beside a clock radio on the bedside table. They were all large coffee-table art books and several of their slipcovers were worn or ripped.

A single, unframed canvas hung on the otherwise plain wall beside the door. The painting was abstract, with horizontal bands of colour and a few dark vertical streaks at the left-hand side. If it represented anything at all, Nina assumed that the grey and purplish horizontal stripes were the sea and sky. Looking closer, she could see flecks of white in the lower strata. The rough vertical parts might have been a building, or perhaps only rock.

'It's unfinished,' Tammy said behind Nina, startling her. 'The last one I ever began. After six months staring at it with brush in hand, I figured I was done with painting. After another year I hung it up. I decided I like it fine as it is.'

She was sitting upright in bed now. The expression on her face was alert, unclouded.

'It's very striking.'

'It is. And it helped me. I was okay with how it turned out.'

Now that Nina was in a position to ask Tammy something about herself, her basic journalistic training – asking open-ended questions to establish communication of any sort – deserted her.

And then she realised that Tammy was weeping.

'It hurts so bad,' she whimpered.

'I'm so sorry,' Nina said. She couldn't decide whether physical contact would be welcomed, or whether it might make Tammy clam up. 'It was all so sudden.'

That same bemused look again, mingled with disgust. Nina actually took a step back.

'You know,' Tammy said, 'I did this to Abram.'

Nina blinked. 'Of course you didn't. Tammy, that doesn't make sense.'

Tammy raised a shaking finger to point at the painting. 'Abram was no kind of island dweller. He had no love for the sea. Why do you think he spent all those years working upstate? He was keeping far away from this place. I made him stay, and I made everything far worse.'

'How?'

'I had my issues with the island too. Abram tried to keep that feeling, that voice inside him, pushed down, but I spoke mine loud and clear. I got preoccupied, I guess, and Abram couldn't help but be affected by it.'

'I'm sorry. I don't understand.'

Abruptly, Tammy threw out both her hands behind her. For a moment Nina thought she was going to fall backwards onto the bed, but she was only leaning back to stare up at Nina from her sitting position.

'Come here.'

Nina edged closer to sit on the edge of the bed.

'See, everybody's got a voice inside them,' Tammy said. 'Everybody knows full well what's in there and what's really going on inside. My Abram, he wasn't as good at hiding his voice as he thought he was. More and more, that voice came on out, but not in the regular way. He wouldn't speak directly about all those things he felt guilty about, but he sure as hell told me.'

Nina thought of Abram's part-confession about his adultery. To know about all that and to remain married to him would have taken some resolve.

Tammy continued in her loud, cracked voice. 'Me, I was better at it. My voice stayed on the inside. But I could hear it, Nina, loud and clear. It told me what was happening out there in the world, and it told me what was happening inside me too. Told me who I really was and that what I was doing was – what's the word? Toxic.' She struggled to make herself comfortable again. 'Now you… We're not much alike. I get the sense that you're not so good at hearing that voice inside you. Not so good at listening to what it's telling you about the way things are.'

She reached out her right hand. Nina stared at it, suddenly appalled at the chipped red nail varnish.

'But that voice is in there all the same,' Tammy said. 'You've only got to listen. It's right… there.'

Her hand darted out, and the flat of her palm made sharp contact with Nina's breastbone.

Nina spasmed and half-fell, half-jumped from the bed. Her eyes widened with shock. Tammy's hand was ice cold. She struggled for breath, trying to reassure herself that Tammy's action hadn't been an attack, no matter how it had felt.

Tammy slumped back. 'Do you want to see more of my paintings?' Somehow it sounded like a threat.

Nina swallowed and smoothed her hair. She nodded slowly, feeling caught in a strange dream. She realised that her ears were ringing again. She wished that she were the one sitting on the bed, in case she became suddenly faint.

'They're all stored away. But they should have been further out of sight.' Tammy released a hollow, barking laugh. 'There's a closet in Abram's room, beside the wardrobe. Go take a look. You'll soon see why they're playing on my mind. But don't bring them in here, you understand?'

Nina hesitated, then left the door open as she crossed the landing to Abram's bedroom. The smell of him hit her as she opened the door. The room was smaller than Tammy's, so narrow that she immediately trod on Abram's slippers placed at the side of the single bed. The room spanned the depth of the house so that it felt like a corridor.

At the far end were the plain white doors of a floor-to-ceiling cupboard. She approached it as slowly as a sleepwalker. When she opened the cupboard door, at first she couldn't understand what she was looking at, then she realised that the paintings were all stacked sideways. She was looking at five tall rows of the edges of stretched canvases. On the vertical pale stripes were paint blemishes like bruises.

She slid out one of the paintings at random.

It was around a metre across and sixty centimetres. It looked rather like the one hanging in Tammy's bedroom: the same configuration of the sea and sky on the right and a similar tall edifice of rock on the left. It was clear that many hours had been spent on this painting, though. The sea was filled with crests and bursts of fountain spray. Rather than a grey swathe, the sky was full of motion, suggesting eddies and gusts. The rock face was meticulously realised, with hints of crimson and gold, its surface riddled with crenulations and dark cubbyholes.

But there was another, starker difference between this painting and the one in Tammy's room. It took Nina a few seconds to spot it, but once noticed it became the focus of the painting.

To the right of the rock, around two-thirds of the way up its height, was a small, dark shape. It was unmistakably a human figure. Its black arms were outstretched. Something, perhaps some item of clothing, appeared to have fallen free as the figure spun through the air. On the cliff top above, where surely the figure had begun the fall, speckles seemed to indicate dirt spilling from the cliff edge.

Nina's mouth was dry. Her headache pulsated. She could hear faint voices from somewhere outside the room. Carefully, she pushed the painting sideways into the rack. She took out another.

It showed the same landscape and the same figure, this time halfway down the cliff face. The sky was redder: dusk. The whorls of paint representing the sea suggested a vortex.

She reached up for a painting on a higher shelf. In this one the figure was closer and more discernible. It was undoubtedly a man. Nina could make out his wide-open mouth, even the stubble on his chin. His hands reached upwards to the cliff top as though he might pull himself back up, even from halfway to the shining wet boulders below.

She looked at others, and they were all essentially the same. Her hands shook as she replaced them all, in as close to their original positions as she could manage.

Shakily, she left the room. Tammy's door was still open. There were voices coming from inside the bedroom. Without wanting to, Nina entered.

Tammy was lying on the bed. She was still clothed, and rather than getting fully under the sheets she had pulled them around herself while lying upon them, making a cocoon or a shroud. She was facing away from the doorway. Nina edged around the foot of the bed to see that Tammy's eyes were closed. Her mouth hung slackly open as if she were about to speak. The clock radio blared out some talk radio station. It was poorly tuned so that the conversation was interrupted every couple of seconds by a squall of static.

Nina couldn't make herself go any closer to the sleeping woman. She backed away and closed the door silently after her.

＊

As Nina made her way downstairs, she saw light spilling from the open door of the den.

'Laurie?'

There was no answer. She entered the room. Laurie stood in its centre, facing away from the doorway, staring up at the photos of Rob.

'I didn't realise you'd come home already,' Nina said.

'Well, I did.'

'Your gran's in bed.'

Laurie didn't respond.

'I rang your dad again this afternoon,' Nina said. 'Nothing.'

She felt foolish, as though she were to blame for Rob's silence. As if it didn't matter to her, too, that he had made himself uncontactable.

'I don't know what's going on,' she blurted out.

'All right,' Laurie replied quickly. 'You don't have to shout. I thought you said Gran was asleep.'

Nina hadn't even realised she had raised her voice. The jangling in her ears was making it difficult to judge external sounds. She remembered people at work talking about a similar sensation once. It might be stress, or worse. Was she on the cusp of some kind of breakdown?

'I guess you were up at the schoolhouse?'

Laurie only grunted. She turned to look at another collection of photos, but Nina still couldn't see her eyes.

'How's everyone getting on? They must all be rattled.'

'About what?'

'Seriously?' Nina spluttered. 'About two people having been killed on the island within a week.'

'*Killed*? Who said Grumps was killed?'

Nina hesitated. The ringing in her ears was so distracting, muddling her thoughts. 'I didn't mean it how it sounded. There'll be an investigation into Lukas's death. I suppose they'll also try to figure out whether anybody might have had any reason to want to hurt him.'

Laurie turned. Her eyes shone. 'And what about Grumps?'

'What about him?'

'What do you think happened?'

Nina rubbed the skin beneath her right earlobe, where she felt a strange pressure. Her eyes flicked to the futon; she would dearly love to lie down right now.

'It was an accident. That's what I think. I don't believe anybody else had anything to do with it, and I don't think Abram meant to fall.' It didn't matter what she actually thought. She didn't know what she thought anyway. 'He loved walking on the coastal path. It was an accident.'

Laurie watched her carefully. Perhaps she suspected Nina's involvement, however slight. Perhaps she imagined Nina had actually pushed Abram over the edge of the cliff herself.

'I wanted to talk to you about the children,' Nina said.

Laurie flinched. 'What?'

'Thomas, in particular.'

'Oh. Those children.'

Nina frowned. 'Have you noticed anything strange about him recently? Anything a bit off?'

'Mum. What's your problem with Thomas?'

'I don't have one.'

'Is it that we're close? Is that the problem?'

'Of course not.'

'Then spit it out, Mum.'

Where had she learned that phrase? Nina tried to imagine it coming from Tammy's mouth, or Rob's, or even Marie's. Laurie was becoming more adult by the day.

'I'm trying to look out for you,' Nina managed to say.

She shrunk beneath Laurie's glare.

Laurie said, 'You know what I think? I think you're looking for something to worry about that doesn't involve you. I think you're feeling guilty.'

Was it true? Nina honestly didn't know. 'Why should I feel guilty?' she said, asking the question of herself as much as her daughter.

Laurie pointed above her head. Nina turned to look at the Robs smiling down at her.

'But your dad walked out on me, not the other way around. And I don't know how to talk to him.'

'Even so, you've moved on quickly.'

Nina blinked rapidly. This conversation was spinning out of her control.

'I saw you speaking to the fire department guy. Mr Frears?' Laurie said. 'You guys look pretty tight. And then I saw how hippy Clay looks at you, too. Who are you going to go with, Mum? Or have you already picked?'

The thought of hooking up with Egg was absurd. Clay, on the other hand...

But Nina said quickly, 'That's nonsense.'

'So's you going on about Thomas.'

Nina rubbed her jawbone. Laurie's words seemed faint, but she didn't dare ask her to speak up.

Laurie folded her arms over her chest. Her head tilted back so that, despite her shorter stature, she was looking down her nose at Nina.

'*I've* spoken to him,' Laurie said slowly. 'This morning.'

At first Nina had no idea what she was talking about. Egg? Clay? Thomas? Then it struck her. 'Your dad. How did you get through to him?'

'He's been avoiding you, Mum. He figured you'd got me and Gran to do your dirty work.'

'Did you tell him about Abram?'

Laurie rolled her eyes. 'No, I told him about what I had for breakfast. Of course I told him.'

'And?'

'And he's upset.'

'I meant—'

'He's coming. He'll sort out all the funeral stuff, whenever they let him.'

'When?'

'Three days. Two and a half.'

Nina's eyes darted. Her first instinct was flight. She had to get off the island before then. The thought of encountering Rob *here*, on his territory, was unbearable. She would have no solid ground, nothing familiar to orient herself. No escape.

The buzzing in her head increased. The sound seemed to swell within her like something physical, like water with its level gradually rising, threatening to drown her. She lifted her arms as though she might swim free.

'What's wrong with you?' Laurie said, her voice full of disdain. She sounded further away all the time.

Nina's body felt alien and heavy. She felt she was drowning. Like in her dream, she had lost all sense of where her hands were located.

She spun suddenly, wrenching herself away from Laurie's intense stare. Something collided with something; one of them was her hand. At first the pain felt like relief, a glimmer of light suggesting the water's surface and air beyond. Then her knuckles began to sing. She looked down and saw three parallel tracks of blood on the back of her hand.

The other something fell from the wall.

Nina bent to pick it up carefully. The glass of the picture frame was punctured at its centre; slivers continued to fall from it. Rob gazed out from beneath the crazed surface, grinning. He was in his mid-teens and wearing a tuxedo. A school prom, by the looks of it. He was handsome and happy.

Nina and Laurie exchanged looks. Nothing needed to be said – the accidental symbolism of what Nina had done was clear. Nina concentrated on her breathing. The sensation of drowning was lessening.

Slowly, Laurie reached into the back pocket of her jeans. She pulled out a folded piece of card, crumpled at the corners. She held it up to the light.

It was another picture of Rob. It had been taken in bright sunlight, which seemed almost obscene contrasted with the dim glow of Tammy's house. It was a selfie taken by Rob himself, judging from the angle and his looming, bulbous appearance.

Beside him was a woman. She had an open, circular face, an easy smile. She wore too much mascara, perhaps, but she was pretty. Her hair was fair.

Squeezed between Rob and Kaytee – it could only be her – were two boys. Both toddlers, though Nina struggled to tell how many years apart they might be. The younger wore a red cap with a Formula One chequered flag. The other boy's curly blond hair almost covered his eyes. He was pulling a face, his index fingers tugging at the edges of his mouth, his tongue poking out at one side.

Nina gulped for air, failed to fill her lungs, gave up. She felt a calmness wash over her. Perhaps it was acceptance.

'They look happy,' she said.

Laurie nodded.

'How long have you had this photo?'

'I've seen Dad a couple of times since he left. Just him, on his own. I haven't met these guys.'

'But you will.'

'Of course I will, Mum.'

Nina rubbed her eyes. 'Because they're family.'

Laurie hesitated. 'Not yet.'

'That's a strange thing to say. Unless...'

Laurie reached out to take Nina's hands. Her touch was warm and more comforting than Nina could bear. She wriggled free.

'You can't blame me, Mum.'

Nina shook her head. No, she couldn't blame Laurie.

Laurie continued, 'It's been a lot to take in. And I have to think about what's right for me.'

Nina told herself she wouldn't cry in front of her daughter, and then she told herself it was exactly this sort of decision that made her so unapproachable.

She could hardly blame Laurie for her own failings.

'You're thinking about going to live with them,' she said.

'I have to think it over, at least. But I'll always be yours too, whatever happens. This doesn't change the fact that you're my mum. I won't leave you alone.'

Nina shook her head, though she wasn't certain what she was refuting. She glanced at the doorway. Where could she run to?

Laurie was still looking at her strangely. 'I'm sorry you're upset. I didn't want to tell you like this. Look, I'm going to go to my room, all right? But we can talk later, or in the morning. Maybe you should rest.'

Laurie squeezed past Nina without their bodies touching. Nina listened to her light footsteps on the stairs, then pushed the door of the den closed. Laurie had taken the photo of Rob's new family with her, but Nina realised now that she was still holding the photo with the smashed frame. The cut on her hand wasn't too serious, but droplets of blood had dripped onto the glass.

CHAPTER NINETEEN

In the morning Nina avoided her daughter. She understood that it was irrational. It wasn't even that she was playing for time; if anything, time was running out. She made an elaborate dance around the house to ensure that she and Laurie were never in the same room at the same time.

The initial urge to escape had become something else. Nina turned it over in her mind. She felt a growing impulse to make the trip to Hope Island not entirely a negative experience. She couldn't return home having failed in every respect. She had established contact with Laurie, and it had done her no good.

But she had also been accused of not listening or paying attention. She could overcome that failing, at least. She might yet make herself useful in untangling the mystery about Lukas's death.

She had made it to the front door without being noticed when the doorbell rang. Reluctantly, she opened it.

Her heart leapt at the sight of Clay on the doorstep. In the lane behind him was one of the Siblings' enormous, mud-streaked four-wheel drive. Mikhail sat in the driver's seat.

'The top of the morning,' said Clay, pushing a strand of hair behind his ear as if that might make him presentable. He was still wearing his overalls spattered with dried cement. He was shabbily beautiful. 'Today we are limousine service.'

'To where?'

'Sanctuary.'

'I don't think we—'

She sensed movement behind her, and turned to see Laurie helping Tammy on with her thick coat.

'This is what Gran needs,' Laurie said. 'It's Sunday. The Siblings love her.'

The thought of encouraging Tammy's artistic side gave Nina the shudders. Tammy had spoken about a voice inside her, but since Nina had seen her paintings of the falling man, she worried that the voice might be vindictive rather than simply mean.

Tammy herself seemed energised, shooing Laurie away to fuss with the buttons of her coat. Nina hadn't seen any pink to her cheeks since the morning they had learnt about Abram's death. Tammy provided a loud running commentary of her actions: 'I'll need a scarf, now where is it? In the closet or hanging up? Yes, right here. But perhaps a thicker one, perhaps, perhaps.'

'And you, Mum?' Laurie said, one eyebrow raised.

Nina turned to Clay. Spending more time with him would be pleasant, but she remembered Laurie's accusation about their overfamiliarity. The effort required to demonstrate that she had no particular feelings towards him would take more energy than she possessed.

'It has been a strange time,' Clay said, perhaps sensing her uncertainty. 'We all need something to take our mind off of all that happens.'

He slapped his knee; Nina marvelled that he didn't laugh at his own ridiculousness. 'I have it! I will take you all on a tour of the house. I will show which artists stayed where, the original decors in some parts, the murals… It is safe, I assure. You will all need tough hats, but we have many.'

'Perfect. Gran will love it. Thank you,' Laurie replied.

She and Tammy approached the car, Laurie's thin hands clasped around Tammy's, enormous in their woollen mittens. Mikhail leapt out to open the rear door for them.

Clay waited patiently on the porch.

'It sounds wonderful,' Nina said. She turned briefly in the doorway, her eyes darting until she spotted Tammy's car keys nestled in the bowl on the sideboard. 'But I have a few things I ought to get done. And I'm afraid I have a bad headache.'

It was only after she said it that she realised it was true.

*

She finally found Si Michaud on the headland above the south bay. His body was hunched as he performed some task low on the ground, his posture reminding Nina of Lukas Weber kneeling face-down on the beach. Despite the wind that whirled up the steep slope from the bay, Si's heavy storm jacket and cap meant that his outline was entirely motionless.

As she came closer, she saw the knife in his right hand. His arm made jerky movements away from his body, hacking at ropes that glinted with internal steel threads.

'Mr Michaud?' she called. 'Si?'

When he rose and turned, Nina felt she had made a mistake. The wind urged her away, but she pressed on, closing the gap.

The rope fell from Si's hand; now Nina saw the debris of old lobster traps which had until now been hidden in the long grass. In a fluid motion he folded the knife into its handle and slipped it into a coat pocket.

'I hope you don't mind me visiting you.'

Si glared at the landscape. 'Can't stop you from coming along this way. It's all common land.'

'But I came to see you, not the views.'

His eyes narrowed. 'So? What do you want?'

She forced her eyes not to stray to the pocket that contained the knife. 'I wanted to ask you a couple of questions about Lukas.'

'Marine Patrol already did that.'

'I understand. And I'm not from the Marine Patrol, or the police.'

'What are you?'

Don't say 'journalist'.

'I want to help find out what happened.'

'You're a tourist.'

His meaning was clear. She wasn't only a visitor to the island – what Nina had heard described with disdain in the north-west of England as an 'offcomer'. It was worse than that: she was relishing this mystery. She was feeding on grief.

'I just want to help.'

He began gathering the cut pieces of rope. 'Got things I need to be doing.'

He had turned his back to her again. Nina had a sudden certainty that he was trying to hide his face. What did he fear she might see there?

'You were scared,' she said.

Si stopped rummaging. He gathered the sections of rope to his chest as if they were precious. 'I'm busy. You get on back to the harbour.'

Beyond the grassy area, Nina saw a small clapboard shack. She wondered what she might find in there.

Perhaps Si anticipated her line of thinking. 'You come back round here again, I'll teach you to mind your own business.'

'Lukas Weber lived with you. Isn't that right?'

'He slept in one of my barns, over the rise. Others have before him. Doesn't mean anything. The Marine Patrol said they were satisfied so you should be too.'

It was an interesting response. Clearly, he bore no trace of guilt about his involvement with Lukas.

Si turned to leave. She had only seconds left.

'But you were scared when you found his body. And you're scared now.'

His shoulders twitched. She made her way through the long grass, close enough to touch his back.

'You don't think Lukas's death was an accident.'

'Course it was.' The reply was too quick. When Si had first entered the Open Arms, he hadn't even been able to express what he'd seen. His shock had suggested something even more dreadful than Lukas's corpse.

'Because you saw something. Some*one*. Where were you standing when you spotted Lukas? Near your workshop over there?'

He faced her. The ropes were now cradled in his huge hands, hanging down like strands of hair.

'Yeah. Now stop asking questions.' His words were barely audible against the rush of the wind.

'You have to tell me what you saw.'

'I don't have to do anything.'

Nina told herself to amend her tone. Her desperation was too evident, her need to make progress in this case in order to validate her being here on Hope Island.

She took a deep breath. 'I saw Lukas. I saw the state he was in. What could he have hit his head against, to make that kind of a hole?'

'Not for me to say.'

'Somebody did that to him. Did that and ran away. And you didn't even go down to the bay to check if Lukas was alive or dead.'

Si tilted his head. He seemed interested in her, despite his impulse to avoid her questions.

Nina pointed at the clapboard building. 'Because if you were up here at your workshop, and then you went to where Lukas's body was, you'd have taken a direct route. Straight down this slope, then directly across the beach at its widest point. It makes sense that whoever killed Lukas – with a rock, or whatever it might have been – didn't leave footprints, because they were on the shoreline, and then could have darted straight into the grassy dunes, where nobody would stand a chance of finding tracks. But you would have left prints that would have lasted hours. If you'd gone down there.'

Si stared at her. His mouth opened, then shut again. Jackpot.

'I didn't see any of them,' he said slowly. 'You got to believe me. I didn't see a thing.'

He swung away from her. The wind caught at his coat and billowed it out, and Nina imagined it might carry him away. She watched as he fumbled to zip it up, dropping the ropes in the process. He hurried away without looking back.

Nina watched him until he disappeared over the headland, then turned her attention to the lobster pots. Beside them was a thick wooden pole. A voice inside her told her to pick it up. She obeyed the voice, and raised the pole above her head, and brought it down upon the lobster pots, once, twice. The sharp splintering sound was glorious. She threw back her head and laughed.

She dropped the pole.

The impulse to smash the pots had been overwhelming. Where had it come from? Frustration about Rob, or Abram, or Laurie, perhaps – or Hope Island itself? It didn't make sense – though she had to admit that the destruction had been cathartic.

She bowed her head and strode north, forcing her mind back to the mystery surrounding Lukas Weber.

There were other possible lines of enquiry. She could ask around at the harbour, gather opinions about Si and his trustworthiness. If she could be sure that Si would remain here with his lobster pots for a little longer, she could sneak onto his farm and take a look at the barn where Lukas had been staying.

But this first conversation with Si hadn't been a waste of time. She had something, however small, to take away and hold up to the light to see if it might lead her further.

I didn't see any of them, Si had said.

Them.

CHAPTER TWENTY

The wave of dizziness hit her as she was driving to the harbour. She lost control of the car and had to swerve to avoid a concrete bollard at the entrance to the jetty where the ferry idled. This prompted a flashback to the day she had arrived on Hope Island, her near-miss with the girl on the road. Her hands shook uncontrollably and the sound in her head was as high-pitched and unrelenting as a drill.

Reluctantly, she pulled at the wheel of the car, turning into the narrow road that led up the hillside towards Cat's Ear Cottage. It would still be empty. She ought to use the time while Tammy and Laurie were absent to rest and recover. Then she would resume her investigation.

But the quiet of the house was oppressive rather than soothing. Nina stood in the hallway still wearing her coat, unnerved by the silence. Placing the car keys into the bowl full of glass pebbles produced a sharp *snick*. She lifted the keys and dropped them again, then repeated the action. The sound echoed from the plain walls and from the glass of the picture frames.

No, it wasn't quietness that she wanted, it was the ability to control her environment. She had been hiding away in the den for days, self-conscious whenever she was in the main part of the house. This was Tammy's realm, and Laurie's, and Rob's. She had been trying not to make a sound.

Previously she had noticed the old stereo in the den, but hadn't yet turned it on. It was an old MIDI system with built-in CD player, two tape decks and a turntable on top. Its front was a single piece of moulded plastic designed to look like hi-fi separates. Perhaps it had been Rob's stereo when he was growing up. She couldn't see any CDs but spotted a plastic carry case tucked beside the stereo. Inside were vinyl records crammed so tight that she had to tip the crate sideways to tease a few out. Some were clearly Rob's: Smashing Pumpkins, NOFX, *A Christmas Together* by John Denver and the Muppets. Others must have been handed down from his parents. The Neil Young albums must have been Abram's, and perhaps also the Rush, Sly and the Family Stone and King Crimson. Nina rifled through the pile, then stopped at Dolly Parton's *Jolene*. She cued up her favourite track, but no sound came from the speakers until she flicked the power switch on one of them. She lay back on the futon.

The delicate, bassy guitar lick of 'Early Morning Breeze' began, then Dolly Parton's voice rang out. She sounded more fragile than Nina remembered. Quiet, too. Nina screwed her eyes shut and tried to focus on the song – hadn't she adored it once? But now it seemed insipid. She flipped onto her knees and cranked up the volume. Better, but only a little. She resumed digging through the box of records. She pulled out one of Rob's heavy-metal albums: *Roots* by Sepultura. On the front cover Rob had scrawled band logos in silver pen. On the back were more doodles. Arrows pointed to one of the track titles: 'Ratamahatta'. Nina cued it up.

A chanting filled the air, a suggestion of a tribal drum beat that stopped as soon as it started. After a pause, it began again, this time pounded on a drum kit. Then a sawing, raw guitar and then a singer bellowing in Portuguese. It sounded like a voodoo ceremony. It was chaotic and *loud* even before Nina turned up the volume, twice. She danced in circles, bouncing on the futon. She spun around, relishing the straightforward dizziness that overwhelmed the muzziness in her head. She fell back with her arms sprawled, letting the music wash over her. She thought of the weightlessness she had experienced in the Crow's Nest.

When the track ended, she rolled onto the floor and stood up. She wanted to run herself a bath, but leaving the music behind would be a shame. She examined the speakers, which were newer than the hi-fi, wood-effect rather than scuffed black. The fact that they had a separate switch suggested that there was a separate power source, and perhaps an inbuilt amplifier. A pair of speakers like these were fixed into the shelves above her viewing window in the *North West Tonight* studio.

She unplugged the speakers and hauled them, cable trailing, upstairs. She plugged them into a socket on the landing and angled them towards the bathroom door. She ran the taps of the wide bathtub and returned downstairs.

The speakers were one thing, but the hi-fi was enormous and, given its age, it might easily get damaged if she carted it upstairs. She pulled out her phone and opened the Music app. The only track was a single song that had been preinstalled on the phone, with a title that included as many numerals as letters. As she jammed the phone back into her pocket, she noticed Clay's MiniDisc player on the bedside table. A quick rifle on the sideboard beside the hi-fi uncovered a ragged auxiliary cable.

On the landing she plugged in the MiniDisc player and set it playing. The sounds of the shell midden were barely audible. She turned the volume to full on both the player and the speakers. Now the hum of the recorded wind was something she felt in her chest. She heard variations she hadn't noticed before, suggestions of words. The silence of the gaps between the sighing and burbling were somehow loud, too. It was very beautiful. She set the two-minute track to repeat on a loop.

She stripped and settled into the water. The roar of the taps mingled with the groans from the speakers outside the door. When the water reached her chin, she turned off the taps with her toes.

It felt good. She felt that she had no body. She was the wind and the sea. She concentrated on the precise sounds of the shell midden song, noting each variation as it repeated on its two-minute rotation. She wondered if she might take up some kind of meditation when she returned to the UK. Maybe she could convince Laurie to join her, a replacement for her primal screaming. If Laurie did decide to move in with Rob and Kaytee – and Nina had already decided that she couldn't possibly stand in her way if that was her choice – then perhaps they might build a different kind of relationship. Nina could become a confidante, somebody remote from day-to-day difficulties. If she could only get to a better place herself, she might influence Laurie in some positive way.

Yes. But she was…

…she was drifting…

…into sleep? Or something like it.

The water was no longer against her skin. She shivered at its absence. The surface of the water was beneath her. She tried to turn, to see how far the fall might be, but she could only stare upward at the gathering clouds that scudded too fast above her.

This was wrong. The roar of the wind was distant as though she were hearing it through some solid barrier. She needed it. She craved it. She gasped and began to panic. Her arms wouldn't lift from her sides: they encountered some invisible obstacle.

She willed her body to turn, but it only tipped so that her head was now lower than her feet. Her toes ached with the cold. She struggled, uncertain whether she was trying to right herself or come closer to the water. She was falling. Like a bullet she hurtled towards the surface of the water, entering it head first, and a great sense of *rightness* flowed through her body, and then she could no longer breathe.

She opened her eyes. The water stung. She tried to rub them, but her arms were trapped.

They really were. This was real.

She was underwater and this was real.

She braced herself, then forced her eyes open again. The surface of the water seemed only inches above her. Why couldn't she lift her head?

It was only now that she recognised the dark stripes above her as limbs. They were stretched out and their trajectory corresponded with the flashes of pain that she identified in her forearms. To her left, above the white horizon of the bathtub, she saw two black ovals, or maybe more. The heads of whoever was holding her down.

She was drowning and this was real.

She opened her mouth but couldn't tell whether she made any noise along with the bubbles, so great was the shrieking inside her. She shook her head, but something was pressing down on her forehead, holding her under. How many people were doing this to her?

She made the word 'No!' and tried to push it out.

She cast from side to side, her eyes rolling. She kicked her feet, striking them painfully against the taps to no avail. She felt blackness rise up within her. She wouldn't have long before she passed out.

The limbs flashed above her, dizzying in their number. Heads bent over the bathtub, hair making the silhouettes ragged.

The limbs were thin. Children. She thought of the boys in the photo Laurie had showed her – Kaytee and Rob's boys – and she could see their faces suddenly superimposed onto the black shapes above.

Amid the burbling of the water and her own struggles she could still hear the looped booming of the shell midden recordings. And then something else, sharper and more sudden. It had the urgent quality of something physical: it was within the house.

Abruptly, the black shapes disappeared. It took Nina a moment before she realised what this meant. She pushed up from the floor of the bathtub and emerged from the water coughing, heaving air into her lungs. Each breath was a knife.

She heaved herself up and out and fell panting onto the bath mat, retching into the centre of its concentric circles.

'Mum!'

Laurie burst into the bathroom, almost tripping over Nina crouching there. Nina's breath caught as something enveloped her. But it was only a towel thrown over her back.

'What's wrong? Are you sick?'

Nina spat a dollop of phlegm onto the mat. She wiped her mouth and leered up at her daughter, whose face appeared doubled but who, Nina realised, was immensely beautiful.

The sounds of the shell midden continued to blare from the speakers outside the bathroom.

Nina shook her head balefully and looked up. The tall window above the sink was wide open to reveal a swaying, leafless birch outside.

'Someone tried to kill me,' Nina said. Her voice was croaky and small. She said it again, more forcefully. 'Somebody tried to kill me. More than one of them. Tried to drown me in the bath.'

Laurie straightened and stood. She looked at the blaring speakers on the landing and frowned. She stared into Nina's eyes.

Nina looked down. She could see no marks on her forearms, but she could still feel the grip of those black hands.

Laurie reached out to support Nina by the arms. Her fingers fitted neatly into the precise locations of the pain.

CHAPTER TWENTY-ONE

Tammy returned home in the early afternoon, escorted up the porch steps by Clay. As usual, he appeared carefree, a blond Scandinavian puppy.

'You look dreadful,' Tammy said.

Nina sunk deeper into Rob's baseball jersey that she had discovered folded in the den cupboard. She had only partially towelled her hair dry and the strands were already rising. She hadn't so much as glanced in a mirror. She must look a state. At least she had stopped shaking, and the pain in her forearms was only an echo.

Clay peered at her. 'Tammy is right. You look very bad.'

'Why didn't you come home earlier with Laurie?' Nina asked.

Tammy craned her neck to peer into the sitting room. 'Laurie wasn't so interested in the tour. Which was a shame, because it was fascinating – oh, like you wouldn't believe! Clay made for a wonderful guide. You know there are still some rooms perfectly intact in the main building? It's like walking back in time. Part of me imagined moving in right there and then.'

'Feel free to do just this,' Clay said. 'We have a room all ready for you in the big house. It seems that Zain and Mischa have left the island without farewells. We would be more than glad to host for you.'

Tammy looked up at Clay and blushed girlishly. Nina felt a twinge of jealousy.

'So, Laurie walked home?' she said. How long would it have taken to walk from the Sanctuary? How long might she have been in the house before she entered the bathroom?

'She said she'd go visit Thomas,' Tammy replied. 'Is she here?'

Nina stifled a shudder at the mention of Thomas. She pictured the spindly limbs that had forced her under the water.

'She's in her room,' she said. 'She won't come out.'

Tammy scowled. 'What did you say to the girl?'

This was new, this idea that Nina might be an actively malign influence on her daughter. What did it suggest about Tammy's conversations with Laurie?

'I think I gave her a scare.' Nina thought about adding, *and she gave me a scare too*. Laurie had burst in just in time to save her, but the idea that this convenience was a little too neat had burrowed into Nina's mind. Now, an hour and a half later, Laurie's appearance and the attempted drowning had merged into the same event. And there had been more than one pair of hands pushing her down.

The voice inside her that suggested that Laurie was involved had to be ignored, but the possibility was no more absurd than the idea that Nina might have imagined the attack. That was what Laurie had said, after her initial sympathy had turned to dismay.

'Thanks for bringing Tammy back,' Nina said to Clay. Then, to Tammy, 'And now that you *are* back, there's somewhere I need to be. I'll see you later.' She winced at the rise in pitch that made the statement more like a question. She plucked the keys from the bowl and hurried to the doorway. She felt their gazes on her back as she jogged down the porch steps. Tammy's attitude would be far more accusatory when Nina returned, once she'd had a chance to compare notes with her granddaughter.

*

It took more than a minute for Marie to appear at the door of the schoolhouse. She looked older. Somewhere within the building, Niall screamed.

Marie's forehead creased. 'Are you okay?'

Nina shivered and pulled her jacket around her. The wind was cold today. Her ears stung with the chill.

Marie stepped aside. 'You'd better come in.'

Nina followed her into the warmth. 'I'm sorry if I'm intruding. It sounds like you're having a tough time.'

In the kitchen Marie gestured at the coffee pot on the stove. But it was late afternoon and the pot was empty, anyway. Nina stood before the stove, enjoying its heat.

'I won't stay long,' she said. 'I was actually hoping to speak to Thomas. Is he here?'

Marie frowned. 'He wouldn't usually be.'

'So he's in the house? Laurie's at home, so I figured he might be indoors too. And it's cold out there.'

'That wouldn't have stopped him being up there in the

woods, normally.'

'It feels like today isn't a normal day. Would you mind if I spoke to him?' Even as she said it, she wished she could retract the request. The reality of the scenario hit her. Seeing Thomas was last thing she wanted. She felt suddenly cold and bloated, as if she were still underwater.

Niall screamed again. It seemed to Nina an honest sound, almost enjoyable. Marie looked at the doorway. 'Give me a second.'

When she returned she held Niall in her arms. Her chin was tilted to one side, to prevent the baby from scratching at her. But Nina noticed that her neck and chest were criss-crossed with pale lines.

Thomas plodded behind his mother into the kitchen. Nina gripped the back of a chair. She examined his sullen expression and his arms. Though they were thin, they showed the first knots of adolescent muscles. Was he strong enough to push her under the water? If he was determined to hurt her, yes.

'Is this about Laurie?' Marie said.

Nina watched the boy's posture. He shifted from foot to foot.

'Partly,' she said. Then, to Thomas, 'Is there anything you'd like to say to me?'

Thomas glanced up through his dark fringe. Then his eyes dropped to the floor. 'No.'

Even if there hadn't been a physical attack, even if he had only crept into the house and seen her naked in the bath, this whole thing would be intolerable. Nina marvelled at her ability to remain calm, even though a large part of her wanted to flee not only from the schoolhouse but from the island, the continent.

She cleared her throat quietly. 'Where were you earlier this afternoon?'

'What's this about, Nina?' Marie said sharply.

Nina held up a hand, in control now. It was important not to lead an interviewee down a particular path. 'Thomas? Where were you at around half past two?'

Thomas's cheeks had reddened. He clicked his jaw. 'I was with Laurie.'

'Where?'

'The den. In the woods. We met up there.'

'And then where did you go?'

'Nowhere.'

A phrase came to Nina's mind: *Everybody knows this is nowhere.* How dare he lie to her face. How dare he have his claws not only in her but in her daughter too. He was a vicious child, evil, and surely everybody could see that. Her neutral facade crumbled. This would be her only chance to question him face-to-face. 'Did you go to our house? Tammy Fisher's house?'

Thomas's eyes flicked up again. He was doing a good impression of confusion. 'No.'

'But Laurie did.'

Thomas shrugged. 'She left first.'

'And what did you do?'

He rubbed at an eye. Was that a crocodile tear? 'I came home.'

'He's been here since before three,' Marie said. In a lower voice, she said, 'I want you to know that Thomas has been amazing these last few days. He's come out the other side of whatever's been chewing away at him. Okay? So get to the point, Nina. What is it you want to know?'

The rush of the wind and the sea echoed in Nina's ears. She glanced through the door into the schoolroom and the display of shells on its wall. 'I want to know whether Thomas and Laurie did anything wrong this afternoon. Anything bad.'

Thomas raised his head. His eyes were red. 'It wasn't bad! It wasn't my fault!'

Nina forced herself to maintain an even tone, though she hated herself for not lashing out, protecting her daughter. 'What did you do?'

Thomas's eyes darted from his mother to Nina. 'I thought we both felt the same way. I was wrong. I swear I didn't mean to upset her or ask her to do anything she didn't like.'

Nina blinked. 'What are you talking about?'

Thomas turned to Marie. 'Mom, you have to believe me. Laurie got upset, but I swear I backed off as soon as she said no.'

Marie's face had already been pale. Now it was white. 'You tried to have sex with her?'

'No! Mum, no! She's like a year younger than me.'

'Then what?'

Thomas looked around, as if hoping an exit might appear, or that some other calamity might outrank his predicament. 'Just kissing... Maybe a bit more. I thought she was into it.

But she wasn't.' He gazed pleadingly up at Nina. 'You have to believe me. Laurie will back me up. I hope she'll back me up. I really like her, for real. I'm so sorry.'

Nina struggled to process what he was saying. Even stranger was the transformation in the boy's body language. All his stiffness and aloofness had disappeared. He now appeared exactly what he was: a fifteen-year-old boy full of hormones and confusion and uncertainty.

'Does Laurie back up this story?' Marie asked Nina. 'What has she said about all this?'

Nina puffed out her cheeks. 'Nothing.'

'Nothing? And how does she seem? Is she upset?'

Slowly, Nina shook her head.

'Then that's something.' She crouched before her son, wincing as the baby in her arms reached up to nip the skin of her throat. 'Thomas? You understand that none of this is okay?'

Thomas nodded tearfully.

'But if things were as you say they were… Well, I appreciate that you listened to Laurie.'

She turned to Nina. 'So. We should maybe all get together, all four of us, and talk this through, if we feel that'd help. But I guess you want to get back to Laurie, right? Are we all good for now?'

Nina realised that she hadn't stopped shaking her head. It seemed to help with the dizziness and the noise, somehow. Marie's expression became colder.

'That's not what I came here for,' Nina managed to say.

'It isn't?'

Nina watched Thomas closely. He pressed his hands to his cheeks, rubbing away tears with his fingertips. He blinked rapidly. It didn't look like an expression of deeper guilt, only bafflement.

She felt lightheaded. She felt that she was drifting away.

'I was taking a bath,' she said haltingly, 'and I think someone tried to drown me.'

Marie rose from her haunches. '*You think*?'

'I was confused. I mean, I was asleep. But I saw someone.' She glanced at Thomas.

'Christ. Nina, think about what you're saying. What did you see?'

Nina's bottom lip trembled uncontrollably. 'I don't know.'

'Well, I hope to God you're not accusing—'

'I didn't do anything!' Thomas shouted. His hands were cupping his chin awkwardly, his fingers spread beneath his ears.

'There you go,' Marie said pointedly. 'I think we've had enough accusations for one day. You'd better get on back to Laurie. Now.'

'I don't trust him!' Nina blurted. The chair back seemed to give way beneath her hands: she stumbled and caught herself against the table.

'I told you what I did,' Thomas yelled. His baby brother screamed, too, as if in wordless support. 'Isn't that bad enough?'

Through her tears, Nina saw him rubbing and rubbing at the skin beneath his ears.

'What's wrong, Tom?' Marie said, rushing over to put an arm around him.

Thomas's mouth opened and closed again and again. 'It *hurts*, Mom. Inside my head. It hurts.'

He flopped onto his knees, a prayer pose. His eyes rolled back, exposing the bright whites.

Marie swung around to face Nina.

'Get out,' she hissed. 'Get out right this second.'

CHAPTER TWENTY-TWO

The man who answered the door had several-days-old stubble. He peered up at Nina through thick glasses.

'Hello. I've come directly from the school,' she said, appalled at her enunciation, her emphasis of her Britishness. She looked down at the binder she had stolen from the teacher's desk on her way out of the schoolroom. 'I was hoping that your daughter might be at home.'

'Genie ain't here,' he said.

'She isn't at the schoolhouse, either. I mean, I know it's Sunday, but I really would like to speak to her.'

'Let kids be kids, I say. She's around somewhere.' He emitted a sound that was part cough, part laugh. 'No way off an island, huh?'

'Mr Mason? It would be really helpful if I could speak to your daughter.'

'Who are you? Got a weird way of talking.'

'I'm a friend of Marie Maddox.'

'This is about school?'

'Sort of.'

'It's vacation. She in trouble?'

Nina frowned. Genie Mason was, what, seven years old? The idea of her attempting to drown an adult was absurd. But she might at least know something about Thomas or one of the other older kids. 'Not that I know of. Is your wife at home?'

'Nope.'

'Do you expect her to be home soon?'

A shrug.

'Could I leave a message? For Eugenie?'

He scrutinised her with his black eyes. He began to press the door shut. 'No.'

＊

The stolen island directory was only useful up to a point. It contained names and addresses, and even low-resolution passport photo images, though they were almost indecipherable due to the degradations of photocopying. But the photos were only of adults and there was no obvious way to determine which addresses any children lived at. If she had managed to steal a class register too, cross-referencing would have taken mere moments. Nina resorted to hanging around at the harbour and asking passers-by for the names of children's parents, though it was soon clear that she was attracting suspicion.

Nine-year-old Ali Jenner had been at home. He had stared up at Nina so innocently while his parents watched, that all questions left Nina's mind. David Priest's mother had tracked him down in the meadow behind their fenced yard. He had refused to speak to Nina, and after a couple of minutes Jess Priest insisted that unless she had some sort of documentation she should leave. Chase Pickthall refused to come out of his bedroom. When pressed, his father insisted that Chase had been there all afternoon, though his glances at the ceiling might easily have betrayed a lie.

Sal and Landon Curtiz were standing behind the low white garden fence, watching Nina as she approached. Nina's eyes were on Sal, the older of the two. She guessed the girl was around ten or eleven. Not strong, but not weak either. How much force did it take to stop somebody from rising out of water?

'Hi guys,' she called out in a cheerful voice that instantly made her feel nauseous and a sham. 'How's things?'

The children exchanged looks. They didn't reply.

'Are your parents home?'

Sal turned to the front door.

'No,' Nina said quickly. 'Before you go and get them, I wanted to ask you something. Have you been away from home this afternoon?'

Another look passed between the children.

'Playing, maybe?'

Silence.

'Up at the woods? The den you guys made? Or somewhere else?'

Landon bent to pluck a dandelion from the grass. He blew three times and watched the seeds parachute away. He was only around six or seven. Even Sal, despite her surliness and her older years, couldn't possibly be any kind of a threat. They were only kids.

'What's going on?' a voice called.

A woman strode around the corner of the building. 'I've had a phone call about you. Charlie Jenner says you've been poking around all over the place today. What gives?'

Nina raised her hands. 'I'm sorry. I wanted to say hi.'

'Sure. It's creepy as all hell, you know that? You with your Mary Poppins accent.'

Nina backed away. 'I'm confused about what happened this afternoon. Some children came into my house.' She tested the idea again. Is that still what she believed? She understood it was significant that she hadn't been back to Cat's Ear Cottage, hadn't wanted to question Laurie further about her movements that afternoon. Making oblique accusations against a bunch of kids wasn't normal behaviour.

'Go be confused somewhere else,' the woman said, advancing upon the gate so that Nina had no choice but to turn and hurry away.

*

She was ready to give up and return to Tammy's house when a memory rose to the surface. Back when she had introduced the children one by one in the schoolhouse kitchen, Marie had mentioned two absent children. Their surname had been the same as a friend Nina had had when she was at school herself. Hutchinson. Noah and May Hutchinson.

She riffled through the pages of the directory.

After several false starts she consulted a woman hurrying from the harbour grocery store. Atlantic Avenue might sound grand, but it was merely a lane, on the northern hillside far beyond the main village.

By the time she arrived Nina was sweating. The distinction between the rumble of the sea and the churning inside her head was impossible to determine. The house was a wooden-walled bungalow with pillars supporting a wide porch. It looked like a small-scale copy of the White House, with hints of grandeur despite the weather-worn slats and chips in the white paint. Nina took a moment to gather herself before she pushed the doorbell.

She heard sounds from within the building. Scuffling and voices. Nobody answered the door.

She pressed the bell again, then rapped on the glass panel. 'Hello?'

There was a distant slam. Then footsteps.

The door opened a few inches.

'Yes?' It was a woman's voice. Nina could only see a hint of dark hair, a flash of pale cheek.

'My name's Nina Scaife. I was hoping to speak to you.' Again, she kept her voice level, denying the inner hiss that made her want to shout.

'Why?'

'It's nothing to worry about. Have you been in touch with any of the other parents on the island? The Jenners, or the Curtiz family?'

'No. Nobody.' The voice was strained. Tired.

Nina tilted her head but couldn't see the woman fully. 'What's your name?'

A pause. 'Dee.'

'Hello Dee. I'm Nina, as I said. I'd like you to open the door a little more. Is that okay?'

After a few seconds the door swung inwards to reveal a woman standing in a dark corridor. The place smelled sweet and musty, as though the windows hadn't been opened for a long time. Dee's hair was a mess – Nina wondered if she looked similarly bedraggled herself – and what Nina first took to be make-up were actually dark bags under her eyes. A red mark lined one cheek. There were bruises on the insides of both of her arms. Nina had seen those kinds of marks many times before, in interviews that contained appalling enough details that they required a warning before they were broadcast on TV. She imagined that there might be worse marks hidden beneath Dee's baggy T-shirt.

'Is your husband in the house?' she said softly.

'No.' Her answer was too quick, as if she had rehearsed a denial.

'I heard voices. I was told your children were ill?' She craned her neck but the corridor behind Dee was a void.

'No.'

'Are they here?'

'They're sleeping.'

'What kind of illness is it?'

Dee's mouth curled, but it wasn't a smile. She was trying to stop herself from crying.

'Some kind of bug? That's what their teacher said.'

'I don't know.'

'Have they seen a doctor?'

Suddenly a cry came from somewhere inside the house. A deep voice, a man's. Dee's head flicked around, then back to Nina. Weakly, she tried to push Nina away. Nina pressed herself against the door, holding it open.

'I'm sorry,' she said with a grunt. 'I need to come in.'

Nina pushed past Dee, who released a groan as though Nina had hit her in the stomach. The first doorway along the corridor opened into a kitchen. The blinds were pulled down. There was nobody inside. On the other side of the corridor Nina saw a small sitting room. The only light was from a muted TV showing a garish Nickelodeon cartoon. Dee scrabbled at Nina's arm as she hurried along the corridor. The next door had a latch on its outside, though the bolt was slid open. She pushed at the door. It gave a little but wouldn't open. Nina glanced at Dee, whose face was dark and filled with dismay.

Nina flicked the light switch, to no effect. She looked up to see that the bulb in the corridor was smashed. She knew that she ought to get out, consult Egg, return with backup or let somebody more capable do the job.

But instead she shoved again at the door. It gave but then slammed tight. Somebody was pressing on it from the other side.

'Mr Hutchinson!' she yelled. 'Please come out here right now!'

To Dee she said, 'Does he have any kind of a weapon?'

Instantly, Dee replied, 'God, no! Harvey would never do anything.' Her arms were hugging her chest, hiding the bruises.

Nina took a step back. 'All right,' she said loudly to the door. 'All right. I'm leaving. Okay?' She stamped a few times on the linoleum.

Then she charged at the door, hitting it with the full force of her body. It opened immediately, swinging freely until it impacted with the man who had been blocking it, with a slapping sound like a plank of wood falling on concrete. Nina pressed her body against the door, shoving the man away.

He had fallen to the floor. He now sat like a child during a school assembly, his legs tucked up. His hands were on top of his head as though he was trying to protect himself. His shoulders were wrenching up and down in heavy sobs.

Nina peered into the dark room. A pile of plastic toys was pushed to one wall like flotsam washed up on a shore. The mattress of one of the single beds was on its side, a hole ripped in its centre to reveal coiled wire springs. In the centre of the room was a pile of cereal flakes, bread, open tins. There were no plates and food was smeared on the floor, baked beans and rice trodden into the gaps in the floorboards.

At the far side of the room Nina saw two small figures. The young boy wore only a pair of shorts and his torso was covered in grime. The girl wore a school uniform. The blouse was ripped, and there was a large hole in one leg of her grey tights. Nina gasped as she recognised the girl she had almost run over on her first day on Hope Island.

Like their mother, the children's hair was wild. Whereas Dee's expression had produced only pity in Nina, the children's glares filled her with horror. Their chins were pressed against their chests, watching her from under lowered brows. Their bodies were oddly stooped, their knees bent. Nina imagined them leaning over a bathtub, pressing, pressing, pressing down.

She realised too late what they looked like. Animals, ready to pounce.

Within seconds they were upon her, their nails scratching for purchase on her arms as though trying to climb her body to reach her face.

Nina gasped and fell backwards out of the room. In a flurry, something leapt upon her and she batted at it. She pushed her attacker away and with a start she realised that it was the father, not the children. Harvey Hutchinson's face hung suspended over her ghoulishly, his arms outstretched as he straddled her. Then he jumped to his feet. In a single motion he grabbed at the door handle, slammed it closed, then crunched the latch into place. From a pocket he produced a padlock and threaded it into a hole in the latch mechanism with shaking hands.

'What?' Nina said, still on her back, dragging herself away from the doorway instinctively.

Dee bent to help her to her feet.

'Please,' she said, 'don't tell anybody?'

'Are you kidding me?' Nina gasped. 'Have you *seen* them? And they attacked me.'

'They're scared.'

'No.' Nina shook her head. Everything was becoming muddled. 'That's not what I mean. They tried to kill me, in the Fisher house.'

'That's impossible,' Harvey said quickly. 'They haven't been outside since— We've kept them safe in here. I can vouch for that.'

'They're ill,' Dee said in a weak voice.

Harvey put his back to the door, panting. Like his wife, his arms and his face were covered with bruises and cuts. His nose looked as though it might be broken.

'You go talking to anyone about this,' he said, wiping blood from his mouth, 'and I swear I'll find you. Understand?'

Nina felt a surge of shame, yet mixed in amongst the shock she felt a swell of vindication. But she had to get out, collect her thoughts. Send in the cavalry, because this situation was about as fucked up as any she'd encountered in her years of miserable news stories. When she stood her legs were so shaky that she almost collapsed again.

Something hit the bedroom door from inside, then Nina heard the squeak of skin skidding upon it.

Dee's lips pressed together, and tears filled her eyes. Then she went to her husband, put her arm around his waist, and watched as Nina left.

CHAPTER TWENTY-THREE

The fire department office was dark and empty. Nina found Egg in the Open Arms.

'You look like you need a drink,' Egg said, holding up his empty glass. Then he frowned. 'Hey. What's wrong?'

Nina dropped into the seat opposite. The walk from the Hutchinson house had seemed impossibly lengthy, her pace as slow as a sleepwalker. She had stopped several times to collect stones from the path, throwing them as hard as she could and relishing the sound of their impact. She didn't know why.

When she reached the harbour, she had stared at the ferry bobbing beside the jetty, daydreaming of getting as far away from the Hutchinson house as possible. But she was determined to do things in the right order. Egg had to be told about what was happening.

But all she managed to say was, 'I'm not going crazy.'

'Okay. For the record, I didn't say a thing.'

'You're looking at me weird.'

'You seem a bit off, that's all. And you're almost shouting.'

She frowned. 'Yeah. Get me that drink?'

Egg rose and weaved towards the bar. He returned with two beers. 'Unless you wanted shots too?'

'This'll do for now.' Nina slurped at the beer. It was weak but it tasted heavenly. After she had downed half of the drink her confidence was partially restored. 'You're going to need to call in some backup.'

'Has something happened?'

Nina snorted, making a vortex of foam in her glass. 'Yep.'

'Did something happen to *you*?'

She nodded. Abruptly, tears stung her eyes. 'Fuck,' she said, rubbing at her right eye with a knuckle.

Egg waited patiently. Nina found his manner infuriating.

'Someone drowned me,' she said.

She saw Egg's eyes move as he took in her appearance.

'*Tried* to drown me,' she corrected herself. 'More than one person, working together.'

'Where was this?'

'In the bath.'

'In the bath?'

'In Tammy's house. I fell asleep. I know that's dangerous. Don't look at me like that.'

'I wasn't—'

Something rose and fell within Nina's chest. Bile, or disappointment. 'And... they were children.'

A pause. 'Nina...'

'I swear it's true.'

'You have proof?'

'I *saw* them.'

'You saw them clearly? Who was this?'

Nina hesitated. 'I was under the water. And then they were gone.'

'And you'd been asleep.'

'Fuck.' She slammed her glass onto the table, producing a satisfying sharp sound. A couple of customers looked around. They didn't appear shocked. One or two smiled at her. The TVs were blaring as usual and soon enough they turned back to the screens, their mouths hanging open as if that might improve their capacity to hear.

'Fuck *off*,' she said. 'I know what I saw.'

'Don't take this the wrong way, but I have two things I need to say,' Egg said, excruciatingly reasonable. 'First, you look very tired and… upset, and I need you to calm down. Second, I'd need evidence to even begin looking into any kind of accusation like this. Third, I note that you haven't actually accused anyone, which makes me wonder—'

'May and Noah Hutchinson.'

Without so much as blinking, Egg raised his glass and sipped. 'May and Noah Hutchinson. What about them?'

'I am accusing them. And you're the only authority on this turd of an island so I expect you to—'

Egg put a hand upon hers. Immediately, she burst into tears.

'I just…' she began, but her throat closed up.

'Hush,' Egg said, as if soothing an infant, and Nina thought of baby Niall when she had held him in her arms, and then she thought of Laurie all those years ago.

She nodded, choking on her tears. She was so tired, and her head ached terribly. She felt Egg put his arm around her and she knew that everybody in the Open Arms must be watching them now, and it didn't feel *good* so much as not quite as alone. She cried and cried, doing nothing to prevent the volume of her sobs from rising.

She wiped her forearm over her face, transferring mucus to the fine hair on her arm. She looked up. Nobody was watching her, after all. The hubbub of the other customers and the sports commentary had risen as if to mask her outburst.

'Something awful is happening,' she said to Egg. 'I went to the Hutchinson house. The parents were trying to cover for the kids. I forced my way in – I know, I know, that's not okay – and if you could have seen those children…'

Egg stiffened. 'I know Harvey and Dee very well. I've known them my whole life.'

'But May and Noah—'

'Are, what, eleven and six respectively? Think about what you're saying.'

'They tried to drown me.'

'At the Hutchinson house?'

'No, at Tammy's house. You're not listening. I know I didn't see them when they were doing it. I know how this all sounds. But they did it, I'm sure. And what about Abram's death? What about Lukas?'

Egg's demeanour was becoming more formal by the second. 'Please try not to bundle everything together. Try to keep things related to your actual grievance here.'

An image of children formed in Nina's mind. They weren't May and Noah, they were even younger, both boys. Kaytee and Rob's kids.

Quietly, she said, 'Those children look like death.'

'I heard they've been ill.'

Nina nodded, her head bobbing heavily. 'Something's terribly wrong. We should call social services on the mainland.'

'No. Nina, no. I'll go up and check in on them.'

'You shouldn't go alone.'

Egg didn't reply.

'Tell me that you believe me?'

Egg finished his drink. 'I'll visit them. In my own time, you understand? I'll see if they need anything, at the very least. But I need you to tell me that you're not going to go back up there. Do you need me to show you my badge, make it clear this is an official demand?'

'I won't go back up there,' Nina said, feeling like a scolded child.

*

When she emerged from the Open Arms she looked around, pulling her coat tight and rubbing the tears from her eyes. She was grateful that there were only a few people milling around in the harbour area. Though it was only mid-afternoon the sky had darkened and the cloud cover looked solid, like a low roof.

It took her a few moments to register that somebody was standing on the opposite side of the seawater-slicked paved area, on the decking outside the fire department, because the figure was so slight. It was Eugenie Mason. Her hands were in the pockets of her duffel coat, but her arms were held straight, making the open coat taut and spread like a fin or wings.

They faced each other across the distance. Genie didn't move; only the wind pulling at her coat made her more than a statue.

Nina stepped from the hotel porch.

Genie didn't move.

Nina walked a few paces towards the start of the hill road, which necessarily took her closer to the fire department. Her neck was stiff; she had to turn her entire upper body in order to watch the girl.

Genie hadn't moved from her position but she, too, turned to face inland. Now that Nina was nearer to her, she could see the beads of drizzle on her coat and in her hair.

Nina walked faster to where the concrete ended and the road began. At a sharp sound from behind she whirled around, but there was nobody there.

The track seemed steeper than she remembered, so steep that she wondered if she might need to use her hands as well as her feet. She was panting with exertion by the time the road levelled out, and she barely had enough breath to gasp when she saw the twin outlines on the bank where the road veered left. Sal and Landon Curtiz stood above her, watching impassively as she stumbled along the track.

'Go home!' she managed to call out, but she didn't slow down and the children didn't respond. She glanced downhill. The Open Arms was still close, and she could sprint at a fair pace on the downward slope… but the thought of Genie Mason still down there somewhere, out of sight, made her tremble.

This whole thing was absurd, she knew.

But then she saw Sal Curtiz reach out and take the hand of her younger brother, and all Nina could think was to escape. She dashed further inland, keeping to the road that led to Cat's Ear Cottage. On the horizon close to the woodland she saw more black figures, and she tried to count in her mind all the island children, to account for them and to prepare herself for the appearance of more, but her mind wouldn't think in straight lines and she was almost there.

*

Nina could hear Laurie and Tammy talking in the dining room. She caught a whiff of melted cheese and her stomach lurched. She hadn't eaten since breakfast.

It had been May and Noah all along. Laurie was innocent. That voice inside Nina that continually accused Laurie was wrong.

She marched directly upstairs to Laurie's empty bedroom, then immediately went to the window. She saw no sign of the island children. She fished under the bed for Laurie's tartan-patterned suitcase, then threw in the items of clothing that were scattered over the carpet, without taking particular care to be thorough. Rob would be arriving at some point the day after tomorrow: if she left anything behind, he could bring it home. She collected her own case from the den – she hadn't unpacked and had returned each laundered item to it, folded neatly. Outside, she tossed the suitcases into the back of the Chrysler, then returned to the house. She stumbled back upstairs and stared at herself in the bathroom mirror, appalled at how little of herself she recognised. The window was still open and the room was cold. She pulled one of Tammy's hairbrushes through her matted hair, then splashed water on her face. It felt good, so she did it again and then she found herself scouring her cheeks and forehead, her palms abrasive against her tender skin. She looked into the mirror again and saw a woman cleaner but no more familiar. She brushed her teeth and spat.

Her legs shook as she descended the stairs, and she clung to the banister to prevent herself from toppling. Beside the bowl of glass pebbles, she found an envelope and stationery.

'Hey,' she said, louder than she meant to, as she passed through the sitting room and into the dining room.

Tammy did a double-take, then tried to disguise it with a cough.

Laurie was sitting at the table. 'Mum?' she said, and the single word made Nina want to cry again or maybe die.

'I'm good,' Nina said. She stood at the end of the dining table. In its centre was a Pyrex dish containing the remnants of a meal.

'I made mac and cheese,' Laurie said, gesturing at the bowl. 'Even Gran had to admit that I can cook.'

Nina nodded stiffly.

'Don't worry,' Laurie said. 'I saved you some. It's in the oven, still warm.'

'I'm not hungry,' Nina replied. 'I think I need to get some air. Clear the mind.' It was what Abram had said to her once, she realised with a shiver. Her voice cracked a little as she said, 'Will you come with me, Laurie?'

Laurie glanced at Tammy. 'You're okay here, Gran?'

Tammy smiled. 'I have my shows.'

Laurie helped Tammy up from her chair and escorted her to the sitting room. She flicked on the TV and turned up the volume. Tammy settled into her usual position, mouth hanging open, as the commercial-break sting of *Project Runway* began.

Rob would arrive in less than two days. He could care for his mother. She'd be all right alone until then.

'Goodbye, Tammy,' Nina said quietly.

'Okay,' Laurie said to Nina, with forced brightness. 'Ready when you are.'

Laurie protested a little when Nina ushered her into the passenger seat of the car, but relented. Nina drove to the harbour slowly, scanning the horizon for signs of the children. She saw nobody, child or adult.

'I thought you said you wanted air,' Laurie said.

'I realised we haven't walked down by the water's edge since we arrived.' Out of the corner of her eye Nina saw her daughter shoot her a glance, but she didn't say anything.

She parked at the end of the jetty. The ferry bobbed alongside it. They were ten minutes early. Nina glanced at the fire department but saw no sign of Genie Mason.

'Shall we sit over there?' Nina said, pointing at the rocky beach visible beyond the Open Arms. 'Just for a bit. I'm tired suddenly.'

'Sure, Mum.' Laurie took her arm as they walked. Nina felt far older than her years. 'Are you sure you're okay? You had a shock earlier.'

'Which one?' Nina said without thinking.

'When you were in the bathroom, Mum. I was worried. I've never seen you upset like that. I don't think I've ever seen *anybody* upset like that.'

Nina didn't reply. When they reached the rocky beach, she sat heavily on the pebbles, wincing. Laurie remained standing. She picked a flat stone from the beach and hefted it in her hand. Nina thought of the hole in Lukas Weber's head. It would have been a far bigger rock.

Laurie turned and flung the stone into the ocean. The thick cloud cover made the gap between the sky and sea a narrow tunnel. The stone bounced once, then hit a cresting wave and disappeared.

'Better on a flat lake,' Laurie said, 'and Dad was always the master.'

'What?'

'Dad was always good at skimming stones.'

'Yes.'

Laurie hesitated. 'Are you afraid to see him in a couple of days, Mum?'

'Of course not.' But she would have been afraid, if she was going to be here.

'Kaytee isn't coming, you know. Or her kids.'

Nina wanted to hug her for saying 'her kids' rather than 'their kids'. There was nothing to fear from Laurie, despite what the voice inside her said. Laurie was on her side. Nina had alerted the island authorities, so now saving Laurie from the children of Hope Island was the only thing that mattered.

'Okay,' she said.

'She seems nice.'

'Have you met her?' Nina choked on her words slightly.

'No. I'm going by what Dad's said.'

'I'm sure she's wonderful.'

'I didn't say that.'

Laurie sat beside Nina. She took her hand.

'This trip hasn't panned out as I'd hoped,' Nina said.

Laurie laughed. 'What were you expecting – Disneyland?'

'I hoped I might get closer to you.'

'You're my *mum*, Mum.'

'That doesn't mean anything. Hold on, I don't mean that how it sounds. I'm saying that just because I'm your mother, it doesn't give me any right over you. You make your own choices. I have to… Well, I guess I have to earn the right to spend time with you.'

'I swear I haven't even talked to Dad yet about living with him.'

'That's not it. I want things to be more equal between us. I was never good at being a parent.'

Laurie sat on the pebbles beside Nina, then snuggled up against her. She didn't speak.

Nina sighed. 'Thanks.'

'For what?'

'I know I've been weird. Thanks for not making me feel even weirder.'

'Want to keep walking?'

Nina shook her head. 'Wait here. I'll be back in a tick.'

She returned to the car, opened the boot and removed the two suitcases. After locking the car again, she nipped up the few steps to the fire department, wary of encountering

Genie Mason. She put the car keys into the envelope upon which she had written *FOR TAMMY FISHER* and pushed it through the letterbox.

The ferry operator was loitering at the end of the jetty. He wore a padded blue jacket, and his black waterproof trousers and boots shone wet up to his knees. His face looked bottom-heavy with dark stubble and his eyes were hidden under the brim of his baseball cap.

A voice inside Nina told her that what she was doing was wrong. She should stay on Hope Island. But the voice could no longer be trusted.

'I'd like a crossing for two, please,' Nina said.

The man scowled at her. 'Which crossing?'

'This one. The one leaving in a few minutes.'

'Not happening. There's a storm coming. No more ferries today.'

Nina scanned the clouds overhead. The only glimpse of sky was a reddening haze. 'It looks fine to me.'

The ferry operator shook his head. 'Ever heard of a weather forecast?'

'I'm surprised anyone here has. I can't even access emails, let alone the Met Office. Seriously, I want to get to the mainland and I need you to take me.'

'I thought you said two tickets.'

Nina looked past the jetty to the rocky beach. Laurie's neck was craning, meerkat-like, her head moving from side to side.

'How much do you want?' Nina said. 'I need to go.'

'There's no ferry for you.'

Nina paused. 'For me? For me specifically, you mean?' A thought hit her. 'What's your name?'

'Ed.'

'Ed what?'

'Ed Curtiz.'

Nina exhaled. 'I knew it. So let me guess, you've spoken to your wife and she's told you I was bothering your kids, and now you all have some pig-headed small-town vendetta against me. Am I close?'

To her surprise, Ed displayed no signs of relishing his role as gatekeeper. 'Sure, I heard from Becks,' he said slowly, adjusting his cap. 'I know who you are. But don't get overblown ideas about your importance, Nina Scaife. The ferry's running for nobody. There's a storm coming this way, fast.'

'What's going on, Mum?'

Nina whirled around. The thought crossed her mind to hide the suitcases, even to fling them into the water.

Laurie's eyes flicked down to look at the cases. A look of disgust flashed onto her face. 'All that talk about being equal. You know I actually fell for that?'

'We need to go,' Nina said. 'We need to get away from this place.'

'I'm not leaving Gran,' Laurie said. 'And Dad's coming the day after tomorrow. What are you thinking, Mum? What's going on in your head?'

Nina stared at her and she allowed herself to dwell on the same question: *What's going on in my head*? Nothing seemed quite real. Nothing was right. The squealing sound in her ears was maddening.

'I have to go,' she said. 'With or without you.'

Laurie stared.

Then Ed said, as slowly as before, 'I already told you, nobody's going anywhere.'

When Nina saw the fist, she thought it was somebody else's. It was only when it connected with Ed's stubbly cheek and she felt the ricochet in her bones that she realised she had hit him.

CHAPTER TWENTY-FOUR

The storm hit a couple of hours later. From her booth in the barroom of the Open Arms, Nina watched the rain lashing against the window, but soon got bored despite its pleasant rumbling background drone.

She hadn't protested when Laurie had begun climbing the hill back towards Tammy's house, her suitcase bumping against her leg. Nina hadn't offered to drive Laurie back up there – and getting the keys back would have presented difficulties anyway – as she knew Laurie would refuse to get into the car with her.

There had been a strange glint in Kelly Brady's eyes when she'd asked about room vacancies, but whether that was due to news of her hitting Ed Curtiz travelling fast, or something else entirely, she had no idea. With exaggerated politeness, Kelly had suggested that she might like to eat in the barroom before heading upstairs, '…and maybe a drink to wash it down?'

It was as good a plan as any. In these conditions there could be no escape from the island, and even if she could escape, she couldn't abandon Laurie. And yet she had already failed her daughter, by virtue of not being with her at this very moment. She had retreated, as she had always retreated from Laurie. And here and now, there wasn't even Rob to step in and do the job of parenting properly.

If the islanders relished watching her crumble, she didn't care. Nobody approached her. She ate the twig-thin fries that came with her burger, but nothing else. She drank red wine and she watched two of the TVs idly. One was showing a basketball game, the other one of the *Fast and the Furious* sequels. She found both absorbing – not so much the visuals, but the twin roars of the crowd and the car engines, mixing pleasingly with the fury of the storm outside the hotel. After a while she realised that she had stopped eating or drinking, and that her mouth was hanging open. She must appear moronic.

At eleven o'clock she hauled herself upstairs to room fourteen and lay spreadeagled on top of the starched bed-linen without undressing. The sounds of the storm were louder here – the window was slightly open – and it was warm. She was sweating and her body was weak and she wished she had the energy to strip off her clothes. She fell asleep fantasising about taking a shower, an act that seemed remote and impossible.

She was grateful when her body lifted from the bedclothes. Her shirt clung to her back for several seconds until she felt it come free, weighed down by its wetness. The storm intensified, the rain pounding on the window until the window didn't so much open as stop being there, and then she was away, soaring into the sky, the rain lashing harder as she rose, until the downfall was an unbroken sheet like the upper reaches of a waterfall. She was drenched to the skin and she might as well not have been wearing clothes at all and it was glorious. Slowly she began to corkscrew, burrowing through the water as though it were something solid, and spray was flung from her spinning body like sparks from a Catherine wheel. Her ears rang with the whooshes of displaced water, but even so she heard people far below, remarking on her beauty.

Something lurched within her. She cursed. She was so far up, even a slight deviation from her corkscrew path might make her fall.

Those voices were distracting her. They weren't commenting on her beauty, or anything about her. They were muttered and furtive. She tried to concentrate on the sound of the rain hitting the window.

The window. It was back.

Her eyes opened. She stared at the ceiling fan, which at first she mistook for a ship's propeller, and then her body righted itself and she found herself lying on the bed, her arms pressed tightly to her sides like a diver making herself more streamlined.

The voices continued.

She felt around for her phone. It was just after three o'clock in the morning.

The rain was soothing. Her eyelids were heavy.

At least one of the voices was a child's.

She leapt up and stood swaying at the foot of the bed. From the window she could see nothing but roiling blackness and she cursed Kelly Brady's obsequious insistence on giving her a sea view.

She pulled on her shoes and burst out of the room, clattering down the back stairs which doubled as a fire exit, then outside into the dark.

Her shirt was sodden within seconds. She looked back; the door had already clicked shut. She held her breath, listening for voices. She pulled her phone out of her pocket and flicked on the torch, then hurriedly turned it off again before she even had a chance to look around. She noted wryly that she had no phone signal. She crept along the front of the hotel, where an overhang gave slight protection from the rain.

There was a single lamp post at the edge of the concreted section of the harbour, where it gave way to the packed gravel of the main road inland. With the lack of moonlight or even stars overhead, the light of the lamp seemed the only anchor point in an ocean of gloom. Beyond, Nina could make out the silhouettes of three figures. From the angular cap and the bouncing gait, she recognised the person in the centre immediately: it was Egg. To either side of him were children, one smaller than the other, though from the rear it was impossible to identify them. He was holding their hands.

She exhaled in relief and then shivered, only partly in response to the cold rain. Egg's nonchalance in the barroom of the Open Arms must have been an act for her benefit. He must have followed up on her lead about the Hutchinson children, or at least mounted an investigation of his own. Perhaps he had been waiting at the harbour, watching out for any unusual activity. In the morning, the mystery would begin to be unravelled.

She wept. Soon this would be over. Laurie would be safe and one or both of them would leave Hope Island.

Except Egg had already led the children past the fire department. And as Nina watched they took a sharp turn to the left, leaving the gravel road behind to climb the hillside.

She left the porch shelter of the Open Arms and hurried in their wake, though an instinct told her not to reveal herself. Her hair slapped against her face and stuck there, making runnels for more water to drip along. She pulled her hair aside and plastered the strands to her cheeks, then made a visor with her hand to afford a clearer view.

She skirted the pool of lamplight, which meant that she took longer than her quarry to reach the path. It was barely defined, a route worn by people taking a shortcut down the hillside from the residential areas to the harbour. The rain made the soil slick and in places mud flowed freely. Nina skidded and her arms windmilled but there was nothing to grab onto. She forced herself to take her time. If she fell to the left and slid more than a couple of feet towards the cliff edge, it would be a long drop to the concrete surface of the harbour.

She could no longer see Egg or the children.

Several times she bent almost double to keep her balance. Her fingers sunk into the ooze; she wiped them on her slick shirt, grimacing at the dark trail they left behind. The wind changed direction so often that she wasn't able to lean into it, and the rain seemed to gather for each new gust, depositing buckets-worth of water onto her at unpredictable intervals.

The slope became shallower. The sky was a slab of black. She saw no sign of Egg.

She swayed with the sideways push of the rain. She wondered whether she had been out long enough to kickstart hypothermia. The battering rain and the wind and the sea applauded her as she tramped along.

'Quiet,' she muttered. She turned her head from side to side and wished that she was wearing Clay's binaural microphones. 'Please. Let me listen.'

From somewhere ahead came a rhythmic pulsing. It was less insistent than a drill, but no less regular and sharp. She turned on the spot, then followed the sound.

She heard rather than saw the hollow: the thudding changed in pitch, the treble rising to match the bass as she drew closer. She hunkered down and then shuffled forward.

It was only a very shallow dip in the landscape, wide and circular. Standing in its centre was a group of people. One of them was far taller than the others. Nina's stomach alternated between feeling desperately empty and full to bursting, and the shrill sound within her head was excruciating.

She watched the children and told herself this was a nightmare. She dug the fingernails of her right hand into the palm of her left.

There was no waking up from this.

Were they all there, all of the island children? Had they all been involved from the start, from Thomas all the way down to perhaps even Marie's baby? No explanation seemed impossible, no matter how ridiculous.

She tried to count the number of children, but they kept shifting, sidestepping in a circle but always keeping Egg in the centre. Whatever they were holding in their hands was what was producing the rhythm. Nina saw swift movements. Sticks hitting rocks in perfect regularity. The rhythm dictated the tempo of Nina's thoughts.

Please—

Please don't let—

Please don't let Laurie be down there.

It was impossible to see clearly.

Nina fumbled for her phone. Water streamed down her arms and trickled in rivulets along her fingers. The fingerprint scanner didn't recognise her. What was her passcode?

She looked up again and her breath caught. The group had tightened into a huddle and Egg had disappeared.

'Please,' she mouthed. 'Don't.'

No. Egg was still there, still in the middle, but he had been forced to his knees.

Nina's legs screamed with pain due to her odd posture, but she couldn't straighten, couldn't make any move to bring her closer to the hollow.

She opened her mouth to shout. Nothing came out. There was something wrong with her. She hadn't been able to scream in Laurie's cubbyhole, the Crow's Nest, either.

Down there in the hollow she saw one of the dark children raise something smooth and round into the air. It came down on Egg's head.

The pounding rhythm stopped and even the wind seemed to abate. Nina watched aghast as the stone lifted and came down again. Egg gave no cry, so the only new sound was an echoing *chuck*.

When the stone was drawn up again, Nina rediscovered her ability to control her body. She sprang forwards with her arms outstretched, shouting 'Stop!' or something like it.

And—

Oh, that shriek, that sound, that voice inside her. She hung frozen above the ground, mid-leap.

And—

And the children stopped moving around their captive and the blackness of their heads perhaps turned towards her and at the same moment the stone came down again and then there was a scream. A real one, not within her own body but out there in the world, in that hollow below her, a shout like nothing she had ever heard. It was the most dreadful glorious excruciating sound Nina could imagine: a piercing screech that seemed drawn not from the depths of a body but from the earth itself, a cleaving of continents.

Everything seemed to stutter, both visually and aurally: was she blacking out? Perhaps she shouted 'Egg!' or perhaps not. Her hands went to cover her ears, which left her unbalanced as she tumbled forwards.

But the shout from down in the hollow was so large and substantial, such a physical thing. It thumped her in the chest even as she hung in the air. Then, only an instant later, she was hurtling backwards, her momentum reversed to cast her away from the hollow. Dimly, she marvelled at her weightlessness as she corkscrewed and fell with a grunt to the sodden grass.

Pain knifed into her abdomen as she rose to her feet. Disoriented, she spun to locate the hollow.

The only figure that remained in its centre was Egg. His body was crumpled, his arms contorted. She was glad that she couldn't see his head. The children lay like scattered dominoes, their feet pointing to their victim like the hands of a clock. The wind must have flung them aside too.

Now the children rose, faltering as they found their feet, like newborn animals.

They were staring up at her.

With jerky, unnatural movements they began climbing the slope of the hollow, scrambling with hands and feet to make their way towards Nina, their pace increasing and their confidence growing as they learned to grasp the clods of sodden grass.

Nina couldn't move. 'What do you want?' she moaned.

The children remained silent, their only sounds the scratching of their hands and feet, but the storm bellowed its laughter.

Nina saw hints of their faces. Sal Curtiz, David Priest, Chase Pickthall, little Noah Hutchinson smeared with mud or something worse.

Even in her panic Nina scanned the group for Laurie; even in her panic she experienced a glimmer of relief at not being able to see her.

Laurie was her only thought, her only plan. If Laurie wasn't here, she still needed to be protected.

Nina took a last look at the approaching children, then spun and sprinted away.

The world had become nothing like its daylight form. The topography of the island had shifted in the dark and the storm. Nothing was where it should be. Tammy's house might have been anywhere or nowhere.

Nina experienced only a series of tactile surfaces. The uneven ground beneath her feet. The blanket of rain pushing against her, the diagonal plane of the wind. The sky that had lowered to become a jagged rock surface above her head, its stalactites threatening to impale her.

Ahead of her was a wall of black within which she gradually perceived vertical strips. The woodland. She chanced a glance behind her before she reached it. The children had spread out, beginning to flank her. They were fast and she was tired, and everything hurt.

She plunged into the forest. The nicks of the branches were almost a relief: minor wounds in place of a more serious injury. She weaved through the trees at random, not even attempting to visualise a route.

Something tangled around her legs, tripping her so that her palms skidded and scuffed on a tree trunk, pain springing instantly from them. When she hit the ground something hard crunched beneath her; she thought of the bones in the shell midden. She whimpered and looked down, certain that she would see the outstretched arms of one of the children, but it was only a tarpaulin that had wrapped around her legs, and only a box of crackers that she had fallen upon. This must be Thomas's den, his base ready for when he and his friends were required to fend for themselves. Robin Hood and Davy Crockett; it had sounded like a childish game. Nina considered huddling under the tarpaulin and praying that the children would pass by, but even in her panic she saw that it was the worst plan imaginable. This was their territory. She had to find somewhere out of their reach, or unfamiliar to them – but on an island this size, and with her so exhausted, the idea seemed nonsensical. She struggled to tug the tarpaulin away, rose to her feet, and staggered on. She used the trunks of the trees as handholds as if she were climbing rather than running.

She tried to summon remembered details about her location. On one side of the rectangular woodland were homes and the schoolhouse, she knew, but she had no idea which way she was facing now. The forest creaked and snicked and cackled around her. She heard new sounds of movement, too. Even though the children moved lightly – they must know every inch of this place – she heard the snapping of twigs, the brush of fabric on bark.

The children were everywhere around her.

She knew the woodland was small, but even so, she burst out of the trees before she was ready. She must have simply passed across one corner of the forest. Her momentum was difficult to check, even when she recognised that the glints ahead of her were far away – far *below* – and that she was fast running out of ground.

And then suddenly she was teetering on the cliff edge.

She gazed out at the sea and at the boulders far below and she wondered whether a fall might be a preferable end.

CHAPTER TWENTY-FIVE

The rain prickled on Nina's arms, which were wrapped around her knees. Its tapping and teasing was soothing. She shivered with pleasure.

Her eyes opened and she found herself still within her dream. Everything was black at the edges. She blinked and tried to make sense of the pale circle above— no, in front of her. Her eyes closed again. It hardly mattered.

Seconds or minutes or hours later, something gripped her arm. She shook it off and gasped, then clamped her mouth shut for fear she might swallow water and drown – wasn't she underwater, still? Her vision was blurred. She saw a thin stripe bisecting a blue circle and then, obscenely interrupting that neat pattern, an arm. It cast around and a hand grasped her again.

She yelped and pushed backwards with her feet, but her shoulders met something hard. She made a sound from her mouth that was no kind of language. They were going to drown her again. Her shirt clung to her, wet and heavy as canvas.

'Mum?'

It was Laurie's voice, clear and not filtered through water. Nina was unable to process what it meant.

'Come out of there, Mum, okay?'

Nina brushed the hand away and thankfully Laurie released her grip.

She looked around. Rock. She was in a cavern. The Crow's Nest. She didn't remember climbing in here, but of course she must have done.

She opened her mouth. The last time she had been in here, she had been asked to scream. Now she found that she couldn't even speak.

'It's only me, Mum,' Laurie said.

That was hardly comforting. There was no guarantee Laurie could be trusted. Even if Laurie hadn't been there in the hollow last night...

The vision of Egg being brought to his knees filled her mind. In her memory, he and the children around him all moved jerkily, like stop-frame animation.

He was dead. They killed him and Nina had only watched. She was weeping now, silently.

'It's okay,' Laurie's voice said, so softly that Nina might have imagined it.

Nina's sobs became bitter, almost laughter. It would not be okay. But staying trapped in this tiny cave was hardly an option. Her spine spiked with flashes of pain.

With difficulty, she shuffled to the mouth of the cavern, wincing at the rain and the sunlight reflected on the broad gleaming shield of the sea. She turned on the plateau and when she straightened her back it emitted several sharp clicks.

She sidestepped gingerly on the slick rock until she found her footing on the larger boulder beside the Crow's Nest.

Beneath the dripping hood of her cagoule, Laurie's fair hair made a halo. Her lips were puckered in concern. She looked at Nina's sodden shirt and her jeans black with wetness.

'Hi,' Nina said. She stifled a shiver.

'What's going on, Mum?'

'I could ask you the same thing. Where were you last night?'

'You know where I was. Gran didn't know a thing about your plan, but I felt awful, like she'd been left behind.'

'What brought you to the Crow's Nest, though? Was it a coincidence that you happened to be passing this way?' Nina had no idea if she was feeling her way towards an accusation.

Laurie's forehead creased. 'Don't be an idiot. I was looking for you.'

'You thought I was at the Open Arms.'

'And I went there. I went to your hotel room, Mum. The door was wide open. People are worried.'

'People?'

'Just me, then. I've been all over. And now it's way past lunchtime and I've found you.'

Somehow the accusations seemed to be going in the wrong direction. In her disorientation, Nina didn't feel able to vouch for what she had seen during the night. The world around her hadn't yet become solid enough for her to trust her memories; the cliff edge made her feel lopsided and defensive. Even so, she cursed herself for the urge to give herself an alibi, however weak. 'I wanted to see this place again. It's important to you.'

Laurie shrugged. 'It was, yeah. I don't know.'

Silence fell. They both looked out at the ocean. The wind drove tall humps towards the rock to burst in showers of spray. Nina shivered and thought of the driving rain the night before, and the corresponding dampness of her clothes now. It had been real. She had seen what she had seen. The children had murdered Egg.

She wondered if her grief would continue to grow, accumulating for Abram and Egg together. Egg had been a real human being, and she had liked him because of, rather than in spite of, his hopelessness. She hadn't known him long, but she had already begun to think of him as a younger brother.

A voice inside her insisted that, however distant and ridiculous the idea, Laurie might somehow be a part of it all.

'Do you want me dead?' Nina said suddenly. Then she clamped both her hands over her mouth.

Laurie was so close to her that her hood almost protected Nina's face from the rain as well as her own. She didn't answer. Nina blinked to clear her vision, then stared into her daughter's eyes. There was nothing there that was bad or cruel. There was fear, certainly, and panic and perhaps revulsion, but no animosity.

'Mum, you're shivering.'

Nina nodded and then found that she couldn't stop. Her shoulders chugged to amplify the motion until her entire body shook uncontrollably.

*

She was still shivering when they reached the cottage. The walk had taken longer than it ought to; the rain had picked up again, and the wind had gained ferocity. Nina had stumbled often, and each time Laurie took her arm she had flinched and pulled away. She had checked her phone every few minutes, but there was no reception; it was the same with Laurie's. Nina hadn't said anything to Laurie about the events during the night, though she had tried to summon her courage several times. She had been struck by the unsettling feeling that this was the same conversation as when they had arrived on Hope Island. Then, she had been attempting to speak the truth about Laurie's father. To deliver the even more awful news about Egg was impossible.

Nina was grateful that Tammy wasn't in the house. It wasn't just that she was reluctant to face Tammy after having tried to flee the island. Tammy couldn't be trusted any more than any other islander. Her paintings of men falling from cliffs were a nightmare that predated everything that had happened to Nina on Hope Island.

She fell upon the phone in the hallway, dialled 999, hung up, dialled 911. She did it again, twice, before she registered that there was no dial tone. She stared at the receiver, then at Laurie, who took it, listened and frowned.

'Gran said that it goes sometimes,' Laurie said. 'And there was a storm last night.'

Nina nodded. She remembered Marie referring to the same problem.

For the first time, it occurred to Nina to wonder if Egg's body was still up there on the hilltop, or whether the children would have dragged it away somewhere. Bile rose in her throat along with the image of his cracked skull.

She took the receiver from Laurie, careful not to let their fingers touch, and replaced it on its stand. The water dripping from her clothes had already made a dark pool on the carpet.

'You have to warm up, and fast,' Laurie said. 'Do you want a bath?'

'No,' Nina replied instantly.

But Laurie was right about needing to get herself dry. Her shivering was uncontrollable.

She climbed the stairs slowly, stopping each time her shudders made progress impossible. Laurie followed her. Nina felt vulnerable: Laurie could trip her and send her toppling down the steps at any moment. But why here and why now?

They reached the landing. Nina watched her daughter warily.

Laurie opened the door of her bedroom. 'Take off those wet clothes, Mum.'

Nina entered the room. She sat on the edge of the bed, grimacing at the sensation of sinking. She stood and obeyed Laurie's command meekly. Her jeans were sodden, making a rigid shell, a denim exoskeleton. When she finally managed to peel them off, her legs looked sickly pale and thin. Laurie brought in a towel as she was bending to shrug off her long-sleeved T-shirt. They stood watching each other, the towel held out like a peace offering or a gauntlet.

Nothing in Laurie's eyes suggested anything more than concern. If anything was unnatural, it was her ability to remain calm in the face of Nina's erratic behaviour. But Nina had no idea whether Laurie would ordinarily be capable of such tolerance. She had no idea what Laurie was like.

The image of the night before was a static tableau in her mind. That view from above the hollow. The group of dark shadows within, and Egg – poor, dear Egg – on his knees in the centre. Nina found that she was able to insert or remove Laurie from the tableau at will, as though she were flicking between two spot-the-difference images. Laurie was there. Laurie wasn't there. Laurie was part of this. Laurie was innocent. Nina tried to listen to the voice within her, but the shrill ringing sound in her ears overwhelmed everything.

She took the towel and began rubbing at her hair. The darkness beneath the towel was a relief. She balled her hands, pressing the fabric hard to her face. She pushed fluffy folds of it into her mouth.

She ought to scream. Let it all out. It would do her good. That's what Laurie had told her on their first full day on the island.

No sound came from her mouth. The towel only made her feel hot. She pulled it away and continued drying herself.

Laurie knelt before her open suitcase and the clothes Nina had crammed into it – was that really only yesterday?

'I don't have my clothes,' Nina said, finally cottoning on.

'I figured you'd rather wear mine than Gran's. There's no way my jeans will fit, but these might do.'

Nina let her drape the items of clothing over her outstretched arms. A plain black skirt and black leggings. A slouchy red woollen jumper. A grey vest with *Oh yeah*? scrawled in white.

'Thank you,' Nina said in the quietest voice.

When she was dressed, she felt like a different person. It was good. The jumper was wide in the neck and slipped off one shoulder. Nina finished towelling her hair.

'I need to find a way to contact the mainland,' she said. It was the only way of interrupting the madness of Hope Island. Out there in the real world, everything must still be normal, people were predictable, children were not murderous. Even when Egg had been alive, Hope Island had been close to lawless, and now there was nothing to hold back the chaos. 'And I'm scared to leave you here alone.'

Laurie folded her arms. 'Why?'

She couldn't hold the truth in abeyance indefinitely. And she felt a sudden urge to tell someone what had happened, to hold the truth up to the light, to see its flaws.

'Because last night Egg was killed.'

Laurie blinked but didn't look away. Nina was unsure what reaction would signal guilt. Then she sighed. 'Mum. You know that isn't true.'

'I saw it.'

'And this was when you were prowling around in the dark, in the rain?'

'Yes.'

'And after you tried to leave the island because you don't want to be here when Dad arrives.' Laurie pressed her fingertips to the bridge of her nose, an action that seemed to Nina absurdly adult.

'No. I mean yes, but that's— There's no link between those two things.'

Gently, Laurie took the towel from her and dropped it onto the bed. 'Mum… I don't know how you're supposed to say this sort of thing… but you're not acting like yourself.'

'Me?'

'You keep accusing people. Me, for one. You're saying things that don't make sense. What do you really think has happened to Mr Frears?' She had the forced neutral manner of a therapist, but her meaning was clear. *Tell me about these hallucinations.*

Traps were springing up everywhere. Nina's throat was dry and the act of towelling her hair had made her head spin. She could hear the rush of the ocean.

'I don't know,' she said carefully. 'I'm sorry. But I do need to call the mainland. They need to know about the phone lines being down, and they can tell us when it'll be safe for the ferry to run. Will you come with me? The fire department have a radio line.'

Laurie hesitated, watching her with an unreadable expression. Then she nodded and led the way downstairs.

*

They saw hints of the commotion as they approached the harbour. Nina lifted the visor of the pink raincoat she had taken from the coat rack in the cottage, and peered through the driving rain to see figures hurrying in the area between the shops and the fire department. The sound of raised voices came from somewhere out of sight. She felt Laurie's gaze as heat upon her face.

The door of the fire department hung open. The doorway was blocked with bodies and through the window Nina could see people in Egg's office. She recognised almost all of them. They were the parents she had met on her doorstepping tour.

They were all shouting over one another. Nina couldn't make out a single word. She rubbed her ears. The odd thing was that the noise, mingling with the thud of the rain and the hissing in her ears, was almost pleasurable, a soundscape richer than the sum of its parts.

'Mum?' Laurie said, small and far away.

Nina glanced at her but couldn't begin to think what to say. She pushed between the people standing in the doorway. A few noticed her arrival and the change in atmosphere spread like a ripple in water. The shouting abated but the muttering seemed almost as loud. They all seemed wreathed in fog; steam rose from them as the rainwater on their clothing evaporated in the heat of the small room.

She tried to remember some of their names, but realised she had never learned most of them. Charlene Jenner, Ed Curtiz… Marie was missing, as were Dee and Harvey Hutchinson. The rest were a mass of faces with only one expression between them: utter mistrust.

She checked her recollection of the night again. It still seemed as real and certain as ever.

She cleared her throat. 'You're here because of your children.' She had meant for it to be a question.

'What do you know about them?' Genie Mason's father said.

'Are they missing?' an unknown, exhausted-looking woman said in a shrill voice.

'What in the hell do *you* think?' David Priest's mother shouted at her. All of her homeliness of yesterday had vanished. Nina caught a glimpse of red pyjamas beneath her thick parka.

'And what are you doing here?' another man she didn't recognise said. Nina wondered whether by *here* he meant the fire department or the island.

Charlene Jenner said, 'I reckon her and Egg have been at it like rabbits. I bet he's sleeping it off in her bed still.' To Nina she demanded, 'Where is he?'

The hissing in Nina's ears was so severe, she couldn't remember what words ought to sound like. She looked down at her right hand as somebody took it. Laurie was clutching her and pressing against her side. It was clear she was terrified.

Charlene's attention shifted to Laurie. In a voice more pleading than accusatory, though no less loud, she said, 'You know where our kids are, don't you?'

'I don't,' Laurie replied. 'I don't know what's going on.'

'Liar! Little liar!'

All of the adults began jostling, each trying to get closer to Nina and Laurie. The hubbub became a roar as they bellowed questions and accusations.

Nina swallowed and pushed the nausea down. There was nothing for it but to tell the truth, as unwelcome as it would be.

'I know what's going on,' she said, her thin voice somehow cutting through the cacophony. 'But I'm sorry. You're not going to like it and there's no way to dress it up. Your children have hidden themselves away somewhere because last night they murdered Egg.'

Some faces displayed pure shock; but in others Nina thought she saw hints of guilt. She felt certain that some of them already had their suspicions about what their children might be prepared to do. None of them spoke.

The silence didn't last long.

Amid the suddenly restored clamour, Nina shouted, 'Let me get to that phone!'

Ed Curtiz blocked her way. 'There's no fucking way you're doing that, missy. We have questions that need answering.'

'You can ask them. But we have to call the police.' She looked him straight in the eyes. It didn't matter what they did to her, as long as Laurie was safe and as long as she could reintroduce the outside world to Hope Island. It was the only way the nightmare could end. 'Your children are missing. Even if it were only that, surely you'd want the help of the authorities to find them?'

'We already have a fire officer on the island and there's rescue equipment in that there locked cupboard,' Ed replied. 'You tell us where we'll find Egg and we can sort this out ourselves, all right?'

'He's *dead*. I think you've all experienced strange things happening recently. I think you're on the defensive, and that you're lying to yourselves. You've seen strange behaviour in your children, particularly when they're together. And last night Egg was killed with a rock, or at least I think that's what it was, and it was one of your children who did it while the others watched.' Her matter-of-fact tone deteriorated at the end. She gulped for air, almost sobbing as she saw Egg's kneeling silhouette again in her mind's eye.

The parents all roared once again. Nina heard nothing but the shout of the storm of the night before. The noise entered her, whirling around in her head like the wind in the shell midden. It was disorienting yet somehow satisfying.

Laurie had edged away but Ed pushed her back to huddle against Nina. Poor Laurie. But when it was finally proved that Nina was telling the truth, Laurie's suspicion of a nervous breakdown would disappear. They would be on the same side.

'Where will we find Egg?' Ed shouted.

'If his body hasn't been moved, you'll find it in a grassy hollow on the hilltop right above this fire department. Go up the dirt track that leads from the building, then I'm guessing you can't miss it. I'll show you. Once you let me call the police.'

Ed swooped over to Egg's desk and yanked the radio phone from its base. He jammed it into the pocket of his coat.

'No fucking way,' he said again. 'And you're not coming with us. This is the closest we have to a police station, and you're staying in it until we figure out what the hell you are.' He held up a set of keys. Nina wondered whether he acted as some kind of deputy to Egg, or perhaps the keys were held in some publicly accessible place. It hardly mattered.

A sharp sound from outside made Ed and the rest of the parents turn. Through the grimy window Nina saw Tammy's car lurch towards the jutting rocks that its bumper must already have struck once. Revving madly, it catapulted forwards in a bunny hop. The horn sounded briefly but Nina couldn't tell whether it was deliberate or the result of the driver hitting the centre of the wheel by accident.

'I got the keys back from Mr Frears yesterday,' Laurie said quietly.

'Quick,' Nina hissed, far louder.

They held hands as they charged into the people standing behind them. Chase Pickthall's parents parted in surprise at the sudden attack, leaving a clear route to the door.

'Don't let them go!' Ed Curtiz roared.

But Nina and Laurie were already outside in the rain. Skidding on the wet and cracked concrete, Nina sprinted to the rear door, flung it open, and hurled herself into the back seat. She heard the front door open and close and the car revving to the point where she expected something to explode. Then it was moving, and she scrabbled to turn and claw at the back door as people emerged from the fire department and sought to gain purchase on its handle. The door was still flapping as Laurie in the front passenger seat yelped and Tammy – whooping and thumping the rim of the steering wheel – pulled the car in a sharp left turn and gunned the engine as they hurtled away from the harbour, producing a wake of spray in which Nina glimpsed, for a fraction of a second, a rainbow.

CHAPTER TWENTY-SIX

They were halfway up the hill before Nina managed to wrestle the rear door fully closed, reducing the outside roar to the distant sound of pebbles springing up against the wheel arches of the car. Tammy was hunched over the steering wheel and hadn't even glanced into the back seat.

Nina caught her breath. 'They'll follow us to your house.'

She flailed and grabbed at the door handle for balance as the car tipped violently. Tammy's driving style was to keep the accelerator pedal jammed down and then try to intuit a safe route over the bumpy terrain. The wipers were doing a poor job of clearing the windscreen and it looked as though Tammy was being forced to squint through a small patch where both wipers overlapped and where the glass wasn't smeared with white streaks.

'Put your seat belt on, Mum,' Laurie said without turning in the front passenger seat. Her right hand was clamped onto the dashboard to steady her.

Chastened, Nina did as she was told. Though she no longer feared that Laurie was responsible for Egg's murder, a voice inside told her to remain wary. Keeping on her good side was sensible. Moreover, Laurie seemed more and more adult, and it felt strangely reassuring to let her adopt the maternal role. Nina almost giggled at the thought of asking, 'Are we nearly there yet?'

Tammy leaned into the turn as she wrenched the car off the main road. She didn't slow as they approached and then passed the lane that led to her house.

'Where are you taking us?' Nina said. 'This is ridiculous. We need to get off the island, and the only way to do that is from the harbour.'

Tammy only emitted a grunt and bent even closer to the steering wheel.

Nina watched the tree line as they careered past the woodland. Perhaps the children were hiding in there. Perhaps Tammy was taking her directly to them. Keeping a firm hold of the handle, she pulled gently at the door release. The door remained closed; there must be child locks. If she wound down the window it would probably stop halfway, too small a gap for anybody to climb out. Suddenly, the idea of being forced into the role of a child in this topsy-turvy family petrified her.

'Where are you taking me?' she said weakly.

The answer lay before them as they surmounted the apex of the hill. Below them, spread out like elements of a model train set, were the buildings of the Sanctuary within their perimeter fence.

In there she would be as much a prisoner as if the islanders had locked her up in the fire department.

She tried to review her options, though they seemed comically few. She must escape from Tammy and Laurie, somehow. Whatever their intentions might be, they weren't in Nina's interests. After all, Laurie clearly still felt the simplest explanation of recent events was that Nina was hallucinating.

She must find her way back to the harbour. Steal one of the smaller boats – a rowing boat, if necessary. Reaching the mainland would be too great a distance, but Monhegan was a possibility. For a second, she relished the thought of landing at one of the other Hope Islands in the gulf, and starting her visit afresh there. She prayed that whatever madness had consumed this Hope Island hadn't spread to anywhere else.

The gates of the complex were wide open. As Tammy guided the car through – nicking the left-hand mirror as she did and producing a squeal of alarm from Laurie – Nina noticed that there was nobody manning the gate to close it after them.

The thought of escaping from her own family was ridiculous, but no less ridiculous than anything else that had occurred in the last twenty-four hours. Nina forced her breathing to slow, and tried to stifle the ringing in her ears that was becoming ever more distracting. Her eyes watered but she couldn't let herself release all her anguish. She needed to act, and she needed to choose her moment carefully.

As the car barrelled towards the gravel area between the Portakabins she released her seat belt silently. She planted her feet on the floor and angled her body so that she was ready to leap out of the car as soon as the door was opened from the outside.

The car stopped. Laurie got out and went straight to Nina's door. It opened.

Nina thumped the inside of the door with both hands, snapping it fully open. She winced as she registered that the impact had knocked Laurie off her feet, but she didn't stop to look. Her spine twisted as she veered away, aiming towards the still-open gates several hundred metres away. Her sodden shoes skidded on the gravel.

All of her momentum disappeared as she came to an abrupt halt. What had she hit?

Her face was pressed against Clay's chest; he must have emerged unseen from his workshop. Nina's feet scrabbled in vain and she slid down his torso. She felt his arms fold around her shoulders easily, as though this were an anticipated and welcome hug.

Despite the inappropriate timing, Nina suddenly recognised how attracted to Clay she was and – a thought that arrived in tandem – how little she was attracted to Rob nowadays. She and Rob had been growing apart for many years. Her fondness towards him was rooted in their early life together. They had never been destined to remain together for good.

All strength left Nina's body. She turned to see Laurie rise and brush the gravel from her backside, then splay out her hands at Nina in a *what the fuck* gesture.

Tammy struggled out of the driver's seat. As she and Laurie approached, Nina tried once again to push Clay away. He didn't so much restrain her as place himself in her direct line of movement, a fleshy obstacle that she hadn't the energy to circumnavigate.

'Clay,' Tammy said. 'We need your help.'

The 'we' was confusing, but Nina assumed she wasn't included in it. She was the problem that Tammy and Laurie needed help to solve. She was the bacteria in the bloodstream.

She found her voice and when she spoke, she had to raise her volume over the scream in her ears. 'Let me go! All of you. I don't understand this.'

And then she cried openly. She didn't even raise her hands to her eyes. The tears flowed into her mouth, as salty as seawater. Laurie wept too, which only made things worse.

Tammy frowned and said to Clay, 'Nina is in real trouble. And that means that we all are.'

Nina blinked and sniffled and stared up at this unknowable woman.

Clay nodded at Tammy and waited patiently, as if she were only recounting a trivial anecdote.

'A number of people are accusing Nina of crimes,' Tammy continued in her foghorn voice. 'And there are others who mean her harm. I don't know the truth of it all, but she's no liar.'

Then Tammy smiled, a warm honest smile, and looked directly into Nina's eyes, and suddenly it felt like it might all be okay.

*

Nina watched Clay's deft movements as he made his way across the scrubland, hopping from rock to tuft and avoiding the pools of rainwater that had collected in the hollows. She tried to replicate his route, without success. At least the wellington boots that Clay had lent her meant that her failures weren't punished with wet feet.

A little behind her, Laurie tramped in a straight line, her head bowed against the driving rain as she squelched through the mire. Their matching, moss-coloured army-surplus ponchos whipped in the wind. Nina imagined that they must look like a pair of wraiths.

The lighthouse rose before them, jutting from the tip of the island like a stalagmite.

She stumble-jogged to catch up with Clay. 'How confident are you that we'll be able to contact the mainland?'

'We will see,' Clay replied in a neutral tone. His view of the world seemed utterly straightforward. Nina imagined that he might consider predicting any aspect of the future, to any degree, pointless.

'But there's a radio phone in there?'

'Something like it.' Clay noticed Nina glancing back at Laurie. 'All is fine and good here in the grounds owned by the Siblings. What is the phrase you British like? As safe as houses?'

Nina resisted the temptation to make a snide remark about the derelict state of the Sanctuary mansion, its status as a health-and-safety nightmare.

They exchanged no more words until they arrived at the lighthouse. Nina thought she could see white paint flaking off and falling like snow, dislodged by the force of the rain. The place looked sickly.

Clay struggled with the padlock on the rusted iron door. Its handle was missing; he fished in his rucksack to retrieve a crowbar, which he inserted into the slot where the handle would fit. He grunted as he pulled the door open, scrabbling at its edge with his free hand. Each of his fingertips was flecked with something dark, but Nina couldn't tell whether it was rust or blood. Clay rolled a biggish rock to hold the iron door open.

When Laurie joined them, her nose wrinkled as she peered inside. Nina wished that her daughter had obeyed her instruction to stay with Tammy.

Nina flicked on the torch she had been given at the same moment Laurie switched hers on, so that the black interior of the tower was penetrated by two criss-crossing beams which seemed to suggest movement all around. Nina held her breath but reassured herself that the only things moving were dust motes. Clay strode inside without illumination of his own.

Within the base of the building were empty shelves that might once have contained equipment and life vests. In the exact centre of the space was a metal mesh stairwell. They climbed it, each of their footsteps clanging. At a landing the stairs continued up, presumably to the lamp room, but Clay pushed at the only door on this level. Inside, the loose fittings of a tiny window high above Nina's head rattled with the wind. What kind of coastguard base offered no views of the ocean?

At first there seemed barely enough room for them to squeeze in past an empty desk and two wooden chairs, but then Clay disappeared out of sight; Nina realised that the room followed the curve of the exterior wall.

She heard Clay groan. When she found him, he was bending over an ancient steel control console. The microphone on a flexible stand seemed intact, but wires spilled from the angled console front, which appeared to have been levered up forcibly.

'Can you get this thing working?' Nina said.

Clay flicked a switch on the left of the console. A couple of readouts shone a sickly yellow.

'There is power, which is some start.' He swung his rucksack from his shoulder, pulled out a pair of headphones and jammed the jack into a socket. He turned one dial, then another. He shook his head.

'How about broadcasting?' Nina said. 'Can you send out a message, one way?'

Clay tapped the microphone, then the glass of a readout containing a motionless needle. 'Looks like no sound going in, no sound coming out. But do not worry. I can fix this.'

Calmly, he removed his tool belt and laid it out on the flat upper part of the console. From his rucksack he took a fistful of thin cables. He puffed out his cheeks, then selected a pair of pliers.

Laurie's face was softened and made pink by the rain. The balled-up poncho in her hands dripped onto the linoleum floor with echoing plops. She disappeared, then returned with one of the wooden chairs. Clay smiled his thanks and sat before the console, regarding it the way a concert pianist might regard the piano before beginning a complex piece.

*

Forty-five minutes later, Clay was still hard at work, muttering to himself in Finnish as he bobbed up and down, his attention alternating between the nest of wires within the control unit and the exposed ones beneath its removed fascia.

Laurie was standing on a chair, peering out at the storm through the tiny window, her little body flinching with each peal of thunder. She turned, watched Nina and Clay for a few seconds, then rolled her eyes. 'Some engineer.'

Nina made a face. 'He's helping, at least.'

'Is that a dig at me?'

Nina blinked. 'Of course not. That's not what I meant. I'm barely helping myself.'

In truth, she had been at Clay's side the entire time, learning quickly to anticipate which tool he needed, and she had begun to offer her own theories. The console wasn't so different from the technology in her Salford studio, with the main differentiator being the number of wires as opposed to baffling microscopic circuitry. In her studio she made it her business to observe any tinkering that went on – more than once she had sacrificed her Saturday to watch the techies installing new equipment, bugging them with questions and acting offended if they patronised her with simplistic answers. Here on Hope Island she had far more at stake.

Clay was shivering.

'Your jumper's sodden,' Nina said as she approached him.

Clay waved a hand dismissively.

'Here,' she said, moving beside him and putting an arm around him. Her poncho had done a decent job of keeping her red woollen jumper – Laurie's jumper – dry.

Clay's body beneath his baggy clothes was lean, like a knotted rope in bubble wrap. Nina tried to visualise Rob as a comparison, but found she had no mental image of his body, only an impression, his general aura.

Clay didn't look at her, but kept frowning at the console. She gripped his waist tighter.

'I think I am on something,' he murmured.

'Sorry?'

'Onto? I think I am *onto* something.' He held up a fist of frayed wires. 'I will strip these and start again. Maybe they are perished. Then I will figure out what it is that they do.'

'How long do you think it might take?' She wasn't sure what she'd like his answer to be. It did feel good, holding him like this.

'Still some while yet. Or a little longer. You and your daughter, you should go and sleep.'

Nina's eyes flicked to Laurie, absorbed in the storm. 'We're not sleepy. And I'd rather—'

Clay turned to look at her finally.

A lightning slap outside, another rumble. Nina rubbed at an ear. The rushing sound came from both inside and outside her head. She liked it.

She pressed herself against Clay's body. She held his cold face in her warm hands. Their lips met.

He was as cold as a statue, and as unyielding.

Nina staggered backwards as if he had pushed her.

'Sorry,' she said. 'Sorry. You were shivering. That's all.'

Behind her she heard Laurie hop down from her wooden chair. How much had she seen?

'Sorry,' Nina said again.

'I am insisting,' Clay said stiffly. 'You both should go back to the Sanctuary. There are many beds for you there.'

Laurie had already begun fumbling with her poncho. She gave no sign of having witnessed Nina's fumbled seduction. She let out a grunt of frustration as she spun the poncho around, trying to line up her face with the hole. When she had succeeded, she stared at Nina, her arms raised as if to emphasise her absurd, bulbous appearance.

Nina nodded. She stretched her arms and performed a fake yawn, but then a real, enormous yawn rose up from her belly and emerged, paralysing her for several seconds.

'Clay,' she said. 'Once you fix that thing, promise that you'll come straight over to the Sanctuary and tell us?'

Clay had already ducked beneath the console again. His hand emerged, giving a thumbs up.

In a muffled voice he said, 'Enjoy your sweet dream.'

CHAPTER TWENTY-SEVEN

The hollow clanging of their footsteps on the metal gantry of the lighthouse echoed and accumulated, growing louder and louder until it felt to Nina like they were inside a giant tolling bell. With a strange shudder she realised that the sensation was enjoyable. The volume and sonorous insistence overwhelmed her anxieties. She resisted the temptation to close her eyes and wallow in the noise, to let it overcome her entirely. When they reached the bottom of the staircase and stepped onto concrete, she could almost have wept with the loss of comfort.

The noise of the storm was some consolation. As soon as she and Laurie left the lee of the doorway the rain hammered on her hood. Above them the sky growled and flickered occasionally over the black, tumultuous ocean.

Nina glanced over the cliff edge at the rocks fifty metres below. At least, she presumed there were rocks down there: she could hear waves breaking and the acoustics suggested a rocky bay. To the right of the lighthouse she could make out a wooden balustrade, angled diagonally down and disappearing over the crest of the cliff, but after a short stretch it plunged into uniform gloom and its lower reaches were invisible.

'What are you doing?' Laurie shouted behind her.

Nina hurried away from the edge. 'Clay said the Siblings owned a boat. I think it's moored down there.'

'Will he let you use it?'

'He made me promise I wouldn't. It's small, he says. Too small for this storm.'

'Then come *on*. My feet are wet.'

They squelched through the sodden grass while the sky grumbled above them.

'When the radio's fixed, what are you going to tell the police?' Laurie shielded her face with an arm and had to shout to be heard over the rain.

There was a correct answer, an honourable answer. *The truth*. But Nina no longer knew what that might be.

'That bad things are happening here. And that we need help.'

Laurie's cowl shook with her nodding. 'Is Egg really dead?'

'I'm pretty sure. I know that he was attacked. And I heard him scream.'

Laurie said something that Nina couldn't make out.

'You'll have to speak louder!' Nina shouted.

The wind picked up and the sky flashed. Five seconds later, a rumbling came from all around. It seemed to emanate from the ground beneath them as well as the sky above.

Laurie's hood swung her way. 'I said you were the one wandering around the hills at night. So you should know.'

The realisation hit Nina harder than the buffeting wind. It was she who lacked an alibi, not Laurie. Her assertions must sound crazed. And the police would see it the same way.

'When I get through to the Maine police, or whoever, I'll tell them that the island children have all gone missing,' Nina said. 'That's the truth, isn't it? And that their parents refused to let me call the mainland.'

These were facts. They may not be the key details, but anybody would find them worrisome.

Laurie didn't answer.

'I'm scared, Laurie,' Nina said, cupping her hands around her mouth and feeling absurd at this shouted conversation. 'I don't know what's happening. But I know that somebody needs to come here and make it stop.'

Laurie's shroud rose and fell. One wing of the poncho lifted, and a small hand emerged. Nina took it and they stumbled side by side, tethered.

Then Laurie said, 'You're wrong, you know.'

'Wrong, as in just wrong in general? Wrong in the head?'

'I mean you're wrong about Thomas and the others.'

The island children had become a single, compound threat in Nina's mind. Had she seen Thomas at the scene of Egg's murder? He no longer represented a specific fear, particularly since his confession at the schoolhouse.

She realised she hadn't thought much about his confession either.

'I heard Thomas tried to get more physical with you,' Nina said. 'And that you stopped him.'

Laurie froze, a sudden statue if not for her flapping poncho. 'What?'

'Look, I know you like him. But I'm impressed that you didn't let it become anything more than that.'

'What?' Laurie said again after a pause. This time the word was laced with disgust.

'I'm saying that I think you did right. I'm not going to lecture you. I'm saying I approve.'

Laurie pulled her hand away. She stood before Nina, blocking her way.

Nina longed to be back inside the tolling bell of the lighthouse stairwell, where sounds were deafening and unchanging and predictable and good. Laurie's accusations were like the twittering of a bird.

She raised her arms and the wind rushed under her poncho, puffing it out, and she wondered if she might be thrown off the headland, and whether that might not be better than being harangued by a livid teenager.

'You *approve*?' Laurie shrieked. 'You're giving me your *approval*?'

'I'm not giving you anything.'

'No, you never *have*, Mum!'

'This isn't the time. I can't—'

'You can't what? Can't prove all these things you're accusing people of? Can't wait to find a way off this island away from me? Can't manage to be a proper mum for years and years until you feel like telling me when I should be 'getting physical' with boys? Can't win Dad back so you'll let him and me walk away out of your life?

Can't fucking *speak* like a normal human being?'

Nina's mouth opened and closed wordlessly.

She was grateful for the sudden intensification of the storm. Lightning cracked somewhere overhead and the thunder followed immediately, a great thud that reverberated in her ribcage and made her retch, though she was conscious of an equal and opposite internal response, a giddiness and a loss of herself not unlike an orgasm.

In Laurie's face she saw unfiltered terror.

Nina spun around at another sound, closer than the thunder. It was halfway between a sigh and the popping of a cork. It was followed moments later by a crash, accompanied by a juddering that worked its way up from the ground and through her body. Something enormous had impacted nearby. She gazed up at the bulging dark clouds, imagining meteors.

'What the hell was that?' Laurie cried.

'We should go back,' Nina shouted. 'The Sanctuary's too far.'

'No! I want to be with Gran. She might be afraid.'

'I said it's too far!'

'Are you going to tell me you're my mum and so I do what you say?'

Nina reached out, grasping for Laurie's hand.

Laurie yanked it away again, her eyes wide as though she had been struck. She turned and ran.

She was heading in the wrong direction. The thought of Laurie hurtling into the dark was more than Nina could bear. She sprinted after her.

The storm chased them, creaking and cracking, and Nina leapt aside more than once in the fear that something else would be thrown down to Earth. And then she had to sidestep swiftly around some pale obstacle that almost tripped her, and she recognised it dimly as the stone that Clay had heaved to one side to reveal the passage to the shell midden… Except she could see the mud tideline where it had been embedded in the ground, and the mud was at the *top*. The huge rock had been flipped upside down. How was that possible?

'Laurie!' she screamed, understanding only that something was very wrong.

She identified Laurie only by her wraith silhouette, which was blacker than the surrounding dark.

'I'm sorry!' Nina shouted as she approached.

Laurie's poncho flapped. Her arms were waving frantically beneath the shroud. It was only when Laurie turned to face her that Nina realised that until now she had been looking at her daughter's back.

'I don't understand,' Nina bellowed. 'Any of this. I'm sorry! I only want to keep you safe.'

The side wind made Laurie's outline ripple wildly and produced tearing sounds.

For several seconds Laurie didn't reply. Then, in a voice that ought to have been quiet but which Nina heard as clear as if she were whispering directly into her ear, she said, 'You're doing it wrong.'

'I'm trying my best,' Nina replied. 'I'm trying to listen. I'm trying to listen to you and…' She searched for the right phrase. '…to listen to the voice inside me.'

It was Tammy's phrase, she realised. How had Tammy said it, exactly? *Everybody knows full well what's in there and what's really going on inside.* Nina wasn't certain whether it seemed a comforting thought, or terrifying.

She reached out to her daughter, as Tammy had reached out to her.

'You have it too,' she said. 'I'm certain that inside something is telling you that I'm not lying.'

She couldn't see Laurie's face in the gloom, but the hood of the poncho dipped towards her outstretched hand.

'In here,' Nina said. Her fingertips made contact with Laurie's chest, tapping the collarbone.

Laurie's body jerked. And then she was falling backwards, and it was too late for Nina to do anything other than gasp.

In an instant Laurie had disappeared entirely.

Nina fell to the ground in confusion. Wetness immediately began seeping through the knees of her trousers.

The storm roared at her, inside and out.

She hobbled forwards on her hands and knees. Directly behind where Laurie had been standing was an oblong void, the dimensions of a grave plot.

Slow as a dreamer, Nina reached into the black hole.

Her fingers grazed a hard ledge. A little further forwards and lower, another.

Steps.

It was the entrance to the shell midden.

But she had seen the stone, hadn't she? If the entrance to the shell midden was *here*, how had its covering stone ended up so far away?

In a flash she realised what the sigh and the thud of heavy impact had been: the stone thrown forcibly from the hole and then landing elsewhere. It made no sense, but it was true.

'Laurie?' she called into the blackness.

There was no reply.

She rubbed her forearm across her eyes to clear her vision.

Arms outstretched like a sleepwalker, she edged down the steps. The walls of the passage rose to envelop her and the strip of clouds visible above appeared as white as summer cumuli in comparison to the profound blackness below the earth.

Now that Nina was sheltered the wind dropped. She gasped and wept noisily, and then wondered if she had been weeping all along.

'Laurie?' she whimpered.

She remembered she possessed a source of light. She fumbled beneath her dripping poncho to retrieve her phone, then struggled to activate its torch function. Rainwater streamed from her fingers and onto the screen. She hissed at the intensity of the light. Its shifting, harsh beam made the soil to either side of the passageway appear alive.

She turned it to point down the steps. The sight of an empty black wellington boot was like a punch in the guts. Her daughter, whose tiny body she had once carried inside her. What had she done?

The torch blinked out.

'No,' she muttered, prodding at the phone screen with wet fingers, wiping it, trying again. 'No. No.'

The screen remained as black as her surroundings. The battery must be dead, or the water had trickled into some vital part. She shoved it back into her pocket, cursing.

At least she knew where Laurie had fallen. She sidestepped down the remaining steps, pressing her palms against the exposed soil of the passage wall for balance. She thought she felt movement beneath her hands, and she imagined worms.

'I'm here, Laurie,' she spluttered through her sobs. 'I'm here.'

She shuffled into the cavern on her haunches. The floor was uneven, and something crunched beneath her feet; each *crack* she imagined to be the shattering of Laurie's outstretched foot or hand, her nose or jaw.

With a start she recognised that her eyes were closed, as if to make her sense of touch stronger. When she opened them, she could see faint outlines on the ground: tips of shells, perhaps, or struts of bones.

And it was getting lighter. She looked back up the entrance steps, but the sky appeared no brighter, the cloud cover total. The light was coming from somewhere else.

Outside, the volume of the wind rose and rose and somehow Nina related it to the brightness, along with the whirling sound around her, perhaps tracing the unseen periphery of the cavern.

She looked down and saw that her poncho hung limp upon her. There was no wind.

Her breath caught as she saw Laurie splayed out on the hard cavern floor. Nina bent to her, patting her body, uncertain what she was trying to identify. Tears made streaks of her vision. She wished Rob was here and then she wished she'd never met him. She wished that Laurie was someone else's daughter, someone who could look after her. She wished that Laurie were far away from her, safe and well.

'I'm going to lift you,' she said, loudly in order to hear her own voice over a heaving sound that seemed to originate from within the cavern rather than outside. A strange thought occurred to her: the sound was filled with light. She recalled the song that she had heard during her visit with Clay. This was no longer the sound of the wind above and outside, which was brutal and blunt, unlike this deafening whisper.

For a moment the song took her; her eyes fluttered closed and she relished the play of light on her skin, the sense of being embraced both outside and – somehow – from within. The glow was overwhelming. She wanted more.

But…

Laurie was still lying there like a rag doll.

She bent to her daughter and threaded her arms under her neck and knees.

Laurie was lighter than she had imagined. All those stories of mothers displaying incredible strength when their children were at risk. The thought made her heart leap with hope.

Her daughter in her arms, she made her way to the foot of the steps but then a new sound within the cavern made her turn. Had it been a voice?

Something glowed faintly. Nina peered in the blackness. She saw a source of light, pulsing and hypnotic. The illumination seemed to be on the rear wall of the cave. It was a horizontal line, not quite regular, not quite jagged. Light emanated from within it.

She shuddered with sudden fear, with the certainty of another presence in the cavern.

Laurie was all that mattered. She turned away.

With a groan of exertion, she began trudging up the steps, forcing herself to take a moment to make sure of her footing on each new platform. She moaned as Laurie's head bumped on the soft walls.

She burst from the passageway with a gasp of triumph, holding up Laurie's limp body like a newborn.

CHAPTER TWENTY-EIGHT

Nina gasped with terror, flailing to catch hold of anything that might keep her afloat.

She realised she could breathe and that no water clogged her throat. There was no water, except in the heave of the tide that echoed in her ears.

'What?' she said to the darkness.

'We have to go,' Laurie replied. A fumbling, then a flare of brightness that didn't subside. Laurie angled Nina's phone away so that the torch beam shone against the wall rather than in Nina's eyes.

'What? Are you okay?'

When Nina had stumbled into the circle of Portakabins in the late evening Mikhail had tried to take the unconscious Laurie from her, but she had pushed him away. Instead, he had led her to the mansion and up its creaking central staircase, her legs threatening to buckle with each successive step. At first, she had thought she was imagining the wind still howling around her, until she saw that where there ought to have been a stained-glass window at the head of the staircase there were only sharp daggers of colour and its centre was open to the outside world. The corridors of the building were strewn with masonry and wooden beams leaning against the walls, but the room on the first floor which Mikhail had ushered her into was another matter. A single floodlight on a tall pole, the type used by roadside construction crews, was covered with coloured fabric to dim the beam, producing curlicued patterns on the walls of a large, tidy room that contained four old-fashioned beds with brass posts, several chests of drawers – an odd collection presumably salvaged from various other rooms – and, on the wall, a mural depicting boats on the ocean and a sea that seemed more alive than any of its tiny sailors. In one of the beds Tammy's body made a barely-there hump.

Weeping gratefully, Nina had deposited Laurie carefully on the bed furthest from the door.

She had demanded things of Mikhail and, when he appeared, Elliot, but she hadn't let them or any of the other Siblings near Laurie. She wrapped her daughter in blankets, then fussed with the heavy curtains covering the windows and wedged bundles of fabric into the gaps between the glass and the window frames. When she dried the rainwater and it became clear that Laurie was sweating profusely and shivering with a fever, she placed a warm cloth on Laurie's forehead. She hummed a tune – it took her several minutes to identify it as an echo of the song she had heard in the shell midden – and held her daughter's hand and vowed to watch her until the sun rose.

But she had fallen asleep.

'I'm okay,' Laurie said. 'I'm okay now.' She looked it, too. Her eyes were alert, her skin gleaming.

'I'm so sorry about what happened,' Nina said. Memories from the evening washed over her like cold water. 'I shouldn't have pushed you. I didn't know you'd fall.'

'All right. There's no time. We have to go.' Laurie shone the torch at the door, as if seeing it might make Nina hurry.

'But why? What's going on?'

'The children. They're coming for us.'

Nina scratched the sleep from her eyes. The makeshift curtains were still black. She tried to raise herself from her awkward position slumped against the wall. 'Where are they?'

'They've climbed the fence. They're heading this way.'

'You saw them?'

Laurie angled the torch towards her own face. The shadow of her nose became a sundial pointer, indicating one eye and then the other.

'I'm scared, Mum.'

Nina stared at her. If not for the shaking of the phone, Laurie's face would appear completely still. Rather than meeting Nina's eye, she was looking up at the mural on the wall. It was an ugly thing, Nina thought. Maybe the artists that had resided in the Sanctuary retreat weren't as talented as she'd been led to believe.

Then she remembered herself and shuffled on her knees to embrace her daughter. She shushed and patted and smoothed, and it all came naturally, all these things she had never thought to do when Laurie was an infant.

'What should we do?' she said into Laurie's hair. She looked over to where she knew Tammy's bed was, though she couldn't see that far in the gloom. 'We'd better wake your gran.'

Laurie disentangled herself from Nina's arms. She pushed back her hair and stood. 'They aren't interested in her. We have to leave *now.*'

Nina stared up at her daughter, who alternated yellow and dazzling white in the shifting torchlight. She imagined Laurie as a mother, making decisions on behalf of her child. She'd be good at it.

She looked at the black window. 'What time is it?'

'Night. They're coming, Mum. Let's go. Mikhail will hold them off for now, but we have to go. We can use the motorboat. We can leave the island.'

Nina's heart leapt. 'What about Clay?'

'Still working on the transmitter. He'll call ahead so they'll be ready for us on the mainland. Get up, quick.' She pulled Nina by the hand, jolting her shoulder joint.

Nina shook her head, from disorientation rather than as a refusal. How had Laurie made all these plans? How was she even up and about, looking so well? Nina accepted her coat when Laurie passed it to her, and shrugged it on with her help. Laurie bent and cupped each of Nina's feet in turn, putting on her shoes and then tying her shoelaces. She herself was already dressed. She had lost her poncho. A streak of muck on her cheek was the only evidence of her fall into the shell midden.

The corridor was empty other than a metal chair against the wall. Elliot had promised that one of the Siblings would remain there until the morning.

Nina followed Laurie through the wreckage of the building, relying on her torchlight to avoid the obstacles. Several times she bumped into the corridor walls, producing dry puffs of plaster and, once, a thud as a large chunk fell to the wooden floorboards. Laurie took the stairs two at a time, but Nina felt her way down along the banister, trusting neither it nor the groaning steps.

Then they were outside. The rain had stopped but the wind reinvigorated the whirling sound in Nina's head, and it slapped at her; she even looked down to check she was wearing her skirt and leggings because they felt like nothing at all.

Her thoughts were getting muddled. Surely it was wrong to leave Tammy inside the building? But the voice inside her – the same one that had been so wary of Laurie after Nina was attacked in the bath – now told her to trust her daughter.

Laurie sped across the gravel and past the chapel. When Nina hesitated and looked around at the Portakabins and called out as loudly as she dared, 'Mikhail?' there was no answer.

The voice inside her was insistent, rising from a whisper to a demand to a shout. She should go with Laurie, without question. Nina winced and begged the voice to stop.

Laurie was already on the verge of disappearing into the gloom. Nina hurried after her. The cry of the wind might have disguised any sounds of approaching children. She remembered them chasing her, after they had murdered Egg, their pursuit through the woodland. She didn't think she would have the stamina to escape like that again. Even if Laurie was wrong, it was best to assume the worst and find somewhere safe, far away.

Laurie kept several paces ahead. Nina stumbled to keep up. The moon shone only intermittently. Clouds scudded across the sky and, giddily, Nina imagined their movement was the cause of the wind rather than a consequence. The clouds roared and laughed at her foolishness, unable even to walk straight, not feeling like herself at all, and her head hurt, it *hurt*, it hurt and she rubbed at the hollows below her ear and behind her jaw, trying to ease the shrill sound up and out as one might coax an air bubble trapped beneath new wallpaper.

This was real.

All of this was actually happening.

'Slow down,' she might have cried out, and, 'Faster,' Laurie might have replied. Nina looked behind her groggily for signs of anybody in pursuit but there might have been dozens and there might have been none.

It felt as though they had always been stumbling around in this marshy grassland between the Sanctuary and the lighthouse. Everything before seemed like a dream. Any prospect of finding themselves elsewhere seemed like fantasy.

When they finally reached the lighthouse on the tip of the island, Nina made towards its open door, hope rising within her that encountering Clay might wake her from her nightmare. But before she could enter, Laurie took her hand and instead guided her towards and then down the wooden steps on the cliffside. Nina's breath kept being stolen by the howling wind and she watched the dark mass of Laurie's jumper – which was only thin, so why wasn't she shivering with the cold? – and her own feet on the creaking steps which seemed far away, as though she were growing like Alice, as if her head were still level with the cliff top and her legs were stretching and stretching. But then anybody might feel disoriented out here in the cold wind at whatever o'clock in the morning and with so much unseen awfulness everywhere about and she would be sick she was sure of it.

It was easier to imagine that she really was dreaming. Then there would be no consequences to letting Laurie make all the decisions. It was easier and easy felt good. The voice inside her told her that she was right.

After a minute Nina found herself on a level surface once more, though it swayed oddly beneath her. The wood was slick and slippery. She put out her hands like a tightrope walker and she thought of walking the plank in pirate stories or *Peter Pan* and she wondered if Laurie would ever grow up.

'Get in,' Laurie shouted, and her black arm indicated the boat with its hull knocking against the jetty. It was painted white and seemed almost phosphorescent, and Nina gladly stepped into it because it was an escape from the unremitting darkness. She sat facing backwards at its prow like a figurehead the wrong way around.

She remembered.

'Clay said it was too small to use in this storm!' she shouted, and in her giddiness she felt proud of herself for making sense in the midst of the shriek from everywhere.

Laurie started the outboard motor with surprising ease. She crouched before the rope mooring the boat to the jetty.

Nina gripped both sides of the boat as it lurched forward. Within thirty seconds they had passed the rock wall that sheltered the little bay. Then, suddenly, the full force of the storm hit them. Nina gasped and a fist of air filled her throat and made it impossible for a moment to clamp her mouth shut. The wind caught the hull and in tandem with the swell of the sea it pushed the boat up and to the right. Nina pressed herself in the opposite direction, willing herself to be heavy enough to right the vessel.

She so wanted to leave this place; it took great strength to shout, 'Turn back!'

Laurie was hunched at the motor, immune to the wind.

The black land slid away, the only smooth motion in a universe of jolts and heaves. The unlit lamp room of the lighthouse above was a blind eye.

'We won't make it!' Nina said, not even shouting now.

Laurie rose. Her face was shrouded in darkness and Nina saw her as a great black toad.

Nina cried out in panic.

It wasn't that Laurie moved fast but her movements were difficult to predict. All Nina could make out was her stooping to the floor of the boat and then lifting something thin and long. And it was an oar, she realised, but the voice inside her told her not to panic, so she only puzzled idly about it as the motor chugged steadily despite the ferocity of the water. But then an instinct, unrelated to the voice inside her, made her duck and press herself forwards rather than to one side, to avoid the swing of the wood that even in the midst of the storm made a whipping sound beside her ear, and a buzzing like the sound of blowing on a taut piece of grass held clamped in both hands on a summer day.

Laurie swung again and now they had somehow switched ends within the boat, which rocked wildly beneath them.

Panic arrived in a tidal swell.

Not Laurie. Anybody else but please, not Laurie.

Nina stood and held up both hands – a surrender or a plea – but Laurie didn't hesitate. She changed her grip on the oar shaft, now holding it like a javelin, and thrust it at Nina's face. Nina twisted enough for it to glance off the nape of her neck, but the impact produced a jolt of revulsion, pure revulsion that infected every part of her in an instant and the hurt and the bile and the screaming welled up and wanted out.

Nina told herself to beg or to attempt some maternal pronouncement – comforting or scolding, though both seemed absurd – but in the end she made no sound at all. Every part of her was concentrated on her reactions and diving away from harm.

When the jab came again, she was ready for it. She slapped the paddle of the oar away, then darted forwards and grabbed with both hands at the shaft, twisting it free of Laurie's grip and pushing back at her at the same time. Laurie stumbled back against the prow, her mouth contorting but releasing no sound as her spine jarred against the rim of the boat. And now Nina was standing with the oar in both hands, the wind catching the wide paddle and spinning it like a weathercock, the grain of the wood shaft grazing against her palms.

'You're my daughter!' Nina shouted, as if that might achieve anything. And sure enough, Laurie only stared at her like an animal uncovered in its burrow.

Nina made to hurl the oar into the water but then she stopped herself, because Laurie wasn't going to just lie there and watch, she was already up from her reclining position, a peculiar motion as though her feet were clamped and she could simply straighten her legs to rise. And Nina considered her options, which amounted to pleading or attacking or escaping, and neither of the first two seemed tolerable and so she launched herself from the left-hand side of the boat and into the black troughs of the sea, still holding the oar in both hands and still not screaming from the horror of it all.

*

In her dreams she had been above the water, facing the storm and its screaming winds. This was altogether different.

Waves slapped at her face and body, trying to fold her into themselves. An undercurrent gripped her legs and her heavy boots which she couldn't begin to unlace and kick off, driving them to one side and then before her, making an acute angle of her body hinged around the horizontal oar, as if it were the restraining bar of a rollercoaster seat and she were a willing thrill-seeker.

This equilibrium lasted only for a moment, though it was enough for her to get her bearings. Though the tide was pressing in, some suction effect of the cresting waves had already pulled her further out to sea rather than into the bay. She would have no assistance in making her way back. She made to hurl the oar away, but as soon as she pulled it from under her body she dipped beneath the surface and her mouth filled. She retched, spat, and held the oar in both hands again.

A twist revealed the motorboat, to one side rather than behind her. Laurie crouched beside the outboard motor.

Nina groaned, then pushed her face under the water to stifle any louder sound.

She spun to face the bay, ducked her head beneath the surface of the water with the oar held out before her like a child's flotation aid, then propelled herself forward.

It occurred to her how alert she felt now, in comparison to her disorientation when she had been following Laurie from the Sanctuary. Fear provided powerful focus. Down here amid the waves, the shriek within her head was indistinguishable from the roar of wind and water.

A sharp buzzing indicated that the motorboat was nearby. Nina let the oar slide along the lengths of her arms to settle beneath her armpits. She pressed down on it in an attempt to hide it from view.

The sound of the motor slipped from left to right, somewhere behind her. Nina forced herself to kick only lightly until its volume diminished. Then she took a grateful breath and kicked wildly again.

She refused to allow herself to think about Laurie's intentions, about Laurie's state of mind, about Laurie.

Kick. Kick.

Breathe.

Kick. Kick.

Kick. Kick.

Head up. Get bearings.

The bay, or at least the profound blackness that had indicated the shelter of the bay, was gone.

Froth and panic swept at her. The sea had shoved her to one side. She trod water and spun, uncertain even of the location of Hope Island.

The sound of the motor.

She pressed her head down, water filling her mouth and sluicing down her throat, but she didn't choke or push against it. She shouted silently at all of this wrongness and struggle.

The motor came. It went.

A blank black mound. An island.

Head down.

Kick. Kick.

Breathe.

Kick. Kick.

Head up.

Perhaps she cried out with the joy of it, seeing the pale lighthouse tower hanging above her. She hadn't been carried as far as she had thought, only far enough for the building to have been hidden by the outcrop upon which it was perched.

Head down.

Kick. Kick.

This time the engine was a roar directly behind her, distant and then immediately close. Instinctively, Nina altered her grip on the oar, holding its blunt tip against her sternum and forcing the other end knife-like into the depths, a swordfish bill cutting and pushing down, down, and just in time: she spun and watched the hull of the boat become a blot where she had been, then the swirling white chaos produced by the outboard motor.

It was safer down here, and less complex. Pressure built within her head, but she allowed herself only a second above the surface before pushing herself down again, slicing through the depths and in her head a jumble of half-remembered prayers.

The blade of the oar tinked against something hard and the jolt travelled through her and roused her once again.

She pressed herself against the rock, dug her fingers into hollows, and scrabbled upwards.

When her mouth opened to shout at all the horror no sound emerged, but she heard it all the same, screaming within her.

But at least the roiling sea was empty of motorboats and daughters.

The lighthouse had disappeared, though that only meant it must be directly above her and this must be the far side of the island's tip. But there seemed no way up.

She turned and worked her way laterally along the rock, towards the black shore. The tide at her back alternated between encouragement and bloody-minded resistance.

Hand over hand, the oar wedged diagonally across her body, chafing at her jaw, hand over hand. She allowed herself to pause for a few seconds to weep. Then breathe and continue, and hand over hand.

Her knees grazed a rock shelf. She scrambled onto it, using the oar as a staff. Underfoot the black rock was hard and sharp and gnarled as coral.

The blade of the oar caught in a crevice. Stumbling and unable to halt, she wrenched it. When she heard the blade snap she felt the first nauseous pang of real grief, and she held up the paddle and stared at it hanging by a stringy sinew and then falling to clatter on the rock, and she spluttered and cried again and couldn't stop.

The moon chanced a glimpse of the island and the wet rock glimmered.

When Nina put her weight on her right foot the shriek in her head shifted down to her ankle.

She pressed her right hand on the torn end of the oar shaft. Splinters dug into her palm. She drove its other end onto the rock and took a faltering step, then again, then again. Her ankle screamed with pain.

At the top she turned. No motorboats, no daughters.

'I'll come back and help you, Laurie,' she muttered, though she had no idea what that might mean.

The open door at the foot of the lighthouse was only metres away. Nina stumbled to it and pulled herself up the ringing gantry stairs, holding what remained of the snapped oar like a runner's baton. She reached the top without having taken a breath.

And—

And Clay was dead, of course he was dead, slumped beneath the radio transmitter console and blood covering so much of him that it was pointless to even try to determine the location of the wound.

Nina stared at the body, paralysed and gasping for air.

Sobs racked her body, each of which threatened to topple

her and put her beside Clay on the floor, a position from which she might never rise.

She remembered her shame after her attempt to kiss Clay. The voice inside her told her she had cursed him. By other means, the voice insisted, she had also cursed Abram and Egg.

Clay had been a good man. He had hated nobody and would have helped anybody. Nina pictured the island children creeping up on him as he worked on the transmitter, surrounding him and then beating him to death. She prayed that he hadn't had time to react or see who was responsible.

She clutched her head at the sounding of a bell within her, deafening and eclipsing her pounding heart.

She heard echoes of the same tolling bell from outside the room. The ringing stairwell footsteps of not one person, not only Laurie, but *many,* and so the only thing to do was to barricade the double doors with chairs and the oar passed through its tough steel handles and then find a spot on the curve of the wall halfway between this new awful threat and the bloody corpse of Clay and crouch there, waiting and trying to remember how to think.

CHAPTER TWENTY-NINE

She waited and didn't think.

The screeching sound in her head swallowed up the world; perhaps beyond the walls of the lighthouse there was white noise and nothing else.

The doors to the room rocked inwards under the weight of the children, but each time the chair and the oar held the doors shut.

The children were strong, but they were still children. Maybe the door would last a while longer.

Wincing at the pain in her foot, she made her way to the far end of the curved room. She gasped and pushed down her fear in order to approach Clay. She couldn't bear to examine him or allow his blue eyes to stare up at her. She shrugged off her coat and, before she could get a clear impression of his state, she flung it over his head and upper body. Then she pulled at his feet, trying not to visualise his cheeks and nose dragging against the rough hessian flooring, smearing blood into the divots between woven clumps. She pushed him up against the outer wall, turned her back on his body and took gulps of stale air.

She wept for him for more than a minute and then she forced herself to stop.

Her first thought was that he had hardly progressed with his repair of the transmitter console, that his murder must have been soon after she and Laurie had left him. But then she saw a new dent in the horizontal panel of the console, and jagged steel at the edges of this crater. The loose wires had been yanked forcibly from the oblong units beneath the lifted fascia, so hard that several of them had snapped. The children hadn't necessarily known what they were doing, but they had sabotaged the equipment thoroughly.

She fought a wave of despondency. The choice was clear: either set to work here or face the demons outside the room. Each thud at the door reminded her that Laurie was out there, too.

The first task was to repair the wires. She pulled at their plastic coverings; before long, her fingertips stung with abrasions from the wires. She rummaged in Clay's tool belt resting on the console. There must be pliers somewhere. When she couldn't find them, she bent beside her rumpled coat, lifted it just enough to locate Clay's hand, eased from it the pliers still held tight, dropped the coat and exhaled again and again and again. The jaw tips of the pliers were spotted with blood. She wiped them on her coat and hoped that the blood was a child's blood, that Clay had died fighting, and then she retched at the thought.

The thumping at the door stopped her from succumbing to despair. She wasn't going to end up like Clay. She would do what she could with the transmitter, and when she failed, she would open the door and go out fighting.

Once the wires had been repaired, she turned her attention to understanding how close Clay had come to operating the transmitter. She inserted jack leads into sockets, allowing some unconscious sense of fit to determine which seemed right, paying scant attention to labels which were as legible as hieroglyphics anyway.

Nothing. She tried other permutations.

Nothing. Try again.

In her concentration the screeching in her head seemed more distant, less of an attack.

In her concentration the hammering at the doors became only a metronome tick.

Nothing. Another permutation.

Nothing.

Then—

It wasn't much, but she saw it. A flicker of a red needle in one of two similar readouts on the sloped rear of the console. She watched the needle intently, holding her breath.

Nothing.

'Come on,' she whispered, and it flickered again.

She slapped her forehead. The red needle jumped.

'Testing,' she said, louder. 'Testing testing.'

The red needle arced to the halfway mark, then dropped. She leant closer to the microphone on its steel stalk segmented like an earthworm, and said, 'Nina had a little lamb,' and the red needle waved happily.

Outside the room, the children thumped harder.

Nina retrieved the fascia of the console and she leant on it with her full weight until it clicked into place.

Until now she had been standing over the console. Now she felt around for the chair and sat. She turned her attention to the right-hand portion of the console, which dictated the broadcast frequencies. Whoever had struck it had cracked the transparent slider that indicated the selected frequency. She pulled out glass shards, but the slider was jammed. Still, though, the frequency dial gave no sign of obstruction when she twisted it.

'Can you hear me?' she said, watching the left-hand needle rise and fall with her voice. She twisted the dial a fraction. 'Can you hear me?' Another twist. 'Emergency. SOS. Can you hear me?'

The red needle within the right-hand eye of the console lay flat and still.

She continued twisting the dial in tiny increments.

'Help,' she said. Her voice cracked a little. She wondered what she would end up using as a weapon to hold off the children, to club her only daughter around the head. A wave of revulsion swelled up inside her, pulsing in sync with the thumping at the door. She rubbed tears from her eyes and returned her attention to the microphone. 'Calling from Hope Island.' She remembered Laurie's comment about there being more than one Hope Island, but had no idea how to specify which this was. 'Emergency. Coastguard, police, fire service, anybody. Please help.'

The right-hand eye winked for a fraction of a second.

Her hand shook as she rotated the dial back a little, terrified of overshooting, losing her place, starting again.

'SOS. This is Hope Island. We need your help.'

The input needle jumped. She heard no sound. She rocked the dial back and forth, homing in on a point where the needle danced without ever falling flat.

'Can you hear me?' she said.

The only thing she heard, though she barely registered it as sound, was an unwavering, high-pitched mechanical squeal which obliterated the shriek in her head.

She pushed at the volume controls; the readouts insisted stubbornly that the speaker was operational. She shifted the console from the wall to examine the wires trailing from the angled speaker. The wires seemed unmolested and plugged into the only sockets that appeared to make sense. The problem must be within the console. She tried to picture herself removing the fascia to prod around again within the guts of the machine. She found no mental image to suggest that she would do it.

'I can't hear you,' she said slowly, 'but I think maybe you can hear me?'

She gazed at the shipping map pinned on the wall behind the console. It was mostly a blue void.

'This is Hope Island calling. Hope Island, close to Monhegan. We need your help,' she said. 'If you're the coastguard, please send a boat. If you're anybody else, please contact the coastguard or the police and relay this message. There's been a... There's been a dreadful accident. Three adults are dead. The children. The children are—'

Murderous? Ill? She cleared her throat. 'Our children are at risk. Please. I'm begging you. Relay this message to somebody who can take us away from Hope Island.'

The red needle had been almost inert, but when she stopped speaking it bounced several times.

'I can't hear you,' Nina said in a choked voice, 'but I can see the audio indicator moving. If you've received this message, please, make three sharp noises.'

The needle dropped to horizontal.

Then it leapt, one, two, three.

Hot tears stung Nina's eyes. 'Thank you. Thank you. Please hurry. We're all in danger here.'

Another flurry of leaps. Then nothing.

Nina released her grip on the radio dial. She slumped.

The squeal of the radio transmitter was sharp as a blade, replacing the shriek she had heard so often recently. This new sound buoyed her, kept her from slipping into the void of exhaustion.

And also—

There were no—

She could no longer hear the bass beat underpinning the treble.

The children had fallen silent.

Cautiously, she rose from the stool, took a few careful steps, gazed at the door still held with its oar and its tilted chair.

It was true. The children had stopped hammering at the door.

Had they gone?

But there *was* another sound, so quiet as to be almost indistinguishable from silence. Nina forced herself to listen.

Her first thought: bubbles. Gurgles. Water, water, everywhere.

No.

Sobbing.

Then:

'Mum?'

A long, drawn-out word. Piercing, even through a wall. Nina imagined rolling over and prodding Rob in the ribcage. They had an agreement, after all. Rob did the nights, Nina needed her brain intact for work, she did the morning duties anyway, didn't she, except when she had to leave the house early which admittedly was more and more often. Over time, Nina had trained herself so that most nights she was able to sleep through the shouts.

'Mum?' Drawn out into four syllables. Pleading.

There was no Rob here, no ribcage to prod.

'Laurie?' Nina said.

'What's happening?' Laurie's voice was almost smothered by the thickness of the door and the whooshing of the transmitter.

She mustn't let herself be taken in. They might be trying a new tactic to get into the room. 'Who's out there?'

A pause. 'Ten children. They're all upset. And there's me. I'm upset too.'

Laurie sounded like herself. When she had woken Nina in the Sanctuary mansion, her confidence, that offhand dismissal of taking Tammy with them, had been unlike her. She had behaved stiffly and strangely, just like the island children. Nina felt suddenly certain that the island children were acting under the influence of something that had made them murderous, and that Laurie had only recently succumbed to the same malign force. The change had been soon after she had toppled into the shell midden. A vision of the bright light she had seen down there flashed into her mind's eye.

But Laurie sounded like herself, now. Nina had to believe that this was really her.

She wanted to fling open the door, but instead she pressed herself against it and said, 'Tell me what you were doing two minutes ago.'

Another hesitation. 'I was trying to get in there. I wanted to get in.'

'Why?'

Two sobs, the second stifled. 'I wanted to get to you. Not for a good reason. I wanted to hurt you.'

Nina clamped her hand over her mouth. Her chin and the skin below her cheekbones spasmed. Weakly, she said, 'How about now?'

She could hardly hear Laurie's answer and she hated the door for preventing her from seeing her daughter's face. 'I want to get to you,' Laurie said sorrowfully. 'But not to hurt you. I don't, Mum, I don't. I feel—'

'You feel what?'

'My head hurts.'

Nina nodded, then rested her forehead on the door. Tears dropped onto the linoleum floor like rain.

'Mum, what's that awful sound?'

Nina, too, winced at the high-pitched squeal of the operational radio transmitter.

This really was Laurie. If Nina had any maternal instinct, it told her that her daughter was behind the door. At that moment, it was difficult to care if she was wrong. She wanted Laurie in her arms.

With difficulty, she unjammed the chair from its diagonal position against the door.

She slid the snapped oar from the handles.

Then she eased open one of the doors.

On the small concrete landing were bodies. The children closest to the door looked as though they had simply fallen on top of one another. They were racked with sobs. Behind them, other children knelt or sat weeping. Two of them were less familiar than the others, their clothes almost entirely shredded, until Nina recognised them as May and Noah Hutchinson. One older child, the Curtiz girl, stood on the lowest step of the stairwell that led to the lamp room, leaning with her full weight on the guardrail as though she might be sick over it. Nina scanned the group. She saw no sign of Thomas Maddox.

Laurie stood before the group. Water dripped from the hair smeared to her cheeks. Her face was pale as ceramic and her soaking wet jumper clung to her thin body. She was shivering uncontrollably. Her arms stretched out towards Nina.

CHAPTER THIRTY

Nina counted the children at the top of the stairwell, and she counted them again when they reached the bottom. At the doorway she spread her arms to block the route back into the lighthouse, ushering them away like an absurd shepherd.

The children followed her instructions blankly. They wept or snuffled or gazed silently at their feet.

The wind had dropped. The rain had become a fine drizzle. The cloud cover was punctuated with glimpses of blue. Beyond the lighthouse the sun was beginning to rise, giving the ocean shimmering yellow zebra stripes.

Laurie clung to Nina's arm until Nina gently pushed her away. The pain from her ankle meant that the oar was necessary as a staff, and she couldn't support her daughter at the same time. They walked side by side and the other children plodded ahead of them in an untidy chevron. It occurred to Nina that they ought to be behind her, in order for the visuals to match her acting as their Pied Piper.

'I knew I was doing it,' Laurie said without turning to face Nina.

'Then why didn't you stop?'

'I did! I did stop!'

And they had stopped, all of the children, at the moment Nina operated the radio transmitter. Its high-pitched hum, *that awful sound*. She thought of a security device installed under the canopy outside her local newsagent, which emitted a tinny drone that she could barely discern, but which warded off the groups of teenagers on their stolen bikes.

That may have been the explanation – and she reminded herself to be on alert for hints that straying beyond the range of the transmitter might return the children to their murderous state – but what was important at this moment was: 'Do you hate me?'

'No!' Laurie said. 'I mean, I don't always *like* you, but that's not the same. And I didn't hate you even—' She made a circular gesture with her hand that Nina supposed indicated the recent past. 'I knew what I had to do.'

'And what was that?'

Out of the corner of her eye, Nina registered Laurie looking at her, but she found she couldn't meet her daughter's eyes. Their embrace when Nina had opened the door of the transmitter room had been awkward, all limbs. But it was impossible to tell whether the strangeness had been due to something being wrong about Laurie, or simply because they embraced one another so rarely.

'I don't want to do it now,' Laurie said, her voice cracking. 'And I'm sorry. I'm very sorry.'

The clouds rearranged themselves to permit sunlight to fall in beams that looked thick enough and solid enough to climb. They made orange stepping stones that dotted the heath ahead.

Nina shielded her eyes. The Sanctuary mansion and cabins had grown; they must already have travelled half the distance from the tip of the island.

Scattered before the buildings were black specks. They were moving.

'Here comes the welcoming party,' Nina muttered. She counted more than twenty figures; the children's parents must have co-opted assistance from the other islanders. She wondered whether they still considered themselves a search party, or whether they might have mutated into something more akin to a lynching party by now.

None of the children, even those whose heads rose occasionally from staring at their feet, seemed aware of the approaching group. Nina drove them onwards.

'What did you feel?' Nina said to Laurie hurriedly. 'When you were trying to get into the room. To get to me.'

Laurie sniffed and rubbed at her face with her forearm. 'I don't know the word. Not anger. It was sadder than that.'

'Like something necessary but awful.'

'Yes. Is there a word for that?'

Nina watched the backs of the children. She would have killed them, and it wouldn't have been only to save herself. 'I don't know. Mercy.'

'Yes.' One slow plod, then another, another. 'Yes. That's what I felt. Mercy. It had to be done. It would have been a… I don't know. A release?'

Something caught in Nina's throat. 'Killing me.'

'Yeah. Killing you.'

The wind caught Nina's poncho, got beneath it, got under her skin. 'Okay,' she said. It sounded like somebody else's voice. 'Thank you for being honest with me.'

The figures shouted as they approached. Alongside the parents of the children were islanders that Nina recognised from Abram's funeral and from the harbour.

When the two groups finally met the parents enveloped their respective children. Nina thought again of white blood cells attacking and absorbing bacteria.

Once their children were smothered safely, the adults turned to face Nina. Their dark expressions made clear that they didn't consider Nina as having delivered their children, only that here she was, again, inexplicably in the centre of a crisis.

'I found them all,' Nina said. She realised she was crying. She forced her sobs to subside. 'They followed me.'

But despite returning the children, Nina would never be accepted by these people. No explanation for what had happened would be plausible.

Yet still she added, 'They tried to kill me.'

The parents shouted questions, too many at once to be understood.

Nina said, 'What took you so long to get here?'

Somebody stepped out from the throng. On her face was a different expression to the others: concern for Nina.

'Marie,' Nina said, and her own voice sounded too loud, as if she couldn't prevent herself from shouting. She wished she could still hear the comforting ringing in her ears.

Marie was carrying her baby. She was holding hands with her son, Thomas, who gazed at Laurie with a mix of curiosity and horror.

'They found Egg,' Marie said.

'I was right?' Nina said weakly. 'He was dead?'

When Marie nodded Nina felt a surge of triumph along with renewed grief.

A shout: 'How do we know it wasn't you who killed him?'

Nina scanned the crowd. It might have been Charlene Jenner or the Curtiz mother, or any number of other women.

'I didn't,' Nina said simply. 'It was the children.'

A roar from the crowd, which had formed itself into a dense mass before Nina and Laurie.

A man Nina didn't know shouted, 'What about her? Are you accusing your own daughter too?'

Nina turned to Laurie but said nothing.

Laurie's lips moved but at first her words were inaudible over the accusations. She swallowed, then shouted, 'I didn't kill Mr Frears!'

She was met with another swell of rage.

Laurie glanced over at Nina; her eyelids flickered, she gulped air. Then she turned back to the crowd. When she held up a hand, incredibly, the crowd became almost silent.

In a voice louder than before, Laurie announced, 'But I tried to kill my mum. I tried to beat her to death, twice.'

Nina watched as the islanders processed the implications. The loopholes. Two lunatic offcomers to Hope Island, mother and daughter. It hardly mattered which of them had committed which crime. It only mattered that the situation might be contained to the pair of them. The dawning sense of relief was palpable.

Nina clung to Laurie as the white blood cells prepared to absorb them. Kelly Brady had pushed his way to the front of the group, his ordinarily florid face crimson with rage. It seemed conceivable that he and the other islanders might tear them both apart.

'Stop!' a voice bellowed.

Si Michaud had run to the front of the group and now faced it with both hands raised.

'Stop,' he said again, less forcefully but without any reduction in volume. 'I saw them do it.'

Nina pictured Si standing at the rise of the hill, beside his workshop hut, looking down upon the south bay. *I didn't see any of them*, he had said.

'I saw your children,' he continued. 'I saw them arrive and I saw them sneak up on Lukas Weber. And I saw them crush his skull with rocks.'

Nina wished that the wind would pick up to fill the silence. Her head ached. Something inside her craved noise, as cacophonous as possible.

'Ali was there,' Si said, pointing at the Jenner boy wrapped around his father. 'Sal and Landon. Chase, Genie, David.' He turned to Marie standing at his side. 'And Thomas. They all did it together. But this girl Laurie wasn't there.'

Kelly Brady turned to look at his followers. Nina saw a couple of the parents hold their children at arm's length in order to look into their eyes. The children snuffled like animals. Some shook their heads, though perhaps from sorrow more than outright denial.

'It's true.'

Thomas Maddox had stepped up onto a rock. A couple of the adults edged backwards.

Nina glanced at Marie. The baby in her arms gurgled happily as loose strands of her hair tickled his face. Marie began to shake uncontrollably.

Thomas looked older now, barely a child at all. Nina remembered his teary-eyed confession about kissing Laurie. He had been free of his earlier malevolence even then. He was the oldest of the children, almost an adult. Whatever had controlled them had already lost its power over him.

'We had to,' Thomas said. 'It wasn't that we wanted to or didn't want to. We just had to, that's all. Laurie wasn't involved.' He took a deep breath. 'The rest of us... some of us killed Lukas, and most of us killed Egg, and we all killed Abram Fisher.'

A sickening silence.

Then—

David Priest fell from his mother's arms. He stumbled and then came to rest on his side in a foetal position.

'Jess?' the woman's husband said, pulling at her arm. She had dropped her child.

Somebody was shouting in a high-pitched voice, but Nina couldn't determine from which direction the sound came.

'Jess? What's wrong?'

Because there *was* something wrong. Jess Priest stood over her fallen son and her mouth hung open. Her head shook, making her features blurred, her lips a horizontal oblong of pink.

She made no sound even as her husband's cries became more pleading and more desperate.

Then he stopped.

The screaming grew in intensity.

But none of the group made a sound.

It *hurt*.

Nina clasped her hands to her neck, pressing her fingers to the flat skin beneath her ears. She was aware that Laurie was standing before her in an odd position, holding Nina's elbows, looking into her eyes.

Suddenly, Nina felt more afraid than she had ever been in her life. Even the renewed pain in her ears and head wasn't as terrible as this fear.

She raised her head stiffly. All of the adults were inert. The children had either fallen or leapt from their arms and now stood peering up at their parents, as curious and hesitant as tourists scrutinising a collection of standing stones.

They were afraid, too, the children. There was no malice in them any longer. They were only children.

'Mum?' Laurie said. Her voice was so quiet, so distant.

Despite her fear, Nina realised that her own body was motionless. The shudders she felt were internal, like ripples amongst her organs, whereas her external body wasn't shivering at all.

Laurie spoke again, but the voice inside Nina suggested that if something was so quiet, what could be the urgency?

So quiet that it hurt. More than the screaming.

Nina's rush of anger was unexpected and alien. How could Laurie permit herself to be so meek? After everything that had happened, where was her rage, her fury, her celebration of this glorious chaos? Her shouts, her screams?

If she had been able, Nina might have throttled her, just to squeeze out a sound.

No. This voice inside wasn't her. What she was thinking weren't her thoughts. She loved Laurie. She had no desire to harm her.

But this wasn't such an unreasonable demand, the voice inside told her. She only wanted Laurie to shout.

From the group of adults swaying on the spot there came a staccato cough.

Another.

It became—

Better.

A shout.

More than one. Many, mingling. A chorus of joy and the best sort of pain. The islanders had lost any trace of their earlier panic. They all shouted in their happiness.

Nina didn't shout but she knew that she soon would.

Laurie's eyes were wide with fear. She spun, saw the group behind her, spun back to Nina.

'Stop,' she said in a voice so small as to be barely anything at all. 'Stop this. Please. I don't know what it is but—'

A clap.

Applause? No.

Slap, slap.

Nina saw the adults' arms rising and then dropping. Slap went their palms on their trouser legs, like tent canvas billowing in the wind.

The storm had ceased so—

They must become the storm.

Slap slap slap slap.

And still the shouting, a shout of no word at all but meaning everything.

Nina saw Kelly Brady drop to his haunches. She had never seen him display anything close to a smile but now he was grinning, his tongue lolling from a stretched-wide mouth. He slapped his palms on the ground and threw back his head and whooped and slapped again.

Others saw, too, or responded to the same instinct. They dropped, punched the earth, slapped their thighs, their shoes, their faces. Genie Mason's father scooped rocks from hollows in the turf, then beat them together hard enough to produce plumes of grey dust.

The children skittered around like insects, trying to lift their parents to their feet, trying to prevent them from hurting themselves.

Nina didn't want to, but she found herself revelling in

the glory of it. Still she didn't move. She realised that she had dropped the splintered oar that she had been using to prop herself up. When others in the group turned and began to move east, the voice inside her agreed it made sense, and so of course she joined them. Five of them, then six, then seven, striding east. Laurie pulled at Nina's sleeve and then her fingers and then her waist, trying to drag her back but why? Why, when this was necessary and right? So Nina shrugged off her jacket and didn't even look back to see what surely would have been a comical sight of Laurie holding the jacket like a skin with no occupant and Nina kept striding, her movements stiff and her ankle infuriatingly weak, and the lack of the oar a problem but her limbs still singing with the pleasure of movement and being used so correctly. The islanders – eight of them now, perhaps more behind, but why would she look back? – clapped and beat upon their bodies a rhythm that eased the shrill pain in her ears, making sense of a melody that until now had been unaccompanied and unmoored.

Some of the older children danced around their parents' legs, trying to make themselves obstacles, failing. They mewled and they were so quiet as to be almost worthless, but it was something and every contribution was good.

She saw Thomas striding alongside to her left. Laurie was pleading with him now: 'Thomas, what is this? Stop. Talk to me.' But Thomas was no longer a child and so of course it was right for him to join the adults, and he ignored Laurie and walked and howled. Good boy. He had two flat rocks in his hands which he clapped together like cymbals and the snap was intoxicating. Nina wondered if he would spin to hit Laurie with one of them and the voice inside her giggled.

And there it was. The entrance to the shell midden. Its black rectangle represented a purity that made the land and sky sickly with confusion and detail.

The voice inside her told her the correct place to stand and told the others too. They made a neat circle around the hole. It felt like being within a family, a real family. The voice told Nina she belonged, finally, and it was wonderful.

Many of the islanders were bellowing at the sky but she realised that her own mouth was still closed. Why couldn't she join in fully? She felt she might weep at her failure to contribute. All these other adults were so close to achieving what they wanted, and yet Nina was adrift and not yet ready.

Even Thomas Maddox's head fell back. He shouted and wept.

His mother beside him mimicked his actions. She shouted and the baby in her arms was forgotten but little Niall didn't mind, he was so happy for his mother and he clung to her and laughed.

Kelly Brady and his red face shouted.

The Curtizes held one another and bellowed to the sky.

Charlene Jenner threw back her head and

fell to her knees and

her head went back further still and

it was beyond natural movement and

something had snapped, just *gone* and

where the rip was exactly, Nina couldn't see and

now there was a hole and

her forehead swung open cracked like an egg like Egg and oh God the sound of it

trapped in an underground railway tunnel on the tracks facing an oncoming train

a whispering choir in an empty cathedral with chaos inches from its heavy doors

sensational speed and a gut punch of glory

It came up and out of Charlene Jenner, hooting with triumph. There was nothing to see.

It screamed and the voice said it was good. Nina's face hurt from her grin.

That sound.

Charlene Jenner's mouth contributed nothing to the chorus. It was clear her body would be limp if not for the pressure being released from within, which held her arms out straight as a crucifix. What was left of her face sagged and her eyes hadn't rolled back as Nina might have expected, but stared directly ahead, at nothing, with no compulsion of direction other than the push from inside.

There were other shouts. Children. They could hardly be expected to understand. Nina and the voice inside her felt pity.

But her envy of the other adults was overwhelming. That sound. To have it come from inside oneself.

For a flash she wished there were something to see, something writhing and soaring above the body of Charlene Jenner.

There was nothing but it was there.

She closed her eyes and fixated on the sound and its harmony within herself.

'—it, Mum!' cried Laurie.

Nina flinched and frowned, a dreamer interrupted.

how could anyone when she was so close why would anybody

Twin thuds from somewhere and a crack and a sigh and then another voice added to the chorus. So sweet, so good.

At the same moment a child's scream.

Nina searched within herself for a trigger, a means of joining them. It wasn't fair that the islanders had had more time to let the voices inside them grow louder and louder. Ever since—

The shell midden.

She opened her mouth wide.

The voice was buried too deep. She wasn't—

'—on, please, Mum, please—'

It was buried and every time she grasped towards this thing it slipped away. It needed time, it wasn't—

She pushed. Clenched, squeezed, pushed. Her mouth made no sound. The air in her throat stung.

She wasn't ready. She wasn't close.

Because—

She had only been on the island a week, had only entered the shell midden a matter of days ago, long after the islanders had entered it. They had surrendered to its song long ago.

Their voices were strong, whereas hers was a whisper in comparison.

Then she felt something. A cord around her waist, pulling her to the ground, pulling her back to shore. Arms.

'—to, you don't have—'

Laurie.

Why was Laurie?

Why was Laurie still?

That sound. It pushed at her chest. She might melt.

The children.

Were themselves again.

They had been ever since.

that awful sound

The radio transmitter. It started and they stopped.

And now suddenly they were themselves but the parents, the adults, were—

That sound. A different sound, profound, maybe divine.

Mercy. A release.

A release.

The same with Egg, that shriek after the slap of the rock on his skull. A release.

The same with Lukas, perhaps, and perhaps even Abram. Release.

Those rocks dropped by children. Mercy. A release.

But now. The children were no longer. So instead—

Nina opened her eyes.

Three adults were on their knees now, their faces slack and identical, their heads cracked open. Others standing around them watching or not watching, not moving, their delight evident. Their children scurrying, harrying, whimpering around them.

'—see me, Mum, can you hear—'

The voice told Nina that she wasn't ready. She wasn't close. It needed time.

The unfairness of it was a physical thing. Nausea, dully real.

She wasn't ready and she would be sick from grief.

Bile sliding up from her belly.

Like.

The salty slip of that oyster down her throat.

A pedestrian sickness. Something alien and wrong that must find its way out from her.

Push.

You can do it, Nina.

Push.

Those fucking oysters.

And then those stories, Tammy's stories, of sickness, parasites, tapeworms.

Like.

This.

In her.

In all of them.

A release. A sickness too great to find a way out by normal means.

A rock to the head would do it but.

The children no longer.

So instead.

She wasn't ready but everybody else was.

An impulse.

A command.

You can do it.

With difficulty, Nina forced her eyes left to look at the black oblong that led to the shell midden. She wanted to be inside it. They all did, the voice inside her said. It was only natural.

Because.

A conviction, a concept of something like home.

More than home. Warmer and better.

An impulse.

Inside all of them.

A command.

You can do it.

The commands came from somewhere outside of them all.

It had to be.

There had to be.

A mother.

CHAPTER THIRTY-ONE

The islanders strode into the pit willingly and the voice inside Nina said that was only right. And they beat on the ground as it rose up above their ears, until their fingertips could no longer reach but then Nina heard their fists against the mud walls of the corridor beneath. She pictured their knuckles sinking into the silt, feeling for anything hard and sharp upon which they might produce a noise or perhaps burst their own skin to at least allow them to find purchase and release a shout of pain. When the first of them reached the floor of the cavern the *crunch crunch crunch* of shell and bone was the most beautiful sound in the world.

Nina wanted nothing more than to beat her hands upon something to add to the song. And she was impatient to join them underground, but she knew that she would be last.

As the islanders trooped into the hole, the neat circle around the pit became a horseshoe as if they were all observing a burial, an image that was hilarious in its inversion of the truth because this was a celebration, and though nobody was smiling, they were singing, in their way, a howl to the sky and Nina knew that when they were all gathered below the ground, the shell midden would do its work and it would amplify their joy and it would be enough.

✳

Finally, it was time.

Concentrate.

The legs, the feet. Her own legs, her own feet.

Part of her, commanded by her, Nina. Not *her*, the mother.

A small step, a giant leap.

Laurie was watching her. Eyes wide, hands grasping.

'—going, where are you—'

Nina knew her movements amounted only to a shuffle. The smallest variation underfoot, minute differences in hardness or softness, forced her to pause, reconsider, gather her strength to begin again.

She must look very funny, sad and funny, a statue teetering forwards from its plinth.

'—go in there, Mum, please don't, don't you—'

Nina's pace became a little quicker. Her feet moved over the ground no more gracefully, but in the stiffness of her movements she found a clockwork momentum.

The black oblong grew before her.

Part of Nina harboured another ambition: to resist what was happening. But it seemed so small compared to the voice inside her, which urged her to revel in it.

And that sound.

That song. Outside and inside. Louder and purer with every faltering step she took towards the entrance to the shell midden.

Nina bumped gently against those waiting ahead of her. She made tiny marching footsteps on the spot.

Laurie had snuck around her. Now she stood on the uppermost step of the corridor to the shell midden. She was holding the snapped oar in both hands, making it a barrier. She pushed at Nina's waist, teeth gritted.

Nina drove her daughter ahead of her. Down the steps, Laurie backwards, Nina wobbling after her. None of the other children accompanied the group. They huddled, clutching at one another, and then Nina descended and they were gone.

That sound, that song.

It was louder, both within her and all around. It whirled close enough to reach out and touch, and it was all the comfort in the world, all the glory. Nina only wished that she could sing along, but the voice within her was immature compared to those within the islanders.

Laurie shouldn't be down here in the shell midden, but her presence hardly mattered. None of the adults were concerned. They all supported one another. Nina gazed at the bobbing heads tramping ahead of her in the passageway. Were they not her brothers and sisters?

But still, that other part of her remained alert.

That other part of her insisted:

These were not her siblings.

Her own parents were long dead.

Laurie was her daughter.

And whatever was down there was not her mother.

But still. They were almost at the foot of the steps.

Her stiff feet found the crunch of bones and shells. Her

eyes rolled back as she swum in the pleasure of the snare-drum accompaniment to the song, that sound.

She saw her kin stiffly stamping, making a circle around the periphery of the dim cavern. They hooted and groaned with their heads back, staring up at the stalactite nothing above and they were *ready*, so nearly ready and though Nina loved them unconditionally she hated them for not waiting for her to catch up.

In the centre of the cavern was a single person, standing on a mound. The tramping of feet around the edge had made a trench in the fragile white struts and crescents that littered the floor, an annulus encircling a pile of unbroken bones. It was Tammy standing in the middle, wearing only a nightgown. She must have arrived before the other islanders; perhaps that meant that she had been one of the first to enter the shell midden, when it was first discovered by the Siblings. Her face flickered between emotions: panic and joy. Her head shook from side to side.

Nina's envy of her was total.

Laurie ran to Tammy immediately and pulled her away from the mound in the centre of the cavern, but Tammy only stared down at her blankly as though she were atop a tall building and Laurie was a speck far below. Laurie cried, and Tammy's cheeks spasmed, and the old woman allowed herself to be led away.

Nina saw her chance; she could take Tammy's place.

Laurie was saying, '—it, won't you *listen* to me, just stop—'

No more than a gnat.

Then Laurie hit Nina with the oar, a slap to the shoulder. Nina didn't flinch.

A nothing.

Laurie wept and pushed and pulled, trying to hold onto both Tammy and Nina at once.

That sound. It was spinning around the outer edge of the cave, drawing air from the passageway and amplifying it and imbuing it with beauty and meaning. Faster and faster, louder and louder.

Laurie stood before her, eyes red from crying. She turned to the empty centre of the cavern.

Nina yelled silently to her limbs to stop the girl, but she had already gone.

Laurie scrambled over the trodden shells and onto the mound in the centre of the annulus.

The envy.

The sound. Crunching and shearing and splintering and oh it was almost too much.

Laurie jumped and stamped and jumped. She drove the blade of the oar down into the pile, again and again, snapping papery artefacts with each strike.

Laurie was not family. These others were Nina's siblings.

Laurie was family. She was all Nina had left.

The song distorted. Beautiful, still, but a queasiness in its broadcast. Nina tried to hang on to its earlier clarity, but it eluded her. For a moment it was the ugliest of shrieks, a poker in the brain.

The crowd of adults parted to form two lines, all bodies facing towards Laurie in the centre, though all their heads still hanging back, eyes up to the blackness.

And on the rear wall of the cavern, a horizontal line. Not quite regular, not quite jagged. Light emanated from within it.

Warmth and the purest sensation of love.

Mother.

But Laurie was stamping still, a distraction to Nina's devotion. From the corner of her eye she saw her daughter crash and smash and cry out.

And there was love in that too. Duller and dimmer and muddled but real.

More real.

Perhaps Laurie was right to be angry?

A new impulse felt both correct and alien at once. It was aligned with Laurie, not *her*. Nina wanted to see her mother, speak to her.

Tammy caught her eye and shook her head.

Nina had no mother.

But all the same.

So, when she burst forwards, she felt no surprise. Nobody commanded her, she had no parents – and up the mound of shells she climbed. The shattering sound made her eyes roll back in near ecstasy, but her trajectory was fixed. She held out both arms, unsure if this was an embrace, but at the same moment Laurie raised her hands in uncertain defence and so instead Nina grabbed at the oar, that totem bound to her by experience. Oar in hand, her momentum drove her further forward. She wavered at the apex of the mound and time froze but then that sound, that song, and the illumination at the rear of the cavern which was part of her and no part of her.

Was it good or was it bad, this impulse? It was impossible to define what was herself. Everything a muddle.

She pushed off with her injured foot which shouted pain and encouragement. She hobbled or maybe sprinted to the rear of the cave. She was in there, her mother. Not *her* mother. *Their* mother, all these obedient islanders standing in formation.

Nina wasn't as ready as the others. She had entered the shell midden so much later than them. Nina still retained a part of herself.

She kept running towards the rear wall.

Nina still retained a part of herself so this impulse was hers, not *hers*. The voice inside her told her it was wrong.

So.

She raised the oar as she ran. She closed her right hand around its splintered end and that pain was good, too.

She was in that hole, behind that wall.

When the blade hit the wall, it was angled precisely along the sliver of light.

The wall shattered, tearing instantly along the rip.

It made no sound.

Nina worked the blade further in, twisting to bring down rubble and dust. Narrow though it was, she could see light.

Push, twist, push.

No sound at all. Until.

A roar, a squeal, a whisper of rage.

The rock crumbled.

And there was nothing to see but it was coming at her all the same. Enormous and nothing at all. It brought with it the suggestion of deafening sound whilst making not a whisper.

It hit her.

And more.

Push, twist, push.

It found its way into her ears first, slithering down the canals.

And her eyes.

And her nostrils. Her fingertips, her fingernails, her pores.

She was *her* and *she* was her.

CHAPTER THIRTY-TWO

The wind spat itself at her; or she was falling into it.

She looked from side to side but saw only the tunnel of her own hair. She was lucid enough to recognise that it was blowing in the wrong direction as she fell.

It was different this time. The wind blustered but her hair provided a thick barrier and she barely shivered with the chill. Other than a tent-canvas shudder the air around her was silent, and so was the voice within her.

Ahead of her she saw a circle of grey expanse framed by the rippling fronds of her hair.

She found her limbs, flexed her fingers. She felt them move.

Tentatively, she reached up to push her fingers through her hair. Her fingertips appeared before her, emerging from the dark mass like newts from a pond. She smiled at them.

She eased aside clumps of hair and craned her neck to peer through the twin gaps to see only more grey. It was impossible to tell if she was moving in relation to it, or if the sensation of speed was only an effect of the wind.

Her fingers moved as fluidly as a harpist's as they walked their way up and around the tunnel of her hair. At the top she again pushed columns of strands aside, rolled back her eyes to see streaks of white, scudding glimpses of crescents, swift motion and chaos.

She was upside down.

She tipped her shoulders to the right, rolling without feeling it. The expanse above her lightened. Her fingertips appeared below once again, pushing aside once again, and now the ocean was beneath her, perhaps fifty metres below.

Flushed with success, she dipped her head, raised her buttocks, saw the water rise up to meet her.

Then in.

Immediately, chaotic forces heaved at her from all sides, pushing at her arms in one direction, her legs in the other, her torso from the front and back at once, squeezing her ribs to snapping point. Whether her eyes were open or closed made no difference; her hair was now an impenetrable mess shuddering around her, sticking to her eyelids and cheeks.

She kicked, she flailed against the cloying water.

She wished that she could arrange a haircut.

She thought of Laurie's neat blond curls.

And then she was gasping and she was grasping at something.

It took all her remaining strength to cling onto the stonework bobbing in the ocean and then to drag herself out of the clinging water that pulled at her legs and tied her shoelaces together and cackled and spat. She lay retching on the tiled roof of a wide building that was almost completely submerged in the ocean, rocking and spinning like a waltzer carriage.

The earlier calmness had been replaced by the fury of a storm. It punched holes in the roof, knocking away tiles to leave gaps through which Nina could see the intact rooms of the Sanctuary mansion. A mural on a wall depicting the precise nightmare in which she was trapped.

And yet despite the groan of the wind, the creak of masonry wrenched in different directions, the slap of the waves against the stone and the tearing away of wood cladding, Nina found the sound no more troubling than the flapping of geese coming to rest on the surface of a still lake, because these sounds were earthly, and the *other* sound was absent. It was only now that she perceived how shrill the shriek within her had become. It was only now it was gone that she remembered what it was to hear.

Around the mansion and halfway submerging it was the sea, the sea, the sea.

She rose to her haunches, balancing on the sloped roof, resting her hands on the tiles. She smoothed down her hair, which was dry. There was no headland in sight, no indication of anything to interrupt a horizon deformed only by swells and the crests of waves.

Nina understood that she wasn't alone.

She turned to face the person who stood at the apex of the roof, unaffected by the queasy sideways lurch that threatened to overturn the building.

Like Nina's, her hair was dry. Her eyes, too, were wide.

She, too, wore a plain black skirt, a slouchy red woollen jumper that slipped off her right shoulder, and beneath that, Nina knew, a grey vest with *Oh yeah?* scrawled in white.

They watched one another as the storm raged overhead, as Nina found the means of anticipating the boat-like rocking of the building, as she rose to her full height, as the other her remained impassive with arms at her sides.

'Are you inside me?' Nina said.

This other Nina watched her without any indication of recognition or interest.

Nina tried to imagine her body – her real body, outside this nightmare. She tried to sense her real limbs. She could perceive nothing except what was here: the ocean, the masonry beneath her feet, her and another her.

She felt utterly lost. Her facade, based on her triumph at having ignored the voice inside her, crumbled. What had she done to herself?

The other Nina's cheeks creased into a grimace of despondency, mirroring her own. It restored Nina's confidence.

'So,' Nina said, forcing her voice to remain level. 'Explain this.'

The other Nina watched her silently.

'I came to you of my own free will,' Nina said. The mansion wrenched to one side and something like thunder shouted but it was no more than a whisper and she remained standing firm. 'I came here to talk to you.'

Some catalyst brought the other woman to life.

'I came to you,' she repeated—

—and at the same moment Nina clasped her hands over her ears in an attempt to block out the squall of noise that pierced everything, reached everywhere, became everything. More roof tiles shattered and fell into the belly of the building; Nina leapt to one side as the tiles beneath her feet gave way.

But then it was over, and nothing had happened. They were ordinary words from a mouth exactly like her own.

'Who are you?' Nina said.

The other Nina opened her mouth. Nina's body tensed.

Nina shook her head hurriedly. 'That's not my question. Tell me this. Are you their mother?'

Open mouth, showing teeth, a Halloween grin without any discernible difference to the reflection Nina saw every morning.

'Their mother, their queen,' the other Nina said—

—and Nina's mouth contorted at the pain the scream the white the black.

Nina gasped and spat onto the tiles. 'I can't. It's too much. You're too much. Too much like—'

But then she looked up and the other Nina was no longer there.

'Is this better?' the woman before her said and now she was Tammy, from her perm to her poise.

And the pain was gone.

'That's better,' Nina said. 'Now we can talk. That's what you want, isn't it?'

'I want nothing,' Tammy replied, the tiny disapproving shake of the head unmistakably hers. 'None of this is as you perceive it to be. These are impulses, the triggering of synapses. This is not a conversation. This is not a meeting of minds.'

Nina shivered, but refused to succumb to her fear. 'You're inside me, aren't you? This is my territory. Whatever this is, I want you to explain.'

Tammy looked up at thunderclouds the shade of cauliflowers past their best.

'Not all this,' Nina said. 'I want you to explain *yourself*.'

Tammy nodded slowly. 'I come to you in a familiar shape because I – we – have no physical form.'

'You exist as sound?'

'Quite so.'

'But you need physical form. You're in my body right this second.'

Tammy released a tinkling laugh. 'Not so. Consider this a courtesy and nothing more.'

Nina snorted with nervous laughter. Her fingers tugged at the wool of Laurie's jumper.

'And how about these others like you?' Then she ventured, 'Your children.'

'That is another matter. They require physical hosts only while incubating. After that point they are free.'

'And that's what we've been? Hosts? Everybody on Hope Island. Everybody who—' Nina's eyes darted as she processed the facts. 'Everybody who entered the shell midden. We all became hosts.'

'It is a necessary part of the incubation process.'

Nina thought of the shout that Egg had released, not from his mouth but from deep within his body. It had been this mother's child. The same with Lukas and Abram. A child hurtling out from a belly. A beautiful thing.

'There is no malice,' Tammy said plainly.

'But your children are parasites,' Nina said distantly.

Tammy laughed again. She fixed Nina with a level stare.

'Isn't that true of all children?'

Nina didn't allow herself to dwell on that. 'But not everybody on the island responded in the same way. The children – *our* children, human. You affected them differently.'

'Your infants and juveniles are too underdeveloped to accommodate one of our kind. They too were impregnated, but without hope of incubation. They too have fulfilled their role.'

'You've been controlling their actions.'

A nod.

'You ordered them to smash the skulls of the adults carrying your children.'

A coy little smile.

'To release your children once they were fully incubated.'

'When the time came, yes.'

'But now our children can't hear you, can they?' Nina's mind ran over the events at the lighthouse. 'I'm guessing you encountered some interference?'

The high-pitched sound coming from the radio transmitter. Nina had done good work. She and poor Clay.

Tammy raised both hands. What began as a shrug became something more introspective; she turned her hands, examining the lines on her palms, then the veins on the backs.

Lightning arced above her and the roof tiles rattled against their nails.

'No matter,' she said airily. 'In almost every case the incubation of each child is close to completion. And a simple call to release them forcibly requires very little subtlety.'

A wide grin revealed perfect false dentures. A flicker of something in the eyes. Nina had seen it before. Tammy lying on the bed, mouth slackly open, all the pain in the world in her looseness. She wished that she had given the old woman something, then. Forgiveness, understanding. A hug.

'You're lying,' Nina said. 'Yes, I believe you can trigger the release. But until now, you relied on the island children to release your children from the hosts. You wouldn't be here talking to me if you didn't have to. You need me, my body, instead of staying tucked away in the shell midden. Am I acting as a – what? An amplifier?'

Tammy's eyebrows raised in surprise.

Growing in confidence, Nina gestured at the ocean that surrounded them and said, 'I think all of this is costing you.'

A sudden fire in Tammy's eyes. Those terrifying white teeth that might spring wide to consume her.

Tammy fell to her knees, clutching her stomach, then put one hand onto the roof tiles to hold her upright. The building rolled and Nina rolled with it. Tammy slid onto her side and the rocking swilled Nina like brandy in a glass.

Suddenly, with a deafening crack, all of the remaining roof tiles splintered and dropped as one into the interior of the building. Nina sprung away to clutch an angled wooden beam; it hit her smack in the stomach. The pain reminded her that she, too, carried one of these parasite children within her. But she shook the thought away and concentrated on her legs swinging beneath this new skeleton of a rooftop.

Tammy was above her, strolling along the beams like a tightrope walker.

Nina renewed her grip on the beam. Ocean spray slapped at her. The building was sinking. She gazed down to see the room in the Sanctuary mansion where she had watched over Laurie in her fever. Within three of the beds she saw huddled shapes.

She turned to look back up at Tammy's suddenly ancient face.

'I will stop you,' Nina said.

There was a world out there, beyond this cavernous sky and bottomless sea. There was a world out there and everybody she had ever known was in it. There was a world out there and Laurie was somewhere close by, watching all of this, watching Nina struggling with this voice inside her. There was a world out there and there was a way out and a way back, but it wasn't time yet.

Nina pushed herself away from the beam as Tammy reached her. She dropped into the depths of the building.

She had aimed for the only unoccupied bed, but rather than provide a soft landing it exploded like ice upon impact. Agony bloomed from everywhere – not only from within Nina's body, but from the walls and the jagged clouds glimpsed through the hole in the roof.

She scrambled to her feet, ignoring the pain. She approached Laurie's bed, shook the huddle under its covers, pulled the blanket away: nothing. She dashed from bed to bed, exposing the ghosts, gasping at the absences.

The ground shook and the floorboards cleaved and angled sharply as something immensely heavy landed behind her. Nina turned to see a woman sunk into a crater that her landing had made in the floorboards.

The woman raised her head enough to gaze at Nina with rolling eyes, and drooled onto the slats. Then she struggled to her feet and brushed herself down. She wore a tight white T-shirt and stonewashed jeans. Her face was perfectly circular and symmetrical. Too much mascara. Fair hair. At first Nina didn't recognise her or didn't want to, but it was Kaytee. Nina realised she had no idea of her surname.

'That's not fair,' Nina said.

'I bear you no malice,' Kaytee said. 'This is about protecting what's mine.'

'Sure.' Wearily, Nina looked her up and down. 'This is the first time I've seen her. Good body, especially for a mother of two.'

Kaytee glanced at her own body. 'This woman means something to you.'

'Not especially.'

'This woman causes you pain.'

'Only in a roundabout way.'

'No.'

Something hit Nina from within her belly. She gulped air but refused to allow herself to bend double. She smacked her lips, swallowed. A rusty taste in the mouth.

'You tell me there's no malice,' she managed to say, 'but you've killed. People are dead. Because—'

'—because it is the only way. This is about responsibility.'

Kaytee reached out a slim bare arm. She was still a metre away from touching.

Nina was overcome with terror and the knowledge that her life could be extinguished at any moment.

'No—'

Nina puked a stream of yellow onto the floorboards.

She stared at the pool of vomit which became a slithering river matching the violent movement of the building, collecting, returning, collecting, returning.

She raised her head.

Kaytee wiped her mouth. She blinked rapidly. She took her hand away and smiled an easy smile.

'This is costing you,' Nina said again—

—and at the same moment Kaytee said it too.

'This is no courtesy, is it? You're not even trying to punish me,' Nina said. 'You *need* me.'

Kaytee smiled again, though perhaps now with a trace of uncertainty. She raised her right hand, looked at it, turned it, extended her index finger to point at Nina.

Nina felt it as a spear in the gut. Her jaw clacked as her mouth stretched too wide. No scream but all the hurt that ever there was.

With difficulty, Nina said, 'You're doing this to protect your children. I understand that.'

'And you?' Kaytee said.

Nina thought of Laurie, somewhere nearby, her fair hair so much more like Kaytee's than her own, the hurt inside her the day Laurie was born, push, Nina, push, you can do it you can do it, it'll come with time don't worry it just takes time she needs you it's not about liking it's instinct you don't need to be here for her to know that you love her she'll be okay but won't you please just sometimes show your face?

'I'm doing this to protect my child,' Nina said.

Another smile, a leer, full lips and a hint of cheekiness that Rob would surely appreciate.

'When you've released your children, you'll kill *our* children,' Nina said. 'They'll have served their purpose.'

A curt nod, barely a flicker of conscience.

Nina continued, 'But you won't be unscathed. This wasn't your plan, to release them forcibly. This is killing you.'

A hint of a chill in that smile now.

'You're not like your children,' Nina said, feeling increasingly sure of herself. She looked up at the darkening clouds through the splintered beams. 'You're not incubating like the others. You can't exist within a host – within me. You may need my body to act as an amplifier for your command, but being inside me is killing you. But you *want* that. You want out of me, you want my…' She paused to think. '…shout. You want my shout to make it happen. It'll kill me, and you'll die too, and you're doing it for them.'

Kaytee's face was unsuited to grief, and it barely lasted. She covered her eyes, giggled, dropped her hands and then she was Laurie. But not Nina's Laurie, not the Laurie out there in the world; a Laurie yet to come. A leanness to the face, cheekbones where there should be meat. A plain dress, more like Nina's usual attire than Laurie's. Her hands now resting on the bulge of her belly. Pride in her eyes.

'Pain,' Laurie said simply, and Nina doubled up with it.

Nina shook her head, looked at her feet. Twisted her fingers into the wool of Laurie's borrowed red jumper flecked with spittle.

'You're more a mother than me,' Nina said.

'I'm more a mother than you,' Laurie said. Her voice was lower than usual, an assuredness that had grown and would continue to grow like the baby in her womb.

Another hit in the gut.

'You'd do anything for your children,' Nina said without looking up.

'I'd do anything for my children.'

Nina winced, push, push, pushed away the pain. Lightning cracks appeared on the walls of the room. The building seemed moments away from disintegration.

She pulled herself to her feet and grabbed at a chest of drawers painted with roses, their stems interlocking curlicues. She heaved each drawer open only to find her own clothes jammed messily inside. She ignored them and scrambled upwards, using the drawers as steps.

'This is killing you,' Nina said, looking down at Laurie from her vantage point near the skeletal roof. 'But you'd die for your children.'

'I'd die for my children,' Laurie said, and she seemed happy enough about it.

A thud from everywhere.

Nina fought the pain, trying to gather herself enough to consider her next move. She looked up and then at the wall. The cracks in the plaster were so pronounced now that she could press her fingertips into the crevices. Her boots skittered until they found purchase.

Laurie watched from below, her expression unreadable.

Nina scrabbled and grunted as she worked her way upwards, the wall shuddering beneath her body, the building leaning so that sometimes the wall was horizontal, sometimes tipping backwards so that she had to cling on by her nails.

She threw her arm up and hit a roof beam, pushed her palm onto the splinters, used the pain to keep her going.

Somehow, Laurie was already on the rooftop. She shook her head sadly.

The storm clouds gathered to form a grey anvil above their heads.

The sea became a single wave that grew and bent in a gargantuan curl above the mansion roof.

This wasn't Laurie.

Nina heard the thunder the crack the thunder the crash the beating of sticks and feet on rocks and bones and shells.

In the sky she saw Laurie's eyes, her Laurie, the Laurie, enormous and ghostly and staring into hers.

The wave grew, threatening to block this vision of her daughter.

There was a way out.

Nina bent her legs and then dived from the rooftop to meet the wall of the wave in the midst of the roar of everything. Every part of her body sang with pain and relief as she met its vertical surface and it shook her awake and around her the islanders beat upon the ground, the walls, themselves and Laurie was here oh Laurie and they embraced and it would be okay.

CHAPTER THIRTY-THREE

It would be okay.

'It will be okay,' she said, or tried to say.

The islanders encircled Nina. Stamping, slapping upon their bodies, heads back, staring sightlessly upwards. Tammy's eyes had rolled so far back that her pupils had disappeared.

Nina stumbled backwards, tripping on the debris from the rooftop of the mansion, which she knew oughtn't to have been here within the shell midden.

She was still partly within the dream. The dream was still partly within her.

She wasn't free of the queen, the mother. She wouldn't be, until the shout, and then it would all be over.

There were other people standing alongside the islanders, stamping and hollering within the shell midden and on the roof of the mansion beneath the curl of the wave in the dream.

Men and women, grimy with stooped backs, barely clothed.

Nina understood who they were.

These were the earlier hosts of the parasites, the children of sound. The voice inside her moaned at the thought of their tantalisingly warm insides.

More prehistoric people arrived from the cavern opening that was barely discernible against the glare of the sky all around. They dragged shells and bones into the cavern and then beat sticks upon them with magnificent ferocity, hooting and gabbling, their arms grazing the stone roof and piercing the surface of the overhanging tidal wave. Their glorious racket nourished the children – *her* children – that they bore within their flesh, feeding them unadulterated noise.

This was *her* time. She revelled in what was to come. *Her* children would soon be freed.

we can do it we can do it we can do it

The shell midden was no waste ground. It had always been a birthing ground.

The modern islanders retreated to allow the prehistoric tribe more space. When the first skull split open, both groups howled at the glory. Then another, then another, the filthy faces falling apart and *her* children spewing forth.

go go go be free

Though the children were made only of sound, it was as though Nina could see their trajectories. She sensed their confusion and their pain as they ricocheted from unfamiliar surfaces: rock, water, flesh.

Only one member of the tribe remained standing. A man, ancient, with lank hair and scars on his back. He spun and gazed upwards at the opening to the shell midden. He filled his lungs and shouted, but it was an ugly shout, a shout against life and not in favour of it.

Nina froze as she looked up, too, at the coffin-shaped opening which appeared as much part of the hanging tidal wave as part of the cavern.

She felt the panic of the children and of *her* and it was her panic too.

faster faster be free

The echoes, the children of sound, rattled from surface to surface, clawing their way blindly towards the opening.

The queen, the mother, understood what was happening even before Nina saw the silhouettes standing at the hole, framed against the blinding liquid sky.

'No!' they both cried out in horror.

The ancient tribesman raged at the figures outside the hole, gesticulating with raised hands.

The figures drew closer to the hole and then the hole shrunk.

It was closing. A stone was being placed over it, sealing it.

The echoes, the children, understood little of what was happening, other than that it was bad.

The hole snapped shut like an eyelid and the cavern was black.

The children punched at the huge stone, doubling back and charging again, but could find no purchase, no glimmer of a gap.

They whirled around the cavern, around the tunnel beneath the tidal wave, flinging masonry and screaming, slapping against the lifeless bodies of the tribespeople, deafening and driving insane the traitorous elder.

Nina understood.

They would be trapped for their entire lifespan, these echoes, these children. They would whirl around and around this cavern for many hundreds of years, but they would gradually diminish, becoming drones and then hums and then nothing, instead of piercing shrieks of blazing life.

But *she* would survive, though barely. The queen, the mother, would watch her children suffer, becoming nothing more than loops of feedback, and then expire. The waste of it would be intolerable.

But *she* would cling on to her own life and she would raise another brood, when the time was right.

Nina tried to ignore the scattered corpses of the tribespeople. She tried to ignore the modern-day islanders who now circled around her, the whites of their rolled-back eyes shining, their tongues hanging loose as they bellowed.

She turned to face the hole at the rear of the cavern. There was nothing. No light, no sound. *She* was no longer in there.

Laurie was facing her, edging forwards as Nina shuffled back. Her wide eyes were luminous in the dark.

The voice inside Nina told her what to do.

The other part of her lost its grip. She did what the voice wanted.

She found herself atop the pile of bones and shells in the centre of the cavern but at the same time she was tiptoeing lightly on the surface of the water, in the hollow curl of the enormous grey wave.

The voice inside her said yes yes yes.

She felt unbalanced, lacking proprioception, her limbs hardly her own. A shout in her belly her feet her fingers but also a silence that made every shuffle of the men and women that surrounded her a crash of cymbals.

'Mum?' Laurie said in a voice coming from very far away, beyond the roar of the sea.

Nina's eyes watered.

Nina was still in here, too.

It would be okay.

'It will be okay,' she said quietly, but Laurie clapped her hands over her ears and squeezed her eyes tight shut and crumpled to her knees.

I'm sorry, Nina didn't dare say.

From the mouths of the islanders came a droning sound of freight trains and avalanches and the collision of planetary bodies. The tidal wave hung above, enclosing them all, waiting.

Laurie gasped and sniffled and stared up at her mother.

'What are you?'

Nina shook her head. She was *her* and *she* was her.

That sound.

Laurie was staring at Nina's belly and so Nina looked down too. Through the red woollen jumper, through the *Oh yeah?* vest, she saw strips of light. The sound, too, was coming from there. Nina felt a rush of pride at the voice inside her. That sound, that beauty, held within her and ready to come out. And in doing so, she would release all of *her* children from the ugly flesh.

She twisted her fingers into the wool and bunched and lifted.

Stretched across her belly was a lattice of searing light. Her skin looked like stone in contrast to the glimpses of fire.

Beautiful.

You can do it, the voice inside her said.

The queen, the mother, was in there. The mother wanted out. She would burst out of Nina's belly and the shout and the pain of it would release all of the incubating children at once. And Nina and the mother would die, of course, but the voice explained that it was only right and natural.

Nina pushed her fingertips into the cracks in her stomach. Her flesh was brittle at the edges. There was no heat, but the skin of her fingers fizzed and hummed, shaking with the sound. It came from within her and then into her hands, then into her body again and into her hands. The feedback loop amplified the sound with each revolution, not degrading but instead gaining in clarity.

But her fingers didn't have the strength, the purchase.

The oar found its way into her hands. She held the snapped end to her belly. Its splinters teased into the fizzing gaps.

She eased the blade of the oar up, offering it to Laurie, pleading. Laurie held it and stared at it and then at Nina.

Laurie shook her head.

The voice raged. Children were wonderful things, but hateful too. Children should respect their elders.

The mother wanted out. It was only right.

Nina struggled to gain purchase on the flat of the oar, but it was too far away for her to put her fingers around it.

It slipped from her grip.

Inside her the shout out out out.

A swoon.

This had not been Nina's plan. When she had leapt from the rooftop, she had intended to stop this very thing from happening. The queen coming out from her belly would trigger the release of every one of her incubating children. It would kill Nina, and the queen, and more than that, it would mean the deaths of anyone acting as a host, and surely all of the island children, and Laurie too. All that would be left would be dead bodies and blazing sound: the children of a sacrificed mother, rising to meet the wind and then gone.

In the periphery of her vision, at the foot of the curl of the wave, at the edge of the cavern, Nina saw Kelly Brady fall to his knees beside the bodies of the prehistoric tribe. His head broke open and out came the song.

Inside Nina's belly a shout of triumph a sob of sadness.

She pulled the oar towards her and a shout from somewhere of yes.

But another part of Nina plunged her face, her arms, her torso into the water and sought around for another voice and a shout of no.

She thought:

You're more a mother than me.

You'd do anything for your children.

And the voice within her screamed yes.

But then Nina thought:

I'm less of a mother than you.

I am

But

Laurie stared up at her, both hands on Nina's waist, face illuminated by the light from Nina's belly.

For a second Nina saw the older Laurie, lean and mature. She thought:

I am like *her*, this mother.

I too want my child to live.

But I'm not prepared to die.

Because she wanted to see Laurie, to know Laurie, her Laurie and the Laurie yet to come, the Laurie with a baby in her belly and all the Lauries before and after.

It was a weakness.

It was a strength.

It was neither, but it was the difference between them, Nina and this mother, this queen.

The oar dropped from her hands.

The voice inside her screamed no.

Instead, Nina began to push, from the belly upwards. She opened her mouth and the light in her belly dimmed and then became ever more ferocious.

Laurie shouted no.

*

Nina pulled together all of herself that wasn't *her*, gathering herself into a dense bundle, a dazzling sun. And she pushed she pushed you can do it and push and push and the pain was excruciating and everything howled no and yet the sun began to rise, away from her belly but not away from *her*, instead pulling *her* along too, a sun swallowing another sun, dragging *her* despite the fingernails dug into the flesh of her belly, no no no never I won't you can't.

Up from the belly, up through the throat, pushing the tongue flat down in the rush to release.

CHAPTER THIRTY-FOUR

Now scream.

CHAPTER THIRTY-FIVE

Nina screamed.

The wave broke and still Nina screamed.

The water rushed into her mouth and still she screamed.

She felt parts of her snag and be pulled away, dragged upwards from the belly, from the throat, through the mouth, and still she screamed. The queen burst upwards shouting no, tangled within Nina's own echoes, her past and her guilt and her shame, pushing out of her along with everything else, all shouting yes yes yes.

In this scream was everything Nina no longer wanted or needed.

From the crest of the wave Nina saw a man fall, tumbling like a teddy bear.

Rob shouted as he fell.

Nina screamed but it was real and good and there was no pain. It was a scream not of frustration and anger but of letting those things go.

Something large slipped from the sky, following Rob. A structure: a building, a house. At first Nina thought it was the Sanctuary mansion, but no, it was far smaller. It was her own house, with its wall creeper that she had never identified or tended, its dirty windows, its decades of life lived within.

She screamed with the anticipation of future joy.

Along with the spray, bricks and timber fell shredded from the house leaving nothing but the plop of pebbles in the ocean.

*

Nina trod water and cast around. A little way away, Rob raised both arms and then, gasping, bobbed away. She was certain he wouldn't sink. Somebody else would find him.

A final crash of masonry from above. Something floated into Nina's line of vision. The front door of her house, its navy-blue paint peeling to reveal the yellow that she had loved, and which Rob had painted over.

It had been a long time since they had seen eye-to-eye. She pitied them both for their many years of pretence.

She clung to the floating door and kicked her legs, staring up at the enormous tidal wave.

She held her breath and ducked her head. For a fleeting moment she was submerged, but then she was through the body of the wave and out again.

Here the sea was calm and tidy.

The coast was not so far away.

On the shore was Laurie, waving.

✳

Nina screamed with certainty at her triumph. The queen, the mother, grazed and tore at Nina's flesh in her attempts not to leave.

Push, push, up and out.

We can do it.

She screamed and wept for the children still buried within the soft stupid flesh of the islanders and she screamed and wept for Laurie.

One last push.

A shout like nobody ever before. Her nails digging into Rob's forearm. His eyes white and wide with horror and the shame of what he had done to her.

Up and out and scalding with sound.

Her head fell back, and she watched.

She saw nothing emerge.

But she heard it.

The queen, the mother, hurtled through her throat and out of her mouth. It burst directly upwards like water from a blowhole. Nina saw nothing and yet she sensed its path as if it were visible. It struck the roof of the cavern, calved in two, spinning to either side only to hit walls then disperse again, darting to gather itself but baffled by the complexities of its own echo, itself slipping away from itself, chasing itself as though in a centrifuge, roaring over the loss of its children still trapped in heavy flesh, and then the queen, the mother was spat from the corridor and up and out once more, skywards, diminished and scrabbling to draw itself together but more and more lost with every passing second.

The islanders' bodies straightened as they saw that the shout had ended. Nina recognised faces, recognised Tammy, bedraggled and wide-eyed, and she recognised Laurie before her, gazing up at her, holding Nina's hands that Nina now rediscovered for herself. The hands were hers, not *hers*, and she was still here.

*

Somebody raised her to her feet. Somebody wept at the bodies that lay toppled sideways on the snapped shells. Somebody called out of the hole and somebody staggered down to help.

Somebody turned the streaks of dawn to blazing daylight and somebody brought a truck.

Mikhail spoke for the first time. Enunciating slowly and without an accent, he said, 'I will concrete up that fucking hole.'

CHAPTER THIRTY-SIX

Nina watched the helicopter spread a series of concentric circles across the water in the harbour bay, then she waved at it as it slid behind the hillside. She nodded in time with its thuds, then continued nodding in the same rhythm even after they became inaudible.

Laurie, sitting beside her on the harbour wall, was watching her. Nina smiled and Laurie smiled back – a smile that had become less brittle and afraid with each appearance – and that was all that was needed.

Her child.

She thought of the other child that had been inside her, only yesterday, only ever sensed dimly. A child made of sound, growing, waiting. Its absence felt like a loss.

Last night Nina had woken startled in Tammy's bed, where they had huddled with Laurie lying between them. It had been her own shouting that had woken her, a sound that slipped unwanted from her throat, but inert and without anger. Neither Tammy nor Laurie had mentioned it this morning. An unsettling thought had occurred to Nina. An attempt to imagine what a miscarriage might be, to these creatures of sound.

Despite everything, Nina wished *her* well, the queen, the mother. She wished that she might find those few children that had incubated in their hosts and been released. What had happened had been due to instinct, like any other animal, like any other mother. Now that the mother and part of her brood were free, Nina had to believe that they would no longer trouble the islanders or anybody else. They were only echoes.

But a sob broke up within her, forcing its way from her throat. She gave it voice and then bobbed her head drunkenly, gasping with gratefulness as Laurie took her hand and stroked it.

Because, of course, Abram and Egg had been among those hosts. They had given their lives to provide the parasitic children of sound entry to the world. So many had died, including Clay, whose death had been senseless in comparison to the others, and which pained Nina more than any. She knew that her grief for him would accumulate within her, and she knew that when she gave it voice it would be deafening. For now, she felt as silent on this matter as one of Clay's recordings of empty buildings.

She hadn't yet attempted to quantify how many of the island population had perished in the shell midden. The harbour was almost empty of people, though she knew that many were huddled together in the Sanctuary mansion, and some had taken bedrooms in the Open Arms, the hotel having been requisitioned by the islanders following the death of Kelly Brady. The calm this morning was a reflection of the scale of the shock and grief. But the quiet couldn't last.

In the absence of the helicopter's rotor blades, Nina listened to the hulls of small boats bumping against the jetty, the cackle of gulls, the mutter of water lapping against stone and an elderly woman outside the grocery store, fiddling with a vivid orange bag-for-life that rippled in the breeze.

Nina shuddered and pulled the cuffs of her coat down, covering Laurie's fingers gripped in her left hand.

Tammy approached them. She pointed up at the hillside, but she meant the departed helicopter.

'The place will be crawling with them soon enough,' she said.

It was the second visit from the Marine Patrol today, and soon boats would bring police and enough yellow-and-black-striped tape to make a new periphery within the Sanctuary walls, enclosing the bodies of the islanders who had died in the shell midden.

And the police would want to talk.

All that noise.

Perhaps Laurie could read her thought processes. 'They'll need a statement from you, Mum. Maybe more than one.'

Nina nodded. Her neck ached. She loved Laurie.

'What will you say to them?'

Nina cleared her throat, wincing at the sensation of floating, torn ribbons in there. If she let herself notice it, every part of her hurt. Hoarsely, she said, 'I'll play it by ear.'

Tammy smoothed down her lavender skirt and crouched before the pair of them. 'I only wish we could convince you to stay with us. Why in heaven's name would you want to be alone right now?'

Nina mustered a smile for Tammy's benefit, trying to grasp her earlier train of thought that had led to her decision. Sleeping all together in a double bed was a three-way closeness that would never be replicated, though perhaps the fact that it had occurred might underpin her future relationship with Tammy, their shared responsibility for Laurie.

'I know it seems wrong,' she replied. 'But I don't want to be in the way. And honestly, I need the peace and quiet.'

Tammy inhaled, offered a trembling smile and then a sharp couple of nods. Then, to Nina's surprise, she turned on her haunches and settled into a sitting position on the crazy-paving, her shoulders against the low wall, nestled between Nina's dangling left leg and Laurie's right. Nina exchanged glances with her daughter, then turned to face the water. She laid her hand gently on Tammy's head and stroked her hair. The sun came out from behind a cloud, reflecting from the windows of the hotel, making her squint before she allowed her eyelids to slide shut, to enjoy the warmth and marmalade glow.

These two women. The three of them, together. Something like joy, something not for words.

'I can see it,' Laurie said.

When Nina opened her eyes again, she saw the snub white ferry approach. It made swift progress across the still water.

She placed her fingers into the handle of her suitcase, fiddling with the green ribbon that was its only real identifying mark on airport carousels.

The world was nothing like she had thought. There were things out there that she would never understand, no matter how closely she or anyone else investigated them.

But she had other priorities.

'Well then,' she said. 'I guess here he is.'

They all stood.

'You're sure you're sure?' Tammy said.

Nina embraced Tammy, then turned and hugged Laurie twice as hard. The feel of that little body against hers.

Her throat was dry and sore. She looked forward to not speaking to anyone for a while.

'Goodbye for now,' she said.

Laurie blinked rapidly. The tips of her eyelashes glistened. Nina would never in her lifetime love anybody more.

She lifted the suitcase in a waist-high salute. Then, as Laurie and Tammy turned to face the ferry, she left them.

At the foot of the jetty she shielded her eyes to look at the ferry, remembering her own fingers on the peeled white paint of its barrier. She smiled at the row of passengers wearing dark uniforms, gazing out at Hope Island.

She climbed the incline to the Open Arms, then up its two steps to stand on its wooden porch. She put down the suitcase and took a seat in one of four unoccupied reclining chairs.

Within minutes the ferry docked, its crunches and clinks echoing from the hillside and back to the harbour front.

She watched Tammy and Laurie walk to the jetty.

The passengers began to disembark. One jogged ahead of the uniformed police officers.

She smiled as she watched Rob run along the jetty to embrace his daughter. At this distance she was only able to examine his posture, his outline. Neither seemed at all familiar to her.

It wasn't Rob's fault, their growing apart. Regardless of him inheriting Abram's tendency to stray, regardless of his obvious betrayal and the cowardice of taking so long to decide to leave, Nina had no claim over him. More importantly, she realised that she no longer wanted him any more than he wanted her. That wasn't her fault either.

In the nightmare she had found herself face-to-face with women against whom she measured herself. Allowing Rob to float away had been almost emotionless, a decision already made subconsciously, long ago. And she had been given the opportunity to give voice to her frustration, at last. Her scream that had expelled the queen had also expelled her anger.

She wasn't afraid. She would meet with Rob, and they would talk, in time. There was no hurry. Grieving for his father must come first, and being comforted by his mother and daughter. And then a police investigation and – she remembered only now – a funeral, a real one, and of course she would be there because she too had loved Abram.

There was no hurry and her expectations were low, except in one regard.

Laurie, her Laurie.

Nina pushed at the mechanism to recline the chair. Now her vision was filled almost entirely with blue, sea and sky, even the nubbins of islands in the gulf all tinged blue.

She felt weightless, hanging here above the harbour, above everything, but the sensation lacked disorientation.

She gazed at the horizon until sea and sky became barely distinguishable from one another, and she listened to the buried roar in the ocean and the shout of the wind, and they were good things.

ABOUT THE AUTHOR

Tim Major is author of *Snakeskins*, *You Don't Belong Here*, *Blighters*, *Carus & Mitch*, the YA novel *Machineries of Mercy*, the short story collection *And the House Lights Dim*, and a non-fiction book about the silent crime film, *Les Vampires*. His shorts have appeared in *Interzone*, *Not One of Us* and numerous anthologies including *Best of British Science Fiction* and *The Best Horror of the Year*. He lives in York, UK.

ACKNOWLEDGEMENTS

I owe grateful thanks to my editors, Gary Budden and George Sandison, for their terrific work shaping this novel, and to Dan Coxon, Lydia Gittins, Polly Grice and the Titan Books fiction team for their support, enthusiasm and excellent company at writing conventions.

Thanks to Kath Stansfield and Dave Towsey for beta-reading and for their knack of finding a balance between criticism and cheerleading. Thanks to Michael Rowley for his helpful input at the synopsis stage.

Thanks to all the authors, bloggers and reviewers who supported my previous novel, *Snakeskins*, and who kept my imposter syndrome at bay for a short while.

Thanks and love to my family: Arthur, Joe, and the best person in the world, Rose Parkin.

SNAKESKINS

TIM MAJOR

Caitlin Hext's first shedding ceremony is imminent, but she's far from prepared to produce a Snakeskin clone. When her Skin fails to turn to dust as expected, she must decide whether she wishes the newcomer alive or dead. *Snakeskins* is an SF thriller examining the repercussions of rejuvenation and cloning on identity and society, with the tone of classic John Wyndham stories and modern TV series such as Channel 4's *Humans*.

"Another great page-turner from Tim Major!"
Alison Littlewood, author of *The Hidden People*

"A premise worthy of Wyndham becomes a twisty political SF thriller in the hands of Major. *Snakeskins* is full of action and surprise, keeping me reading, but the real hook lies in the rich seam of humanity within."
Aliya Whiteley, author of *The Beauty*

"Tim Major masterfully weaves his plot strands together, studding *Snakeskins* with images of duality and metamorphosis to create a dark and compelling vision of corruption and conspiracy with a subtly satirical edge."
The Financial Times

SKEIN ISLAND

ALIYA WHITELEY

Skein Island is a private refuge twelve miles off the coast of
Devon. Few receive the invitation to stay for one week, free of
charge. If you are chosen, you must pay for your stay with a
story from your past; a Declaration for the Island's vast library.
What happens to your Declaration after you leave the island
is not your concern. Powerful and disturbing, it is a story over
which the characters will fight for control. Until they realise the
true enemy is the story itself.

"Aliya Whiteley's quiet prose is perfect for the slowly
unfolding narrative... Compelling."
SciFiNow

"*The Loosening Skin* is a sensuous, thought provoking
meditation on love that deserves not only a second read,
but a third as well. This book will cement Aliya Whiteley's
reputation as one of the finest of a new generation of weird
fiction writers. More, please."
Helen Marshall, author of *Gifts For the One Who Comes After*

"A fine example of understated horror."
The Guardian

THE BREACH

M.T. HILL

Freya Medlock, a reporter at her local paper, is down on her luck. When she's assigned to cover the death of a young climber named Stephen, she might just have the story she needs. Freya soon meets Shep: a trainee steeplejack with his own secret life. As Shep draws Freya deeper into the urbex scene, the circumstances of Stephen's death become more unsettling – and Freya is risking more and more to get the answers she wants.

"One of the most innovative and outspoken
new writers of British science fiction"
Nina Allan, author of *The Rift*

"Intense and well observed, *Zero Bomb* delves into
our fears and distrust of technology, and our political
anxieties stoked by twenty-four hour news"
Anne Charnock, author of *Dreams Before the Start of Time*

"Hill has created a hero for our times whose journey
towards the truth is compulsively readable"
The Guardian on *Zero Bomb*

For more fantastic fiction, author events,
exclusive excerpts, competitions, limited editions and more

VISIT OUR WEBSITE
titanbooks.com

LIKE US ON FACEBOOK
facebook.com/titanbooks

FOLLOW US ON TWITTER AND INSTAGRAM
@TitanBooks

EMAIL US
readerfeedback@titanemail.com